FREEDOM'S SHADOW

~

MARLO SCHALESKY

CROSSWAY BOOKS • WHEATON, ILLINOIS

A DIVISION OF GOOD NEWS PUBLISHERS

Freedom's Shadow

Copyright © 2001 by Marlo Schalesky

Published by Crossway Books
              A division of Good News Publishers
              1300 Crescent Street
              Wheaton, Illinois 60187

Cover design: Cindy Kiple

Cover illustration: James Griffin

First printing, 2001

Printed in the United States of America

Library of Congress Cataloging-in-Publication Data
Schalesky, Marlo 1967–
    Freedom's shadow / Marlo Schalesky.
      p.   cm. — (The winds of freedom ; bk. 2)
    ISBN 1-58134-266-7 (alk. paper)
      1. United States—History—French and Indian War, 1755-1763—
Fiction. 2. Washington, George, 1732-1799—Fiction. 3. Indians of
North America—Fiction. I. Title.
PS3569.C4728 F74   2001
813'.6—dc21   2001000642
                                                 CIP

15	14	13	12	11	10	09	08	07	06	05	04	03	02	01
15	14	13	12	11	10	9	8	7	6	5	4	3	2	1

To
Bethany Ann
for all her "help"

In my anguish

I cried to the LORD,

and he answered

by setting me free.

PSALM 118:5

~

PROLOGUE

London, England, November 1754

Fog tangled with the faint light of the street lamp overhead, causing the flame to grow dimmer still. From the shadow of a shoe-maker's shop, Inspector General Higgins shivered and pulled his coat closer around his neck. Silence crept through the alley and settled over the cobbled street. Only the relentless dripping of an icicle melting from the eaves above and the occasional pawing of a dog in the alley behind broke the quietness. Before him on the narrow street nothing moved; nothing stirred; nothing even breathed. So Inspector Higgins waited.

Finally in the distance he heard it, the clip-clop of hooves on cobblestone. He shrank farther into the shadows and studied the sound. The gait, he determined, was too quick, too precise, to be the plodding of a dray horse. And yet it was heavier than the stride of a lady's mount. A gentleman's horse, he decided, finely bred and prop-erly trained, the steed of a wealthy aristocrat whose presence seemed as foreign to this part of the city as a preacher at a tavern brawl.

Within minutes the horse, blacker even than the night, came into view. Inspector Higgins leaned forward, being careful to remain within the shadows. The horse came closer until he could see the rider hidden in a cloak as black as his mount. From within the dark-ness of the hooded cape, the rider's head turned toward the street lamp. The horse paused. Eerie silence again descended, except for the drip, drip of water on cobblestone. A chill danced up the inspec-tor's spine. For a moment he closed his eyes and willed the rider to move on. A minute passed, then two. His heart beat a rapid rhythm.

At last the rider turned and guided his horse to the tavern down the street from the inspector's hiding place. The tavern, closed for the night, boasted a sagging porch and a single square window with curtains that reached only halfway down the smoke-smudged pane.

Above the door a ramshackle sign, with its paint worn thin, simply read "Inn."

With the rider's back turned, Inspector Higgins slipped from the corner of the shoemaker's shop and crept across the front of the warehouse beside it until he could just see into the tavern's downstairs window. Inside, a fire blazed in the grate, providing the only illumination. At a table in the back of the room, he thought he could see the outline of a man.

Outside, the rider dismounted and headed toward the tavern door. The inspector crouched behind an empty barrel and listened to the way the rider's footsteps echoed lightly on the wooden planks. Higgins twisted his mustache between his fingers and made a mental note. *He's a smaller man than I thought. The coat is too large for him. It's worn as much for disguise as warmth. But he's quick on his feet despite the bulky garment. A strange stride for a man who rides such a horse . . .*

The rider knocked twice at the door. Higgins watched as the man inside rose and stumbled to open it. When he did, the rider handed him what looked like a parchment scroll.

Higgins crept from behind one barrel to another until he was at a better angle to view the men. He recognized the man from the tavern—Rowley, a champion fighter and a known seller of England's secrets. But it wasn't Rowley he'd been tracking for three long years. It was this black-cloaked aristocrat, this quick-stepping man who rode out of the fog like some dark prince to betray his country. The inspector's eyes narrowed. In a moment he would know the rider's identity. He savored the thought.

Rowley mumbled something to the other man, nodded his head, then stepped back inside and shut the door. The rider turned toward his horse. It was time.

Higgins reached for his pistol. His hand shook. He leaped from the shadows. "Halt!" he shouted.

The black rider didn't pause. He didn't even turn.

Light glinted off the inspector's pistol as the rider swung onto his horse and reined him back toward Higgins. The rider's cry tore through the night. The horse surged forward.

Before the inspector could move, the beast was upon him.

Hooves flashed in the air and glanced off his shoulder. He stumbled sideways, then regained his footing. His grip tightened on the pistol. He lifted it and pointed it at the rider. "Stop!" he cried.

Again the rider urged the horse toward him. For an instant his eyes caught those still shadowed in the cape's darkness. He thought he heard a low laugh. Then something whipped from the rider's hand and crashed down onto his forearm. His pistol and the object spun into the night. He could hear them clatter on the cobblestones beyond. He turned. The horse reared again. Blinding whiteness exploded across his vision. He fell, only then realizing that a hoof had struck him in the forehead.

From the edge of consciousness, he heard the horse race off into the darkness. With sickening clarity Higgins knew that he had again lost his prey. Then he was swallowed in a blackness that swirled up not from the night but from somewhere within. For a while he knew no more.

A moment, an eternity, passed while Higgins lay in the street, oblivious to his pain. Then slowly consciousness crept back through his mind. He opened his eyes. The tavern was dark and deserted. Only the feeble light of the streetlamp greeted him. He rose to his knees and raised one hand to his forehead. Blood, warm and sticky, met his touch. He reached for his handkerchief and dabbed at the wound. His head spun. He blinked.

There in the street, illuminated by the scant light of the streetlamp's flame, he saw his pistol—and something else lying beside it. He hobbled over, picked up the gun, and returned it to its holster. Then he turned his attention to the object beside it. A riding crop of fine leather, delicately tooled—the instrument of a man of power and wealth. But which man?

He turned the crop over in his hand. The light caught the silver insignia on the end. He looked closer and knew he had seen the symbol before, a lion's head surrounded by fire.

Inspector Higgins smiled and tucked the instrument into his coat. "Sleep well, Lord Grant," he whispered, "for judgment cometh with the morning."

PART ONE

The Shadow Falls

~

ONE

~

East of Fort Duquesne, Pennsylvania frontier, July 1755

Fingers of darkness reached through the trees and curled around the feet of an Indian brave. The breeze blew a strand of hair across his eyes. He didn't pause to brush it away.

The brave clutched his bow in one hand and an arrow in the other. His gaze traveled up and down the wooden length of the arrow, noting how the scant moonlight shimmered dully from the tip. He had not held his weapon against another man for ten long years—years of searching, of grief and doubt, years that stretched together in a blur of dark confusion. Now again the time had come for war. And again he must prove himself the warrior.

He sighed and slipped through the tall sycamores, his vision steady on the enemy camp in the distance. Silently he crept forward, like a part of the night fog, his hand firm on the bow. Somewhere in the night a wildcat screamed, sending shivers of doubt racing through the warrior's tall frame. He drew a deep breath. Out there in the darkness the enemy waited, vulnerable in the moments before dawn.

The brave paused. His gaze searched the black sky. "I am White Wolf," he whispered. "I am not afraid." The statement echoed hollowly in his ears. Leaves brushed against White Wolf's shoulders and thighs as he continued. His eyes grew narrow.

Streaks of dawn began to peek through the night's mantle, chasing away the remnants of his fear. Far behind him, on the east side of the French Fort Duquesne, the ground was interlaced with ravines, ditches, and barricades, with ramparts ten feet thick made of squared logs and filled in with earth. All these were preparations for the war that had burst to life between the English and French, a war that had swept him up in it despite his anger, suspicions, and dread. War had come, with Colonel Washington and his English troops, with General Braddock and his red-coated hordes.

He sighed and listened to the gentle rumble of the Monongahela River just beyond him. How had he come to this?

White Wolf shook his head, remembering the night, several moons ago now, when he and others had given their pledge over a belt of wampum. Even now he could see how the firelight flickered off Captain Pierre de Contrecoeur's long face as he regarded them, his eyes both sad and determined.

"My brothers," the man had begun, "in my heart there is a great gladness that you have at last thrown off the shackles of the English and have now realized that your future is tied to the French, your brothers and protectors."

At his words White Wolf felt the fury begin to burn in his chest. Yet he had remained silent, watching the fire dance and the smoke curl up to the ceiling.

As if sensing his distrust, Contrecoeur looked directly at him, his eyes squinting into dark slits before opening wide again to regard the others. "From across the sea your great father, the king of France, and all his country looks upon you with warmth and high praise."

White Wolf's throat tightened at the lie.

"Already he has sent you many gifts, blankets to warm you, pots to cook your stew, jewels to adorn your chiefs, and brandy to make you strong. These gifts honor you for your fidelity, and there will be more to come. An even greater harmony will rise between us, until for all time our races will be as one."

The thought stuck with cold foreboding in White Wolf's mind. He grimaced as the assembled tribesmen nodded and murmured among themselves. Slowly Contrecoeur held up a war belt of deep purple shells. The men gasped and fell silent. Fort Duquesne's commandant held the belt high above his head, allowing both ends to trail to the floor as his eyes pierced each man.

Wampum binds the oath. White Wolf whispered the words to himself, his eyes fixed on the long belt while the face of his sister Kwelik swam before his vision.

The commandant continued, "My brothers, all of you know by

now that the English have murdered my children, just as they have murdered yours. My heart is sick. Now I shall send my French soldiers to take revenge." He paused. "Men of the Sault Sainte Louis, men of the Lake of Two Mountains, men of La Presentation, men of the Far West, I invite you all by this belt of wampum to join your French father and help him crush the assassins." From under his coat Contrecoeur removed a bright new tomahawk with his free hand and stepped to one side where he placed it and the war belt on top of two barrels. "Take this hatchet," he called, "and with it two barrels of wine for a feast. Join me against the English enemy. Revenge is ours!"

Before White Wolf could protest, Pontiac, the great Ottawa chief, had stepped forward and sealed their doom. "We will go with our French brothers to battle. We will fight at your side." His voice rang decisively over the gathering as he grabbed the war belt in one hand and thrust it above his head. "To victory! To the death of the Englishmen!" His face flushed with grim determination.

A loud cheer rose from the throats of the assembled warriors and pierced White Wolf's heart. At that moment he was swept again into the fury of war and revenge, a madness that now drove him on this journey through the coldness of the dawn.

The crack of a branch underfoot startled White Wolf from the memory. He stopped. His head cocked to one side as he listened to the whisperings of the dying night—an owl, the sigh of a breeze through the leaves overhead, and his own breathing, quiet and heavy in his ears.

He crept forward and raised his hand to pull away the branches in front of him. There in a clearing just ahead the English camped for the night. Dozens of tents littered the landscape, and behind them the great cannons of war sat like silent sentinels, waiting for the moment of attack. To his right half a dozen horses swished their tails and stamped their hooves as if impatient for the day to begin.

White Wolf clutched his bow more fiercely. Soon the time for action would be upon him. He crouched low to watch and wait. In the largest tent someone stirred and turned over in his bedroll. *That would be the young George Washington,* White Wolf thought, *or perhaps Braddock himself.*

Across the clearing someone coughed. Then again all grew

quiet, serene, oblivious to the enemy lurking in the bushes. White Wolf took a deep breath and continued his watch, waiting for something, someone, some small turn of events that would show him what he must do.

Then it happened. A man slipped from his tent, stretched his arms, and yawned into the morning air. The sound shimmered across the clearing and stabbed through White Wolf's nerves. The time had come.

The man rubbed his eyes and stumbled toward the trees, alone. White Wolf placed an arrow carefully into the bow, feeling the weight of the tomahawk fastened at his waist. The man frowned and stopped. Then he stepped back to retrieve his musket before continuing into the trees.

White Wolf sucked in his breath and silently followed as the man made his way to a spot where two tall oak trees blocked him from the main camp. The Indian held his breath and squeezed his weapon tight in his damp palm.

The Englishman turned his back to the place where White Wolf waited. He whistled quietly as he set his musket against a nearby tree, beyond easy grasp. He cleared his throat and then began humming to himself.

White Wolf clenched his teeth. His jaw hardened. He pulled back the arrow in the string and aimed at the white man's back. The shot would be a long one. He drew a slow breath and willed his hands to remain steady, his arms to stay taut. Then he released the breath and listened to the blood pounding in his ears. He looked down the long shaft of the arrow as time slowed to an eerie crawl and waited for the quiet whir of death's sharp messenger.

Sweat broke out on White Wolf's brow. His hands trembled. Now it would begin again, the never-ending battle of blood and fire. Twelve years disappeared, and he was again the young boy who had watched his village burn and his people die. He was again the boy who had held the tomahawk in his hand and chosen a life of hate and war.

For ten years he had wandered from tribe to tribe, searching for answers, for peace, for a hint of hope on the long trail of despair. He had tried a hundred different philosophies, spoken to dozens of shamans, but the haunting emptiness remained.

And now after all those years, White Wolf's eyes blurred with unshed tears, until his target swam before his vision. His fingers began to slip on the string. Slowly he lowered the weapon. He had had enough death, enough killing, enough blood. If he hoped to be free, he must walk away now.

White Wolf dropped his bow and turned, then stifled a gasp as his eyes locked with those of another brave standing just behind him. "Pontiac! What are you doing here? Why have you followed me?"

The other warrior lifted one hand. His eyes never left White Wolf's. "Finish what you came to do, Waptumewi." His voice, though barely audible, burned through White Wolf's chest. "Join the holy war. Do not fear—only fight."

White Wolf shook his head. "It has been too long, brother. I am no longer the warrior I once was." He kept his tone low enough so the soldier could not hear.

Pontiac laid one hand gently on White Wolf's shoulder. "You are still a warrior. Come, I will show you."

Before the powerful presence of the other man, White Wolf's doubts faded. He looked into the lean, angular face of the Ottawa chief, a man who had already rallied a dozen tribes behind him. The war parties now gathered all around the French fort, waiting for Pontiac's signal to fight. Here was a leader worthy of his people, worthy of a loyalty White Wolf could no longer give.

White Wolf lowered his gaze and glanced at the soldier, who was now squatting beside the tree with his pants around his ankles. "The war is not ours, Pontiac. It is a white man's war. We are wrong to join them."

Pontiac paused before answering. "You are wise, Waptumewi, but consider this. The French are strong. They will beat back the Englishmen. We will help them to push the English from our land."

White Wolf frowned. "All white men are the enemy, the French as well as the English. The day will come when we will rue this war and the blood we shed." His voice dropped to a deadly whisper. "I know. I have seen it before."

Pontiac studied him for a moment, then nodded. "I will remember your words. But know this, nothing can stop the war to come."

The words reverberated coldly in White Wolf's ears.

Pontiac's face softened. "Come with me, my brother," he repeated, instilling in White Wolf a momentary confidence. "Come, let us make our strike before it is too late." He motioned toward the hapless man who was now pulling his breeches back up around his waist. "Come."

White Wolf nodded as Pontiac picked up the discarded bow and arrow. He glanced only once at White Wolf, holding his eyes in a single penetrating gaze, before drawing back the arrow in the string. "For our people," he whispered.

He released the string, and the arrow split the dawn air. The weapon found its mark in the Englishman's chest, cutting short his scream. With a muted war cry, Pontiac leaped from the trees toward his victim. White Wolf followed.

"There is no other way, brother," Pontiac hissed as he reached the writhing soldier and pulled out a long knife. "This is war."

War. The word echoed through White Wolf's mind as his eyes fixed on Pontiac's blade.

With practiced accuracy, Pontiac ran his knife in a circle around the man's head and then ripped the scalp from his skull. The bloody mass dangled from the older brave's grip. He handed the prize to White Wolf.

Blood flowed over White Wolf's hand as he took the scalp. The sight of it sickened him. Nothing had changed in ten years.

Once long ago, a lifetime ago it seemed, he was happy, at peace. He remembered the feeling like a far-off dream—Kwelik teaching him to fish, his mother laughing, and his father holding him on his knee. But those times had ended with fire and war. Hate and fury and desperation had driven him, until only this was left, only the scalp of the enemy, hot and bloody in his fist.

White Wolf wiped his hand on his breechcloth. His throat tightened. He flung back his head. Despair welled in him, dark and relentless. Would he never be free? *Oh, God, help me.*

It was the first prayer he had uttered in twelve long years.

TWO

~

Annie put her hands on both hips and glared into the steel-gray eyes of the man in front of her. For several seconds she stared up at him, not intimidated by his six-foot-two stance. Gold buttons on his blue coat winked at her in the flickering candlelight, daring her to break her gaze. She held her breath and listened to the tent flap as it shuddered in the evening breeze. Beyond that she could hear the whisper of campfires outside.

Annie's jaw clenched. "Colonel Washington." She squeezed his name through lips stiff with concealed fury. "I know that I'm a woman, but I can fight as good as any man. Just give me a weapon, and I'll show you."

George Washington held her gaze with his own, his voice steady. "I know you can fight, Miss Hill. Sometimes I think that's all you can do." He pulled off his coat and tossed it onto the cot. "In all my twenty-two years, I have never met a woman so stubborn." He sighed and leaned his hands on a small table covered with maps.

Annie frowned and opened her mouth, but Washington waved away her objection with one hand. "What were you thinking, girl? Did you believe the men wouldn't notice a coat missing here, a shirt and breeches gone there?"

Annie lowered her head. "I hoped not." It suddenly seemed terribly hot in the colonel's small tent.

Washington picked up his gun and laid it across the table. His hand rested on the barrel. For a moment he didn't speak. When he did, his gaze shot through her like a lead ball from the musket. "So, Miss Hill, were you planning on stealing your weapon as well?"

She didn't answer.

Suddenly he chuckled. "Ah, your plan was not so well thought out after all." He paused, the corners of his eyes crinkling in a pleasant smile. "As if anyone could possibly mistake you for a soldier."

Annie lifted her chin. "I could be the best soldier in your whole unit."

Washington's voice softened. "I've no doubt you could be."

"Then—"

"No, Miss Hill, I will not change my mind. Tomorrow, God willing, we march to Fort Duquesne to engage the French. When we do, you will stay here." He stabbed his finger toward the ground. "I agreed you could join the army as a washerwoman—and no more." His comment ended in a wracking cough. He sat down on the edge of the cot and rubbed one hand over his forehead.

Annie stomped her foot. "I came to be a soldier, not to wash men's stockings!"

Washington stared at her a moment longer before his lips again turned up into an amused smile. "I do admit that you are a very poor washerwoman."

"Clean breeches aren't going to kill the enemy, Colonel Washington," Annie muttered. "I came here to get my revenge. You can't stop me."

Washington ran one hand through his brown hair, his eyes gentle as he spoke. "Revenge is a sword that turns on its wielder. Is it worth the cost?"

"It is to me."

Washington's next cough left him breathless. Sweat beaded on his forehead and trickled down his temple. He reached up one hand to wipe it away. "I do not have the energy to fight both you and the French," he sighed. "At least not until I recover from this illness."

Annie clenched her fists.

"Listen to me." His words, gentle and compelling, reached out to her. "Go home. The battle you seek cannot be fought here."

She turned away. Anger and grief shot through her chest with sudden intensity. "I have no home anymore. They took it ten years ago—the Indians and the French. I swore then that I would never forgive, never forget. And I won't. Not now. Not ever." She turned back to him and dashed away the moisture that had begun to form in her eyes.

Washington nodded once. His eyes pierced to her soul, as if reading the fear and anguish she hid there. Without a word, he stood and walked to the opening of his tent. He stopped to lean his arm against the stiff canvas and stare into the descending night. "Come here, Annie."

She eyed him suspiciously as she stepped beside him.

He looked down at her. Then with one hand he pulled the tent flap farther back. "Look out there." He tilted his head toward the encampment. "Tell me, what do you see?"

She wrinkled her brow into a frown. "I see red-coated soldiers, Virginians dressed in blue, and a few dusty frontiersmen gathered around their campfires."

Washington nodded. "What else?"

Annie shook her head. "Nothing else."

"Then I will tell you what *I* see." He gazed out again at his men. "I see men called by God to be free, to live in this new land without fear, without oppression."

The words called to Annie's soul. Her voice dropped to a whisper. "That is why I must fight. For freedom."

Washington turned back toward her. His face filled with compassion. "Understand this. These men will go to battle tomorrow. But only God can make us free. In Him we must trust. And so must you."

Old hurt, old desperation clutched Annie's heart. "I don't know how."

"The time will come when God will call you to protect this land. Wait for Him. Now is not the time; nor is this the place." His eyes held hers with grave intensity. "You must let go of the past."

Pain caught in Annie's throat. "I can't."

"Trust in God—not in the musket's fire."

She looked away.

Washington sighed. "Go. Get some rest. Tomorrow we will need you to help the wounded."

Annie nodded mutely, her mind screaming its protest to the words that still rang in her ears.

Washington waved toward the tent opening. "Trust, Annie. Remember. Now go." He paused, his voice turning light with humor as she stepped from the tent. "And do return Percy's breeches. He was quite lost this morning without them."

A rare smile touched Annie's lips as she headed toward her bedroll. *That Colonel Washington,* she thought, *he could have had me punished for thievery, but instead he was kind. I'll have to remember to return those stockings I took from his wash.* She grinned to herself and then brushed past a woman who was sauntering toward the men's beds.

"Watch where you're going, love."

Annie glanced up to notice hair the color of dirty straw and a dress slipping down to expose bare shoulders.

The woman reached down and straightened her worn skirt. "Ye be ruining my wares if you ain't careful."

Annie mumbled an apology, her mind still on her encounter with George Washington. *Trust God. Let go of the past. Wait.* The words stirred through her, commanding, beckoning. But how could she follow them, especially now when she was all alone with nothing but blood-filled memories to keep her company in the night?

"I hope he paid ye well for your services, missy." The woman's strident voice cut through her thoughts.

Annie turned back around. A frown marred her features.

The woman's laugh jangled across her nerves like breaking glass. "He's a handsome devil, that Colonel Washington. And young too. I can't say as I blame you for fancying him. But a pretty girl like you deserves fair pay."

Annie's eyes narrowed at the implication. "Colonel Washington isn't like that, and neither am I."

"Aye, you were in for a wee bit o' tea and conversation, I suppose." The woman crossed her arms, one eyebrow raised in mocking disbelief. "Say what you wish, love, but I'll be going home with a nice little bundle myself." She patted the pouch filled with coins that hung around her waist. "Don't worry, missy. I ain't begrudging you no business. There be plenty of it for all of us."

"I came to fight," Annie muttered in response, "not to . . ."

The woman's loud cackle drowned out Annie's words. "Call it

what you like, love. From the looks of you, it must have been quite a fight."

Annie scowled at the woman's unconcealed mirth.

"If you like, I'll put in a good word for you with General Braddock. For a price, of course." She gave Annie a broad wink. "Or maybe you're doing well enough with just the colonel."

Annie's fists clenched at her sides. She fought the urge to wipe the mocking look from the woman's face. But Kwelik, who had become like a mother to her in the last ten years, had taught her the value of self-control, a lesson she struggled to remember now. *Wherefore, my beloved brethren, let every man be swift to hear, slow to speak, slow to wrath: For the wrath of man worketh not the righteousness of God.* The words from James, spoken in Kwelik's gentle voice, echoed in Annie's mind. But they could not chase the hot anger from her. She leaned toward the woman in front of her. "Watch your tongue, or I may just cut it from your head while you sleep."

The woman took a step backward. "Don't be getting your petticoat all in a ruffle. I didn't mean nothing."

Annie released her hands and pressed her palms against her legs.

"Washington ain't been with any of us girls," the woman continued. "But I wouldn't be surprised if he were to favor the likes of you. You're a fiery one, you are. And with red hair to match your temper." She reached up and touched a curl of Annie's hair. "Like the color of autumn leaves it is, caught fire in the sun." Her voice grew quiet. "Lovely. Men—they like that sort of thing."

Annie pulled away.

The woman sighed. "Mine's just a yellow-brown like a church mouse, my mama used to say." She wiped her hand across her nose. "Not that I was ever in a church long enough to find out."

Disgust and anger churned in Annie's stomach. She scowled and looked away. If not for Kwelik, she might have become just like this woman, crude and licentious. But Kwelik had saved her, taught her, shown her a life that she still could not fully accept. She took a deep breath and let it out again before answering the woman. "Listen, whoever you are—"

"Name's Mary, Mary 'Lizbeth."

Annie nodded. "Listen, Mary, I'm not here to fill my pockets with coins or to entertain the men. There's more at stake than a few pence or even a few pounds. If we don't win this battle, we could all lose our scalps, and that's not a pretty sight." Annie's voice echoed low and deadly in her own ears.

"Eeeiiii," Mary screeched. Her cry echoed over the encampment. "Ye talk a mean talk, love." She lowered her voice. "But we'll beat them Frenchies. Everyone says so."

Annie's features hardened. "You'd better pray to God that it's so." She opened her mouth to say more and then clamped her lips shut again. No one knew, no one understood the stakes of the battle at hand. The lives of every family on the frontier rested on their shoulders. If they lost, no one would be safe from the bite of the tomahawk, from the blade of the French-driven savages. Braddock, Washington, and their troops must win. Annie shook her head. No one should die like her family had. No child should see her mother's scalp ripped from her skull. She shuddered even now at the thought, pushing the memory from her mind with practiced skill.

Without another word, Annie again headed toward her bedroll at the far edge of the camp. She threw herself down on her bed and wiped her hand across one cheek. She sniffed, despising the emotions that welled within her.

Jonathan and Kwelik thought she was away finding her relatives who may have survived the Indian attacks. But she knew the truth. They were all dead. Dead and gone. Now she would avenge their deaths and more. She would make her own life, a new life without fear or shame. And no one, no savage, no Frenchman, no prostitute, no Englishman would take it away from her.

Annie gritted her teeth. "Never forgive. Never forget," she repeated the promise to herself.

The memory of Washington's last words came back to her. *Trust. Let go. Wait.*

Tears again gathered in her eyes. Quickly she dashed them away. She had no time for sorrow or for doubt. She must fight and win. This time she would protect her family and her future. This time she would not stand by, helpless, and watch as death ripped life away from the ones she loved. Tomorrow she would avenge the past and, perhaps, somehow free herself from the memory that haunted her still.

∾

Just as dawn began to break, the snap of a twig woke Annie from a dream she wished she could forget. It was the same nightmare. Lately it came every night—dark, bleak, and inescapable.

She groaned and rolled over in her blankets. Her eyes searched the sky, watching the stars fade from the dark shroud above her. With another low moan, she rubbed her hands over her face, as if by doing so she could erase the image etched into her mind. It was always the same. Yet it never lost its horror, never lessened its terrifying grip on her heart.

In the dream she was ten years old again, and the Indians came. She could see their eyes glimmering in the grayness of twilight. On and on they came, toward her, toward her home, her family. She opened her mouth to scream, to warn the others, but no sound came. Only silence. Always the silence. Still the Indians came closer, their tomahawks bright and luminous in the waning daylight. Then in a quick flurry of terror, they attacked. Suddenly she felt the weight of a musket in her hand. Blood spattered across her face. This time her scream rent the silence. But instead of protecting her family, she dropped the gun. It became a snake that writhed at her feet and looked up at her with her mother's dead eyes.

A breeze blew over Annie and sent a chill over her sweat-drenched back. *It was not like that,* she told herself. *There was no musket, no snake. It's only a dream.* She wrapped her arms around her cold body, unable to shake the feeling of those dead eyes watching her, condemning her for doing nothing as her family perished.

A muffled sound echoed from the trees behind her. Was it a footstep? Annie held her breath, listening. The sound came again, the quiet whoosh of a branch falling back into place. She knew that sound. Indians.

Annie bit her lip. Her eyes narrowed with concentration as she peered into the emerging dawn. A chill of dread plucked at her spine.

Yes, she was sure now. They were out there watching, waiting, their tomahawks ready for the kill. But no one would believe her if she told them. No one would listen to a simple washerwoman, except perhaps Colonel Washington, and she would never go to his tent while the camp slept.

Annie closed her eyes. As soon as she did, the dead eyes from her dream, wide and accusing, sprang before her vision. "You must let go of the past," Washington had said. But he didn't know, no one knew, the secret she kept buried in her memory, the secret that haunted her through her dreams, that threatened to destroy her still.

Annie drew a slow breath, rose silently, and allowed her blankets to fall to one side. Somewhere, close, the enemy waited. This time she would not lie paralyzed with fear.

Like part of the new day's mist, she wafted through the trees, her footsteps silent on the damp turf. Above her an owl hooted before winging its way to the top of a tall oak. A squirrel scampered up a tree to her right and dropped an acorn to the ground below. Annie wove quietly through the trees. Her eyes searched for a sign of the enemy. Before her the trees opened to form a small clearing over-shadowed by half a dozen tall sycamores. *There*, she thought, her eyes narrowing. *The sounds came from the clearing.*

Annie rubbed her hands against her stomach to quell its fluttering before she stepped into the ring of trees and quietly pushed back the leaves that blocked her vision. *Oh no. I'm too late.* Her gaze locked on the scalped body of an English soldier, his breeches still clutched in his dead hands. She stumbled toward him. Her stomach heaved. *Not again. Please, God, not again.* She turned from the sight of the man's bloodstained face. When she did, her eyes fell on the musket that leaned against a nearby tree. A musket unfired, unused, silent, like the gun that haunted her dreams.

Annie's breath came in short gasps as she lifted the weapon from its resting place and ran her hand down the black barrel. The gun felt heavy in her grip. She practiced putting it up to her eye, as she had seen the men do. Her arms shook. She bit her lower lip and tried again. This time she steadied the butt against her shoulder and cocked the gun.

Behind her a branch cracked. The sound ricocheted through the air. Annie whirled, her finger tense on the trigger. A squirrel tumbled from a nearby tree, chattering its indignation before again scrambling up the slender trunk. Annie let out her breath, only then realizing that she'd been holding it. Her hands loosened on the musket. "It's only a squirrel," she whispered to herself, hoping the words would quiet the wild thumping in her chest.

Before the sound of her voice faded from the air, she heard a footstep to her left. She turned and pulled the musket to her shoulder. She drew a sharp breath. Her eyes clashed with those of an Indian brave, his bow still clutched in one hand.

Without a second thought, she aimed the gun and yanked back on the trigger. Nothing happened.

The brave lunged toward her. She swung the bayonet with all her strength. Somehow the blade found its mark. The Indian fell. His hands gripped his thigh as his bow skittered across the wet grass.

Annie stifled a shout of victory. Her gaze locked on the brave's bloody flesh. The sound of her own breathing rasped in her ear. She swallowed once, then again. Her knuckles turned white on the gun's barrel. Before her the Indian struggled to rise, then grimaced as he fell back to the ground.

Annie looked at the bayonet, stained with her enemy's blood. She stood above the felled Indian. The musket shook in her palms. She pointed the weapon at the brave's midsection. Her eyes again fastened on the wound in his leg. Her vision blurred with old fury, old fear.

"Your people killed my parents," she whispered, "and stole my life. I hate you. I hate you all!" Her voice cracked.

For a moment her gaze locked with that of the Indian as they stared at one another over the barrel of the musket. The brave's eyes widened with shock. Annie caught her breath as he reached a bloody hand toward her.

His mouth formed a single word. "Annie?"

The musket slipped from her hands.

THREE

A wave crashed against the ship's side, sending spray over the deck and casting fine droplets onto Jonathan Grant's troubled face. He squinted and looked into the dying afternoon sunlight shimmering off the surface of the turbulent water.

Above, the mast creaked, and the square-rigged sails sagged in white folds as the 200-foot ship dipped and rose on the waves. Jonathan brushed his boot over the rope that lay on the deck and glanced at the ship's sterncastle. Somewhere in there the officers planned their course and adjusted the steering tiller. Somewhere in there the binnacle held a compass that pointed them toward England. Jonathan shivered at the thought and again gazed out over the water. As he watched, the sun slipped behind the horizon, casting a red glow over sky and sea. To Jonathan, it looked like ribbons of fire from heaven.

Fire. He closed his eyes. Even after ten years, he could still see the flames that had licked up around Kwelik, the flames that had come to symbolize his freedom and hers. At that time he had felt God's presence and love. But now? Now he felt nothing but the wet fingers of foreboding.

Jonathan ran his hand through his hair. Before him the ocean spread out vast and endless, and on it the path of sunlight led back to the colonies, to home. But the ship was headed to England. A twinge of revulsion swelled in his chest.

Another wave slammed against the boat and sent water dashing over the railing, making a rainbow of colors that shone, then faded, before his eyes. The time had come to face his past and in it to find the future. For himself and for Richard. Or so he had thought when he received the letter.

Jonathan frowned as he pressed his hand over his cloak pocket and heard the crinkle of the paper he kept there. The letter. He pulled it out and unfolded it, running his fingers lightly over the dog-eared edges and smeared ink. His eyes glanced over the words, not reading them. Slowly he refolded the paper and returned it to his pocket. He knew what it said.

Jonathan, come home quick. They say your brother's in league with the French. They've thrown him in prison, and now he's awful sick. Sneaky business going on here. She's taken over everything.
                                                        Your servant, Tobias

"Jonathan, come home." Those words were like a bitter herb in his soul. He'd struggled to swallow them, struggled to accept the plea that called him to do what he swore he never would. If it had been anyone but Tobias, Jonathan would have torn up the request without a second thought. But Tobias wouldn't write unless there was no other way to save Richard.

Jonathan stared into the black water beneath him. If Richard hanged, no one with the Grant name would be safe from the executioner's rope. Not him, not Kwelik, not his children. All of them would become suspect. Suspicion would ooze across the ocean and find them in their frontier home, just as Richard's jealousy had found him before. Soon the colonial army would be knocking at his door with their questions and allegations, with their letters from England accusing him of treason. But even more than that, the hand of God, strong and unyielding, was pushing him back to England, forcing him to face the brother he had long ago disowned.

Jonathan leaned on the ship's railing, feeling the once-familiar clutching of anger and dread in his chest. He had thought he was finished with such bitterness when he made his peace with God. But now it seemed that the past had reached out and pulled him back into it. He had told himself that he'd forgiven his brother. But what was forgiveness? He found that he didn't know anymore.

Behind him boards squeaked as someone approached. Jonathan turned. A smile replaced his scowl as he watched his wife, seven months pregnant with their second child, stumble across the deck toward him. His smile widened as she rubbed her rounded belly and pushed a strand of black hair behind one ear.

She grimaced, her topaz-blue eyes flashing to his in a wry frown. "I think I'd rather swim to England than spend another day in this wretched bundle of sodden sticks." Her face pulled into a half-smile, stretching the scar that marred her cheek. "I'll never get those sea legs that the sailors boast about." She scowled and gripped the edge with unsteady hands.

Jonathan chuckled as he pulled her into his embrace. She leaned back against his chest. Her cheek rested on his shoulder. "It's just the babe, my love," he whispered in her ear. He leaned down to plant a gentle kiss on her forehead. "We'll reach England within a week if God wills."

"And none too soon." Kwelik groaned as the ship tossed and jolted against another wave.

It is too soon for me. Jonathan tightened his grip on his wife and allowed his eyes to blur on the distant horizon. A vision of his brother materialized before him, just as he was ten years ago—cold, angry, and accusing. Ten years. It was a long time, too long, not long enough. Jonathan sighed.

Kwelik's arm reached around him. She rubbed her hand over his back. "You're doing the right thing, Jonathan." She spoke the words with an assurance he wished he could echo.

Silence settled between them as Jonathan allowed his gaze to follow a group of black clouds that blotted out the last rays of day. The breeze picked up, whipping the sail above their heads. The hard thwack of fabric against wood reverberated through his senses. He looked down at Kwelik, her face thoughtful as dark hair danced around her face in the wind. "A storm is coming, my love," he whispered. His face pulled into a troubled frown. *A storm above and within. I wonder which will be greater?*

Kwelik reached up and gently pushed a lock of hair back from his eyes. Her fingers rested momentarily on his cheek. "God goes with us. I know it." Her voice was quiet, firm. "Besides," she said smiling, "I always wanted to see Papa's world."

Jonathan's gaze met hers in a moment of deep understanding.

Rain spattered across his face, making tiny rivulets down his cheeks and jaw. "Come. We must go below deck." He watched his wife's brow wrinkle at his words.

"So soon?" Kwelik pressed her hand into the small of her back and turned toward the far end of the ship.

Jonathan gripped the rail one last time. A scream sliced through the air. His blood froze. Before the sound dissipated, a small boy darted from the doorway of the sterncastle and sprinted toward them. His arms flailed as another earsplitting shriek came from his throat. "Noooooo. I didn't mean it! Don't hurt me."

The child threw himself at Kwelik. His hands clung to her skirt. "I didn't mean it, Mama," he wailed again.

Behind him a dark sailor stormed from the doorway leading to the crew's quarters. The light from a lantern swung across his face, showing an ominous scowl. The man stomped toward them, with his shirt dripping and a wet parchment in his hand. "Curse you, boy! God help me if I don't throw you to the sharks before another night has passed."

"Noooo," the boy repeated and buried his face in his mother's skirt.

"Shhh, Justin," she whispered, smoothing his hair beneath gentle fingers.

The sailor turned toward Jonathan. "The little savage spilled my ale. Is he your boy?"

Jonathan put one hand on Justin's shoulder and turned toward the man. "Yes, he is." As he spoke, he looked down at his six-year-old son, so much like him at that age, except for those bright blue eyes that mirrored his mother's.

The sailor growled. "Heed my words then, or your son will never make it to England." He reached toward the child and gripped the boy's shirt in a gnarled fist. "You'd better look out, you little devil."

Jonathan took a step forward, ready to protect his child.

The man dropped his grip and glanced from father to son. "Next time," he muttered, "your papa may not be so near." With one quick movement, he pulled aside his shirt to reveal a long knife protruding from his waistband.

Justin gulped and lowered his eyes, his arms still tight around his mother's legs.

The man stepped back. His eyes traveled to Kwelik's swollen belly before he turned and spat on the deck. "Don't know why they let savages or their brats on this ship. I should throw both of you to the sharks." He sneered. His face moved closer to Kwelik's. "Maybe I will." He grabbed her arm.

Rage exploded in Jonathan. Without thought, he slammed his fist into the sailor's chin. The man spun under the blow and dropped to the deck with a hard thud. Water spilled over the side and splashed into the sailor's face as he struggled to rise.

Jonathan leaned over him, his expression dark with fury. "She is my wife. Touch her again at your own risk."

The man's eyes turned to black slits. He stood and stumbled backward. "You'll pay for this, Indian-lover," he growled. "From now on you'd better watch your back." His tongue darted out to lick dry lips. Then he grunted and turned away.

Kwelik drew a sharp breath and remained silent, her arms firm around the small body of her son.

Jonathan scowled. His anger turned to cold dread in his chest. In the distance lightning ripped across the clouds. A moment later thunder rumbled in the evening sky like a portent of trouble to come.

Kwelik's soft hand descended on Jonathan's arm. Her eyes searched his as the rain began to fall in fierce sheets. "The storm has come," she whispered. "And with it the night."

Jonathan watched the sailor disappear below deck as Kwelik's words were lost in another roar of thunder.

FOUR

~

The bright rays of dawn washing over the eastern horizon confirmed Annie's fear. "White Wolf?" She choked on his name. "What have I done?" She dropped to her knees and reached out to staunch the flow of blood that came from his thigh.

White Wolf caught her hand in his. His fingers squeezed hers until she no longer trembled. "So it really is you, Wakon?" he whispered. His voice stumbled over the English words. "After all these years?"

She nodded. Her hand fumbled to tear off a strip of cloth from the bottom of her dress and wrap it tightly around his leg. "Where are the others? The rest of your war band?"

"I am alone."

"Alone?"

"I thought, I tried . . ." He shook his head. "You would not understand."

A chill, left over from the night's mist, crept along Annie's skin.

White Wolf's mouth pulled into a pained smile as she knotted the fabric around his wound. "You always were one to strike first and think later." He grimaced, his eyes steady on her downturned face. This time his speech came more smoothly. "But this is not the greeting I would expect from the girl I saved from the Frenchman's fury." He grew silent as a spasm of pain flitted over his face.

Annie cleared her throat, hoping her voice would cover the sound of her heart beating awkwardly in her ears. "I see that you have not changed in ten years," she hissed, motioning to the dead man lying in the puddle of his own blood. "Still I wouldn't have done it if I had known it was you." She paused. Her face wrinkled into a defensive frown. "Not that I ever had no . . ." She drew a deep breath, hating herself for so easily falling back into the vernacular of the girl she had once been. "What I mean is," she continued, "it's not that I ever had *any* fondness for you, Waptumewi. But for Kwelik's sake, mind you, I wouldn't have slashed you." Her voice cracked and lowered. "She's never stopped worrying and wondering about you." Reverence touched her tone. "And praying for you."

White Wolf leaned forward and gripped Annie's arm. "She is well then?" The question seeped from his lips in a pained whisper.

Annie nodded.

"And Snow Bird?"

Her gaze fell as she shook her head. "Smallpox. Six years ago. She was among the first to die." Annie paused. Her eyes flickered up to his and then fell again. "Why didn't you ever come back, Waptumewi? We needed you."

Long silence fell between them before White Wolf spoke again. "I could not."

Her eyes raised to meet his. In that moment she felt herself caught in the swirling waters of his gaze. There, swimming deep in the dark currents, were the reflections of her own doubts, her own pain, her own hidden guilt. For that single breath of time, understanding flashed between them, and Annie saw that they were both drowning in past pain. Yet neither knew the way to the shore.

Somewhere above her a wood thrush chirped its greeting to the dawn, breaking the spell. A breeze played at the curls of her hair, reminding her that time swept on around them and with it the consequences of her ill-fated bayonet swing.

Annie turned her head away and gave White Wolf's makeshift bandages a final tug. "It matters not now. The past is gone, forgotten." Even as she spoke, she knew the words were a lie. "Now you must go. Quickly." She stood and helped him to his feet. "The soldiers will be waking soon." Her voice turned wry. "Unless you planned to conquer the entire army with just your bow and arrows."

White Wolf scowled at her. "I see you too have not changed so much."

She shrugged. "Perhaps not. Can you walk?"

White Wolf's eyes searched hers one last time, as if seeking answers she could not give. Then they traveled over her right shoulder and widened with sudden fear.

"Pontiac, no!"

A blade flashed in the scant morning light and pressed into the flesh at Annie's throat. A drop of hot blood trickled down her skin. She twisted beneath the warrior's grasp, turning to meet black eyes, cold with the hatred of war. She clenched her teeth.

The brave's arm encircled her head and forced her chin up until she stood immobile beneath his grip. "The English come. They rise from their long slumber. We will kill the woman and flee."

"No!" White Wolf gasped the word.

Pontiac tightened his hold. His knife pressed deeper into the soft hollow of her throat. "Are you a friend of the English, Waptumewi? Is that why you could not kill the soldier?"

Annie's eyes flashed to White Wolf's face, watching it harden into a stern, emotionless mask, belying nothing. Her brows furrowed as she grappled with the thought that White Wolf did not kill the soldier, but this other man did, this brave who now stood behind her, his blade sharp at her neck.

White Wolf's answer came slowly, methodically, as if he had no interest in the outcome of Pontiac's decision. "Of course you may kill the woman if you wish. It's of no consequence to me."

Annie glared at him.

White Wolf's jaw flexed under her angry perusal. "It's only that I had thought she would make a fine gift to our French allies. They have so few white women at the fort." He paused. His eyes locked with Pontiac's. "She looks strong, healthy. But she is only one woman. Taking her scalp holds no honor."

Pontiac sighed. "Perhaps you are right. Come, let us go back and join our brothers at the fort." He squeezed White Wolf's shoulder with his free hand. "We have scouted the enemy. We have lessened their numbers by one. Soon they will all fall beneath our guns and tomahawks." He looked into White Wolf's eyes. "Are you prepared, Waptumewi, for the battle that will come?"

"We will see." White Wolf's answer slipped from his lips in a quiet whisper.

Pontiac nodded. His grip loosened on Annie as he guided them into the trees.

When the knife slipped low enough on her neck, Annie twisted in Pontiac's arm and sank her teeth into his hand. She tasted blood as she wrenched from his grasp. The knife clattered to the ground at her feet.

Before she could escape, Pontiac's hand smacked into her chin. She crumbled to the dirt. Her vision tunneled as she struggled unsuccessfully to rise.

Pontiac yanked her to her feet. One hand retrieved his knife while the other twined through her hair. He spoke over his shoulder. "Hurry, brother. The English approach."

Annie swayed under Pontiac's cruel grip. She swung around. Her fists flailed ineffectually at the Indian's chest. He chuckled.

With a muted cry Annie clawed at him while fear and anger chased each other through her befuddled mind. Pontiac pulled her hair harder, jarring her head back until she looked into his cold stare. He did not need to speak the threat that she saw there.

"Get away from me!" The words slurred from Annie's lips, already swelling from the impact of Pontiac's fist.

With one quick movement, he bound her arms with his belt and shoved her in front of him. "Silence, woman," he commanded. "Speak to me again, and I will cut your throat."

Annie glanced up at the tall warrior and knew that he spoke the truth.

Beside her White Wolf balanced unsteadily on his injured leg. He brushed against her, his mouth near her ear. "Quiet, Wakon," he whispered. "Trust me."

Anger exploded across her vision. *Trust? Like Snow Bird did? Like Kwelik?*

White Wolf must have read her thoughts. A pang of regret stabbed through her as she saw sorrow flash across his face.

From behind them distant English voices called through the morning air. "I thought I heard something over there," a man shouted, his footsteps loud as he pushed through a thicket of brush.

Annie opened her mouth to cry out, but the glint of Pontiac's blade silenced her.

"Did anyone see who was missing at camp?" Annie recognized the deep voice of Colonel Washington.

"Jenkins is gone and the washerwoman," came the muted reply.

"Miss Hill?"

"Aye."

"Go," Pontiac whispered. He nodded to White Wolf as he continued to push Annie in front of him.

She took a step forward and stumbled, hoping the sound would carry back to the soldiers.

Pontiac's knife immediately pressed against the base of her throat. "Make another sound," he whispered, his breath hot in her ear, "break a branch, disturb even a single leaf, and you will not live to see the noonday sun."

Then, as silently as the disappearing mist, the three of them melted into the trees. In moments the English voices grew more distant, until they faded altogether, and with them Annie's hope for escape. On and on the three traveled, slipping through the woods like a quiet breeze, never stopping, never speaking, never looking back. Pontiac's grip remained firm, compelling her forward.

Above her blue jays squawked to their mates, drowning the sounds of the meadowlark in the distance. Leaves rustled behind them like taunting whispers of old memories. Annie could almost hear the words reminding her of every failure, every mistake, every regret that haunted her dreams. She ground her teeth. How could she have allowed herself to be captured again? Had she learned nothing since her family's murder? She was a fool. No wonder Washington had not trusted her to fight with the men.

Annie scowled and stumbled beside White Wolf as Pontiac pushed her over a fallen tree in their path. She caught her breath, not daring to utter a sound as the bark tore through her dress and scraped along her skin. Already the morning dew had soaked the tattered bottom of her skirt, until the cloth wrapped around her legs like icy fingers intent on torment. But it didn't matter, she told herself.

Nothing mattered except that she somehow escape, somehow fight her way out of this nightmare.

She looked over at White Wolf as he limped silently beside her. His shoulders had broadened in the last ten years, and he had added inches to his height. She noticed the dark skin that rippled over his muscular back as he struggled to pull himself over the fallen tree trunk.

As if sensing her scrutiny, White Wolf turned toward her, his eyes unreadable in the morning light. And suddenly she was looking at a stranger.

～

Philippe Reveau stood on the battlement of Fort Duquesne, his gaze steady on the distant horizon. Today the battle would begin. Today the line between life and death would become as narrow as a musket's lead shot. And today through death or freedom, he would escape the endless purgatory of his meaningless existence. With a soft sigh he rubbed his hand over the back of his hair and twisted a single strand around his finger. Silently he watched as the sun climbed higher in the morning sky.

Below him French soldiers scampered about, preparing for battle. Word had come that morning from their Indian allies that the English with their guns and cannons had finally crossed the Monongahela River. Now the moment for war had arrived.

Philippe swallowed hard, ignoring the surge of distaste that welled within him whenever he thought of the battle he would face, a battle for a land he hated, a land he would soon forsake. For months now he'd planned his escape back to France. In the confusion of cannon fire, he would slip away, unnoticed and unmissed. They would think him dead on the battlefield and never guess that instead he'd run away. Then he would find his way home, someway, somehow. And when he did, he would never return to this wretched land again.

Philippe smiled. He could almost taste the ocean breezes that would lead him back to France. And in his mind he could hear the quiet lapping of the Seine River and the pattering of hurried feet on the busy streets of Paris. He could smell the aroma of fresh croissants wafting from the open door of the boulanger's shop, as it beckoned him to come and sample its crusty delicacies.

"Stop your daydreaming, soldier, and join your unit." The shout from below shattered Philippe's reverie. He sighed again. Then his eyes fell to the angry scowl of his lieutenant. He looked away. He was nothing to these men, nothing but a faceless image behind a musket, nothing but a body that filled a spot in the ranks, just one more man to die unmourned from enemy fire.

Philippe grabbed his musket in cold fingers and scurried down the ladder to join the others. Quickly he took his place in the ranks, his face blank as he marched out the fort's gate. The great wooden doors creaked closed behind him. Then the huge brace slammed into place with an air of finality.

Philippe raised his chin. One way or another, it would be the last time he ever heard that sound. He gritted his teeth and listened to the rhythmic thud of boots on the hard-packed earth.

Soon the rat-tat-tat of English drums replaced the sound of their footsteps. On the road ahead of them the English waited. Philippe shifted the horn of gunpowder that hung at his waist. Once, a long time ago, he could have followed an Indian girl and been free of the war that surrounded him now. But he had hesitated, afraid to take the risk of escaping with her. So he'd waited—too long. He rubbed his hand along the barrel of his musket, hoping to still the fear that whispered through him. Soon, if God smiled on him, he would remedy his former mistake.

By rote Philippe whispered a quick "Our Father" as the priests had taught him. The words were meaningless to him, but comforting. He drew a deep breath, allowing the cool morning air to wash through his lungs as his eyes studied the sky above him. Was there really a God out there somewhere? A God who saw and knew and loved? If only it were so. In France he would find the answer to that question, and many others. He would find out who he really was.

From in front of him, the commander's warning boomed through the morning air. Philippe's head jerked up at the sound. There in rows across the tiny road the English stood, their scarlet coats like blood against the trees, their guns pointed and ready. For a moment every man held his breath, waiting for the sound of a musket's fire.

It came. A shot whizzed through the air, the first messenger of the day's death toll. A dozen shots followed. Philippe cringed as a man fell beside him.

Then the world turned dark.

FIVE

~

After the long night's storm, sunlight glimmered across the water's surface, shining like a million jeweled ladies waltzing with the ocean's waves. Jonathan smiled and turned from the sight. His eyes rested on his wife who stood quietly at the ship's stern. Even from across the deck, her gentle beauty touched him. Despite her scars Kwelik had only grown more beautiful in their ten years of marriage.

Unaware of his warm perusal, Kwelik laughed as she watched the water dip and swirl in the ship's wake. *Probably thinking of some similarity between her own life and the waves,* Jonathan thought. He knew her so well, and yet she still surprised him with the depths of her love, still delighted him in so many ways. *What a precious gift You've given me, Lord. I would have never dreamed that such happiness could be mine.*

Kwelik twirled the end of her long black braid in graceful fingers. How he loved the feel of the thick, silky tresses as she snuggled in his arms. He sighed with contentment and allowed his gaze to wander over the endless expanse of ocean. *This ocean is like Your love for me, God, and hers.* He smiled to himself. *My wife's ways are becoming my own. Even I am beginning to see reminders of You in nature.* He brushed a bit of moisture from his shirt and then looked up at the blue sky. *Ah, Lord God, I beseech You, make me a worthy husband. Increase my faith in You.*

Jonathan dropped his gaze. Then a frown settled on his face as he watched a sailor approach Kwelik. Jonathan leaned forward and squinted to get a better look. The man stopped in front of her. His chin tilted so that his face was visible.

Jonathan caught his breath as he recognized the man who had accosted them before the storm. Uneasiness gripped his chest. He started toward his wife. His hands clenched tight, then opened again.

The sailor pointed his finger in Kwelik's face. His mouth twisted with loathing as he spoke words that Jonathan could not hear. Anger and fear marked Kwelik's features. She stepped back, her palm pressed against her abdomen. The man sneered.

Jonathan quickened his stride.

Kwelik shook her head. Her hand reached behind her as she sought to inch away from the red-faced sailor. Just as Jonathan crossed the center of the deck, the man thrust out a gnarled hand and shoved Kwelik to the deck.

"Hold!" Jonathan shouted.

Kwelik struggled to a kneeling position, her face pale as she clutched her midsection.

Fear and fury erupted in Jonathan. He threw himself at the sailor and hurled the man to the deck. The sailor's head hit the wooden planks with a dull thud. They rolled together, Jonathan's grip tight on the man's collar. He pulled back his arm and cocked his fist to slam it into the sailor's leathery face.

"No, Jonathan!" Kwelik's desperate call sounded behind him.

He halted his blow. His hand shook with the intensity of his anger. *Increase my faith.* His prayer echoed in his mind. He gritted his teeth. At that moment he wanted nothing more than to pummel the life out of the man who now trembled in his grip.

"Jonathan." Kwelik repeated his name, softer this time.

With a groan Jonathan shoved the man from him and stumbled to his feet. "Faith, not fists," he whispered to himself, though his breath still came in short bursts of anger. His eyes bored into the sailor at his feet. "Next time," he growled. Then he turned to help Kwelik.

"Behind you!" Kwelik warned.

Jonathan felt the man's hands impact his lower back with a violent shove. Kwelik screamed as he flew toward the ship's railing. With a quick movement, he attempted to turn, to fend off the sailor's attack. His foot skidded on a coil of rope and sent him staggering to the edge of the ship. For a moment Kwelik's frightened face filled his vision. Then the world spun until he saw nothing but green water swelling beneath him like a writhing demon, eager to swallow its prey. Jonathan crashed into its cold jaws. The waves roared in his ears as he plunged beneath the icy surface. He fought his way up to the air, gasping as he coughed and choked for breath. His mouth filled with the bitter water. Cold waves swirled around his head. His arms flailed, and his lungs burned from the intake of sea water as he floundered toward the ship.

Another wave slapped into him and pushed his head below the water's surface. Desperately he struggled against the waves. From somewhere behind him he could hear the excited shouts from the men on deck.

"The rope. Grab the rope," someone yelled.

Jonathan turned. His eyes stung as he stared across the shimmering water. He looked up. There leaning over the railing, four men stood, their hands holding the rope that had sent him hurling into the ocean.

Jonathan blinked as one end of the rope sailed in his direction. It landed a few feet from him, hitting the water with a quiet splash. He swam toward it and grabbed it a few feet up the length. His hands, stiff and shaking with cold, tied the sodden mass around him.

"Haul him up, men," a sailor shouted.

Jonathan felt the rope tighten. The air above him resounded with the grunts of the men tugging on the far end of the rope. Slowly he rose from the water. His knees bumped and scraped along the side of the boat as the men pulled him from the ocean's icy teeth. With a final heave, they dragged him up to the railing. Then a dozen rough hands reached down to yank him onto the deck.

Jonathan fell to his knees. His hair dripped over his face while his hands pressed against the solid surface of the wood planking. He gagged and spewed salt water from his lungs, then struggled to loosen the swollen rope from around him. He groaned, his fingers numb and useless.

Kwelik rushed toward him. "Oh, Jonathan," she breathed. She wrapped one arm around his shoulders as her other hand reached down to touch his face. "Can you stand?"

Jonathan swayed as he rose. He reached up to squeeze her hand reassuringly. Then his head tilted to glare at his adversary who now stood belligerently behind the other men.

"Have you gone mad, sir?" the captain shouted from across the deck. His face wrinkled in an accusatory scowl as he bore down on Jonathan.

"Nay, sir." Jonathan pushed back his sodden hair with one hand. He pointed at Kwelik's attacker. "I was pushed over by that man."

The captain turned to the sailor. "Is that true, Waller?"

A hush fell over the deck as everyone's eyes turned toward the man. Only the slap of the ship's bow against the waves could be heard in the waiting stillness.

Waller dropped his head. "Aye, Cap'n. It's true." He scuffed his booted heel over the deck. His voice sharpened to a whine. "I threw him over."

Jonathan heard a soft intake of breath behind him.

Waller raised his head. A wicked glint shone from his eyes as he regarded Jonathan and then the captain. "And I'd do it again, Cap'n." He licked his lips. "He provoked me sorely, he did, blaspheming God and crown like that. I couldn't stomach it. Things I dare not repeat, sir."

Jonathan lunged forward. "Liar!"

Waller stumbled backward. The captain moved between them. "See there, Cap'n," the man screeched. "He's the devil's own consort, I tell you. Just look at his woman. He's a savage-lover and a French spy, I'd wager. Pah." He thrust his chin forward and spat on the deck.

"Still your lying tongue, or I'll do it for you." Jonathan's fists clenched. He stepped forward.

Kwelik put her hand gently on his arm. "Wait, husband." Her voice spoke softly in his ear. "Something's not right here."

Jonathan looked back at her and noted the suspicion that colored her face as she continued. "He has planned this. His look is the same as the men who once attacked us outside the blacksmith's shop. He desires for you to fight him."

Jonathan nodded once and took a step back, his eyes intent on the man's smug face. Kwelik was right. Even now he could feel the invisible trap that closed in around him.

Behind him a sharp gasp echoed from Kwelik's lips, and her fingers dug into the flesh of his forearm.

Jonathan turned. His arms automatically reached to pull her to him.

Kwelik put her hands on his chest and looked down, her eyes wide. Jonathan's gaze followed hers. Water stained the deck and dripped from beneath her full skirt.

"I pray thee, get the Mistress Sullivan. Hurry." Her voice shook as she spoke.

Jonathan frowned. "What is it?"

Kwelik's eyes locked with his. Her face flooded with sudden fear. "The babe," she whispered. "It comes too soon."

~

Bark bit into Annie's flesh as she struggled to loosen herself from the tree to which she was tied. Pontiac's final words still pulsed in her ears. "From here you will see the death of your mighty army," he had said, "and you will know that your hope is dead with them. After the battle I will take you to the French fort where you will serve them well or die." Annie clenched her jaw, determined to feel no fear.

The pungent smell of sap assaulted her senses as it oozed into her hair and attracted a passing honeybee. She shook her head, irritated by the buzzing insect that settled on her shoulder. She scowled and attempted to blow away the offending bug. Finally the bee rose and flew in a lazy circle around her.

"Bloody bug," she whispered, twisting her head to keep the bee from landing on her again. "If only I were free, I'd squash you with my bare hands."

In a moment the bee was forgotten as Annie saw a dozen Indian warriors slither through the trees beside her. She looked beyond them, down a short hill and through a thicket of brush. There, less than a hundred yards from her, the road twined like a thin worm. And on it, with red coats like bright signals, the English proudly approached.

Annie turned her head and watched as the French materialized from the trees and gathered on the road before the English. Their muskets glimmered in the sun. Both armies stopped. Annie held her breath. For a long second silence descended over the land. Then a French officer lifted his hat and shouted. His voice sent a chill across Annie's skin. At that moment, like the wail of a banshee, a shot split the morning.

Before Annie could draw another breath, a hundred muskets exploded. The earth trembled beneath her as smoke billowed into the air. The haze cleared, revealing a score of men fallen on both sides.

Annie strained forward, her heart hammering as the French regulars gave ground. "Yes," she whispered. "Go. Flee. You cannot win this battle." Her voice gained strength. "You must not."

As if in denial of her plea, the French captain waved his hat to the left and right. In response more Indians dissolved into the forest, intent on taking the English in flank. Annie's eyes flew to the British troops. Her stomach tightened as the men pressed forward, unaware of the invisible enemy.

"They're surrounding you. Get off the road. Hurry," Annie cried, willing the British officers to hear her through the noise of battle. Instead, covering the sound of her voice, chilling war cries echoed from every direction. Annie groaned as the French, encouraged by the howl of their Indian allies, again surged forward.

Ten yards in front of her a brave passed through the trees, momentarily blocking her view. Like a part of the shadows, he crept low to the ground, his musket clenched in one hand. Annie stared at his dark back and then at the tomahawk that swung from his belt. Her breath came more quickly as a ray of sunlight caught the dull blade and threw a sliver of light back into her face. She groaned. If only she could hold the weapon in her own hand, wield it with the strength of her own wrath, stand beside her people, and die if she must.

The brave ducked behind a tall birch and stopped. Then he lifted his musket to aim at the foremost British troops. His shot blasted through the trees. With a shout of success, he moved on, slinking from Annie's sight.

Her gaze fell to the battlefield. Desperately she watched as the

English wheeled their light artillery into line and blasted a thundering salvo that rose above the rattle of the musketry. Black smoke danced above the scene. Annie squinted and waited for the advance of the English troops. Below her a band of regulars ran forward, bayonets flashing, their coats like targets in the haze. They swung into formation.

"Get back, get back!" Annie screamed. But her words were lost.

The Indians shrieked again, their weapons resounding. Countless British soldiers fell beneath their fire. She cringed as the English troops recoiled in confusion, stumbling over one another on the narrow twelve-foot road.

"No, no!" Annie heard her own voice shriek in her ears. "It's too late! Don't retreat! Fight!"

Another volley of fire rained down from the Indians who had ascended a nearby hill. Annie watched with horror as the English regulars continued to scurry backward, only to ram into the front of the approaching baggage wagon. Wedged onto the tiny road, unable to maneuver, the men turned again to fight.

Annie heard the low whistle of an artillery shell a moment before it hit. With a loud blast it slammed into the ground near her. Her heart hammered in her throat as the force of the explosion jarred her shoulders. Clumps of dirt and grass sprayed over her. A cry wrenched from her lips as a rock hurled into her side. She spat dirt from her mouth. "It doesn't matter," she whispered fiercely. "Better to die in battle than at the hands of the French or the Indians."

She drew a deep breath and choked. The acrid smoke of black powder hung densely in the air, making the scarlet coats of the British appear as only a blur of color in the saffron haze. The shouts of the distraught soldiers echoed in her ears. She bit her lip, wishing she could close her eyes, hide from the horror that played itself out below her. But she could not. There her future hung in the smoke and gagged on the bitter taste of it.

Annie coughed. Despair clawed through her as General Braddock galloped into the fray, shouting orders, commands, and imprecations. He beat his befuddled men with flat of his sword, yanking his horse in this direction and that as he sought to drive his troops forward. Annie groaned as she saw Washington, still weak from illness, sitting astride his horse. His musket fired hopelessly into the mass of French troops.

Spurts of flame from the musketry and large guns stabbed through the gloom as gunners fired wildly in every direction. Beside her a small tree burst under a direct hit. Its branches flew through the air and scattered across the rocky ground. Annie shook her head. "The enemy, shoot at the enemy," she shouted. Her words evaporated like mist in the fire.

Again, closer to the English this time, came the Indians' shrill shrieks, like mad laughter among the trees. Annie could see the English soldiers huddled together, as if fear had paralyzed them.

She tightened her muscles and strained at the ropes that bound her. At that moment Washington's horse crumpled beneath him. Annie gasped. He staggered up and pulled a dead man from another mount. Smoothly he swung his long legs over the saddle and continued to fight.

To her left a few frontiersmen glided through the trees as blue-garbed Virginians shot from behind rocks and trees at the French and Indians. But even as the colonists advanced, the English regulars dissolved into a demoralized mob. Bundled together in a frightened heap, they fired aimlessly into the shadowy forest, cutting down their own men. Annie's eyes blurred with tears of fury and frustration. She screamed as frontiersmen fell beneath the friendly fire.

She raised her chin toward the smoky sky. "What sort of God are You?" she shouted. "Are You blind? Are You deaf?" Her voice echoed against the trees above her and then lost itself in the screams of the fallen men. She dropped her head.

A stray shot whizzed by her and burrowed into a tree to her right. Annie shuddered and pressed her back into the rough bark of the oak's trunk. Fury at her own helplessness twined around her. She closed her eyes. If only she could be fighting now instead of sitting trussed to a tree, able to do nothing but mourn as her countrymen fell in the melee of terror and slaughter.

Annie opened her eyes and watched dully as Washington leaped from his horse and rushed toward General Braddock, who had toppled from his mount. In the trees near him, the face of an Indian warrior materialized behind the barrel of a long musket. Annie held her breath as the Indian pointed the gun at Washington's chest. The shot exploded into the air. She groaned, waiting for Washington to fall.

He did not.

Annie's brows drew together in confusion. The Indian was too close to miss. Yet, without flinching, Washington pulled off his jacket and placed it around the shoulders of the wounded general. Annie's eyes narrowed. She drew a quick breath. As far as she could tell, not one spot of blood marred the colonel's tall frame. Washington scanned the battlefield and then turned to help Braddock remount his horse.

Braddock swayed in his saddle, lifted his bayonet, and then shouted above the blasts of musket fire. "Retreat! Retreat! Back to the river!" The words pierced Annie's heart like a sword.

She turned her gaze to the French troops. One of the soldiers cast down his musket. He glanced around him, then disappeared into the trees.

The cheers of the French soldiers and the whoop of Indians resounded in her ears as the remnants of the English army clawed their way toward the narrow strip of ground that still lay open between them and the river. All that was left of her army and her hope was the artillery, abandoned on the road like a child's discarded toys.

"Come back," she choked, her voice hoarse from the thick smoke of battle.

No one listened. No one heard. No one cared.

Cold foreboding clutched her throat and stung her eyes. It was over. "Oh God, God, why have You abandoned me? Abandoned us?" *Trust God*, Washington had said. Now against the backs of the retreating British troops, his words seemed like the ramblings of a madman.

Annie tilted her head to stare into the smoke-covered sky. Her voice squeezed through lips tight with anguish. "How can I trust You, God? How can I now? Look." Her eyes fell to the battlefield and blurred on the scene. Everywhere red-coated soldiers lay dead and dying, scattered over the ground like spilled matchsticks. "Can't You see? Don't You care?"

Then in the smoky haze she saw something that made her stomach tighten with dark fear. Pontiac strode toward her. His skin glistened with blood and sweat. A dozen scalps dangled from his belt.

Bile rose in Annie's throat. Now, she knew, the real terror would begin.

Six

~

The moment had come. Philippe squeezed his musket in his hand and allowed the hot metal to sear his skin one last time. He watched as the English lumbered back toward the Monongahela River, their guns and wounded left like refuse on the battlefield.

The victory shouts of his fellow soldiers rang hollowly in his ears. Victory meant nothing, at least not to him, not in this land, not with the shores of France an ocean away.

Philippe frowned. His eyes traveled down to his musket. He hated the feel of it in his hand. With a snort of disgust, he threw it away from him. The barrel made a sharp thump on the hard-packed dirt. He edged toward the trees. Now he would make good his escape.

When he reached the edge of the woods, he paused and glanced back one final time to search for watching eyes. He saw none. A curl of smoke drifted around him, tickling his nose until he sneezed. The sound echoed in his ears like an artillery shot. But no one else heard. He rubbed his finger across his nose and slipped into the forest.

Around him branches swooped down on all sides, their leaves dusted with the soot of battle. He smiled. Soon he would be free. All he had to do was put as much distance as possible between himself and those who would again enslave him. "I'm going home," he whispered. The words wove like a melody through the trees.

He quickened his pace to a steady trot. In France all would be right again. In France he would live free. In France he would find his destiny. *In France, in France, in France*. Philippe chuckled as his footsteps swished through the grass in time with the chant in his mind. He slowed to push back a spindly branch from his path. Nothing could stop him now.

Before the thought faded from his mind, a brave stepped from the trees to block his escape. Philippe skidded to a halt. His breath stopped. His eyes locked on the tomahawk clenched fiercely in the Indian's right hand. Slowly his gaze traveled up the warrior's muscular form. He trembled as he looked into the brave's face—chiseled cheekbones framed by long dark hair and topped by eyes as black and fathomless as the sea that separated Philippe from his homeland.

The Indian leaned forward. A feathered braid swung across his bare chest. His grip whitened on the weapon.

Philippe attempted to step back, but he found himself frozen beneath the warrior's dark gaze. "*Arrétez*," he whispered, his voice sounding like that of the boy he had once been. "*Non*."

The Indian raised his tomahawk.

Philippe closed his eyes, waiting as his dreams withered like chaff beneath the black fire of the Indian's gaze.

~

White Wolf's hand trembled on the tomahawk as he regarded the Frenchman before him. A *deserter*, he wondered, *even after such a grand victory?* The soldier closed his eyes and waited, as if expecting him to deliver the killing blow.

White Wolf watched the breeze ruffle the man's light brown hair. Ten years ago he would have killed the man without another thought. But not today. Today not even a single scalp hung from his belt. He lowered his weapon. "I am White Wolf. I will not harm you." The French words sputtered awkwardly from his lips as he searched his memory for the lessons learned a lifetime ago. "*Parlez-vous anglais, monsieur?*"

The French soldier responded slowly. "*Oui.* I mean, yes."

White Wolf nodded, English now coming more easily to his tongue. "Who are you, and why do you sneak through the woods like a rabbit escaping the wolf?"

The Frenchman did not flinch as he answered. "I am Philippe Reveau." He lifted his chin. "And I will not go back."

White Wolf's eyes narrowed at the soldier's determined tone. "Where is your musket, Philippe Reveau?"

"There." Philippe motioned toward the battlefield. "I am weary of war, this land, and everything that reminds me of it."

White Wolf frowned. "So you threw away your weapon?"

Philippe nodded.

"Then you are a fool." White Wolf spoke calmly. As if to confirm his words, the victory cry of the Ottawa Indians cut through the air as they gathered scalps from the battlefield.

Philippe's jaw tightened. "I am going back to France. I will not need a musket there."

White Wolf flung back his head and laughed. The sound rang against the leaves overhead as he motioned into the forest. "And you expect to find France just through those trees and over that knoll perhaps?"

Philippe's face reddened.

White Wolf put his hand on Philippe's shoulder. His face sobered. "You do not know how to find France, do you, my friend?"

The red color deepened on Philippe's cheeks. "I have escaped the fort. For now that is enough."

White Wolf raised his eyebrows and waited.

Philippe drew a long breath and thrust out his chest. "You may kill me now or take me back and turn me over to the French officers. I am ready to accept my fate."

For a long moment White Wolf watched Philippe's obstinate expression. Then he smiled. "Why do you wish so much to go to France?"

Philippe's eyes lowered, catching White Wolf's with intensity. "You ask many questions for an Indian," he muttered. "If you must know, I was born there. And for the first years of my life, I was happy there, my family and I." Philippe paused as if this should explain everything.

White Wolf leaned back and crossed his arms in front of him. *Home.* The word whispered through him. He swallowed hard. "Go on," he murmured, his voice tight with unwelcome emotion.

"There I will find myself again." Philippe stepped toward him. His voice lowered. "And I will find God."

The tomahawk shook in White Wolf's hand. He cleared his throat and steadied himself. "So you are going home?"

Philippe nodded.

White Wolf studied him a moment longer before he spoke again. "Then you are a braver man than I thought." A wry smile broke over White Wolf's face. He turned the tomahawk around in his hand and tapped Philippe on the chest with the handle. "I'll help you."

"What?" The word slipped from Philippe's lips in a whisper.

"I'll help you return to France," White Wolf repeated, his voice steady despite the rapid beating of his heart.

Philippe caught his breath. "You know the way?"

White Wolf's voice dropped. "My father taught me many things."

Beyond them a feminine scream echoed from the battlefield. The sound tore through White Wolf's nerves. He shivered. His hand descended onto Philippe's shoulder as he led the Frenchman further into the forest. "I will show you the way to France," he repeated, "but first you must help me."

Philippe frowned and stepped beside White Wolf. "How?"

White Wolf grimaced and twirled his tomahawk in one hand as he attempted to explain. "There is a woman."

For the first time a smile of understanding flickered over Philippe's face. "Ah yes, *l'amour*. We French know it well."

White Wolf stared at him for a moment before his mouth bent in bitter amusement. "Love?" A sharp laugh broke from his lips. "No, I wouldn't call it that, my friend." He rubbed his hand over his bandaged leg. "Anything but that."

Philippe's brows drew together in confusion.

White Wolf chuckled again. "But that is of no matter. It's enough to know that I wish the woman free. She has been captured with some of the English and will soon be brought to the fort."

Philippe scowled. "I told you, I will not go back."

"You will," White Wolf asserted in response. "You'll help me to free her. Then I'll show you how to go home."

Philippe scratched his head and looked back to the west toward the fort. Slowly he dipped his head in quiet acquiescence. "It will be as you say." He gripped White Wolf's forearm to seal the pact. "I will help you and the woman."

White Wolf's eyes caught and held Philippe's. "To finding the way back home then," he whispered, his last words lost in the forest breezes, "for both of us."

∼

Endure. Fight. Show no fear. Annie's head pounded with the strength of renewed resolve as she stumbled behind the band of Indian warriors that followed Pontiac. Ropes chafed her wrists, reminding her of that other day when the Indians had stolen her life, killed her family, and sparked in her the fire of wrath and revenge. She ground her teeth and allowed the fury, terror, and despair to mix together in the hot cauldron of her heart.

Night had just begun to cast its mantle over the Pennsylvania sky. Annie glanced up, welcoming the descending darkness. Night, she hoped, would shroud the persistent horror that plodded before her vision in the form of twenty ponies, their backs arched beneath piles of dripping scalps.

Annie shuddered as her gaze fell to the hunched outlines of a dozen British regulars, their faces painted as black as the coming night, a sign that they were reserved for torture. And beside them, with dresses torn and bloody, staggered six white women, fellow captives from battle.

A pained cry burst from Annie's lips as her toes jammed into a root that jutted from the path. She strained at the ropes that bound her, her hands useless to break her fall. Her shoulder slammed into the hard-packed earth. A rock jabbed into her shin, drawing fresh blood from the myriad tiny cuts that laced her skin. She bit her lip, refusing to make another sound.

A brave stepped beside her. The red coat of a dead Englishman was draped over his bare shoulders. "Get up," he demanded. His rough English splintered her resolve. His fingers wrapped tightly around her arm. She attempted to pull away and failed.

The Indian leaned over her. The back of his hand slapped roughly across her face. The ground swayed beneath her. "This is not happening," she whispered to herself. "Not now. Not again." The brave's fingers dug into her skin as he jerked her to her feet. From in front of the ponies, Pontiac turned briefly. His eyes pierced hers. Annie scowled, then winced at the pain in her cheek.

"Walk," the Indian behind her commanded. The butt of his tomahawk pressed into her back. She faltered forward.

To her left a woman sniffled. Annie's gaze flickered up the woman's stout frame with sudden recognition. "Mary Elizabeth?"

The woman turned, revealing bloodshot eyes in a face wet with tears. "Aye. That you, Miss Hill?"

Annie sidled near her, her voice low. "It is."

Mary Elizabeth tipped her head. "Oh, Miss Hill, you was right. I didn't believe you, but you was right. What's gonna become of us? I don't want to die." The last word ended in a rush of noisy tears.

"Hush, Mary." Annie looked anxiously behind her, relieved that the Indian with the tomahawk had dropped back to speak with another brave. She turned back toward Mary. "Listen to me. If you want to live, you must not draw attention to yourself."

Mary Elizabeth's sobs quickly became a high-pitched wail.

Annie cringed. "No, Mary! Shhh."

"I don't wanna di-i-i-ie."

"Look!" Annie's voice raised above Mary Elizabeth's cry. "The fort."

Mary sniffed and quieted. "The French?" Her brows drew together in sudden thought. "Say, maybe them Frenchies could use a woman of my talents," she whispered, the idea giving her new assurance. "Surely they won't let no Injuns hurt a woman right outside their walls. Will they?"

Annie did not answer. Before her the French fort loomed tall and ominous against the twilight sky. As they approached the gate, the Indians waved their stolen swords and raised the scalp halloo. A dozen musket shots exploded into the air. In response cheers and answering musket fire echoed from atop the fort's walls. Annie held her breath. Now she would discover whether she would live or die.

As if reading her thoughts, a hundred Indian warriors gathered sticks, switches, and thorny branches from the woods around them.

Then without a word, the braves lined up in two rows, making a thin corridor that stretched toward the fort's gate. Their silence had twisted around Annie's heart. Now a shrill shriek burst from every savage throat. Her knees shook beneath her as the Indians pounded the ground with their makeshift clubs.

Beside her Mary Elizabeth's terrified scream rose above the clamor. "Oh God, God!" she howled. "What's going on?"

"It's the gauntlet," Annie answered, her voice dull with remembered fear.

Mary Elizabeth sucked in her breath. "The gauntlet?"

Annie nodded. "The prisoners must run through without falling as the Indians beat them."

A tremor shook Mary Elizabeth's ample frame. "What if they fall?"

Annie turned toward her and remained silent.

For a moment Mary Elizabeth's watery blue eyes met hers. Then the woman swallowed once and promptly crumpled to the ground in a terrified heap.

From behind them an English soldier was thrust forward. The sharp cries of the Indians echoed through the air as they continued to pound the ground in preparation for their first victim.

Annie tightened her jaw, refusing to look away as a brave pulled out a long knife and cut away the soldier's uniform. The brave stepped back. He twirled the soldier's torn shirt over his head as he spoke in broken English. "You run. Fast. Indian hit. No fall, live. Fall, die. Simple. Now run." With another flick of his wrist he sliced the neck and wrist bonds from the soldier and shoved him toward the gauntlet. The soldier backed away, his eyes wide with horror. He looked for a way to escape and found none.

"Run!" the Indian behind him shouted and then lit a torch. The flame sputtered up. Sparks flew toward the sky.

With a gasp the English soldier stumbled toward the Indians. His feet picked up speed as the brave thrust the torch into his back. His first shriek cut through Annie's nerves.

The air filled with the scent of burning flesh. Annie's eyes fastened on the Englishman. He surged forward. Branches beat down on him with frenzied precision. "Go. Hurry," she whispered through clenched teeth. "Faster."

Four steps. Five. Six. The soldier still ran.

Annie stepped closer. Her thoughts urged the man forward. *Push through. Don't stop.*

Seven steps. Eight. A savage blow crashed on the side of the man's head. He wavered. Blood gushed from his ear.

"Stay up!" This time the words burst from Annie's lips in a desperate scream.

The man crumpled.

Annie closed her eyes and listened as the Indians fell upon the soldier with their sticks and switches. Thump, thump, thump. Annie knew that the man's flesh was giving way beneath them. And there in the background sounded Mary Elizabeth's persistent wail.

Moments later the Indians' loud whoop burst into the air and swallowed the cries of Mary Elizabeth and the other prisoners. Annie opened her eyes to see the warriors haul off the bloody mass that was once an English soldier. Her stomach heaved.

Pontiac strode toward her, his eyes steady on hers. A mocking smile twisted his lips as he stepped beside her. Before she could comprehend his intent, his hand bit into the flesh of her upper arm and compelled her forward. The Indians shrieked again. Understanding washed through her. *Endure. Fight. Show no fear.*

Pontiac thrust her toward the gauntlet line. Before her the Indians whacked the ground with their sticks and branches. Despite her resolve a tremor ran through her. Her eyes flashed up to Pontiac.

He looked down at her, his voice emotionless as he spoke. "It is our way."

Annie dropped her gaze. Her eyes focused on the end of the line. "I will survive."

Pontiac stepped closer. "I can spare you." His voice breathed lightly in her ear.

Annie did not hesitate as she answered, "I'm ready. I'm not afraid." Her gaze clashed with his. "Know this, you, you . . ." Her body trembled with the intensity of her hate. "You bloody barbarian! I would rather die a hundred deaths than ever be indebted to you."

To her surprise Pontiac's low chuckle sounded in her ear. "It is a shame that I have promised to give you to the French, if you live." He ran his finger beneath her chin and then tilted her face toward him. "You would make a fine woman for a warrior chief."

Annie's cheeks flushed with fury. "I will live. But I will never be a red man's wife." Her eyes slid from his face to fix on the fort's gate, dimly visible through the line of Indian braves.

Pontiac's hand gripped her arm until her skin turned pale. He leaned forward. His face crossed her vision. "No, you will die." He paused and dropped her arm. A smile flashed across his features, then faded. "But not yet."

Annie felt his grip loosen.

"Bring the next one." Pontiac shouted the command over his shoulder. "I choose to spare this woman for French pleasures." He laughed again.

The sound echoed coldly in Annie's ears. Then she turned and watched with helpless horror as Mary Elizabeth entered the gauntlet line.

SEVEN

~

The wooden planks creaked under Jonathan's feet as he paced back and forth along the narrow corridor outside his cabin. From behind the thick door came his wife's pained moans, interspersed with the low muttering of Mistress Sullivan. He reached the end of the corridor and turned around for the hundredth time in the endless night.

A single lantern swayed from the ceiling and sent a dozen shadows swirling across the bare walls. Jonathan watched the shadows and continued his vigil. Back and forth, back and forth, listen, wait, hope, fear. He ran his hand through his hair and then dropped it to his chin, scarcely noticing the rough stubble that grew there. His bloodshot eyes focused again on the door that separated him from his wife and the child for whom they'd hoped and prayed.

Six years it had taken them to conceive after Justin was born. Six long, doubt-filled years, wondering if God would ever bless them with another child. Then it had finally happened. Oh, how they'd rejoiced! Kwelik had made tiny deerskin booties, and their friend Rosie began work on a patchwork blanket. He and Justin had then made a small cradle that even now waited ready in the room beyond. But now Jonathan feared that cradle could remain forever empty, and not only could he lose the child they'd yearned for, but he could lose the woman he loved.

Jonathan took three steps forward and paused before the cabin door. With a trembling breath, he held out the tips of his fingers and touched its rough exterior. "Oh God, God," he whispered, "don't let them die. Save the child. And save my wife." His prayer came to a choking halt just as it had done countless times during his long watch.

An agonized cry echoed from the room and wrenched through

his heart. Fear shot through him again and brought him to his knees. "Oh, God, help! Have mercy. Please have mercy." He rocked forward and back on his heels. His breath came in quiet sobs as he dropped his head into his hands. "What was I thinking? Only a madman would haul his pregnant wife across the world to save a brother who had tried to kill him. I should have forgotten the note, forgotten that I ever knew a Richard Grant."

Jonathan lifted his face. His eyes searched the damp beams above him. "Am I a fool, God?" His voice cracked.

First be reconciled to thy brother, and then come and offer thy gift. Jonathan's head fell again to his hands as the verse whispered through his mind in Kwelik's quiet voice.

As if in defiance of the words, a scream tore from the room before him. Jonathan leaped to his feet. His fists clenched and unclenched at his sides. "How can I care about my brother now, God? Do You hear my wife's cries? Do You hear her pain?" As his voice faded, Jonathan squeezed his eyes shut and fought to contain the panic that rose within him.

Sudden silence emanated from behind the door. Jonathan leaned closer. A baby's cry split the air. Then again the silence.

A minute passed, then five, then twenty. Still no further sound but muted shuffling came from the room beyond. He turned away and resumed his pacing. Had the child died after its first cry? And Kwelik? Jonathan groaned, unable to bear the thought.

The door squeaked open behind him. He swiveled around. Mistress Sullivan blustered from the room. Her face flushed beneath her crumpled cap as she hurried toward him.

A thousand questions, a million fears, darted through Jonathan's mind. He opened his mouth, but no sound came.

Without a word Mistress Sullivan wrapped her strong arms around him.

Jonathan's eyes jerked to hers. His gaze searched her wrinkled face.

She smiled and pushed back a lock of gray hair from her cheek. "The babe lives, Mr. Grant. A strong girl-child."

Jonathan felt his blood run hot through his veins. "A daughter?" he whispered. Wonder filled his voice.

Mistress Sullivan grinned. "A beautiful little girl. With the face of an angel." She laughed and clapped her hands together at Jonathan's bewildered expression. "You may breathe again, sir. All is well." She stepped back, gripped Jonathan's face in both hands, and planted a kiss on each cheek. "God is with you, Mr. Grant. 'Twas a difficult time, to be sure. But the wee child lived. Thanks be to God."

Jonathan's heart beat faster as he touched the woman's arm with a trembling finger. "And my wife?"

Mistress Sullivan smiled and wiped a hand across her forehead. "Weak but alive, Mr. Grant. I've never seen a woman with such a tenacity for life." She shook her head and chuckled. "Most women would have just given up and died last night. But not your wife. She's quite a woman."

Jonathan closed his eyes and felt the tight grip of fear loosen from around his heart. He opened his eyes again and nodded, scarcely hearing any more of the woman's chatter.

A broad grin flashed over her round face as she patted his shoulder. "You may see for yourself, sir." She motioned toward the door. "Go on in now. They're both waiting for you."

Jonathan smiled and placed his hand on the door that had symbolized the worst of his fears. He took a deep breath and cautiously pushed it open.

There, propped up on the small bed, lay his wife with a blanket-wrapped bundle in her arms. Jonathan paused, noticing how her hair fell in damp clumps down her pale forehead, though her cheeks remained colored by a fine blush of weariness and joy.

"Kwelik?" His voice stumbled over her name.

"It's all right, Jonathan. Look." She smiled up at him and pulled back the corner of the blanket in her arms.

Jonathan's breath caught as his eyes fell to the tiny face peeking from the folds. Then his gaze traveled back to Kwelik. "Is she . . ."

Kwelik nodded. "She's perfect. Come and see."

He chuckled softly and hurried to them. Then he knelt and encircled both her and the child in his arms.

"A month and a half early," Kwelik continued. "Yet she is perfect. Only her little fingernails and toenails are missing." She disengaged the child's tiny hand from the covers and placed it in her palm. "And Mistress Sullivan says they'll grow in a few weeks." Her free hand reached out to intertwine with Jonathan's. "God is gracious."

Jonathan tilted his head toward her. "And merciful." He lifted his arm. His finger gently touched the flushed cheek of his daughter. Awe filled him. "She's so beautiful, so delicate. I never dreamed . . ."

Kwelik raised his hand to her lips and kissed it. Her eyes shone with joy. "What shall we name her?"

Jonathan's finger traveled up to his daughter's dark hair where it lay in drying curls around her face. He caught a strand between his thumb and forefinger. "I would like to call her Brenna, my mother's name."

Kwelik smiled. "May she be as gentle and faithful as the woman you have told me about." Her gaze rested on the baby. "You shall be called Brenna." She looked again at Jonathan. "But, if you are willing, her Indian name will be Hanaholend. It means River Loving."

Jonathan reached down and gathered the baby in his arms. The warmth of her tiny body spread through him. He brushed his lips gently over her forehead. "Brenna Hanaholend, do you know how much you are loved?"

The baby jerked her arm in his direction and grunted in response.

Jonathan laughed. His eyes caught Kwelik's. "Already she knows her papa's voice."

An exuberant knock sounded on the door just before it opened. Jonathan lifted his head as a small face pushed through the opening. "Can I come in too?" Justin's voice barely concealed his excitement. "Mistress Sullivan said it would be all right now."

"Come, Justin. Meet your baby sister." Kwelik reached out her hand to beckon the boy.

Jonathan turned and grinned at his son. "You're a big brother now. Look who God has given you—given us." He placed his arm around the boy's shoulder and drew him close.

Justin took a deep breath. "She's so little. Is she real? Did she cry a lot when she was born? Is she too small for our cradle? Was I ever that tiny?" His words tumbled over one another. He snuggled closer to Jonathan's chest while his head leaned over the small bundle in his father's arms. "What's her name? Does she know I'm her big brother? Can I hold her?" He did not stop his barrage of questions until Jonathan lifted his hand in mock exasperation.

"Shhh, son." Jonathan chuckled as he spoke. "You may hold her only if you still your wagging tongue."

Justin gulped once. His eyes grew wide as he pressed his lips together tightly. He stretched out his arms and held his breath.

Jonathan grinned and laid the baby in them. "Now cradle her head, son," he instructed. "She's not strong enough yet to hold it up on her own."

Justin nodded vigorously and carefully rearranged his arms.

Jonathan smiled at the boy's tender care. "Son," his voice rose with authority.

Justin's head darted up.

"It's your duty to protect your sister. She will look to you for wisdom and guidance. This is a high calling from God." Bitterness against Richard slithered through Jonathan's mind. Fiercely he pushed it aside. "Do you understand?"

Justin's face fell into solemn lines. "I understand, sir." His childish voice deepened with the gravity of his vow. "I won't let anything hurt her. Ever. I promise."

And Jonathan knew that his son spoke the truth.

～

Somewhere across the ocean a woman stared into the descending night. Her hazel eyes flashed as she plotted her long-awaited revenge. Outside, the wind howled with the hint of storm. The woman smiled at the sound and then placed one carefully manicured hand on her hip. With her chin lifted toward the sky, she studied her dim reflection in the window's pane.

"The years have only served to accentuate your beauty," she whispered to herself. A low chuckle gathered in her throat. "A fool indeed is the man who scorned you. Now he will pay for his error.

They will all pay." She touched her blonde hair with one finger and noted that the deep red of her gown presented an alluring picture in the glass.

From a shadowy hallway, a child approached. Her slippered feet padded across the plush rug. The young girl rubbed her arm over her sleepy eyes and frowned. "Why are your fingers tapping that way on the windowsill, Mama?"

"Silence, Katherine." The woman did not turn as she issued her command. "I'm listening to the wind."

The child cocked her head to one side. "What does it say, Mama?"

The woman's voice dropped. Her lips again stretched into a taut smile. "It says that my enemy is near." The words fell like jagged ice into the night.

～

Darkness covered the sky and reached its cold fingers into the hidden recesses of Annie's heart. She groaned and pulled at the stocks that bound her. Tiny slivers scraped her skin as the wood resisted her. She took a deep breath and smelled the pungent aroma of sweat, smoke, and her own black fear.

Around her the fort's walls rose high and unyielding, their tops like the deadly teeth of a cougar, with her as the helpless prey swallowed in the monster's jaws. She licked her lips and tasted the salt and blood that had dried there. Her eyes watered from the smoke drifting from the huge Indian bonfires that spat and crackled outside the fort's walls. An orange glow splashed across the sky. She blinked.

"The flames," she whispered. Her mind stumbled between past and present, between reality and nightmare. "Kwelik!"

As her mind swirled in the blackness, Annie watched an image of her younger self racing toward the fire as red tongues licked up around the only person Annie still loved. "Stop!" In conjunction with her shout, the shadowy figure from a decade ago crumpled to the ground. The fire roared up to conceal its victim.

Then, as if the words themselves could reach through the years to bind her, Annie heard her own voice speaking the pledge she had made as that child. "I will never forget what they've done. I will make them pay."

A chill raced through her. She drew a choking breath as a present-day shriek reached her ears. In a moment reality refocused.

"I'm not afraid!" she shouted in an attempt to clear her mind from the dark images of the past.

As if in response, the screams of tortured English soldiers ricocheted through her senses, reminding her of the price of capture and defeat. "Die, just die," she cried, knowing that her words were useless, knowing that the men would live for half the night yet, knowing that the Indians had tied them only near enough to the flames to cause their flesh to burn and peel as they slowly cooked like spitted quails. Just as they had planned to do to Kwelik. But someone had stopped them. Who? Annie couldn't remember anymore.

She twisted her wrists in the narrow stocks and wished she could press her hands to her ears to shut out the piercing shrieks. She even wished for Mary Elizabeth's senseless chatter to drown the screams. But Mary Elizabeth was dead. Annie had watched her fall beneath a wicked blow that had crushed half her skull. The woman died before she could take three steps. Death, quick and decisive, with no room for lingering hope.

Annie closed her eyes as the horror again swayed before her vision, then faded. Mary Elizabeth screaming, weeping, stumbling forward, then falling silent in sudden death. Annie twisted her head to stare into the night sky. *It should have been me, God. I should have been the one who ran the gauntlet, not Mary Elizabeth. I should have felt the deadly blows. It should have been my life that gushed out dark and red as vivid proof of the savagery of the Indians. But it wasn't. Again You have denied me the right to face the enemy, to show them I will not be afraid.* Annie dropped her gaze. Nothing made sense anymore. Maybe it never had.

I will not forget. I will make them pay. Her pledge rang eerily through her mind. She pressed her chin against the wooden enclosure that held her head. If only she could fight her way free, but the wood was a senseless adversary, immune to her fury.

Beside her, her hands dangled ineffectually, already swelling from her futile attempts to pull them loose. Somehow she must escape and make Pontiac regret what he did to Mary Elizabeth and to her.

Annie clenched her fists, refusing to wince as pain shot up her arms and lodged in her shoulders. Frustration pounded in her head. With a bruised foot she kicked the bottom of her stocks and shouted her demands. "Let me out of here. Now!"

But nobody listened. Only a burst of distant laughter met her shrill cry.

Eventually a group of French soldiers strolled by her, their muskets slung casually over slumped shoulders. One laughed and struck his tinderbox to light the pipe that dangled from his lips. A yellow glow illuminated his features as his hands cupped the pipe's bowl. Annie turned her eyes from the sight of rotted teeth flashing in the darkness as the man smiled to his companions.

Beyond him a few stray Indians milled about the fort and gathered with the French over small fires. The group of soldiers meandered toward a spurt of flame. Their raucous shouts echoed back to Annie as they patted each other on the back and recounted their stories of battle. The unfamiliar voices swirled around Annie's head. She struggled to understand the words, groping through her memory for the lessons Kwelik had tried to teach her. Slowly the speech became clearer.

"The English, they retreated like dogs," guffawed a thin soldier.

The men laughed.

"It was quite a victory," boomed a deeper voice. "Besides a thousand dead, the Brits left all their artillery, provisions, supplies, and stores."

Slowly Annie translated the words in her mind. Her face darkened at the implication of the soldier's words.

"At least dogs would have taken their bones with them as they ran away," the man continued.

The soldiers howled at the man's wit.

"Not only that," another man boasted, "but we got ourselves over 100 new oxen and about 500 horses. Even got the general's military chest."

"*Mon Dieu!* I hadn't heard," exclaimed the man with the pipe.

"*Oui, mon ami.* It had £25,000 in gold and all his official papers. And we only lost sixteen men."

Annie squinted to make out the scowl on the first man's face.

The man tapped his pipe in one hand and shook his head. "*Oui,* but Beaujeu was one of them. He was quite a loss."

Annie strained at her bonds. The wood splintered into her flesh. "A curse on this Beaujeu," she shouted. Her broken French carried over the gathering. "May he rot in purgatory forever!" She spat the words toward the soldiers, daring them to ignore her any longer.

Heads swiveled in Annie's direction. One Frenchman rose from his squatting position around the fire. Shadows from his long pipe danced wickedly across his face. "Who is she that speaks such things?" His voice was harsh as he approached her.

"Some fool Englishwoman," one of his companions answered. "Even the Indians didn't want her."

The men chuckled among themselves. Then they turned back to the fire. But the soldier with the pipe continued toward Annie. His eyes narrowed as he stepped close to her. "An English whore?" he whispered, his voice filled with contempt.

Annie raised her chin and remained silent.

The Frenchman scratched the end of his pipe over his jaw. Slowly he leaned forward until his face was only inches from hers. He placed one finger under her chin to tilt it toward him. A bitter smile crept over his features as his other hand traced the bruise on her cheek. "Does the *mademoiselle* wish to speak again?"

Annie glared into his dark eyes. Her fury exploded as a hot blush beneath her skin. "Come closer, big man," she whispered, her voice low and sultry.

As the soldier's face bent closer, Annie spat on his cheek. Liquid dripped from the side of his nose down his chin.

He pulled sharply away from her. "*Femme diabolique.* Devil woman," he sputtered as he reached up one hand to wipe away the spittle. With a deliberate move, he ran his damp finger over her lips. His eyes never left her face. "Make peace while you can, woman." His voice hardened. "Lest we return you to your Indian friends.

Listen." He put a hand to his ear. His dark eyes mocked her. "You can hear the sounds of their welcome."

Annie could not stop the shiver that raced over her at the screams of the British prisoners. She stiffened her jaw. "I'm not afraid."

The Frenchman laughed. "No? But you should be." He twirled his pipe in his fingers and turned away. "Tomorrow you will see what your defiance gets you, *mademoiselle*." He spoke the threat casually over his shoulder as he walked back to his companions. "You will not be able to spit in the face of death." He turned back and flicked his fingers contemptuously in her direction.

His words chanted coldly in Annie's ears. She dropped her head. The man was right. Her anger had gained her nothing. She had not helped her army or made the frontier safer for her friends or even caused her enemies to pause before the strength of her wrath. Her efforts had been meaningless, useless, futile. Nothing had changed, and tomorrow she would die, unnoticed and unmourned. She would never be free.

Annie's eyes raised one last time. She scanned the fort's occupants. No one looked her way. No one cared if she screamed in anger or wept with sorrow. No one even saw her. Even God had turned His back.

Just as the thought lodged in her mind, Annie's eyes met those of an Indian brave who stood near the fort's wall. Her breath stopped in her throat. "White Wolf?" She whispered his name.

As if he could hear her words, the brave nodded once and pressed a finger to his lips. Then he turned away.

EIGHT

~

Splinters of pale moonlight drifted through the slats above Annie's head. She rubbed her hands along her bruised arms and felt dried blood crusted around her wrists. A lifetime ago, it seemed, she had been released from the stocks only to be thrown into this shack that smelled of mold and stale urine. Horizontal logs formed the short sides, half buried in the damp earth. Two broken boxes sat in a corner, and old straw littered the dirt floor. She shivered and glanced at the thick webs that reached across the ceiling. *There must be a hundred bugs in here*, she thought. *I hate bugs.* She sighed.

The hours had passed, each an eternity, as if they too were conscripted for her torture. She had tried several times to push open the small hatch in the ceiling above her, but it was blocked from the outside.

She leaned back against the damp wall, closed her eyes, and allowed the blackness to rush in around her like a living creature. "Come, darkness," she whispered. "What more can you do to me?"

In the shadows beside her mice dug in the straw. She turned her head from the sound. It was always the same. Always the darkness. Always the endless rustling of things she didn't want to see—memories that couldn't be silenced.

She opened her eyes and tilted her head toward the blackest corner of her pit. "It wasn't supposed to be like this, you know," she said to the mice. "I'd planned to fight a glorious battle and savor victory at the end."

The mice paused in their burrowing, as if listening to her complaint.

Annie pressed her hands into the cold dirt beneath her. "Father always said that life was an adventure to be lived to its fullest. Even Kwelik said the same. But she called it the freedom of living in God's will." Her eyes fell to the cuts on her hands and arms. "But I've found neither adventure nor freedom. I've found nothing but this dark, stinking cell. I've become nothing but the companion of spiders and mice. Some soldier I turned out to be."

Annie rubbed her fingers along the raw skin of her neck and winced. "Now here I am, stuck in a hole with mice that scratch and burrow and will not be tamed." She swept her hand toward the shadows and laughed, a bitter sound that echoed hollowly off the cold walls and died there. "How did it ever come to this?"

Even as she asked, she knew. She could feel the hatred stirring within her, even more tangible than the darkness that surrounded her. She rested her head against the wall. "It's too late, God. I don't know how to forgive them. I can't." She crossed her arms. "I won't. But if You get me out of here, I'll do whatever else You ask of me. I promise."

As her words faded, the hatch creaked open above her. A Frenchman's face appeared in the opening. His brown eyes were illuminated by the dim glow of a candle. He lifted the light higher, casting wild shadows into the corners of her cell.

Annie leaped to her feet. Her body stiffened into a defensive posture. "Stay away from me," she shouted.

The man's hand remained steady on the candle as he raised a finger to his lips. "Shhh. Would you be quiet," he whispered. A thick French accent masked his English words.

Annie scowled. Her fists tightened as she lifted them to her chest. "Who are you?" She did not lower her voice.

The Frenchman frowned. "I am Philippe. Now if you'd just be quiet, I'll tell you why I've come."

Annie took a step back. "I don't care. Just go away."

"You don't care?" His tone colored with mockery. "Even if I told you that I've come to get you out of here?" He lowered himself into the cell, leaving the hatch open.

Her eyes raked his tall frame, his muscular arms, the hard set of his chin. "Stay away from me," she warned again.

Philippe took one step forward. With a quick move, she lifted her foot and slammed it into his shin. Philippe grunted and fell to the straw. His hands reached for his injured leg as the candle flew to the ground.

Annie bolted toward the hatch. But before she could make her escape, his arm snaked out and tripped her. She tumbled to the ground beside him. His hand clamped onto her arm. He glared at her.

Annie opened her mouth to bite his hand when a sight behind him stopped her. There, where the candle had fallen next to a box, a flame sputtered and grew. Then the straw caught fire.

Philippe glanced over his shoulder and leaped to his feet. His hand remained steady on her arm. "Now look what you've done. I ought to just leave you here to burn." A low growl sounded from his throat as the fire gained strength. "But I've made a promise, fool that I am."

Annie trembled. "The fire," she whispered. "I've got to get out of here."

Philippe rubbed his free hand over the back of his neck and shook his head. "Why any man would bother to save your hide, I don't know." He motioned toward the hatch. "Make haste, woman, before I decide to leave you here after all."

Annie did not move. "I'm not afraid," she stated, forcing herself to believe the words as she said them. Slowly her eyes turned to Philippe. "I'm not going to no man's bed. I'll take my chances with the flames first."

A queer smile of approval flickered over Philippe's face. "I guess the Indian was right about the two of you." He stepped toward the hatch. Fire licked up around the box. "Nevertheless, you can take that up with him."

Annie caught her breath. "The Indian? Pontiac?"

Philippe frowned. "No, the great Ottawa chief doesn't seem to care if you live or die."

"Who then?"

"So there is something, or someone, you fear." Philippe's lips twisted into another smile as Annie scowled at him. He sighed and relented. "The brave said that his name was White Wolf. Now," he pointed to the hatch, "will you please climb out of here before we both cook like a couple of rabbits." Philippe's voice remained calm. The fire crackled as it skittered across the ground to a fresh pile of straw.

Annie drew a deep breath, positioned herself beneath the hatch, and reached up to pull herself through.

"I see you have a little sense at least," Philippe muttered below her. "Now stop your wild kicking, and I'll help you."

Annie felt Philippe's hands on her legs. Then he thrust her through the hatch. Her fingernails scraped on the top of the shack as her body cleared the opening. She rolled and toppled to the ground outside her prison. Her chin slammed into the dirt before she could regain her footing. She staggered to her feet and then turned back toward the enclosure.

In a moment the Frenchman stood beside her.

"So if you've been sent to rescue me, how do we escape the fort?"

Philippe brushed off his trousers and then turned to carefully close and latch the hatch door.

Annie scowled. "What are you doing that for?"

Philippe looked back at her. Scorn marred his features. "If we're lucky, they will think you dead in the fire and not pursue us." His fingers gripped her arm as he propelled her forward. "What did you think? That we would just dance out the front gates unnoticed?"

Annie swallowed and remained silent.

Philippe gave her a single deprecating glance. "Now come, if you please." His voice dripped with false chivalry. Then he dropped her arm and slipped into the darkness.

Annie lifted her skirts and scurried after him. She glanced back and saw flames just beginning to lick through the hatch cover. Smoke stained the air around her.

"This way," Philippe whispered. "To the western wall."

From the far side of the fort, Annie heard the shouts of French soldiers as they discovered the fire. "Is the woman still in there?" a man yelled above the melee.

"Can't say," responded another.

"Start the bucket brigade," an authoritative voice commanded.

"Let her burn," shrieked a soldier.

Annie recognized the voice of the man with the pipe. She shivered and pressed closer to Philippe. They raced through stacks of crates toward a small door in the fort wall.

"Hurry." Philippe motioned for her to follow as he quickly opened the door and slid through. His hand reached back to help her.

"Freedom," she whispered and ducked through the opening after him. Behind her a box tipped from its precarious position and sent several crates crashing to the ground. The wood split, spilling the contents with a loud clatter.

Annie cringed.

"*Arrétez!*" a Frenchman shouted in the distance.

Annie looked over her shoulder to see men running toward her. "They've found us!"

"Now you've done it," Philippe muttered. "Run!"

Annie's feet took flight beneath her as she sprinted toward the trees. Fort Duquesne's gates swung open behind her. Blood pounded in her ears and drowned the sound of the soldiers' angry shouts. A shot whizzed past her. She shuddered, her eyes never leaving Philippe's back as he darted into the forest.

"This way!" White Wolf materialized from the trees ahead and motioned for them to follow.

Annie drew abreast of him. She averted her eyes from his face.

"Come." White Wolf grabbed her arm and pulled her behind him. "This way will lead us away from the Indian camps. Hurry." His glance flickered over her. "You look well for an escaped prisoner." A smile twitched at his lips, then disappeared.

Annie did not answer. Another musket shot shook the leaves above them.

"They're closing in." White Wolf had scarcely spoken the words when a pained cry burst from his lips. Shock etched his features as he fell headlong. His hands clutched his side.

"No!" The word echoed through Annie's frame as her vision focused on the blood, dark and red, that gushed from between White Wolf's fingers.

～

England. Jonathan rubbed his hand along the tattered velvet of the carriage seat and fixed his eyes on the floor at his feet. England. Even after three hours of bumping along cobbled roads, he still could not believe that he had truly returned. He drew a deep breath and allowed the misty air to sift through his lungs with old familiarity. England, the symbol of everything he had hoped to escape, everything he wanted to forget.

Beside him the dreary summer sun leaked through the open window and sent shards of light scampering across the carriage walls. On the opposite seat his new daughter nursed beneath a borrowed blanket. The child gurgled, her tiny fist breaking free of its constraints to wave in the moist air.

Jonathan listened to the muted sucking and felt again the pattering of worry through his mind. His thoughts returned to the sailor who had accosted them. Even as they were leaving the dock, the sailor had shouted from the deck above, "I ain't the only one who knows who you are, Jonathan Grant. You ain't got no idea what's waiting for you, do ya?" His dissonant laugh still clanged in Jonathan's ears.

Little Brenna grunted as she finished feeding. He reached over and touched her small hand and then leaned back to tousle the hair of his son sitting beside him.

Justin grinned up at him. "Where are we going, Papa? Is that the house?" Justin pointed to a cottage tucked in the rolling hills.

Jonathan raised his head. "No, Justin, that belongs to Paul Stafford. And that," he nodded out the other window, "is the home of the Breckenridges. When I was your age, their son went off to India to be a merchant."

Justin turned his inquisitive eyes to his father. "When will we get to Uncle Richard's house? Are we almost there? Is it a very big house? Will I meet Uncle Richard? What does he look like? Is he very old?"

Jonathan smiled. "Quiet, son. We'll be there soon. But you must remember, Uncle Richard is not living there now."

Justin's forehead wrinkled at the thought. "Why not?"

The question jabbed through Jonathan.

Kwelik leaned over and pressed her finger against Justin's lips. "Shush, son," she whispered. "You ask too many questions. Would you like to hold your sister for a while?"

Justin's face beamed his assent. His questions were forgotten as soon as Kwelik placed the child in his arms. He clucked his tongue. His finger gently rubbed the baby's chest and chin. A huge grin spread over his face.

Kwelik turned back to Jonathan. "This is a beautiful land, husband, so green and lush. It's a wonder you left it." She smiled.

"I was never happy here," he muttered in response.

"Never, Papa?" Justin's blue eyes darted from his sister's face to pierce through Jonathan.

Jonathan sighed. "Well, perhaps for a time, when I was very young."

"England is where you lived when you were little like me and like Brenna." Justin's head nodded once for emphasis.

"Yes, that's right." Jonathan smiled at his son's enthusiasm.

Justin's face grew solemn. "Did you run away?"

Jonathan was silent a moment before answering. "I suppose I did."

"Hmm." Justin's brow creased into a thoughtful frown. "Was it 'cause you didn't like Uncle Richard no more?"

"Something like that."

Justin's frown deepened. "Mama says we got to love everyone. Don't you, Mama?"

Jonathan glanced at his wife. A tiny smile played at the corner of her lips. "Yes, son," she answered. She leaned over to pat the boy on the leg. "Your father loves your uncle now." She turned her eyes to capture Jonathan's. One eyebrow raised as she regarded him. "Don't you?"

"Yes." The word felt dry on Jonathan's lips.

"But you said . . ." Justin's voice trailed off as Kwelik shook her head.

Jonathan sighed. "Listen, son, people don't always say what they mean." *Like me*, he thought, *and like Richard*. "We were young once, happy, and mischievous just like you."

Jonathan brushed a bit of dampness from his cheek and watched as Justin studied him with a trusting expression. He had been innocent once too, a hundred years ago it seemed, an eternity ago. Jonathan closed his eyes and allowed the memory to swirl around him.

"What do you see, Jonathan?" Kwelik's words drifted over him—gentle, peaceful.

"It was a long time ago," he muttered. His eyes opened to rest on her face.

"Not so very long," she countered.

Jonathan motioned out the window. "Do you see that field?"

Kwelik nodded.

"That's where I would ride Sir Charles." Jonathan smiled. "Mother, Richard, and I used to have picnics under that old oak. Richard always liked ham, but I liked roast beef. Sometimes I can still taste the biscuits Mother would bake especially for the occasion. Those were happy times." Jonathan's gaze fell to his hands clasped tightly in his lap.

Kwelik tucked Brenna's blanket under the baby's tiny chin and then reached over to grip Jonathan's hand in her own. "Tell me about Richard," she urged. "How he was back then."

"Richard." Jonathan rolled the name on his tongue. "Richard would bring storybooks and read to us. Sometimes he would write poetry—silly rhymes mostly, that would make me laugh." His gaze blurred on the distant landscape. "'Billy the butler was a crazy old coot./He had only shoes and flowers for a suit./He sat on a rose thorn and raised a great hoot./So Billy the butler wore only his boots.'"

Kwelik chuckled.

Jonathan's eyes refocused on his wife, then drifted to his young son. "But we grew up, Richard and I, and everything changed."

"Don't think about that, Jonathan. Not now." Kwelik's hand tightened on his.

He scowled and looked away from her searching eyes. They saw too much, knew too much of what he still hid in his soul. "And now we're here. I'm a fool indeed." He muttered the last sentence to himself.

For a moment Kwelik watched him. Then she spoke. "You're a new man now, new in Christ Jesus. Never forget that."

Her assurance was like a healing touch. "I hope so." He did not know if he spoke the words aloud.

The carriage jostled around a bend, and the Grant mansion loomed against the afternoon sky. Jonathan's breath stopped in his throat. The massive structure, its gray stones covered with ivy, dominated the landscape. Green fields spread like grand carpets in all directions.

"It's—it's quite striking, isn't it?" Kwelik spoke in a hushed voice. She took the baby from Justin's arms.

Smoke curled from the front chimney like a dark ribbon. Jonathan frowned and fought the rush of conflicting emotions that swirled within him. "Someone's there."

Kwelik leaned forward. "Servants?"

Jonathan shook his head. "No, that's the main fireplace. The servants' quarters are around the back."

"Perhaps it's Uncle Richard," spouted Justin, his young voice sprinkled with unconcealed anticipation.

Suspicion clutched Jonathan's heart. He leaned out the carriage window. "Here, driver."

"Aye, sir." The driver turned down the long driveway. Several minutes later he pulled up the horse's reins and stopped the carriage in front of the wide entrance of the Grant mansion.

Slowly Jonathan descended from the carriage. A shiver raced through him. "Nothing has changed." He whispered the words to no one. Green lawns met a stone walkway that led beneath a trellised arch toward the front of the mansion. Pink roses laced through the trellis from bushes on either side. Jonathan's gaze fell to the multicolored irises that lined each side of the walk. Yellows, blues, and purples—his mother's favorite. She had planted them herself so long ago. And there they still bloomed, those or others like them. He allowed a faint smile to brush his lips. Tobias had not forgotten. He had kept the irises just as they'd always been.

Jonathan glanced to his left. Even the garden looked the same—a large pond covered with water lilies and surrounded by tall yews on three sides. And in the center a statue that resembled his father. Jonathan shuddered and turned from the sight.

As he did, Justin hopped down behind him. His small fist burrowed into his father's hand as his face tilted up to study the house. His jaw dropped. "Papa, it's so big."

For a long moment Jonathan stood silently in front of the massive building as his heart beat furiously in his chest. The time had come to face the past. He took a deep breath and continued up the walkway. As he reached the front of the mansion, the tall oak door pulled open with a hushed groan. A slim figure appeared in the ivy-shadowed opening.

Jonathan stopped short.

Then the person spoke. "I knew you'd come."

Their words froze between them. "Elizabeth!"

NINE

~

Pain spread as red heat through White Wolf's limbs. He clamped his lips shut over the searing agony.

A warrior never cries out. A warrior endures. A warrior fights on. Taquachi's words, cold and ruthless, came back to him. Blood oozed hot and sticky over his side. His heart pounded wildly in his ears. Perhaps he was a warrior no longer. Perhaps he was only a man, a man who now stood on the edge of death and knew that home did not await him on the other side.

Above him Annie's face appeared out of the blur, her eyes wide and fixed on the wound in his side. White Wolf's gaze followed hers. His breath escaped in a shocked rush as he focused on the tatters of flesh that bled beneath his trembling hand. His stomach heaved. *A warrior feels no pain.*

"I'm no warrior." White Wolf closed his eyes, unable to fight the sick fear that spread through him like an icy wind. The soldiers were coming. He could feel their pursuit, closer and closer, muskets hot in their hands. He could see them in his mind, hard and merciless, like reflections of the man he had once chosen to become.

White Wolf dragged his legs beneath him and struggled to rise despite the onslaught of pain. Dizziness swirled through him. He opened his eyes. His vision tunneled.

"White Wolf!"

He heard Annie's voice as if from a great distance. With effort he focused on the sound.

"They're just ahead!" A Frenchman's cry rose from behind them.

He had to get up, run, escape. Why did his legs refuse his command? Why did he lie here still with hot fire coursing through his veins?

"Get up, Waptumewi. Hurry!"

White Wolf groaned. His thoughts twirled through his mind, jumbled, confused, mixed with blood that he knew was his own. *A warrior endures.* This time, Taquachi's harsh laugh accompanied the memory. The dead brave's face swayed across White Wolf's vision.

"Leave me alone!" The words gurgled in his throat. He batted at the image with his free hand.

"Stop that!" Annie gripped his hand with her own. Her arm cradled his shoulder and pulled him to his feet. "I will not let you die rescuing me, Waptumewi."

White Wolf glanced up. His eyes focused on the blood that covered Annie's skirt. He reached out and clutched at the fabric. Dull terror rose within him.

"Let go. I'm not hurt." Her words broke through his confusion.

Another blast of a French musket echoed through White Wolf's senses.

"They're coming!" Philippe's urgent cry sent a chill across White Wolf's skin as the Frenchman sped back toward them.

Annie's grip loosened. She motioned to Philippe. "Help me!"

Philippe sprinted to White Wolf's side. White Wolf grabbed Philippe's shoulder. The Frenchman's strong arm reached around him.

White Wolf attempted to run but failed. "I can't," he whispered.

Concern dug deep furrows in Philippe's face as he carried White Wolf into the trees. "They are just behind us," he muttered. "We will try to lose them in the brush." He paused. His voice turned grim. "But I don't know if we shall."

A rustling sound came from the woods behind them. A soldier shouted, "One of them's hit, sir. Ground's stained with blood. They can't be far."

White Wolf pressed his hand harder into his wound as they stumbled forward. Trees loomed black and menacing before him, their branches like crooked fingers reaching to squeeze the life from his soul. He shuddered. *A warrior knows no fear.*

"Stay with me, brother." A chill of warning sounded in Philippe's tone. He did not slow his pace as his fingers dug into White Wolf's skin. He turned his head, his eyes dark as he spoke words only White Wolf could hear. "We may die together, *mon ami*. But not yet. You must not faint."

White Wolf's breath came ragged to his throat. His jaw tightened over renewed pain. He steadied his breathing as Philippe changed course.

"No! The rocks." The words sputtered from White Wolf's lips.

Philippe stopped. "What rocks?"

To their right torches glowed in the trees.

White Wolf turned from the sight. "The rocks." He repeated the phrase, struggling to make his tongue obey his will. "Scouted. Last night."

Annie turned, her eyes wide and questioning.

Philippe shook his head. "Pay no heed, woman. He knows not what he's saying. He's lost too much blood."

White Wolf's hand tightened on Philippe's shoulder. "Listen!" His lips trembled. "Hide. The rocks."

Annie stared at him. "Do you hear that, Waptumewi?" Her voice grew fierce. "That is the sound of death. Yours and mine." She squeezed his arm with one hand. "We must keep going."

"No." White Wolf drew a shuddering breath. "Trust me."

For a moment she regarded him. He could see the memories in her eyes, memories that even now accused him, condemned him. He dropped his gaze.

Annie turned to Philippe. "Do as he says." The strength of her statement came like a balm to old wounds. She stepped beside him and reached her arm beneath his elbow. She leaned closer. "Trust is a slippery thing, Waptumewi," she whispered. "Do not ask me for it again." She straightened and cleared her throat. "Which way do we go?"

White Wolf tilted his head. "Southeast toward the river." He felt new blood surge from his wound. From the darkness behind him, he heard the sounds of pursuit—the echo of branches thudding back into place, the crackle of leaves underfoot.

But slowly as they twined through the trees, the soldiers dropped away, leaving only an occasional shout to jar White Wolf's nerves.

And each time a Frenchman cried, "I've lost them," their captain would again call, "Push on, men. They aren't far. Through those trees." Those words whirled through White Wolf's mind until they grew into a hard knot, urging him on, despite the pain, despite the blood, despite the crazed pounding of his heart in his chest.

"There!" White Wolf coughed. He pointed toward a hillside hemmed in by large boulders, their surfaces lit by moonlight.

Philippe and Annie hurried toward the spot and stopped. White Wolf waved his hand to a hole beneath the rocks.

"That?" Annie's voice was incredulous. "That's our hiding place?"

White Wolf's head lolled to one side as he nodded.

"All three of us?"

"Quickly!" Philippe wiped his hand across his forehead as he spoke.

White Wolf shuddered. His hand pulled at Annie's sleeve as he stumbled toward the hole. "Opens. Bear cave." The words gained clarity.

"There's not even an arm's length between the ground and the bottom of the rock," Annie muttered as she dropped to her knees before the opening.

White Wolf drew a deep breath. "Squeeze through. Enough room. Go!" The last word ended in a gasp.

Philippe frowned. "The men will be following the blood. We will not lose them long in the trees."

White Wolf did not glance at him as he fell to his knees and crawled through the hole. The rocky earth scraped his wound. He bit his lip, refusing to make a sound. The smell of warm earth surrounded him as he pulled himself inside the enclosure and collapsed. A *warrior endures*. The words taunted him.

Philippe crawled noiselessly beside White Wolf and drew his legs to his chest. "Perhaps they will not find us," he muttered. "Perhaps we will live." His eyes, shadowed by the darkness, fell to White Wolf. "All of us."

Annie frowned and eased White Wolf's head into her lap with unusual gentleness. Her fingers lingered over his torn side before she turned away. "What do we do now?" White Wolf felt her question slip away from him and dissolve in the darkness, though her arm remained steady around him.

"We wait." Philippe's tone betrayed nothing.

White Wolf felt Annie's fingers press into his arm. She rested her head against the rock wall. "Well, I certainly hope the bear doesn't live here anymore."

White Wolf raised his head. His eyes met hers in a tiny shaft of moonlight that came in through the roof of the cave. Then his eyelids fell shut again. "But it does," he whispered. Even as he spoke, pain washed through him like a black wave, drowning him in an ocean of night.

∽

Annie turned her head to see White Wolf's eyes roll closed. His body became limp in her grasp. Her breath stopped in her throat. "White Wolf! No!" Terror shot through her as she leaned cautiously over him.

"Is he . . ." Philippe whispered the question.

She touched the hollow of White Wolf's neck. His flesh felt cold and clammy. Yet underneath came the faint, fluttering beat of a warrior's heart. She closed her eyes and willed herself to ignore the ache that shot through her with the thought of White Wolf's death. She turned back to Philippe. "It's all right. He lives. But barely."

Philippe nodded. "We must stop the bleeding."

Annie gripped her sleeve and yanked until the material tore at the seam. "This will not help for long." She shook her head and pressed the cloth over the gap in White Wolf's side. "You hang on, Waptumewi. You live."

White Wolf's eyes fluttered open. "Kwelik?" His voice was ragged.

"Shhh," Annie whispered. She gripped his shoulder in steel fingers. "You're going to live, Waptumewi. You will not die. Do you hear me?"

He groaned and thrashed his head from side to side.

"Over here!" The shout of a French soldier echoed through the tiny cave. Annie's eyes caught Philippe's. They both froze. She pulled White Wolf closer to her while her hand kept steady pressure on the wound.

Outside, booted feet crunched through the underbrush toward them. Annie dared not breathe as the footsteps drew nearer. Nearer. Nearer. Tension congealed in the air. A branch cracked just outside the cave. Every muscle in Annie's body grew taut. Another moment, another breath, another step closer.

"Look!" the soldier shouted.

Annie felt her heart thump madly in her chest.

"There's blood on this rock." The man's voice rose with excitement. "They came this way."

Oh, God. The plea flew through Annie's mind. *If You're out there like Kwelik says, then You've got to save us.* The words came faster now. *I know I ain't much to You, but this Indian here, well, he's Kwelik's brother. He needs another chance. Don't let the French catch us, and don't let him die.* She paused and added, *For Kwelik's sake.*

Annie's eyes lifted to the opening of the cave. She caught her breath. There two pant legs draped around booted heels. *I could reach out and touch him,* she thought. The idea sent a chill of dread racing through her.

Philippe's gaze flickered to hers and then returned to the cave's opening.

Annie pressed her back against the rock wall and watched the butt of the soldier's musket tap the ground with rhythmic impatience. From the corner of her eye, she could see a drop of sweat, touched by moonlight, trickle down Philippe's face. She swallowed once. Then her eyes again fixed on the gray pants. She bit her lip and wished that by the sheer strength of her will, she could make the legs disappear into the night's haze.

But the boots remained. And the musket steadily rapped— thump, thump, thump—on the ground beside them.

Go away!

The soldier did not move.

Annie clenched her teeth. *Make him pass on, God. Please.*

"Captain's going back to the fort," another Frenchman shouted from the distance. "We'll search again at morning light."

"They won't get far with one wounded," the soldier outside the cave called back. He picked up his musket and strode away.

Annie's breath escaped her lips in a rush. "That was close." She wiped one hand across her forehead to dry the beads of perspiration.

Philippe's hand descended on her arm. "Quiet." He lifted his hand, his voice barely audible. "They will come back. Wait."

Doubt flashed across Annie's mind.

Philippe shook his head. "They will see if we betray ourselves. We French always watch for the fool."

Annie stopped her movement. Her arm tightened around White Wolf's shoulders. As if sensing her fear, White Wolf jerked in her grip and moaned softly. The sound reverberated in the cave. Within moments footsteps again passed quietly and quickly in front of the cave. This time they did not stop.

As the sound faded, Philippe nodded at Annie. His voice returned to normal tones as he spoke. "*Trés bien.* Now they're gone." He pulled a tinderbox from his breast pocket and struck it. He then used the flame to light a small stick. A weary smile crossed his face as he handed the light to Annie. "We have survived the first test, *mademoiselle.*" He leaned over and looked closely at White Wolf's wound. His fingers touched the inflamed flesh. "This, though, is not good. We must act quickly." Philippe sat up, his voice suddenly heavy. "I must go back to Fort Duquesne."

Annie's eyes narrowed. "You will abandon us?"

Philippe's brows drew together. "*Non.* You, I would leave, but not the Indian. He will lead me home."

"Home?" She frowned. The word meant nothing to her.

Philippe picked up another stick from the cave floor and scratched absently at the dirt before answering. "To France."

Annie scowled. "Is that why you stay with us then? Because you don't know the way?"

Philippe snapped the stick in two. His eyes bored a hole through her. "No, it is not the only reason. The Indian is my friend. But you—" He pointed the ragged edge of the stick toward her chest.

"You are only an annoyance. Remember that," he growled and tossed the broken branch at her feet. "Make the fire there." He pointed to the farthest corner of the cave.

"What?" Annie's brow furrowed.

Philippe sighed. "Must you question everything? Here." He reached over and pulled the knife from White Wolf's belt.

Annie's eyes grew wide.

Philippe chuckled. "I will not hurt you, woman. This is for the Indian. If he is to live, you must remove the shot. It is near the surface and will not be difficult to find." If Philippe heard her sharp intake of breath, he did not stop to take notice. "Then heat the knife in the fire and sear the wound to stop the bleeding. Do you understand?"

Annie nodded.

"You must not allow him to cry out lest the fort scouts hear him. And the fire must burn hot and quickly with little smoke." He tossed his tinderbox to her. "Put it out as soon as the work is done. I will bring the proper wood. If you work quickly, you will finish before you are discovered."

And if I don't, then White Wolf and I die, and you're no worse for the adventure. Annie clamped her lips over the thought. "Then what will you do?"

"I will get the medicine the Indian needs and perhaps a few supplies. If I am seen, they will not know that I am the one who freed you. They will think I am returning from the search. But it will make my escape more difficult." His frown deepened. "They were supposed to believe me dead on the battlefield."

"Now they'll know you're a deserter."

"Only if I am caught, *mademoiselle.* You do want food, don't you?"

Annie nodded.

A crooked smile replaced Philippe's frown. "Well, then, I am a poor hunter, I fear. And he," he waved his hand at White Wolf, "will not be of much help for many days. With luck we will not die tonight." His eyes lingered on White Wolf. "And with a miracle, we might survive the morrow." He grimaced. "Are you ready?"

Annie nodded again.

"Then let us finish what we have begun." Before she could disagree, Philippe disappeared out the cave's opening.

Within minutes branches were pushed into the cave. Their ends scraped eerily against the stone walls. Quickly she started the fire and watched as its flames flickered up to cast crazed shadows over the rocks.

"This should be enough." Philippe's voice sounded from outside the cave as he shoved a final branch through the opening. "I'll return as soon as I can. And remember, don't let him scream." Then Philippe was gone.

Annie held the knife in her trembling hand. Her eyes fixed on its shiny surface as if she had never seen such a weapon before. The glow of firelight shimmered across the blade.

Work quickly. Philippe's words rang in her mind.

She clutched the knife more firmly and knelt over White Wolf. "This will hurt," she whispered. "You must be silent. It'll be over soon." *I hope.* She did not utter the last words aloud.

"A warrior never cries out." White Wolf's voice slurred as he spoke from his delirium.

Annie lowered the knife. Her hand shook more violently. She gripped her wrist with the opposite hand, steadying the knife. Slowly the blade slipped into White Wolf's flesh. She worked at the handle, twisting it until the weapon's tip pulled the shot free from its bloody bindings.

White Wolf's eyes widened.

Annie did not pause. "You're doing well, Waptumewi," she muttered as she lifted the ball from his flesh. She shuddered and tossed it to the far side of the cave. The ball impacted the rock wall and clattered to the earth beneath. Carefully she laid the knife across the fire, making sure the handle rested outside the flames. "Only a moment more."

White Wolf stared at the boulder above him.

Annie rocked back and forth as she waited for the fire to do its work. When the blade took on a red glow, she tore yet another tattered strip from the bottom of her dress and wrapped it around her hand before removing the knife from the heat. She held the weapon over White Wolf's side.

Outside, a rumble of thunder rolled across the evening sky. Annie shivered as raindrops began to fall, the sound of their dropping like the persistent patter of her fears.

"Trust me," White Wolf had said. But did he know what he asked? Did he know that now he must trust her? But trust was for people who had not seen brutality or betrayal. Trust was not for the likes of her or White Wolf.

Annie's vision cleared. Dampness stole in around her, evasive, threatening. She renewed her grip on the knife. "Hang on, Waptumewi."

The knife descended to White Wolf's skin. Annie pressed two fingers to her nose as the odor of seared flesh filled the air. She coughed. Only one more second. Done. At last. She dropped the knife, doused the fire, and then bound the charred wound with the cloth that had been wrapped around her hand.

For a moment White Wolf roused. He raised his head and stared blankly in her direction. "A warrior endures," he muttered, then fell back again, unconscious.

Annie brushed back the hair from his forehead with trembling fingers. "You're a warrior, Waptumewi," she whispered. "You'll survive." She tightened her jaw. "And so will I."

The sound of scraping came from the cave's opening. Annie turned. "Philippe?"

It was not Philippe.

TEN

~

Dread pounded in Philippe's ears as he slipped through the forest. Each footstep brought him nearer to the place he had hoped to escape. Behind him the moon peeked through gathering thunderclouds and cast his shadow onto the silver path that led back to captivity.

Run. Run. Run. His mind screamed the words in time with his quiet steps. But Philippe continued, knowing he must not turn back. He must not think of France waiting there somewhere beyond the horizon.

What am I doing? I should just slip away to France. I'd find it somehow. He dismissed the thought. Something about the Indian held him, made him do this thing that threatened his very life. There was something about the grief hidden in those black eyes, eyes that told stories of a past best forgotten, of sorrows surpassing Philippe's own.

"For the Indian." Philippe whispered the words aloud. All he needed was some of Jean-Pierre's salve and perhaps a bit of dried meat for the journey.

With that thought he skirted the outer wall of the fort until he reached the same door from which he and the woman had escaped earlier. Above and to his right, a soldier paced along the wall. Philippe drew a quick breath and pushed open the small door with one hand. He was thankful that no one had yet replaced the bar that would have locked him out. He would have hated to have to go to the front gate and explain why he hadn't returned earlier with the others. Luckily for him, victory had made the soldiers lax. Without a sound he slid through the opening and carefully stepped over the fallen box that had betrayed their escape. He touched a wooden crate softly with his fingers and grimaced.

A cloud swept over the moon and darkened his path. He inched forward. His eyes strained toward the light flickering from the candles on Jean-Pierre's windowsill.

Only a few more steps.

His foot slipped on a stone. Philippe caught his breath. Rough laughter echoed from across the fort. Then silence. He continued forward. His feet slid along the wall as he edged around a corner.

A man stepped from a building beyond him. The light from within crowned his head with a golden glow. He cracked his knuckles and stretched as his gaze swept the darkness. Philippe slipped into the shadows and pressed his back into the rough wood that formed the side of Jean-Pierre's cabin. He closed his eyes. The man grunted once and then entered another room. The door swung shut behind him with a gentle thump.

Philippe let out his breath and hurried toward Jean-Pierre's door. He raised his hand and tapped lightly on the wooden frame. A low creak echoed through the night as the door swung open. Philippe stepped forward and smiled into the weathered face of the old soldier-turned-medic who stood with his hand clutching the door's handle.

"Philippe, my boy!" Jean-Pierre squinted into the darkness. His face wrinkled into a toothless grin. "Come in." He patted Philippe on the shoulder and drew him inside. "Rain's coming in, you know. I feel it in my bones. Come, sit by my fire, boy."

Philippe shivered at the suggestion and pulled the door shut behind him.

"It will be a long night for those outside, I'd say. *Une nuit longue* indeed." The old man sighed, rubbed a finger under his large nose, and smiled up at Philippe. "Well, boy, I'm glad to see you weren't felled on the battlefield like the captain thought. Though by the looks of your clothes, it was a rough fight."

Philippe glanced down at the blood on his pants and coat.

"It's been a long time since you came to visit me. Got better company these days, eh?" Jean-Pierre chuckled, waddled toward the fire, and leaned over to pick up a charred stick that had fallen to the floor. He winked at Philippe as he stirred up the fire in the grate. Sparks spat into the air and settled back again into the glowing coals.

Philippe smiled and remembered the days when this old man's fire was the only refuge he could find from Berneau's cruel schemes. But Berneau was gone now—dead.

Philippe pulled a chair toward the fire, away from the window, and leaned his head back against the wall. For a moment he closed his eyes. The image of a France he scarcely remembered materialized in his mind. Someday soon he would go home.

"Did you hear all the commotion this evening, boy?"

Philippe's eyes flashed open. "Commotion?"

"Don't tell me you slept through it. Why, 'twas the best time I've had in months, maybe years." Jean-Pierre grinned, oblivious of Philippe's sudden discomfort. "Fool soldiers. Think they know so much. Can't even keep one Englishwoman prisoner. She slips away in the night. Right from under their fool noses." He laughed. "Ain't that something? You should have seen their faces when they came back with nothing but a few burrs and some scratches to show for their efforts." Jean-Pierre sat down and slapped his knee. "Then they needed ol' Jean-Pierre, you know. No more looking down their noses at me." A smug smile replaced his grin. "What a day it's been, what a grand and glorious day." He sighed again.

Philippe cleared his throat and struggled to keep his voice calm. "I suppose they'll be going after the woman again tomorrow. Do they know where she's gone?"

"Aw, they don't know a thing." The old man waved his hand in the air. "Won't even go out, I'm thinking. They got one of the English aristocrats lapping at their feet, and that's enough, I figure."

Philippe scowled. "Another prisoner? Here?"

Jean-Pierre shook his head. "No, no, not here. Back in England, you know. Gives us secrets for no more than a pittance and a promise." He flicked his fingers in the air as he continued, "I'd like to see the look on ol' Braddock's face, arrogant Englishman that he is, if I could tell him that one of his own people foiled his plans. They'll be calling our battle 'Braddock's Defeat' for years to come, unless I miss my guess. And all 'cause of some English traitor." He chuckled and dropped his head. "No one will ever know though. 'Tis a pity. So many secrets hidden by time. Ah, well, enough of my gab."

He opened his eyes wider and leaned toward Philippe. "So, my boy, what you be needin' from ol' Jean-Pierre on this damp evening?"

Philippe scooted forward. "I need a jar of that salve you make, the kind for treating gunshot wounds."

"Some of my salve, eh?" Jean-Pierre squinted his eyes and looked carefully up and down Philippe's frame. "So that's not enemy blood on your coat then, is it?" His voice dropped as one finger traced the crusted handprint on Philippe's shoulder. "You got a wound I should be lookin' at, boy?"

"No, no." Philippe shook his head. "It's not for me. It's for a friend."

"A friend, you say?" Jean-Pierre's voice raised to an interested squeak. "Well, what are you waiting for? From the looks of your clothes, he's lost a lot of blood. Bring him in."

Philippe rubbed his hand over the back of his neck. His gaze fell to the smoldering fire. He sighed and turned back to the old man. "My friend cannot come in." His words hung awkwardly between them. For a moment he looked at Jean-Pierre while his mind willed the man to remember the days when Philippe used to come and mix medicines, stir the fire, and tell him a hundred dreams of France.

Jean-Pierre waited, for once silent.

Slowly Philippe stood. "Will you give me the salve?"

The old man scowled and shifted in his chair. "*Oui, oui*, if you're so anxious." He bobbed his head up and down. "You once liked to sit and talk to ol' Jean-Pierre. But now it's just 'give me salve,' and that's it. What's the matter, boy? Ashamed to be seen with an old man, is it? Aye? Speak up now."

Remorse shot through Philippe. If only he could sit and talk. If only he could tell Jean-Pierre everything, like he used to do when he was a boy. He'd tell him about his escape from the battlefield, about White Wolf, about the girl White Wolf risked his life to save, about his plans, his hopes, his fears. But now he couldn't risk it. He couldn't make his lips say the words. Instead he lowered his head and let shame color his cheeks. "I'm sorry, Jean-Pierre. I wish I could stay awhile and talk, but I must hurry. My friend . . ." His voice trailed off.

Jean-Pierre's momentary frown softened into a look of understanding. "That's okay, boy. Here." He reached to an upper shelf, drew a clay jar from its place, and set it in Philippe's hand. "Use it twice a day for a week or so. Keeps down the swelling, helps it heal. My own mixture, you know." He smiled, his face crinkling into a sad mask.

Philippe smiled back. "I know. The best medicine in all New France."

Jean-Pierre clapped Philippe on the back. "You're a good boy. I was sorry when your mama died. Fine woman. She'd have been proud of the man you've become."

"I hope so, Jean-Pierre. I truly do." Philippe straightened and gripped the man's thin arm in his own firm grasp. "I must go now. My friend is waiting." His eyes met Jean-Pierre's for a long moment. "Thank you."

A quizzical look crossed the old man's face. "Stop by anytime, my boy," he muttered. "Anytime."

Philippe nodded once. His eyes blurred as he slipped from the room. "Good-bye, my old friend," he whispered under his breath. Then he tucked Jean-Pierre's salve inside his coat and hurried toward the unopened supply barrels.

As he reached them, he pried two open and grabbed a sack of dried meat, a few potatoes, and some flour. Slowly he lowered the lid and looked around. No one had seen him. No one knew. And no one, except maybe Jean-Pierre, would care that he was gone.

Philippe headed for the fort wall, his gaze fixed on the tiny door. He turned sideways, careful not to touch any of the crates. This time he would slip away unnoticed, and this time he would not return.

Philippe stepped through the outer door and closed it behind him. A smile touched his lips as he hurried toward the trees. He did not look back.

Above him lightning sizzled across the cloudy sky. Thunder cracked. Its rumble sent a shiver through his bones. Philippe clutched his plunder more tightly and darted into the trees, using them and the brush as a cover from the watching eyes on the fort walls. Rain hit his face like tiny pellets shot from heaven. He lifted his head, hoping the force of the water could wash the feel of the fort from his skin.

It did not.

He lowered his face and raced toward the cave. A chill of foreboding tore through him as rain soaked his breeches. *I am too late.*

As if to confirm his fear, the roar of a bear sounded from the trees before him.

ELEVEN

He had come. Elizabeth felt a thrill of anticipation. She closed her eyes and savored the first taste of victory. Then she opened them and smiled. "Welcome home, Jonathan. It's been a long time."

Jonathan's gaze met hers. "Not nearly long enough."

She studied his frame. If anything, he had become more attractive in the last ten years. His shoulders were broader, his arms more muscular, his face more rugged. She felt her heartbeat quicken. He was here, and soon he would pay for what he did to her.

She placed one hand on her hip and turned slightly so that he could see how her perfectly tailored gown accentuated her figure. The deep purple velvet swirled around her ankles. She pursed her lips just as she had practiced in the mirror a dozen times that day. "Well, are you coming in?"

Jonathan didn't answer. Instead he stared at her, stared through her. "What are you doing here?" His voice seemed to choke on the question.

She raised her hand so that the light would glint off the emerald ring she wore there. "This is all mine." She swept her arm toward the grounds and watched for his reaction.

He gave none.

She twirled a strand of hair around one finger. Her voice lowered. "I am Lady Grant now."

Jonathan inclined his head toward her. "So you married Richard." It was not a question.

"Yes."

Jonathan nodded. "A good match." The way he said it made it sound like an insult.

Elizabeth tightened her jaw. "So you've come back at last." Her gaze flickered to the tattered carriage behind him. The single horse stamped its feet and snorted. She lifted one eyebrow and looked again at Jonathan.

"I've come to see Richard."

"He's not here."

"So I heard." Jonathan reached behind him.

Only then did she look at the woman standing there. Elizabeth's lips drew into a thin line as her gaze raked over the woman's thick black hair, high cheekbones, and bright blue eyes. The woman wore a simple cotton dress with only a plain ribbon woven through the braid in her hair. *A savage!* Elizabeth's eyes narrowed with disdain. Then she glanced at the blanket in the woman's arms. She caught her breath. *A baby? It couldn't be.* She cleared her throat and returned her attention to Jonathan. "Your servant may wait here."

Jonathan's face turned dark red. "She's not my servant!"

"No?" She lifted her eyebrows.

Jonathan put his arm around the Indian woman. "Elizabeth, I'd like you to meet Kwelik, my wife." He emphasized the last two words.

A trill of sarcastic laughter burst from Elizabeth's throat. "Your wife? How droll!" She stepped gracefully from the doorway. Her hand fluttered toward Jonathan's arm, but her gaze rested on the Indian. "Has he told you, my dear, that we were lovers once?"

Jonathan moved beyond her reach.

She laughed again, hoping her words would hurt the other woman who stood so calmly before her, hoping they would break that quiet demeanor with the same pain Jonathan had long ago inflicted upon her. But the woman didn't flinch.

Elizabeth frowned. "Does she speak English?"

Jonathan opened his mouth to respond, but the amused look on Kwelik's face seemed to stop him.

Elizabeth flicked her fingers in the air. "It matters not."

Jonathan clenched his fists and stepped toward her.

Now she would get a response from him. He would act and later be ashamed. And his guilt would be her weapon. She almost smiled.

But Jonathan stopped before he reached her. Elizabeth looked down to see the woman's hand lying gently on Jonathan's arm. His gaze rested briefly on his wife's face. A look passed between them. Respect. Understanding. And something she refused to name. It made her sick to see it.

Hot fury pounded through Elizabeth's temples. How could Jonathan have chosen this Indian, this savage, over her? It was ridiculous, insulting. She felt resolve harden in her chest. He would live to regret what he had done. She cleared her throat. "And the child?" She nodded toward the blanket in the other woman's arms.

A smile touched Jonathan's lips. It was the first one she had seen there, and the look made her stomach tighten with old longing. "My daughter," he whispered. "Just born."

"A girl, you say?" She leaned over and glanced at the tiny face peeking from the blankets. Then she turned away. *The child looks like a monkey. How could Jonathan love such a thing?*

She sighed. "Do come in, Jonathan. The woman and child too."

But Jonathan didn't move.

Her brows drew together. "Surely you don't plan to stand out here all day?"

"I ain't going nowhere with that mean lady," a young voice shouted from behind a clump of ivy.

"Justin, come out here," Jonathan commanded.

A small boy stepped out from the ivy and looked up at her with wide, blue eyes. Elizabeth reached out a hand to steady herself. She had not counted on a son. Something would have to be done. She drew herself up to full height, then relaxed. *Not now*, she told herself. The time would come. She just had to wait a little longer.

She watched as Jonathan offered his arm to his wife, guided his son in front of him, and stepped past her. When he did, she pulled something from her sleeve and slipped it into his pocket. Now she would have her revenge.

～

Rage exploded across Annie's nerves and drowned the sound of the bear's roar. Teeth, sharp and yellow, barely visible in the descending night, flashed across her vision.

The bear pushed forward until its head and shoulders were just inside the cave. Annie lunged toward it, fists flailing.

The bear, hampered by the small opening, struggled to respond. A claw reached toward her and ripped through the bottom of her dress. A sliver of pain shot through her leg. She fell to her knees. Wildly she again lashed out with both arms. Her hands pummeled into coarse black fur. Something warm knocked against her side. A paw? Or a sharp-toothed snout? She didn't know. She didn't want to know.

"Get out! Get away from us!" she shouted. Her voice bounced off the cave's walls and resonated in her ears. As the sound died, she again heard claws scraping against the bare earth. She reached behind her. Her fingers closed over the first thing they touched—a stick burned from the fire.

The bear pushed forward, its chest still pinned by the cave's opening. Hot and pungent breath blew across her face. She gagged and swung the stick at the beast's forehead. The branch, charred by the flames, broke easily, sending the tip spinning to the side of the cave. Fury and darkness clouded her vision until the bear became every enemy who'd ever hurt her, everyone who'd ever done her wrong.

"I hate you, I hate you, I hate you," she screamed as she brought the crumbling branch down again and again until it was nothing but ashes in her hand.

Claws lashed toward her and missed. A snout, warm and wet, shoved against her chest and knocked her backwards. She twisted and kicked out with both feet. The bear roared again. Annie glanced up to see its mouth, blacker than the cave's darkness, plunging toward her.

A voice penetrated through the haze of her anger. "Hit it in the nose." She slammed her fist into the animal's snout.

With a sharp cry, the bear pulled away and began to back out of the cave.

Annie picked up a rock and threw it at the retreating creature just as its head disappeared from the opening. Then she sat down.

Her breath came in heaving gasps. "I did it," she whispered. "I saved us."

Outside, the patter of rain penetrated her senses. She shivered and glanced over at White Wolf. A flash of lightning shot a beam of light through a crack in the rocks overhead, and she could see the strange smile that played over his lips.

"It was only a black bear," he muttered. A chuckle accompanied his words.

She lifted her chin. "What do you mean, only a black bear?"

White Wolf didn't answer immediately. Instead, she heard him rustle about. Then a small flame flickered up from a stick in his hand. She saw Philippe's tinderbox lying next to him.

He raised to one elbow, though she could tell the action hurt him, and lit a second stick. A tiny flame sputtered and grew. He placed the first stick next to the second, grimaced, and then grinned up at her. "Black bears are easily frightened. You gave that one quite a scare. He'll be telling all his friends about the crazy white woman who fought like a cougar." His words ended in a groan.

Thunder boomed outside as Annie scooted closer to him and pointed to the new tear in her already mangled dress and the thin line of blood beneath it. "I suppose you think it was just playing when it did that?" She snorted. "That bear would have ripped us to shreds if I hadn't fought it off."

White Wolf laughed weakly as he lay back flat. "Whatever you say. Poor bear." He added the last words in an undertone.

"That's more like it." Annie felt a smile tug at the corners of her lips. She leaned over him. "How's your side?"

"Better than that bear's nose."

Annie stared down at him, noting the peculiar expression on his face, the amusement mixed with pain in his eyes. It was almost as if—but, no, it couldn't be—yet . . . it was almost as if he was proud of her.

She studied him for a moment longer, then sat back, wrapped her arms around her knees, and grinned down at him. When she did, something stirred in her, something that she hadn't felt in a long, long time, something that felt suspiciously like laughter.

～

Silence settled in the cave like a warm blanket, punctured only by the soft whisper of flames. Despite the throbbing of pain in his side, White Wolf felt a strange peace wash through him. His gaze lingered on Annie's face. The light from the tiny fire flickered over the cave's walls and illuminated her features. Her eyes sparkled in the dim light. She was almost pretty when she smiled, he decided, with that autumn-leaf hair and eyes the color of moss beneath the water. She had grown into quite a woman. But then he never doubted that she would. He'd never forget the first time he saw her. He closed his eyes and remembered.

He and Taquachi's war band had attacked the frontier farm through the cornfield. The stalks had long ago dried in the winter cold and stood as dead sentinels, guarding nothing. They crackled as the raiders passed through. But no one heard, or so they thought.

Taquachi and Gray Bear went first to the small ramshackle cabin. Smoke curled from the chimney, beckoning them. They threw the door open without knocking and rushed inside. Before White Wolf could draw two breaths, a scream rent the air, then stopped short. A second scream ended the same way. And a third. Moments later Taquachi strode from the cabin with three new scalps attached to his waistband and a burning torch held in one hand.

"Check the barn," he shouted. Then he turned back to the cabin and lit the curtains, the porch, and the roof on fire.

White Wolf turned toward the barn. He could hear the sound the fire made as it crackled through the cabin's roof and began to devour the dark interior. He rounded the corner. Hunger for white man's blood burned in his gut. Then he saw her.

She stood there, a girl of maybe ten summers, with her mouth open, her eyes wide, and her father's musket held in both hands. A cornhusk doll lay facedown at her feet. She closed her mouth into a tight line and pointed the gun at his chest. She did not say a word.

He waited.

They stared at each other for a moment. But she did not shoot. Then Taquachi had come. She whirled away from White Wolf and fired at Taquachi. But the bullet missed. He could still remember the look of horror in her eyes.

Before the sound of the shot faded from the air, Taquachi rushed toward her, his tomahawk raised for the kill. She'd tried to run, but fell, and Taquachi was instantly upon her. White Wolf could see it all again in his mind. He remembered how he had rushed to them, gripped Taquachi's wrist, and stopped the killing blow. He remembered how Annie had looked, white-faced and without tears, when he pulled her to her feet and suggested she be allowed to live to replace the daughter Gray Bear had lost the previous summer. And last of all, he remembered the cornhusk doll that lay abandoned on the ground as they turned and headed back to the village.

But that was a long time ago. She was a child then. They had both been children really. And now, though everything had changed, he could still see that little girl if he looked closely enough. And he wondered, if she looked into him, could she find the boy he once had been before all the killing began?

White Wolf sighed, opened his eyes, and looked at the smoldering sticks. A spattering of rain leaked through a crack overhead and dripped onto his thigh. He brushed away the moisture.

"Does it still hurt?" He heard Annie's voice as if from far away.

"Yes," he answered without looking up. But he didn't mean his wound. The hurt he felt went deeper than a musket shot.

"Philippe will bring something to help it."

As if conjured by her words, footsteps sounded outside the cave's opening. Annie picked up another stick.

"*C'est moi*. It's me," a harsh whisper echoed into the cave before Philippe's head poked through the opening. His hair stood out from his head, and an odd lump made one shoulder look misshapen. "Are you two okay? I heard a bear."

Annie tossed down the stick and shifted away from White Wolf. "We're fine. The bear decided not to stay. What did you get?" She reached toward Philippe's shoulder.

The Frenchman finished pulling himself through the opening and threw two sacks from his shoulder onto the ground before her.

He pulled off his wet coat and glared at the two-stick fire. "Didn't I tell you to put that out?"

"The rain will mask the smoke. No one will see." White Wolf spoke the words with more confidence than he felt.

Philippe sighed. "I hope you're right." He pulled a jar from his pocket and held it up. Shadows danced across its surface. "The bags have some food and water. And this," he said, holding the jar so the light turned the clay a rosy red, "is Jean-Pierre's famous salve. Here." He handed the jar to Annie. "Put this on the wound and then wrap it with clean bandages."

Philippe squatted next to White Wolf. "The bandages are in the first sack." He motioned over his shoulder toward the bag nearest to the fire's ashes. Then he bent over and studied White Wolf's face. "You look better than I expected. Did she get the bullet out?"

White Wolf nodded.

"And did it without killing you? Now that's a miracle."

At another time White Wolf would have joined in Philippe's sarcasm, but now he laid back and looked at the rock that formed the cave's ceiling. A drop of water was gathering just above him. In a moment it would fall. "She did well," he muttered. "I will heal quickly."

"Do you think you can walk? We should leave tonight if we can." Philippe's voice lowered. "It would be better not to risk waiting until the morning."

The drop fell, a single tiny gem that glowed golden in the fire-light before it splattered across White Wolf's chest. He grimaced. "I'll walk."

Philippe put both hands on his knees and stood. "Good. We'll eat first and then head east. Yes?"

"Not me. I'm heading north." Annie stood over White Wolf with the jar in her hand.

"We'll all go north." White Wolf paused. His gaze flickered to Philippe and then back again. "North first, then east."

Philippe frowned. "You promised me."

"It will be safer this way. We don't want to risk running into the English army."

Philippe nodded slowly. "Very well." He turned toward Annie. "Are you going to administer that salve or just stand there with the jar in your hand?"

Annie opened her mouth and then seemed to think better of it. She opened the jar. Pungent odor filled the air. White Wolf coughed. Annie bent over his wound, peeled back the old bandages, and smeared on the salve. For a moment it stung. Then coolness spread over his side. He sighed with relief.

As Annie closed the jar and began to rewrap the wound, Philippe turned and pulled some dried meat from the second bag. He handed a piece to White Wolf. "You will need strength for the journey."

White Wolf took the meat and bit into it. It tasted old and poorly dried, nothing like the fresh deer meat he had once hunted for his tribe. But it would do. It would have to. He took a drink of water from the canteen Philippe had set beside him and then handed it to Annie.

She swallowed the meat that was in her mouth and then drank. As she lowered the canteen, she licked away a stray drop of water from her lip. "Thank you," she mumbled, as if the words were foreign to her. Then she closed the canteen, slapped her hands together, and turned toward the cave's opening. "Are we ready?"

Philippe shoved the remaining meat and water back into the bag and glanced at White Wolf. "The woman and I must carry the sacks. Can you walk without our aid?"

White Wolf lifted himself onto his elbows. "I'll manage."

Philippe nodded to Annie. She grabbed White Wolf's left arm while Philippe took hold of the other. Pain seared through his side as they helped him to his knees. He staggered, then righted himself. Philippe tossed the sacks out the opening and exited the cave. White Wolf took a deep breath and followed. In a moment all three were outside.

Rain splashed across White Wolf's cheeks as he searched for an opening in the clouds above. After a minute of watching, the wind blew a hole in the cloud cover, and he spotted the North Star. "That way." He motioned toward a dark clump of trees and blinked. Water trickled down his forehead. He dashed it away and lurched forward. Wet mud oozed between his toes. He felt his knees begin to buckle. A warm arm reached out and held him upright.

"I'm here." A voice, calm and confident, spoke in his ear. He turned and looked into eyes the color of wet moss.

And for that one breath, he knew she saw the boy within.

TWELVE

~

Jonathan stepped across the mansion's threshold and felt the fist of old fears clutch his stomach. *It was a long time ago*, he told himself again. *I'm a different man now*. His heels clicked on the marble floor. The sound made him shiver. How many times had he heard his father's boots clicking on this same tile? Always that sound had sent waves of foreboding rushing through him. Even now he felt the urge to hide.

Kwelik's shoulder brushed his arm. He heard her soft intake of breath as they stepped past the foyer. "It's okay," she whispered. "God is with us."

Yes, he reminded himself. God had led him here. Surely the Lord wouldn't abandon him now. Jonathan fingered the piece of antler tied with a leather thong around his neck. It had been a gift from his wife on the day of their marriage, to remind him of God's faithfulness and love. He gripped the emblem now and struggled to keep the memories at bay.

To his right a grand staircase spiraled up to the second floor, its mahogany railing polished to a brilliant shine. As a small boy he had slid down that railing, once into the back of his father. He didn't want to remember what happened after that.

Jonathan turned away from the stairs and noticed the crystal oil lamps, lit even in the day, that lined the wall. Above, a magnificent rug imported from India hung over the entrance to the ballroom. He'd always been fascinated by the rug's deep colors and intricate design. On each side of the ballroom's great double doors stood huge columns of milky white marble. Jonathan remembered how the pillars had been added after one of his father's trips to Paris. One more monument to a man obsessed with power.

A stone statue of a lion leered at him as he passed. He looked away. He'd always hated that lion with its blank white eyes and open mouth. Movement caught the corner of his gaze. He turned.

"No, Justin, don't touch!" Jonathan grabbed his son's collar and yanked him away from the statue. "Never touch that!" His voice rang loudly in his ears.

Elizabeth stopped in front of him and turned around. Her gaze slid over the boy, then up to him.

Beside him Kwelik frowned. "Is something wrong?" she murmured.

Jonathan shook his head. "No, nothing. It's just . . . It's just . . ." He let the sentence die, not wanting to remember how his father beat him for touching that same statue when he was little more than Justin's age. He swallowed the memory and lifted his chin. *I can do this. This place will not defeat me again.* But his words seemed weak. So little had changed while he'd been gone. Too little had changed.

"You remember the way to the parlor, do you not, Jonathan?" Elizabeth's voice resounded against the marble floor and elegant hangings as she swept her arm toward the room beyond the stairs.

Yes, he remembered the way to the parlor, remembered only too well. In the parlor Richard had slapped their mother across the face and banished her from the house forever. There Jonathan had read the letter telling of his mother's death, and he'd sworn he would never set foot in this house again. Yet it was there that Elizabeth now led them.

A thick carpet from Persia masked the sound of their footsteps. Through the doorway beyond him, he could just glimpse the great stone fireplace that dominated the dining room. The sight caused his skin to grow cold. It was almost as if he could still see his father standing there, glowering down at him, could almost hear the sound of a hand slapping his mother's face, could almost feel the thud of her body as she fell to the floor. Jonathan shook his head. That was a long time ago—long enough that he should be able to forget. Yet the images came back to him with cruel clarity.

Quickly he averted his gaze and entered the parlor. The floor creaked as he crossed the threshold, the same way it had always done.

He rubbed his hands over his forehead and glanced around the room. Behind him Kwelik and Justin entered quietly, stepping past him to the red velvet couch.

As always his gaze was drawn to the fireplace. This one was smaller, made of brick, and cleaned of its ashes. A small portrait of his mother graced the mantel, and above, a huge painting of Richard, added sometime in the last ten years, glared down at him. Richard's round chin was tilted into the air. His eyes were narrowed slightly beneath a pompous white wig. Every button on his deep purple coat gleamed golden. Even the buckles of his shoes were gold and seemed to glint in the sunlight that streamed from the two windows on the far side of the room. One of Richard's hands was tucked into his coat at the waist, and the other rested on the family Bible on a small table beside him. No hint of humor, or regret, or kindness softened his brother's stance or marked his features. Only coldness, pride, and arrogant disdain rested there. Jonathan scowled and turned away from the portrait.

A white bearskin rug covered part of the floor and stretched beneath the couch and two armchairs, also upholstered in red velvet. A lamp sat on the oak side table and sent shards of light across the old black Bible that lay next to it. Jonathan looked at the Bible and took a deep breath. God was with him, he must remember that. With God all things were possible, even facing the past.

Justin and Kwelik, with the babe still in her arms, sat on the edge of the couch and looked up at him.

Elizabeth didn't even glance at them as she took her seat in one of the empty chairs. "Sit down, Jonathan." She motioned to the other chair. "You needn't pace the floor like a tiger on the hunt." Then she reached over and rang a small bell that had been setting on the table.

Immediately a short, thin woman bustled into the room. She wiped her hands nervously on her apron and bowed once. Frizzled yellow hair poked from beneath her bonnet. "Yes, Milady?" When she straightened, her gaze jumped from Jonathan to Justin and then fluttered quickly back to Elizabeth. Her jaw slackened in surprise.

Elizabeth scowled. "Close your mouth, Betsy, and bring us some tea."

Betsy bobbed back and forth and then twisted the ties of her apron around one finger. "Yes, ma'am. Right away, ma'am." She bowed again and remained standing before Elizabeth.

Elizabeth's frown deepened. "Why are you still standing there? Did you not hear my instructions?"

"Yes, ma'am. No, ma'am. I mean . . ." Betsy's face turned as red as the strawberries dotting her bonnet. She drew a quick breath. "Perhaps Milady would like some biscuits with her tea?"

"I do not remember telling the cook to make biscuits."

Betsy stared so hard at the floor that Jonathan thought her gaze would dent the wood.

Elizabeth cleared her throat. "You may bring the biscuits as well."

"And some marmalade for the young sir perhaps?" Betsy's voice turned into a high squeak. Her gaze rose and flickered to Justin. A faint smile touched her lips and then disappeared.

"No jam. Now go." Elizabeth's voice resounded like a slap.

Betsy took a step back and turned toward the door. Before she reached it, Justin leaped to his feet and scampered toward her. "Thank you very kindly, Miss Betsy, for thinking of me," he said in a voice too solemn for his age.

Betsy's eyes darted toward Elizabeth and then again rested on Justin. She reached into her apron pocket. "Perhaps the young sir would like to play with this while he's here," she murmured and handed a tin soldier to Justin.

Jonathan caught his breath. "Where did you get that?"

Fear flashed across Betsy's features. She rubbed her hands over her apron. "From the nursery, sir."

"The nursery?"

"I wasn't stealing it, sir." Betsy's words escaped in a rush.

Jonathan reached out and took the soldier from Justin's grip. He turned it over in his hand. His voice lowered. "I wasn't accusing you, Betsy. It's just . . ." He paused and examined the soldier more closely. "It's just that this was mine when I was a boy."

"Lord Jonathan?" Betsy's voice cracked.

Jonathan smiled. "Just Jonathan, please."

She bobbed a quick curtsy. "Welcome home, sir."

Jonathan put the soldier in his pocket. "Thank you."

Betsy smiled. "Glad to be of service, Milord."

He cringed.

"That's quite enough." Elizabeth's voice cut through the room.

Betsy gulped. "Yes, yes, the tea and biscuits. I'll get them now."
She turned to Kwelik. "And perhaps a few crumpets for the la . . ."
Her words sputtered to a halt as her gaze focused on Kwelik for the
first time.

Jonathan stepped forward, ready to intervene, but Kwelik's smile
stopped him. To his surprise Betsy smiled back, a great, yellow-
toothed grin that crinkled her face into a thousand tiny lines. She
clapped her hands together and let out an excited squeal. "Why, a
visitor *from the New World!* Oh." Her hands flew to her cheeks. "Just
wait until I tell Lydia. And Evie. And—"

"You will say nothing of our guests!" Elizabeth's words shot
through the room like gunfire.

Betsy's face fell. "Oh, no, of course not, Milady. So sorry." Her
shoulders slumped as she headed for the door.

"You may escort the woman and boy to the dining room and give
them something to eat. When they are finished, show them to their
rooms."

"We will not be staying." Jonathan's voice boomed with con-
viction.

Elizabeth raised her eyebrows. "Surely you don't plan to go all
the way back into town?"

Betsy glanced from Elizabeth to Jonathan and back again.

Jonathan crossed his arms over his chest. "I will not stay in this
house."

"Honestly, Jonathan, you haven't changed one bit. Still the stubborn mule, I see." She arched a perfectly shaped eyebrow. "Perhaps
you prefer the servants' quarters?"

"I do."

Elizabeth's hands fluttered toward him. "Don't be silly, Jonathan.
I wasn't serious."

"I was." He could feel Kwelik and Justin watching him, waiting, wondering what he would do. He saw Betsy's startled expression, and he could feel the undercurrent of tense fury that could not be masked by Elizabeth's light words. Still, he held his ground.

Finally Elizabeth sighed. "Oh, very well then. Do as you wish. I suppose you won't allow your family any food either?"

"They may eat in here with me."

"Stubborn man," she muttered. She turned to Betsy. "Bring the tea and biscuits. We will all eat here in the parlor."

"Yes, Milady. Right away, Milady." Betsy bobbed another curtsy and turned to leave. But before she did, Jonathan saw her cast another wondering glance at Kwelik. Then she caught Justin's eye and gave him a friendly wink.

"Use the good silver," Elizabeth called as Betsy left the room. She tilted her head toward Jonathan. "It's nearly impossible to get good help these days. Most of the servants left, of course, when Richard was arrested. Betsy was the only one who stayed. Pity, since I had planned to dismiss her." Elizabeth smoothed the lace doily on the table. "A servant must know her place, I say." Her gaze slid over to Kwelik and then returned to Jonathan.

Jonathan frowned. "Tobias wouldn't have quit. I know him too well. So where is he? I've come at his request."

"Yes, I know about that little note he sent. He's out. His sister has taken suddenly ill, and he's gone to care for her. I don't know when he'll return." Elizabeth leaned forward. Her voice dropped. "Tobias is an old fool. You can't trust him, Jonathan. Not like you used to." A chill seemed to spread through the air at her words.

Jonathan shook off the feeling. "And Richard? He's still imprisoned, I assume."

Elizabeth tapped her long fingernails on the table. "Another fool." She looked down at her hands. "Caught by Inspector Higgins. His riding crop left at the scene of the crime. Selling secrets to the French, I was told." Her eyes filled with tears, though her expression remained cold. "I had no idea when I married him, of course." She looked up suddenly. Her eyes pierced Jonathan's. "You could have saved me from this shame. You should have. Instead, you forced me to marry a traitor."

"I forced you into nothing. You chose of your own free will."

"You would have had me return from the colonies unmarried? What would have been said about me then, pray tell? You left me no choice when you broke our engagement." Her gaze now turned on Kwelik.

"You're an ugly, old liar!" Justin shouted. Jonathan looked down at the red face of his son, but Justin was still glaring at Elizabeth. "You look real pretty, with that curly yellow hair and fancy purple dress, but you aren't very nice. I bet your mama's ashamed of you."

"Justin, hush." Kwelik leaned over the boy and squeezed his knee with one hand.

Elizabeth blanched, then quickly recovered. "You have taught him well, Jonathan. Like you, he's quick to judge that which he knows not."

Jonathan looked at his son, but the boy was now studying the way the sunlight flickered off his shoes. "He's a boy who speaks his mind. Too freely, I admit. He has not yet learned the games of trickery and deceit that are so common in the old world."

"It seems they are just as common in the new. At least, that's what I remember from ten years ago when you broke faith with me. Has so much changed since then?"

Jonathan clenched his teeth. "I will not play this game of words with you, Elizabeth. We both know the truth about what happened in Boston. And now what's in the past is forgotten."

She bent toward him, her voice suddenly low and sultry. "Is it, Jonathan?" She reached forward and brushed her fingers over his arm. He pulled from her touch as from a hot poker.

Then she leaned back and laughed softly. "We will see how forgotten it is. We will see."

THIRTEEN

~

Rain. Annie was growing to hate it. The ever-persistent sogginess, the constant pattering, the long gray sheets of wetness that never stopped falling. For three long days and nights now it had pelted them, until all they could do was stumble forward, heads down, with water streaming into their eyes. Their food was wet, their clothes soaked, and mud oozed into her shoes with every step. But all that would have been all right, Annie thought, if it weren't for Philippe's singing. If she heard "Frère Jacques" one more time, she thought she would have to shut his mouth with her fist.

"Ding, dang, dong. Ding, dang, dong," he sang to the rhythm of their footsteps.

"I'm going to ding-dong you in a minute, Philippe," she called over her shoulder. Then she lifted one hand and wiped it across her forehead.

Behind her Philippe started another song, this one a long, drawling dirge about "l'amour toute la nuit." She shifted her sack of food from her left arm to her right and squinted into the gray twilight. Around her blue spruce, sycamore, and a few oaks rustled their leaves in the wind. A hundred snails crawled over fallen twigs and clumps of moss, their antennae poking in and out as the rain spattered on their heads. Annie watched the slimy creatures and for once envied them. They at least could withdraw into their shells to escape the weather. She sneezed. As she maneuvered around a fat juniper bush, her foot sank into a wide puddle. Mud splattered up her leg and drizzled down her ankle. "I hate this weather!" she sputtered.

"Frère Jacques, Frère Jacques," Philippe sang in response.

She raised her fist over her head and shook it. "How would you like to be put to sleep permanently?" She paused. "What's that?" She lowered her hand and pointed to a dull light shining through the trees ahead.

Philippe's song ended abruptly as he and White Wolf stopped beside her. "A—how do you call it?—torch light from a cabin?" Philippe suggested.

"It flickers like fire dying," White Wolf muttered. "A fire that burns despite the rain. It's not a good sign."

Annie scowled. "Nothing's ever a good sign with you, is it?" She tightened her grip on the sack. A large droplet gathered on the end of her nose. She dashed it away. "It's probably just a cabin, like Philippe said. Maybe they'll let us come in and dry off. We could use a good rest under a real roof for a change."

"It may be a cabin," White Wolf replied, "but we won't be able to rest there."

Philippe patted White Wolf's shoulder. "You and I may not be welcomed, *mon ami*, but the woman could get us more supplies. We shall see." He motioned toward the light. "Let us discover if fortune will smile on us tonight."

Annie waited as Philippe and White Wolf stepped past her. Then she followed. *Philippe may be right, of course. What settler would take in a Delaware brave, a Frenchman, and a wild-haired Englishwoman?* Still it was worth the chance. The New Light settlers she had grown to trust over these past ten years were kind to all, friend and enemy alike. Besides, at this point she would risk much just to be dry again.

White Wolf stumbled in front of her. His hand immediately clutched his side. She hurried toward him. "Are you okay?"

He did not look at her. "I'll live. The pain is only a dull thudding. Nothing to make a warrior even wince."

"But you did wince. You almost fell just now."

He sighed. "It's because I'm a poor warrior."

Annie shook her head. "We'll find help ahead. You'll be better once we rest."

"There will be no help."

She glared at him for a moment and then quickened her pace to pass him. He would see. The English weren't like savage Indians or cruel Frenchmen. They would help strangers in need, even a band of the most unlikely strangers.

Annie glanced at her companions. What was she doing with an Indian and a Frenchman? When she left the settlement just four months ago, she would have scorned anyone who would have suggested such a thing. Yet here she was, not only with them but helping them. Perhaps she should just leave and find her own way. But deserting them at this point somehow seemed cowardly. God had thrown down this challenge, and now she would see it through, as promised.

Annie bumped into Philippe's back as he stepped through a grove of trees and stopped short. "What are you . . ." Her words faded as she saw what lay in front of her.

A charred cabin, its porch destroyed, its door demolished, sagged in the chilling rain. Inside, fire still flickered, devouring the remnants of what had once been a home. The flames, weak now and dying, glowed yellow in the darkened interior. A black patch on the cabin's roof showed where a torch had been thrown, only to be snuffed out by the rain. But the fire inside had not been dampened.

A wave of coldness spread through Annie. White Wolf stumbled forward and stopped beside her. "It's the work of one of Pontiac's war bands," he muttered. "See there." He pointed to a spear embedded in the cabin's outer wall. He hobbled over and yanked it from the wood. When he turned with the spear in his right hand, the glow from the fire made his features seem hard and lifeless. The sight made her stomach roil with old memories. Annie turned away.

A scream tore from her lips. The sack fell from her hand. Three bodies—a man, a woman, and a young boy—lay facedown and scalpless in the mud. Something snapped within her, and she was once again the ten-year-old girl who had failed to stop the massacre of her family. Fury and horror erupted within her. She turned toward White Wolf. "You did this! You and your people. I should have killed you when I had the chance!"

But White Wolf did not seem to hear. Instead, he too stared at the dead settlers, his face pale in the firelight.

Annie ran at him and pounded her fists into his chest. Tears blurred her vision. "You did this, you did this, you did this," she shouted.

White Wolf wrapped his arms tight around her and held her close. His grip pinned her elbows to her sides, so all she could do was cry against his chest and allow her tears to mingle with the rainwater that covered him. "Shhhh," she heard him whisper in her ear. "I know it hurts. I know."

"How could you do it? How could you?" The words bubbled up from somewhere deep inside her and spilled against his skin. She felt his hand on her hair. She jerked back. "I hate you! I hate you all!" Her voice sounded hoarse in her ears.

White Wolf continued to hold her until her racking sobs quieted, and in their place was left only an aching hollowness, a pain like a blade in her throat. Then he released her. She stumbled backward.

Philippe squatted near the bodies. "They are cold and stiff," he called. "I'd say the war band is a day ahead of us, maybe more." He rose to his feet.

White Wolf walked over and stood beside Philippe. His face hardened. "This is just the beginning." His voice was icy. "It will not stop here. No one is safe. Not anymore."

Annie wrapped her arms around herself and averted her eyes from the bodies. "It is as I feared."

White Wolf turned and looked at her with unseeing eyes. "The victory at Fort Duquesne has made them bold. They'll kill without thought, without mercy." His voice lowered, and she could tell he was no longer talking to her. "So I've come again to the edge of hell." He fell to his knees.

Philippe placed his hand on White Wolf's back. "We must go. We need to find shelter for the night. There is nothing for us here."

"No!" The word was out before Annie could stop it. "We can't just leave them like that. We have to bury them." Her gaze rested only briefly on the settlers, then again darted away.

Philippe hoisted his sack higher on his shoulder. "There is no time. They are dead. They can hurt no more."

"No, we can't leave them." Her voice raised to a shrill pitch. *Not like my family was left.*

Philippe's knuckles tightened on his sack. "*C'est la vie*, Annie. You can stay and bury them if you wish. We're going on. Come, *mon ami*." He patted White Wolf's shoulder again.

White Wolf shook off the touch. He turned toward Annie. His gaze caught and held hers. "No, we'll stay. All of us." He stood and headed toward a small lean-to that had not been burned.

"Where are you going?" she called after him.

He did not answer. Instead, he searched inside for a few moments and then returned with two wooden spades and an old cloth. He handed the spades to Philippe and Annie. "You dig. I'll prepare the bodies."

Annie gripped the spade in her hand and began to dig. With each spade full of dirt, the memories became clearer—and with them the old questions. Did anyone ever come to bury her parents? What if she had been braver?

Silently they worked side by side until the hole was dug and the bodies were wrapped in cloth. Then Philippe and Annie lowered the settlers into the hole and covered them.

"Someone should say something," Annie whispered as they stood at the graveside with their eyes downcast. "Someone should say a prayer." But no one spoke—only the rain with its persistent muttering, only the splash of water on the already drenched ground.

Annie opened her mouth. No words came. How could she pray to a God who stood silent while this family was massacred? How could she speak a blessing when her heart burned with cold fury? She looked at White Wolf. His jaw was clenched, and his hand rested against the spear that he'd again picked up.

Finally Philippe spoke. "I will do it, though I am no priest." He cleared his throat. "May God accept these souls, and may they find peace on the other side."

Peace. The thought pierced Annie with an ache of longing, but Philippe's next words drove it from her. "And may their deaths serve as a warning against the sin of hatred and war."

Annie's heart rebelled against the words. Then Philippe raised his eyes to hers. "Can we go now? Or shall we wait for the Indians to return?"

White Wolf stepped between them, the spear still in his hand. "We go. I can walk farther tonight before I'm too weary." He motioned toward the trees with the spear and started in that direction. Annie picked up her sack and trudged after him.

Miles later, just as the clouds began to break and the moon started to shine through, they came to another settlement. This one too had been burned and ransacked. But this time no bodies were sprawled on the ground. To the left of the clearing a small stable stood unharmed. Three sides were enclosed, with the fourth open to the night air.

"We will shelter there tonight," Philippe said and headed toward the structure. Annie followed with White Wolf behind her. In minutes the sacks sat open on one side of the stable, and a small fire flickered from a few dry branches and a pile of hay. Annie knelt between White Wolf and Philippe. Silence hovered over them.

White Wolf handed her a bit of dried meat and the flask of water. She bit off a piece and chewed thoughtfully. Warmth from the fire brushed her cheeks and dried the rain from her hands. She watched the dance of the flame, flickering yellow and orange against the darkness of the night. Before her stood two burned cabins and a broken fence. On the far side of the clearing a chicken coop, its occupants long gone, leaned against an ash tree. A wooden plow and two old harnesses lay inches deep in the mud. Annie took another bite of meat and turned her eyes back to the fire.

On the other side of the flames, White Wolf gripped his new spear. He took the knife from his waistband and began to sharpen the spear's end with long, methodical strokes. Sweat glistened on his chest, and she noticed the tiny flecks of ash that spotted his skin as he worked. Ash. Everything she cared for, it seemed, always turned to ash. And now, she knew, it would happen again unless she could stop it.

The war band was heading right toward the New Light settlement and her friends—Rosie with her graying red hair and jovial "mark me words, lassie"; Tom with his belt always buckled a little too tight; Tim with his stories of the old country; and Jonathan, Kwelik, and little Justin. And, of course, the boy. But he might be spared.

Those people were her family now, and she couldn't lose them—not again. She would go straight back and warn them, help them prepare, fight alongside them. Her warning had saved them once before. If they hurried, they might still be in time.

Annie reached across the fire and took the spear from White Wolf's hand. She felt the weight of it in her palm as her fingers wrapped around the warm shaft. This time, she promised herself, she would fight and win. This time she would not be afraid.

That night the rain cleared.

FOURTEEN

~

"It's not at all like I imagined." White Wolf's words drifted quietly into the morning air. After two more days of walking, they finally stood on the outskirts of the New Light settlement. A decade ago he, with the warriors of his tribe, had attacked these settlers. He'd hoped to drive them from the land and water the ground with their blood. The tribe had lost that battle, and their chief had lost his life. He would never have believed that now he would be asking these people for help. Here he would find his sister again, and with her, he hoped, he would regain his soul.

Annie turned and quirked one eyebrow at him. "No scalps hanging from lodge poles, you'll notice."

White Wolf didn't rise to the bait. Instead, he allowed his gaze to wander over the parts of the settlement that were visible from where he stood. Above a thick log wall he could just see the peaked roofs of two cabins and a larger building with a cross on top. Beyond that and outside the log walls the outlines of three more cabins were visible, one to the east of the clearing and two scattered in the trees to the west. As he watched, a woman stepped from the eastern cabin with a basket held in both arms. She headed across the clearing.

Beside him Annie cleared her throat. "Sarah's had her baby, I see." She paused. "I wonder what else has changed."

As she spoke, a boy darted across an opening in the fort-like wall. White Wolf saw a flash of black hair and something like a stick that the boy was waving above his head. "Aiiiieeeee," came a shrill cry as he disappeared from view.

"Ashton, you get back here this minute!" a woman called from the cabin inside the wall. Ashton—the name caused White Wolf to tremble. He hadn't heard it in a long time. It was the surname of his father's family, a name he hadn't used since he was a boy. Strange that he should hear it again now, as if God was calling him to remember the boy he used to be, remember the man his father had hoped he'd become. But that hope had died with Thomas Ashton, had died as surely as the village his father had given his life to protect.

White Wolf shook his head, willing himself to forget that dark day when his home was attacked and burned, when his father was killed, and when a young boy named Tankawon had first set foot on the warpath that would change him into White Wolf, a man driven by hate and fury.

"I suppose I'd better go first." Annie's comment chased away the memories. "They'll really think I've lost my mind this time."

"You're sure they'll help us?" Philippe's forehead furrowed into deep lines as he brushed his hand over his wrinkled French uniform.

Annie nodded. "I'm sure. They're not all like me, you know."

"Humph," Philippe grunted.

Annie chuckled, a sound so rare that White Wolf stared at her. She caught his eye and frowned. "What's the matter?"

He shrugged. "It's good to see you happy. You're glad to be back."

She looked away. "I'd be gladder if I could bring news of victory with me."

White Wolf studied her for a moment and then motioned toward the clearing. "Go. We'll wait—"

The unmistakable sound of a cocking gun stopped White Wolf's words. He turned and found himself looking down the long barrel of an Englishman's musket. *I didn't hear his approach*, was his first thought. *I'm a warrior, and yet I didn't sense the enemy. What has happened to me?* His gaze traveled up the gun's shiny surface to meet eyes, hard and steady, staring into his own.

"Put down your weapons," the man commanded. "Come quietly, and no one will get hurt." Two other men stepped from the trees, their guns pointed at Annie and Philippe.

White Wolf felt an awkward thudding in his chest. Annie moved toward him. He dropped his spear on the ground and waited.

"Tom?" Annie's voice sounded strained.

The man in front of White Wolf lowered his weapon. A grin

spread across his face. "Well, bless my soul, it's Miss Annie. What're you doing here?"

Annie returned his grin. "Well, of course, it's me. Who did you expect? Indians?"

Tom set down his gun and wrapped her in his thin arms. "Rosie's been so worried," he said. "When we heard the news about Braddock's loss, we thought . . . Well, never mind what we thought. The important thing is that you're safe, and you're home."

White Wolf edged toward the musket.

"Hold on there, Injun," said the second settler. His gun moved to White Wolf's chest. Brown eyes squinted in a freckled face as the man regarded him.

Tom released Annie. His brow furrowed. "These are your friends?"

Annie put her hand on Philippe's shoulder. "This is Philippe Reveau. He helped me escape the French fort."

Tom's eyebrows shot up. "You were captured? Are you okay? Did they hurt you?"

Annie raised her hand to stop the questions. "I'm unharmed. Thanks to Philippe—and to White Wolf."

Three sets of eyes fixed on him. The other guns lowered. "White Wolf?" he heard the third man whisper. "*The* White Wolf?"

White Wolf felt like a wooden carving put on display.

Finally Tom stepped forward. "Welcome, brother of Kwelik. You are among friends." He extended his hand.

White Wolf stared at the hand for a moment before taking it in his own. Tom's fingers closed around his in a firm grip. He looked into the older man's eyes, and this time he saw warmth there, warmth so like his father's that it made his palms sweat.

Tom let go of his hand and turned toward Philippe. "You are welcome too. Though our governments be enemies, we shall be friends, if you are willing."

Philippe gave a small bow. "I am. Thank you."

Tom clapped his hands together and again smiled at Annie. "And now this deserves a celebration! The prodigal daughter has come home at last. Rosie will be so pleased. It's too bad Kwelik isn't here to see it."

"Kwelik's not here? What happened?" Annie's voice raised in alarm.

White Wolf felt as if his breath was suddenly stolen from him.

"Oh, nothing to be worried about." Tom smiled. "Jonathan got a letter from England, so they headed out soon after you left. Don't know when they'll return. We miss them a mighty lot with these Indian attacks all around. Could use Jonathan's battle sense." He glanced at White Wolf and then motioned toward the log wall. "That was Jonathan's idea. Said you can't be too careful. The missus and me put our cabin inside along with Jonathan and Kwelik's and the church. Reckon that'll keep the Indians out?"

White Wolf looked again at the settlement's defenses. "For your sake I hope so. They're not far behind us." He bent over and picked up his spear.

Tom nodded. His voice lowered. "Aye. We know they're coming, but we're ready."

White Wolf glanced at the muskets in their hands. "Yes, I see that."

"Enough yammering. Tonight we celebrate." Tom grabbed his gun and headed toward the opening in the log wall.

The rest of them followed. With each footstep the realization that Kwelik was not there thudded through White Wolf. She had gone. He might never see her again. He should have come months ago, years ago. Maybe he should have never left.

White Wolf shifted his spear from his left to right hand and glanced over his shoulder. The freckle-faced man was staring at him. "Sorry 'bout that welcome," the man said as he drew abreast.

White Wolf's gaze swept over the man's curly brown hair and round, flushed face.

"Name's Tim. Timothy McKnighton."

White Wolf searched his memory for the proper response to such an introduction but found nothing. He remained silent.

Tim McKnighton rubbed his hand over his chin and sniffed. "Been on the watch day and night since Braddock lost the battle at

Fort Duquesne. Attacks up and down the frontier ever since. Them savages—oops, oh, begging your pardon."

White Wolf did not bother to respond.

"Those Indians don't much care who they kill, whether we be peaceful, God-fearing folk or not. Women and children too. Rider came through yesterday with the most gruesome tales ever been heard. Children scalped and slaughtered. Men cut in pieces and fed to the dogs. Women . . ." He shuddered. "I can't even repeat what's been done to the women."

White Wolf felt something tighten in his chest. "And the English are innocent in all this? They have done nothing to the Lenape, to the Shawnee, to the Ottawa? They have not brought disease that has ravaged whole villages at a time? They have not taken our land, forced us from our homes? They have not shot our children? Stolen our women? There is no blood on their hands?"

"Oh, well, I didn't say that exactly. There've been stories, you know. But I don't believe everything I hear."

White Wolf raised his eyebrows.

The man's face turned red.

They walked through the opening in the log wall, and Tom's voice boomed toward the smaller cabin on the right. "Rosie!" he called. "Take out the good dishes. We've got company."

A gray-haired woman bustled out the door. She paused beside a wooden chair and a half-barrel overflowing with marigolds. The sun shone directly into her face, illuminating features wrinkled by years of hard work. She wiped her hands on her apron and squinted up at the visitors. Her hands flew to her cheeks. "Oh, the good Lord be praised!" she exclaimed.

She hurried toward them and swept Annie into her embrace. "Welcome home, child. Bless me, but I thought you'd gone forever," she mumbled into Annie's hair. Then she turned toward White Wolf.

Before he knew what was happening, he too was engulfed in her strong arms. Her grizzled hair poked him in the chin while the scent of fresh bread and strawberries filled his senses. "Oh, laddie, it's so good to meet you at last," he heard her say. "You don't know how I've prayed for you all these years."

Her words were like cold water poured down his spine. He pulled back. "How did you know . . ."

She smiled up at him. "Why, who else would you be but Kwelik's brother? It's in your eyes, lad."

White Wolf felt his hand slipping on his spear. He tightened his grip. The action steadied him.

The woman called Rosie patted him twice on the arm and turned toward Philippe. Her gaze flickered over his ragged uniform. "A French deserter?" she questioned.

"A friend," Tom answered. "Philippe Reveau."

She immediately extended both hands toward Philippe. "Welcome, son. Our home is yours." She smiled up at him.

Philippe took her right hand in his, raised it to his lips, and kissed it. "*Merci*, Madame Rosie. Your beauty is only surpassed by your kindness."

Rosie flushed. "A French flatterer, I see." But White Wolf could tell that she was pleased.

Philippe chuckled. "Is this how you greet all your enemies?"

Rosie put her hands on her hips and cocked her head to one side. "Only the handsome ones, *monsieur*." Her accent so distorted the French word that it was nearly unrecognizable.

They both laughed.

Philippe turned toward Annie. "You were right, *mademoiselle*. They are not at all like you."

Rosie again focused on White Wolf. "You'll be staying, o' course? Jonathan and Kwelik's cabin is empty."

He shook his head. "No, we must move on. We only came to warn you of the approaching war band. We will rest and eat. Then Philippe and I will be on our way. We have a long journey ahead of us." He stabbed his spear into the ground. "And we don't want to be here when the war band arrives." His gaze fastened on Rosie. "Though perhaps your God will save you again."

Rosie looked at him for a long time. Her eyes were unreadable. "I know you were one of those who attacked us when Blacker was killed. I know you hated us. But we have forgiven you. It's God you must deal with now."

"God? He no longer remembers my name."

"He remembers, Tankawon. He always remembers."

White Wolf shivered.

He felt a hand on his arm. He turned to see Annie looking at him, looking through him. "Come, let me show you your sister's home. We can rest there." He nodded and pulled the spear from the dirt.

Annie led him to the second cabin, with Philippe and the others behind them. Tiny violets lined the front of the cabin and drooped in the growing heat. Two buckets lay to the right of the short porch, and beneath them sprouted a tuft of thick brown grass.

White Wolf stepped onto the porch and watched a tiny spider scuttle across the wooden doorframe. A dew-covered web hung from the corner of the door. Sunlight shone on the droplets, making them glitter like glass beads reflecting fire. Annie opened the door and pushed it wide. She disappeared inside.

White Wolf took a deep breath and followed. As soon as he entered the cabin, he could tell it belonged to his sister. He could almost feel her presence in the air. He could nearly see her curled on the high-backed chair in front of the fireplace, could almost hear her voice calling him from the room beyond. His gaze fell to a basket next to the fireplace. A red and blue woven blanket lay across one corner, and small booties hung from the side. He turned back to Rosie.

She smiled at him. "For her second child. The first is six now. A fine, strong boy."

He closed his eyes for a moment and tried to picture it—his sister, her arms holding a tiny baby, a young boy with black hair and blue eyes at her side, and a man like a shadow in the distance. He frowned and opened his eyes.

"We'll leave you all alone for a while," he heard Tom say. "Tim will bring some fresh water. You can clean up and get some rest. We'll come for you when the food is ready." White Wolf heard footsteps behind him. Then the door closed quietly, leaving just himself, Annie, and Philippe together in the house.

"My room is over there." Annie motioned to the left. "I'm going to go lie down. You two can use Jonathan and Kwelik's room." She pointed to a doorway on the right. "Justin's room is next to it. It's small, but it will afford some privacy if you need it."

Philippe stepped past White Wolf and gave another small bow. "*Merci, mademoiselle.*"

The corners of Annie's mouth twitched. "At least coming here has done one thing," she smirked. "It's put a civil tongue in your head. *Mademoiselle* . . ." Her shoulders shook in a silent chuckle. "Yesterday it was 'you, woman.'"

Philippe threw his hands in the air. "*La femme!* There is no pleasing them." He turned toward the doorway on the right and disappeared behind it.

Annie flicked her fingers in Philippe's direction and then stomped off toward her room, leaving White Wolf alone.

For a moment he did nothing but listen to the silence and try to imagine the room with his sister in it. He could hear her laugh. He could see her hand touching the basket ever so gently. He could envision her topaz-blue eyes boring into him, questioning him. He shook off the image.

A few rough paintings lined the wall adjacent to the fireplace. He walked over to them. The first was a picture of a huge Irish wolfhound. Milap, Kwelik's dog. He had been killed the day their village was destroyed. The second was a picture of a dark man that White Wolf had only seen once before—during an Indian attack. That time he, White Wolf, had been the aggressor. The third was a picture of himself as a boy. He paused to study this one for a long moment. Kwelik had painted him at the age of eight or nine summers. He wore a wide grin on his face and held up a fistful of freshly speared trout. It was autumn. He could tell by the way the sun glinted through the ash trees onto the dots of red, purple, and yellow flowers. He'd always loved the fall. But that had all changed.

White Wolf sighed and turned to the last portrait. His breath stopped in his throat. There his parents stared at him through eyes of paint. His father's white-gray hair stood out at awkward angles, just as it always did, while his mother's long black braids cascaded over her chest. His father held a black book that White Wolf knew was a Bible. But it was the look in their faces that caused him to lean closer for a better view. Joy, as if in the next moment they would break out in merry laughter. Kwelik had captured it perfectly. And now that look pierced him with all the longing for home.

He averted his eyes.

When he did, his gaze fell on the wampum belt hanging over the fireplace. *Wampum binds the oath.* He remembered the words from the night Kwelik had nearly lost her life. It seemed like yesterday. It seemed like forever. He reached up and touched the smooth white and purple shells. They felt cool to his touch. White Wolf turned. There, illuminated by a shaft of light, a thick book lay open on a table. He knew he should ignore it, but he could not. Instead, he found himself drawn toward it until he stood over the open page. The print swam before his vision.

From whence come wars and fightings among you? Come they not hence, even of your lusts that war in your members? Ye lust, and have not: ye kill, and desire to have, and cannot obtain: ye fight and war, yet ye have not, because ye ask not. Ye ask, and receive not, because ye ask amiss, that ye may consume it upon your lusts.

White Wolf felt his limbs tremble. The words of James shouted at him, accused him, condemned him. Yet he continued to read.

Submit yourselves therefore to God. Resist the devil, and he will flee from you. Draw nigh to God, and he will draw nigh to you. Cleanse your hands, ye sinners; and purify your hearts, ye double-minded. Be afflicted, and mourn, and weep: let your laughter be turned to mourning, and your joy to heaviness. Humble yourselves in the sight of the Lord, and he shall lift you up.

Those words weren't for him anymore, he reminded himself. Maybe they never had been. But what if . . .

"Do you think a person can start again?" The question shot through him. He looked up. Annie was standing beside him. A strange fire sparked in her moss-green eyes.

And suddenly something long dead in him began to stir once again.

Fifteen

~

It was the most dismal place Jonathan had ever seen. The stone prison crouched on the misty moor like a toothless monster waiting to devour its prey. Twin turrets rose as horns through the fog. A dozen windows, tiny and black, peered out onto the thin gravel road that led up to the gated entrance.

Jonathan stood there for a moment, watching the prison as if waiting for something to beckon him forward. Nothing did. The stray call of a raven echoed across the moor. In the distance rows of black trees thrust their branches into the fog. The air smelled of a rotting dampness that reached all the way to his bones.

He took one step forward and stopped. It was not too late to turn back. Even now as he looked at the bleak walls of the prison, he couldn't help but believe that Richard deserved what he had gotten. After what he had done to Uncle Archibald, after what he had tried to do to Jonathan, and especially after what he'd done to their mother, Richard deserved prison and more. Much more. He deserved to die.

The sudden croaking of a frog near his feet startled Jonathan. He squatted down and looked at the bumpy creature as it hopped across the road. It stopped only once and blinked at him with round gray eyes.

"Hello, little friend," Jonathan whispered.

The frog croaked again and continued on its way. Before it could get to the other side, a snake slithered from the rushes. Oblivious, the frog took another hop. In one sudden movement the snake attacked. Jonathan watched in disgust as the frog oozed down the snake's throat and disappeared. Then the snake looked up at him with eyes like yellow slits, as if to say, "Will you be next?"

"Get away from me," Jonathan answered. He stood up and shivered.

The snake flicked its tongue at him and glided into the rushes.

Jonathan turned back to the prison. *Go on*, a voice inside him whispered. *You must face him.* He forced his feet forward, every step a struggle against the bitterness in his heart. He wished he were back in the mansion with Kwelik and his children; he wished he were back home on the frontier; most of all he wished he could forget that he had a brother who had once tried to kill him. He squared his shoulders and turned to the carriage behind him. "You may leave," he called to the driver. "I'll go alone from here." *Alone.* The word pricked and left him chilled.

The driver nodded and reined his horse back down the narrow road toward town.

Gravel crunched under Jonathan's feet as he walked up to the heavy iron doors and pulled them open. The hinges creaked loudly, drowning the sound of his own uneven breathing. He stepped through the door. Two guards stood on either side. He nodded to them and walked past.

Gray stone walls greeted his vision. He turned toward a wide doorway on his right. There the warden sat behind an old desk. His pen's plume jiggled back and forth as he wrote. Jonathan approached the desk and cleared his throat. The man did not look up. The warden's portly frame barely squeezed into the wide, high-backed chair. Rolls of fat spilled over the top of the armrests and pushed out the buttons on his once-fashionable coat.

"Pardon me, sir." Jonathan's voice echoed eerily off the masonry.

And still the man continued to write.

"I've come to see Lord Grant."

The warden finished writing his sentence, slowly returned the pen to its inkwell, and looked up. Narrow-set eyes studied him from beneath the greasy yellow wig. The man sniffed. "*Lord* Grant, is it? Fancy titles don't mean so much here, as you'll see."

Jonathan frowned. "What do you mean by that?"

The man ran his finger over the feathered portion of his pen. "You are Jonathan Grant, are you not?"

"I am."

"We don't have much pity for traitors to the crown, Mr. Grant, be they lords," he said, his eyes raking up and down Jonathan's frame, "or woodsmen. You would do well to remember that."

Jonathan bristled. "I've come to see my brother. Take me to him."

The man's eyebrows lifted. "You dare to order me?"

Jonathan bowed his head. "I humbly request audience with the Lord Grant who is, I am told, under your," he glanced around, "care."

The man smiled. "Ah, the proper attitude at last."

Jonathan did not respond. He had seen this kind of man before. But even men such as this, he knew, could be changed by the powerful hand of God. He had seen that before as well. An image of his uncle flashed before his vision. He had despised Archibald then, but he would not make that mistake again. Even obese wardens, he reminded himself, were to be afforded proper respect.

The warden's gaze flicked from him to a hallway on the left. "Tibbs," he called into the darkness, "take this man to the dungeon to see Lord Grant." He slurred the title. Then he picked up his quill again and began to scratch on the piece of parchment before him.

A tall, lanky man materialized from the shadows. He wore a tattered guard's uniform and clenched a pipe between crooked teeth. Keys jangled from his belt as he made his way across the room. He rubbed his hand over sallow cheeks. "Follow me," he muttered.

Jonathan followed down the dim hallway. Tibbs looked back at him. "You be Grant's first visitor." He pulled a lantern from a hook on the wall and lit it with his pipe. Light flickered over his crooked nose and scampered into the corners of the hall.

Jonathan's brow furrowed. "No one has come?"

Tibbs shook his head. "Not a soul."

"Not even his wife?"

"The high-and-mighty Lady Grant?" he scoffed. "No, sir."

"You know her?"

Tibbs's lips twisted into a strange smile. "Only by reputation. A colder woman's never been born, they say."

Jonathan watched the man's back as they descended a narrow flight of stairs. Their footsteps echoed hollowly against the stone walls. Ribbons of light darted from the lantern to make wicked patterns on the rock. Water dripped somewhere below them, and the cry of a prisoner echoed up through the darkness. Jonathan sucked in his breath.

Finally they reached the bottom. Tibbs pulled the keys from his waist and unlocked a large metal door. Iron scraped against stone as he pulled the door back and motioned for Jonathan to enter. "This place has a way of making all men equal, as you will see," he muttered over the loud moans of the prisoners.

Coldness, like the slap of a hand, hit Jonathan in the face as he stepped into the dungeon. Cells, each closed with similar iron doors, stretched in a long line into the blackness. The click of the key in a lock behind him indicated that Tibbs had again locked the door. Jonathan looked back.

Tibbs squinted at him through one eye. "That be Grant's cell, third one on the right. You sure you want to see 'im?"

Jonathan drew a breath and choked on the stale air. "I'm sure."

A groan, louder than the others, came from behind a door on his left. Farther down in the darkness someone began shrieking.

Tibbs grinned. "You get used to it after a while. That one's always screamin'. Grant, though—he never utters a sound. Would never know he was here except that the food tray's empty when I come back to get it."

They reached the third door. Tibbs took another key and opened it. "You got a visitor, Grant," he called. He looked at Jonathan. "I'll be back later." He hung the lantern on a peg on the wall and headed toward the outer door.

Jonathan stepped into the foul-smelling cell. In the corner a tall, gaunt figure with scraggly hair and slumped shoulders stood with his back to the door. The man turned, and Jonathan looked into a face he barely recognized.

"So you've come to me at last," Richard rasped.

Words failed Jonathan. Was this his brother? This pale ghost of a man who looked out from dark and sunken eyes?

Richard's gaze bored into his. "Come, brother," he sighed. "I offer you the only seat I have." He motioned toward a moldy straw mattress in the corner. Jonathan did not sit down.

Richard shrugged his shoulders and plopped down on the mattress. He glanced up at Jonathan. "I suppose you think I've gotten what I deserve."

The accuracy of the statement pierced Jonathan. Yet could anyone really deserve this? His gaze wandered over the damp stone walls, the dirty straw, the dark streaks of mildew growing in the crevices of the doorframe.

Richard laughed—a dry, wheezing sound that ended in a cough. Jonathan shivered.

"You need not say it. I can read it in your face," Richard said. "You never could hide your feelings, Johnny. Mother always said so." He paused. "You're right, you know."

Jonathan finally found his voice. "About what?"

"I do deserve this. I deserve it all."

Jonathan's jaw tightened. "So you did what they say?"

A cold smile twisted Richard's lips. "Is that what you think?"

"Well, did you? Did you betray our country to the French?"

Richard's smile widened. Jonathan noticed a tooth missing. "So it's 'our' country now, is it? I thought you hated England, and yet here you are." He waved his hand in the air.

"I'm here because Tobias asked me to come."

"Tobias always thought you were our savior."

"There is only one Savior. I'm not Him."

"Nor am I." Richard stared intently at Jonathan. "But I'll answer your question. I didn't betray England. Not this time." His voice lowered. "Ironic, isn't it? So many things they could have charged me with. Yet I'm here for a crime committed by another."

"How did it happen?"

"The deceiver was carrying my riding crop." His gaze fixed on the corner of his cell where the light didn't reach. "Betrayed by a bit of leather. Who would have believed it?" Richard fell silent.

Jonathan shifted his weight from one foot to the other. He tapped his fingers on his pant legs, then held them still. "I don't know if I believe you or not. You've lied to me before." Richard didn't flinch. Jonathan continued, "I'm here to help you. What can I do?"

Richard's gaze slid in Jonathan's direction. "Is that why you've come, brother? To help me? Despite what has gone between us?"

"If you are innocent, yes. And if you are guilty, then to make things right."

"I'm not innocent. You can't make things right."

Jonathan turned away. "Then I have no business here. I'll go." He started toward the door.

"Jonathan, wait."

He turned back. Richard stood behind him, one hand outstretched. "Stay, brother. I'm sorry. Sorry for so many things. I've been a fool."

Jonathan didn't disagree.

"These walls do something to a man, you know. They change you. They can cause you to go mad, like that poor fellow a few cells down. Or they make you see."

"And what have they done for you?"

"They've shown me the truth. About me and about Father." His expression softened. "I would never have believed it, but here with the mildew, the rats, and the screams in the night, I've found a piece of heaven. Here I've found God."

Jonathan snorted. "You? Found God?"

"You don't have to believe me. But there's one thing I need from you before I can be free."

"What's that?"

Richard began to pace back and forth in the cell. "I wonder if you'll be able? The past is a powerful enemy. Too powerful, methinks, for a man to overcome alone."

Jonathan crossed his arms. "Enough riddles, Richard. Ask what you will of me."

"I ask you to forgive me."

A hundred thoughts flew through Jonathan's mind. He remembered Uncle Archibald's final words: "Forgive Richard." He remembered his mother's face, bruised and pained, the day Richard had banished her. He remembered Kwelik's words spoken years ago: "He that saith he is in the light, and hateth his brother, is in darkness even until now." He had told himself then that he'd forgiven his brother. But now he knew it was lie. *Oh, God,* he prayed, *I've tried to forgive, but I can't. I can't forget what he's done.*

As the prayer faded from his mind, Jonathan looked into the eyes of his hate and saw there the reflection of the frog.

∽

Annie leaned over White Wolf's side as he lay cross-wise over Justin's bed. A ray of sunlight glinted through the window to illuminate his midsection. Annie pressed her finger along the edges of his wound and frowned. "If you would just hold still a minute, I could see how it's healing."

"I am holding still."

Annie glanced up White Wolf's lean frame to see eyebrows drawn together in a dark scowl. "You're twitching," she said.

"You're poking me. What do you expect?"

"I need to see if the skin is coming back healthy."

"Hurry up." White Wolf's voice was sharp.

"It seems to be healing well, I think. But you should have Doc Bradley take a look at it."

White Wolf bent into a sitting position. "It's bad enough to have you prodding at me. I don't want some white man doctor doing the same."

Annie threw her hands in the air. "Fine. Sit here and rot then, for all I care."

White Wolf reached out and grabbed her hand. "I'm sorry. I didn't mean to be rude. I know you're trying to help."

Annie pulled her hand from his. "Don't try to be nice, Waptumewi. It doesn't suit you."

White Wolf folded his legs beneath him until he was sitting cross-legged in the center of the bed. "Why are you so angry? You're home safe, aren't you? Thanks to the Frenchman and me."

"Safe? What do you know about safe? What do you know about anything?" Annie's emotions crashed against one another and tumbled from her lips in bitter words. "You say I'm home, but I don't have a home anymore. You took that from me, remember?"

White Wolf's head lowered. His gaze dropped to his hands in his lap. "I know that. I'm sorry."

"Sorry doesn't make it okay."

White Wolf remained silent for so long that Annie wasn't sure he would ever respond. Finally he looked up. "The past is gone. It can't be changed."

His words pierced her with a strange desperation. *No, it's not gone. It will never be gone*, she felt like screaming. *It lives with me day to day. How else can I explain this pain?* But she didn't say those things. Instead, she turned and looked out the window. "It may be gone," she muttered, "but it's still all that matters."

"Is it?" White Wolf shook his head, unfolded his legs, and rose from the bed. "Maybe you're right."

Silence again settled between them. She could see him smoothing the quilt on the bed with one hand. Yet she continued to stare out the window. A robin flitted to the ground nearby and chirped. Then it flew away. Just like her fleeting hopes for peace. Always they took flight, leaving only the need for revenge in their place.

Annie spoke without turning. "I'm so angry with you, I could, I could . . ."

"I know that." White Wolf's voice belied no emotion.

"It's not just about my family," she said.

"What else then?"

A hundred conflicting feelings raced through Annie—anger, sorrow, guilt, confusion. Finally they crystallized into three simple words. "You left us."

The bed creaked as White Wolf sat down on the edge. She could tell he was looking at her. "It was better for me to go."

Annie did not turn toward him. "You don't know how hard it was. We needed you. The pox came and . . . and it was horrible."

"I was a drunk then—worthless to you or to Snowbird."

"She died at dawn. We burned her with the others."

"How many died?"

"Why do you care?"

"How many, Wakon?"

Annie crossed her arms. "All but ten of us. The settlers helped. None of us would have survived without them. We didn't think Kwelik was going to make it, but she did. Then I got sick too."

"There would have been nothing I could have done."

"You're a coward, Waptumewi. You always were."

"Are you two still arguing?" Philippe walked into the room and tossed his uniform jacket onto the bed. Annie noticed that it looked considerably cleaner.

She uncrossed her arms, put her hands on her hips, and turned toward the door.

Philippe looked from her to White Wolf and back again. "You are like two turkeys, flapping your wings and gobbling at each other. It's time you saw the truth."

"What truth?" Annie and White Wolf spoke together.

Philippe raised both hands and looked at the ceiling. "*Mon Dieu*. They are blind." With that, he turned and left the room.

White Wolf started to follow him. When he reached the door, he stopped. "Why do we still fight about the past? Why can't we let it go?"

"I won't," Annie said. "Not until I make them pay."

"You can't fight forever." White Wolf's voice dropped with sudden intensity. "Someday you will find you have won nothing but shame."

Annie lifted her chin and remained silent

White Wolf fingered the tomahawk at his waist. The sunlight reflected in his black eyes as they caught and held hers. "Believe me, Annie, I know."

Outside, a bell tolled with two loud rings.

"What is that?"

"A gathering," Annie said. "It rings twice to call everyone together. Four times in a rapid pattern is for danger. Three means all is well again."

A knock sounded on the outer door.

"You ready in there?" Rosie's voice drifted in from the open window.

"We're coming," Annie called. She followed White Wolf into the main room.

"You behave yourself tonight," she said as she stepped beside him.

White Wolf's jaw tightened. "What do you mean by that?"

She crossed her arms. "These are good people. You be nice."

"It's not me you should worry about," he mumbled.

Rosie's head poked through the doorway. She grinned. "We're going to have quite a night. Mark's brought that newfangled banjo thing to play, and Tim's got his flute."

Philippe walked into the room. "I'm ready."

"Let's go," Annie said.

They all filed through the door. Candles flickered from the windows of the church, casting a warm yellow glow into the evening air. The doors were open, and the soft rumble of voices floated from within.

"News travels faster around here than a coon with his tail on fire," Rosie muttered. "Hardly needed the bell. Most folks heard you all had come and hustled here before we could even call 'em."

Annie glanced through the doors. "Where's . . ."

Rosie's gaze darted to White Wolf. She motioned toward the trees. "Snaring rabbits, I suspect. Can't keep that boy still."

Annie nodded and then entered the little church. Dozens of friendly faces swarmed before her vision. Suddenly she was caught up in a huge bear hug. The face of old William Conner flashed in front of her. Then she swung away. Lily Conner planted a kiss on her cheek. A child, the Conners' grandson, she assumed, grabbed her around the knees and squeezed. For several minutes she spun from person to person as each expressed joy at her return. From the corner of her eye, she could see White Wolf and Philippe surrounded by a group of the settlers. Rosie stood beside White Wolf with her arm hooked through his and her other hand on Philippe's shoulder. Her acceptance, Annie knew, would influence the others.

A laugh rang out from the front of the church. Annie turned to see Tim McKnighton brandishing his flute in the air like a sword.

Behind him a simple platform held the rough-hewn pulpit. Here there was no stained glass, no paintings, no fine linens over tables of marble. Instead, the church had only a plain wooden cross hanging between two thin windows. Short benches were pushed to each side as people milled around in the center of the building.

Snippets of conversation danced around her. "Washington's tried to beat them back," she heard one man say, "but he ain't got enough troops to make the difference."

"Got to protect ourselves, I tell ya," commented another. "Can't expect help from outside."

"That Pontiac's a bloodthirsty savage." Tim's voice rose above the others.

"No more so than the white man." White Wolf's statement caused the room to go quiet.

Finally Tim spoke again. "It ain't us killin' innocent women and children."

"Boys," Rosie's voice silenced the other two, "this is no time for such talk. Tonight we celebrate God's goodness."

Annie watched as something akin to fury flashed across White Wolf's face before he hid it beneath stone-cold features.

Tom stepped to the front of the church. "Rosie's right." His words carried over the gathering. "We're here to thank God for Annie's safe return and for Kwelik's brother and our new French friend. Let us bow our heads."

Every head bent except White Wolf's and hers.

"We give thanks to You, Lord, for Your kindness and gracious love. We praise You for Your greatness," Tom's voice thundered. "And now we ask Your blessing for us and our new friends. And for our enemies we ask Your mercy."

As he finished, the twang of the banjo filled the sanctuary. Tim raised his flute to his lips and blew. Sweet music filled the air, followed by the swell of voices. "Praise God from whom all blessings flow . . ."

Annie did not join in the singing. Nor, she noticed, did White Wolf. After a few minutes he disengaged himself from Rosie's grip and slipped out the front door. Tom started another song. They would go on singing, praying, and reading Scripture, Annie knew, for hours.

She lowered herself onto a bench and closed her eyes for a moment to listen. The high notes from the flute wove their spell around her. If she listened closely enough, she could almost hear the voice of her mother in the music. "*Come home, come back,*" the voice seemed to say.

"I can't," she whispered in response. "There's no going home again. Not anymore."

"*Come home, come back.*" Was it God's voice now? She couldn't tell.

"How could You let them die, God?" she murmured. "Why didn't You save them? Why did they die, and yet I had to live?"

"*Come home . . .*"

"Not until I make them pay."

The music stopped.

Annie opened her eyes and saw Tom opening the large Bible on the pulpit. Before he could begin reading, she stood up and followed White Wolf. A cool breeze massaged her skin as she stepped from the building. She threw her head back and looked into the sky. "Leave me alone," she whispered.

"He won't." White Wolf materialized from the shadows. He stared into the forest. In his hand he held his tomahawk. "He never does."

The evening wrapped quiet arms around them. Eventually White Wolf spoke again. "I don't belong here." He turned the tomahawk over in his hand.

Annie lowered her gaze.

"You were right, you know," he continued.

"Was I? About what?"

"I am a coward."

Annie drew a deep breath. "We both are."

A boy ran out of the trees and bumped into White Wolf. His wide brown eyes peered up from beneath jet-black hair. "W-who are you?" he sputtered.

White Wolf squatted slightly until he was at eye level with the boy. "I'm a Lenape warrior. Who are you? Kwelik's son?" His gaze darted to Annie's.

Annie reached over and pulled the child toward her. Her hands rested on his shoulders. "This is Ashton." Her voice broke. She cleared her throat and started again. "Ashton, this man is your father."

The tomahawk fell from White Wolf's hand.

SIXTEEN

~

"My son?" White Wolf's eyes widened as he looked from the boy to Annie. A rush of confused emotions—fear, wonder, hope, disbelief—stole his breath. "How?" he gasped.

Annie ran her fingers over the boy's hair and dropped them to his collar. "He was born eight months after you left."

"Ashton." White Wolf rolled the name on his tongue. "I should have known. I should have guessed."

"His Lenape name is Tankawon."

"Tankawon. That was my name as a boy. And now you tell me it's my son's name." The words escaped White Wolf's lips in a reverent whisper.

"Snowbird wanted it that way."

White Wolf leaned over to look the boy in the face and found himself gazing into eyes so like his own that he wondered why he didn't notice it immediately.

Ashton's cheeks reddened. His eyes narrowed. "I don't have a father!" he shouted in a sudden outburst. Then he spun around and raced away.

White Wolf watched him go. Then he straightened. His eyes never left the place where his son had disappeared. "Why didn't you tell me?"

"I didn't know how."

Rosie appeared in the church's doorway. She glanced from him to Annie and then back again. "He knows." It was not a question.

Annie nodded.

Rosie descended the steps and put her hand on White Wolf's shoulder. "I'd hoped you wouldn't find out like this. I wanted to introduce you proper."

White Wolf turned. "He's my son." He spoke as if talking to no one but himself.

"He's a good boy—strong, determined like his father. We've raised him the best we could."

When he didn't respond, Rosie sighed. "Come, lad, sit here with me." She sat on the steps and patted the spot next to her.

Slowly White Wolf lowered himself beside her. Annie brushed by him. Her skirt touched his arm as she passed. He did not look up at her. He couldn't.

"I'm sorry," he heard her mutter. "I should have told you." The door creaked open and closed again.

Then it was only him and Rosie and the scent of fire carried on the breeze. It swirled around him like the smoke of old memories. Snowbird, Kwelik, Taquachi, his father. And now his own son. Tankawon, Ashton. Son of White Wolf. It was incredible, unbelievable, and somehow . . . frightening.

Rosie's voice reached out to him and drew him back from the past. "We didn't know where to find you. Then when the pox came, and Snowbird died . . ."

"She was with child. I never knew. I never suspected." He turned to Rosie. "The boy looks well. You're the one who has cared for him?"

"Aye. Tom and I, with Kwelik and Jonathan. He has suffered no harm here. His Aunt Kwelik taught him languages and the ways of your people. Tom has taught him the Bible and brought him up in the beliefs of your father. And I," she grinned, "I have tried to keep him in one piece." She paused. "We have long believed that you would return."

Shame flooded through White Wolf. "Tom has been his father then?"

She shook her head. "We have loved him as our own son, but you have always been his father."

"He deserves better."

She squeezed his hand. "God has given you a great gift, lad. He has given you a son. With His help, you will make a good father."

White Wolf raised his chin. "I don't want His help."

Rosie did not flinch. "Why is that?"

"He betrayed me once. I will not give Him the chance to do so again."

He expected a rebuke, but Rosie didn't give him one or even draw back her hand. Instead, she simply raised her eyebrows and nodded. "Betrayed you, did He? Tell me."

With all his heart White Wolf wanted to tell her, wanted to pour out his doubts, his fears, and fury. He wanted to share his darkest memories and have her tell him it was all right, that God loved him still. If he told her what God had done, what He had not done, could she convince him that he had been wrong all these years? Could she dispel the hurt that had driven him from his father's faith?

He would tell her, he decided. But not everything. Some things could not be spoken aloud. "How could a God who loves me do nothing as my village was destroyed, as my father was murdered and everyone I loved killed? What kind of God is that?"

Rosie didn't answer. She just kept holding his hand and looking into his eyes.

White Wolf turned from her gaze. He stared up into the evening sky. The first stars were beginning to peek from the mantle of gray. The light winked at him, daring him to speak his doubts. Then the silhouette of an eagle crossed in front of the moon, darkening it. Somehow the sight made his heart yearn for truth. "I was told God loved me. I was told I could trust Him." He felt the old anger hardening in his chest. "But my sister trusted Him, and look what it got her. How could He stand by and watch her walk into the flames for Him?"

Rosie's answer was quiet. "He saved her from that, with your help, she says."

"Yes, but tell me the truth." He lowered his eyes until they were level with hers. "Does she still have the scars?"

"Aye, son, that she does." Rosie's voice was soft.

White Wolf pulled his hand from hers and stood. "So how can you say God cares? How can you say He's trustworthy?"

She shook her head again. "I can't answer that for you. I ain't the one you should be asking."

"Then who?"

She stood beside him and leaned over and brushed a leaf from her skirt. "Ask Him who knows. He's the only one who has the answers." This time she was the one who looked up into the sky. "Seek Him, laddie. Ask Him yerself. Rage at Him if you have to, but take some time to listen too."

"Will He answer, do you think?"

"He will, I believe." She patted his arm and smiled. "Though I doubt it'll be the answer you expect. It never is." Her grin broadened. "Mark me words."

"No," he stated coldly. "I'll never trust Him. Not again." As he spoke, he looked up to see the light from two dozen torches snaking through the trees.

"They've come." Rosie's voice dropped to a hushed whisper.

Behind him the church bell rang four times. The others too had seen the enemy approach.

"Where is your God now?" he heard himself say. As his words faded, the first flaming arrow arched through the night sky.

～

The door creaked open behind Jonathan. Tibbs stepped into the cell and grabbed the lantern. As he did, Richard melted back into the shadows.

"Come with me, Jonathan Grant," Tibbs ordered. His fingers reached out and pressed into Jonathan's arm.

"What's wrong?" Jonathan sputtered.

Tibbs didn't answer. He only tightened his grip and pulled Jonathan out of the cell. The door slammed shut behind him. He hung the lantern on a peg on the wall. Then with his free hand Tibbs turned his key in the lock and glanced toward the outer door. "Here he is, sir."

The warden stood there with a handkerchief pressed to his nose. He adjusted his wig and then drew a pistol from his belt. He aimed directly at Jonathan's chest. "Search him." His voice dripped with malevolence.

Tibbs spun Jonathan toward him and began to search his pockets. He pawed through Jonathan's jacket, his breeches, and even his shoes. When he reached the inner pocket of the coat, he pulled out the tin soldier. "What's this?" he mumbled and held it up in the light.

"A child's toy?" the warden mocked. "Give it back to him, Tibbs, and continue the search."

Jonathan trembled with barely suppressed fury. He glared at the pistol in the warden's hand and then at the warden himself. "Do you always treat visitors with such hospitality?" he asked.

The warden's lips twitched into a slight smile. "Only the treasonous ones."

"It ain't here," Tibbs muttered.

"You won't find anything but the soldier," Jonathan replied.

Richard peered out from the small barred window in his door. "What are you doing?" he croaked. "Let him be. Leave him alone, I say."

"Shut up, you foul piece of vermin," the warden shouted.

The lantern flickered and dimmed. A high-pitched howling rose from the darkness beyond.

Jonathan suddenly felt cold. "What're you looking for?"

Tibbs stared him in the face. "Where have you hidden it? In the lining?" He patted Jonathan's jacket up and down the seams. "Maybe in the tie in your hair?" He yanked the tie from the back of Jonathan's head and squashed the material between his fingers. "Nothing."

"Look again, Tibbs," the warden roared. "It must be there. The note said it would be in his pocket." He waved his gun toward Jonathan's coat.

Jonathan stiffened.

"Yes, sir." Tibbs repeated his search.

In the other cells the prisoners began to bang their chains against the iron doors. A crazed laugh echoed from a nearby chamber. It grew louder before it died completely, leaving only the sound of clanging metal.

The warden's face turned bright red. "They're brothers," he shrieked over the din. "We know he's guilty. You must find it!"

Jonathan's eyes met Richard's. Richard's face appeared even more pale than before. "He's innocent, I tell you!" Richard shouted.

The warden sneered at him. "And we should take your word over our loyal informant?"

"Ain't got no choice for the moment." Tibbs's voice rose above the sound of the other prisoners. "There ain't nothing here."

"There must be!"

"There is not, sir!" yelled Jonathan and Tibbs in unison.

The warden wadded up his handkerchief and threw it into the corner. Then he turned and stomped out of the dungeon. "Let him go. For now." His voice dropped, becoming barely audible over the screaming of the inmate down the hall. "But I'll get you, Jonathan Grant," he warned. "Somehow you'll pay for what you've done."

The outer door slammed shut behind the warden. Immediately the howling stopped, and with it the clatter of chains against iron. Eerie quietness descended over the dungeon until Jonathan could hear his own breath rasping in his throat.

"Go, Jonathan," he heard his brother say.

He turned toward Richard's cell. Only eyes, reflecting the light, were visible through the tiny opening.

Richard spoke again. "Don't come back, Johnny. Return to the colonies and forget what you've seen. Forget that you ever had a brother."

For one moment Jonathan longed to reach out and tell his brother that he forgave him, that he would somehow get him out of there, and everything would all right. But Richard disappeared into the shadows, and the moment passed.

"I wish I could forget," Jonathan whispered to the emptiness. "But some things are not to be."

Tibbs unhooked the lantern and motioned toward the outer door. "Get out, Jonathan Grant," he said. "Get out while you still can."

～

As soon as the arrow hit, Philippe knew his life would never be the same again. Flames shot from the corner of the church, then sputtered, and died. Another arrow followed.

Before it could land, Tom reached the wall's gate. He yanked it closed as the men poured out of the church. Their faces were set in grim lines. Most gripped muskets.

"To the wall, men," Tom shouted.

The settlers rushed to the small openings positioned around the log wall. They slid their guns through narrow slits between logs. From somewhere inside the church, a woman wailed.

Tim raced down the steps, three muskets in his arms, and tossed one to Tom. Then he turned to Philippe. A question spoke silently from his eyes.

Philippe extended his arm.

Tim nodded once and handed him the weapon. The sound of a dozen shots exploded into the air. Smoke puffed from the guns and obscured Philippe's vision. He loaded his musket, spilling powder over the ground in his haste to finish the task. His limbs trembled. He'd always hated battle. It made his stomach flip like a fish caught on the hook.

He hurried toward an open spot in the wall. Tom knelt a few feet away, the butt of his gun steadied against his shoulder. Flames shot from the musket's primer as Tom fired the weapon.

Philippe fell to his knees, shoved his gun through the slit in the wall, and pulled back on the trigger. The kick of the gun threw him backward. Smoke burned his nostrils.

An eerie war whoop keened from outside. The sound sent shivers of dread slicing across Philippe's nerves. More flaming arrows arched across the sky. From the corner of his vision, he could see White Wolf hunched beside the wall, his arms over his head. And next to him Annie furiously shot and reloaded her musket faster than any of the men. A look of crazed rage marred her face.

Philippe pulled back to reload. This time the powder slid into the barrel without spilling. When he again crouched before the hole in the wall, he could see three Indian braves running toward him. Torches flamed from their hands. Their arms bent back, preparing to throw the missiles into the settlement. Philippe aimed and shot again. The second brave spun and fell. Two others lunged forward, knelt, and drew back their bows. A third Indian lit their arrows from his torch. Then fire again split the sky.

Philippe's gaze followed their flight. One arrow landed harmlessly on the ground in front of the church. But the other fell squarely onto the roof of Tom and Rosie's cabin. Rosie and four other women dragged buckets of water from the barrels on the side of the church. They threw the water onto the flames as Philippe again loaded his gun. Then he turned and shot again.

"Tucker, get back here!" Tom's shout pierced the air.

Philippe peered through the opening in the wall to see a man running toward the cabin on the far end of the clearing, outside the wall's protection and directly into the face of the enemy. His wife followed behind him. Philippe recognized the woman by the bundle in her arms. Was the man mad? They would never make it alive.

"Get away from my home, you savages!" the man shrieked.

Flames licked from the cabin's windows.

"Tucker! Don't be a fool," Tom cried. But it was too late. Tucker did not turn back. Instead, he waved his empty musket in the air and continued toward his cabin. Before he could reach it, the Indians converged.

"God have mercy," Philippe heard Tom say before his voice was drowned beneath another volley of musket fire.

Philippe reached into his pocket for a lead shot but found none. "I'm out," he called to Tom. "I need more ammunition."

"In the church," Tom yelled back.

Philippe stood and started toward the church. Flames crackled from the rooftop. Rosie and the women continued to throw water onto the fire, but the roar of flames only grew hotter. Philippe's eyes stung as he reached the steps. He blinked away the dryness. Behind him he could hear Annie's voice shouting at the enemy. Muskets blasted. Indians shrieked their defiance.

What am I doing here? He asked himself. But no answer came. *I only wanted to go home.*

"Look out!" he heard Tom shout above the fray.

Before he could turn, searing pain drove through his right shoulder. Someone screamed. A memory of the Seine River, calm and peaceful, flashed across his vision. Then he saw no more.

Seventeen

~

Fog draped over the countryside in heavy folds, masking the features of the land. Jonathan turned up his collar against the penetrating dampness and urged his horse to a trot. The gentle thump of hooves on hard dirt comforted him. Almost, if he closed his eyes, he could remember how it felt to ride across his farm on the frontier. He longed to smell the hay drying in the fields, to hear the sound of the plow cutting through the earth. *Lord, let me go back home. I hate it here. I don't want to help Richard. I don't care if he lives or dies. If You want him saved, find someone else.*

He reined the horse toward the road leading to the Grant estate. Before he reached the mansion, he turned onto a narrow path that led to the old cottage where he and Kwelik were staying with the children. With any luck he could get their trunks packed and his family on the way to Portsmouth before nightfall.

He nudged the horse to a gentle canter. Tall yew bushes, cut in the shapes of chess figures, lined the path on either side. He'd always thought they were eerie, looking out over the grounds like silent guards, ever watching, ever wary. Why his mother had designed them this way, he'd never known. Skinny pawns led to fat knights and ended with a tall king and queen, except on the right side. There the queen was missing. When Jonathan was eleven, he'd asked about the queen, but his mother had only said, "She ran away to Ireland, and no one's seen her since." Sometimes Jonathan would look out his bedroom window toward the old cottage and imagine that the queen had returned. But when he came down to check, her spot was still empty. "It blew down in the wind," was his father's answer. But somehow he never quite believed him.

Jonathan turned a corner and saw the tiny cottage ahead of him. A simple wooden porch held a small table and rocking chair while dozens of wild rose vines twisted through the railing. A few crimson blossoms peeked from between the slats as if determined to flourish despite the chill of the fog. Behind, mismatched stones formed the wall that rose toward the thick thatched roof. Dual windows, unevenly set, gave the impression of a face cocked to one side. It reminded Jonathan of an old grandmother who could no longer be bothered with coiffed hair and perfumed handkerchiefs. And that, perhaps, is why he preferred the cottage to any other building on the grounds.

Jonathan unsaddled his horse, watered her, and jogged up to the cottage door. Inside, he smiled at Kwelik who sat in a rocking chair with Brenna in her arms. She pressed a finger to her lips.

"Is she sleeping?" Jonathan mouthed.

Kwelik nodded. The chair creaked slightly as she rocked. She had one foot tucked beneath her while the other pushed against the fur rug on the floor. A small fire crackled in the grate.

Jonathan removed his coat and hung it on a hook behind the door. In the next room he could see a teapot steaming on the stove, causing tiny droplets to gather on the wall behind. Curtains of buttercup yellow were pulled closed to shield the room from any wisp of sunlight that might happen to pierce the fog.

He leaned over to kiss Kwelik on the forehead. His fingers brushed Brenna's black hair as he straightened. Kwelik caught him with her gaze, and as always he found himself turned inside out by those topaz eyes. He quickly looked away. Today there were things in him that he didn't want her to see.

Above her, old paintings lined the stone wall. A small one of Sir Charles, the horse, hung beside one of their dog and a larger one of his mother with her head down and just the wide brim of her hat showing. These were Richard's early efforts. Even here, it seemed, Jonathan could not escape the reminder of his brother. He sighed and again looked down at his wife.

She was still studying him.

"Where's Justin?" he whispered.

"Outside playing. He couldn't keep still, so I sent him out to explore." She tilted her head toward the baby asleep against her chest. "Brenna's just fallen asleep. I'll go put her down." She rose in one graceful movement and walked into the bedroom. After a minute she returned.

"I want to go home. Can you get ready to leave by tonight?" Jonathan asked.

Kwelik frowned. "Tonight? Why?"

"I can't endure this place anymore," he answered.

Kwelik sat back in the rocking chair.

Jonathan lowered himself onto the couch and pulled off his boots. He stretched out his legs. "Well, what do you think?"

She was uncommonly silent. He looked up at her. She was staring at him, her face set in serious lines.

"What's wrong?"

"I wonder if your haste to leave has anything to do with this." She reached into her skirt and pulled out a piece of parchment folded into a small square. "I found it in the pocket of your other jacket." She handed him the parchment.

Jonathan unfolded it. His fingers brushed the red seal, now broken. He lifted it closer and studied the markings in the wax. Cold realization washed through him. He'd seen that seal before on a French communiquè left at the fort at Louisbourg. This mark alone would have been enough to convict him at the prison had the letter been found on him. He turned the parchment over and began to read.

> *Bonjour, mon ami.*
>
> *We received your information. Braddock will find a surprise waiting when he gets to Fort Duquesne. Your payment is on its way. And the settlement we spoke of will be spared as promised.*

The letter was not signed. Jonathan refolded the note and placed it carefully in his boot. Braddock had been found out. And, it seemed, the knowledge had come in time for the French to gather their Indian allies. The thought turned in Jonathan's stomach. Braddock, he knew, would not have been prepared for the Indians' type of warfare. If he had lost . . . Jonathan shuddered. His voice grew hard. "So this is what they were looking for."

"Who?"

"Tibbs and the warden. They searched me. If they'd found it, I would have been imprisoned too."

"You were searched?"

Jonathan nodded. "All the more reason for us to get out of here and go home."

Kwelik shook her head. Her voice softened. "We can't, though I would like nothing more. You know we can't. Not until you've finished whatever God wants you to do here." She paused. Her right eyebrow arched toward her hairline. "Have you done that?"

Jonathan ignored the question. "How did this letter get into my pocket?"

Kwelik rose from her chair and came over to sit beside him. "I don't know. But the more important question is why. What do you know about Braddock?"

"Too much, not enough." Jonathan rubbed his hands over his face and groaned. "Washington spoke to me of their plans after the battle at Great Meadows. He feared that Braddock had started a war there. Now I'm afraid that he did. Afterward the fort he was building fell to the French. Not many of us knew that Braddock was coming from England to retake the fort. But somebody knew, somebody who sold that knowledge to the French."

"Somebody who wants you accused of treason."

"But why?"

"That," she tapped him on the shoulder, "is the question."

The whinny of a horse stopped their conversation. Jonathan leaped to his feet. "Someone's coming." He parted the curtains and looked out the window. "Get Brenna and go. Hurry."

"What is it?"

"Just go!"

Jonathan dropped the curtain and pulled on his boots. Then he flung open the door and stood squarely in the opening. He straightened his shoulders.

Outside, a line of soldiers rode down the path toward the cottage with the fat warden in the lead.

~

Annie saw the arrow just before it hit. "He's down," she screamed as Philippe plunged facedown into the dirt. She threw down her musket and ran toward him. The Tucker family and now Philippe. She didn't think she could stand it. "Cursed savages," she muttered under her breath. "I'll get you for this too."

Philippe didn't move.

White Wolf reached him first. He knelt beside Philippe and gently probed the place where the arrow had penetrated. "It's just into the shoulder," he shouted over the sound of gunfire. "He'll live."

Annie knelt on the other side of Philippe. Fury pounded in her temples. If it were possible, she'd storm out the gates and kill those Indians with her bare hands. Somehow, somewhere, the ax of justice would fall. Only then would she be free. Another volley of shots boomed in her ears. She reached down to pull out the arrow.

"No!" White Wolf grabbed her wrist and squeezed. "Not yet."

Annie wrenched her arm from his grip. "Whose side are you on?" Sweat trickled down her back and dampened her waistband. She sneezed. Her eyes watered from the smoke, blurring her view.

White Wolf looked at her. Gone was the man who had moments before cowered beside the settlers' wall, and in his place was someone Annie barely recognized. Something about him made her anger dissolve back into concern for Philippe.

"Help me pull him back there." He motioned to a spot behind the water barrels. There, she realized, the wall of the church would shield them from any further arrows.

She bent over and grabbed Philippe's feet. White Wolf tucked his hands beneath the Frenchman's arms and carefully lifted his torso without jarring the arrow. "Move quickly but smoothly," he instructed.

Annie nodded. Together they moved Philippe and laid him gently on his side.

With one hand Annie brushed back the hair from Philippe's pale face. "Why doesn't he move?" Her voice quivered.

White Wolf's voice remained steady. "He has wilted like a violet left too long in the sun. I don't think the French will miss him in their ranks." White Wolf ran his hand over the place where the arrow pierced Philippe's shoulder. Then he pulled out his knife and carefully cut away the cloth surrounding the wound. With one finger he felt gently around the torn flesh. "It will come out easily, I think. Here, you take this." He pulled off his shirt, borrowed from Jonathan's closet, and handed it to Annie. "Press the wound when I pull out the arrow. You must be quick."

Annie caught her bottom lip between her teeth and nodded. "I'm ready." Blood pounded so loudly in her ears that she could barely hear the screams of the Indians outside, the shouts of the settlers, or the persistent booming of gunfire.

Bits of ash landed on White Wolf's bare shoulders. His muscles tensed as he gripped the arrow. "Now," he gasped.

The arrow pulled free.

Annie pushed the shirt into the wound to staunch the flow of blood.

"Now tie it."

She wrapped the shirt around Philippe's shoulder and tied a tight knot.

"Well done." His eyes touched hers. "You are a good warrior."

Annie felt her cheeks redden.

White Wolf turned Philippe onto his back, then stood, and plunged his cupped hands into a barrel of water. He stepped over to Philippe and dashed the liquid into the Frenchman's face.

"What're you doing?" Annie hit his hand away.

White Wolf glared at her. "He must awaken." He scooped another handful of water and dropped it onto Philippe's face.

Philippe's eyes flew open. He spat the water from his lips. "Wh-what happened?" he sputtered.

"You fainted," came White Wolf's quick reply.

Philippe attempted to roll onto one elbow but fell back again. "Ooh," he groaned. "My shoulder is on fire." He started to reach toward the wound.

White Wolf stopped his hand. "An arrow pierced your shoulder. We've removed it. You'll recover."

Philippe winced. "Are you sure?"

White Wolf's lips twitched. "You're not much of a soldier, my friend, to be felled by such a small arrow."

Philippe attempted a lopsided smile. "I never said I was."

Behind them the settlers' shouts suddenly turned into cheers. "They're retreating!" Tom yelled.

Annie sprang to her feet and raced to a hole in the wall. There she saw the Indians disappearing into the trees. Tim grabbed her, swung her around, and planted a kiss on her cheek. Then he did the same to Tom. Doc Bradley leaped up and down and waved his musket in the air. "We beat 'em back!" he whooped. Someone else laughed.

Rosie appeared from around the side of the church. She wiped a hand across her soot-covered face. "We saved the church too," she called. "Fire's out, and only part of the roof was lost."

Tom strode over and swept her up in his long arms. "Thanks be to God!" he cried.

"Amen!" chorused the other settlers.

As the noise began to abate, Annie returned to Philippe. White Wolf still knelt beside him. Rosie and Tom joined them. "How many did we lose?" Annie asked.

"Only Tucker with his wife and daughter. Poor fools." Tom switched his musket from his left to right hand. "No one else even injured, except for the Frenchman here." He pointed the gun's butt at Philippe. "Not very quick at ducking, he isn't. But it looks like he'll be all right."

Annie noticed that White Wolf had not stood or even moved. Tom glanced at him. "You okay, son?"

Slowly White Wolf rose to his feet. His eyes met Tom's. "I could not . . ."

Tom reached out and patted him on the shoulder. "I understand. Not against your own people. We didn't expect it."

White Wolf motioned toward Philippe. "But he fought at your side."

"Not my countrymen outside those walls," Philippe muttered, his voice slurred.

White Wolf turned his head so that he seemed to be looking over the wall toward the treetops. His features appeared like chiseled stone. Annie knew that he had again withdrawn into a world where he walked alone, with only his pain for company. She too knew that place—and dreaded it.

She shifted her focus to Tom. "What're we going to do about Sarah?"

Tom sighed. "Do? We can do nothing now but pray."

Annie threw her hands in the air and scowled. "Pray? What good is that?" Her voice raised. "We have to go after them. They might still be alive. We need to rescue them. You can't leave a mother and daughter to die at the hands of the savages. I've seen what the Indians can do to their prisoners. Horrible, nightmarish things." She shuddered.

"We can't leave the settlement unprotected. We haven't a man to spare. You know that." Tom's voice was gentle.

Annie crossed her arms. "I'll go myself."

Tom frowned. "You saw what happened to Tucker. Don't be foolish."

"I can't sit here and do nothing."

"We won't be doing nothing. We'll be praying."

"Then you pray, and I'll go."

Rosie stepped forward and laid a hand on Annie's arm. She looked intently into her face.

Annie lifted her chin.

"Is it only for revenge that you be so determined, lass?" Rosie's question was spoken gently, and yet it pierced Annie's defenses.

Shame stained her face. She lowered her head. "I don't know. But I must go. I can't sit here and wait, knowing what's happening to them out there." She waved her hand toward the trees.

Rosie nodded. "Then our prayers will go with you as well. Go in God's grace, lassie."

"It's madness! Suicide!" Tom broke in. "She can't go alone, and I can't risk sending anyone with her."

"She must do this thing, husband." Rosie put her arm around Annie's shoulders.

Warmth spread through Annie until she finally felt the strings of tension loosening in her back. Someone understood. Someone was standing with her.

"She will do it with our blessing or without it," Rosie continued. "Even if she must go alone."

"She will not go alone." White Wolf's statement dropped like a stone into water.

Annie turned toward him.

He was looking directly at her, his eyes narrowed as if in challenge. "I'll go with her."

"No," she whispered.

White Wolf pulled his tomahawk from his belt and stared at it. "Perhaps it's time for me to go back. Perhaps it's time I remembered how to fight."

"Don't . . ." Annie's voice trailed off.

White Wolf's lips curved into a grim smile. "Peace runs from me like a rabbit chased by a dog, and when I think it's in my reach, you manage to come like a hawk and snatch it away again. So I'll go with you back to war, back to battle, back to where I belong."

"That ain't where you belong, laddie," Rosie spoke softly. "Ye can find peace, God's peace, though ye may have to go through the devil's own fire first."

White Wolf ran his finger across the blade of his tomahawk. Then he raised his head. "So that's where we're going then?"

"I fear so, lad."

"I'll go too." Philippe's voice rose weakly from where he lay on the ground.

White Wolf crouched next to him and placed his hand on his arm. "You would so quickly delay your dreams of France?" he asked.

Philippe struggled to a sitting position. "My dreams have waited this long. A little longer won't matter. Besides," he forced a small grin, "perhaps I can throw a little water in your face to cool the devil's flames."

"Thank you, my brother." White Wolf spoke the words as if bestowing a gift. "But this time the woman and I will go alone. You're in no condition to travel quickly." He raised his hand as Philippe began to interrupt. "No, you will stay and recover. When you are well, you will head to the coast. These people will help you. And if we make it back alive, I will come after you. I promise it."

Finally Philippe nodded. "I will see you again, *mon ami*. This will not be the end for us."

They gripped one another's arms in farewell. Then White Wolf stood and turned toward Annie. "We must go quickly. We can't let them get far ahead."

"Wait," Rosie said. She hurried to her cabin. A few moments later she reappeared with a sack in her hand. "Some food for your journey and a little medicine." Rosie sniffed. "I'm gonna miss you, child." She caught Annie in her strong arms. "You take care of yourself now, and may God go with you." She pulled back and held Annie at arm's length. "Oh, lassie," she whispered, "somewhere out there I pray you'll be able let go of yer hate and see the truth."

Truth. Both Philippe and Rosie had spoken of it, but the truth they saw still eluded her. Was it buried, she wondered, beneath her pain?

"Take this." Rosie handed her a long knife. "We can't spare a musket, but may this serve you just as well."

Annie gripped the handle and felt the coolness of polished bone. It felt good in her hand. She slipped it into her waistband.

Tom pulled open the gate and stood beside it. "May God give you strength and wisdom for your task," he said as she and White Wolf passed into the clearing. On the other side of the meadow the blackened skeleton of the Tucker cabin stood as a silent reminder of what they needed to do.

"Are you prepared for what will come?" White Wolf spoke quietly beside her.

"I am," she stated firmly. And suddenly she knew that she was not.

EIGHTEEN

~

White Wolf suspected that he'd made a mistake the minute he left the settlement. As soon as the gate creaked closed behind him, he told himself that he should have stayed until Philippe recovered and then set out toward the coast like he'd promised. But something that no one else had seen drove him from the settlement. And that something was two young eyes watching him from beneath the porch of Tom and Rosie's cabin. Two eyes filled with anger and disgust, glaring at him as he failed to fight with the others. Eyes that belonged to the son he never knew he had and now was afraid to face.

He'd planned to prove himself to his son in some other way, but Annie had changed all that. And now he wondered why he hadn't let her go alone. Why did he always have to protect her? Something intangible drew them together and bound them. It always had, and try as he might, he couldn't seem to break it.

White Wolf adjusted the tomahawk at his waist. Not much had changed between them over the years. She was still the fierce, fiery girl she'd always been. And he, it seemed, was still the fool. Only she had ever stood toe to toe with him and told him what she thought of him. Snowbird never had the strength for it, and Kwelik was too kind. But Annie had spoken straight from her heart. And, as usual, her heart was now leading her directly into the path of danger.

White Wolf glanced over at her red-brown hair streaming down her back, unruly like the rest of her, the freckled nose, the pale skin. She was, he told himself, a white woman, a member of a people he'd sworn to hate. But that was a long time ago. Being with the settlers reminded him that he was half white man too. He'd once declared that part of him dead, but could he really kill half of who he was? Could the lessons learned at his father's knee be wiped away forever?

He had believed so, but now he wondered. Yet if he faced his English heritage, would he also have to face its God? That was one thing he could not, would not do.

"Where are we going?" Annie's question interrupted his thoughts.

He looked up and saw that he was across the clearing and headed toward a tall clump of ash trees. He brushed aside a branch and turned toward the sound of the rumbling river. "They will camp by the water tonight. I know the spot." He cocked his head to one side and listened. He heard nothing but the tumbling of water. "They move swiftly and silently. We will not be able to catch them until they stop for the night."

"Oh," Annie muttered, then fell quiet.

Above him White Wolf heard the soft hoot of an owl. He looked up to see moonlight filtering through the leaves overhead. Trees rose on either side of him, their trunks like thin pillars holding up a roof. They walked in silence as he led the way.

"Hold up a minute," Annie called. "I've got a stone in my shoe." She stopped and sat on a large boulder. White Wolf waited while she removed her shoe and shook it. A small pebble tumbled out. She wiggled her toes. "That feels better." She stood. "Let's go."

Before he turned back to the path, White Wolf noticed the lichens, illuminated by the moonlight, on the rocks around him. The sight made him remember times almost forgotten. "Rock men," he whispered to himself, and the memory became clearer. Kwelik had always told the best stories about the rock men. Those were good days, happy days, when she would sit and make up tales, and he would laugh and beg for just one more. He had forgotten those stories until now. Somehow walking here in the woods beside Annie caused those old memories to brush through his mind like the flutter of butterfly wings. And that made him see just how far he had fallen.

They walked in silence until the moon rose high in the sky to cast shadows over the path before them. A cool breeze whispered through the trees and rustled the leaves overhead. Annie stopped abruptly beside him. "Look." She pointed through the trees. "Light up ahead."

White Wolf paused. He too had seen the light. "It's the camp. We must be very careful." He took her arm and guided her toward a clump of bushes on their right.

Quietly they crept between the trees. Three times White Wolf paused to listen. Even the crack of a twig could give them away. But as they drew closer, it didn't seem that the braves were on guard against intruders. The sounds of conversation and rough laughter drifted from the camp.

Closer, closer, they stole, until White Wolf could smell the fire burning and hear the low chanting of braves.

"Hurry," he motioned to Annie.

She stumbled behind him.

"Shhh," he hissed.

But she wasn't listening. He turned to see her staring blankly at the camp. He followed her gaze and felt his breath stop. There in the center of the camp the braves sat in a circle around a pillar of fire. And in the fire the man called Tucker writhed and burned. White Wolf could see that his right hand and foot were cut off and hanging above his head, and part of his scalp was missing. His wife huddled on the other side of the camp, the babe clutched to her breast. Her face was deathly pale, as if she had seen in the last hours more horrors than any human should.

Annie tried to plunge forward, but he stopped her. "No! There's nothing we can do for him now. We must think only of the woman and child."

She didn't respond but kept straining against his grip, her eyes like glass staring past him, reflecting the fire.

He shook her. "We must keep our heads."

She started to tremble, and then turned and retched in the bushes.

White Wolf scowled. "Control yourself. They'll hear us."

Annie wiped off her mouth. She tried to speak. No words came.

"Sarah and the baby are not hurt," he whispered. "We'll try to sneak around and untie them. Are you ready?"

The muscles in Annie's neck tightened as she nodded. Before

they could move, her hand reached out to clutch his arm. Her jaw dropped open.

"What is it?" he whispered. Then he felt the sharp tip of a spear in his back. Slowly he turned and found himself staring into the face of Pontiac.

Pontiac lowered the spear. He smiled. "Welcome back, brother." His gaze flickered to Annie. "I see you have brought me a prize."

Words fled from White Wolf's mind.

~

"So we meet again, Jonathan Grant," sneered the warden. He pulled his pony up in front of the porch and dismounted. The pony pawed at the ground and snorted. The soldiers stopped their horses in a straight line beside the warden. They too dismounted and turned stony faces toward Jonathan. No one looked him in the eye. Snowy white cravats peeked at him over jackets the color of fresh blood.

Jonathan stood taller. "What're you doing here?" The note seemed to burn against his ankle as he spoke. He could have thrown it into the fire the moment he saw the soldiers, but something had stopped him. Perhaps it was because that small piece of parchment was his only link to the real traitor, his only hope of finding who was really to blame.

The warden didn't even blink. "I think you know why I'm here."

"You won't find whatever you're looking for," Jonathan said aloud. Inwardly he prayed, *Lord, don't let them find it. Keep us safe, please.*

The warden pulled his riding crop from the fleshy folds beneath his arm. He pointed it at the cottage. "Search it. Search every corner." He swished the crop in the air and jabbed it in Jonathan's direction. "Do not interfere, or you will be arrested."

As one, the soldiers dropped the reins of their horses and swarmed over the cottage like hornets. Four brushed past him to the interior of the house; two swept around the outside; another stood guard beside Jonathan. He turned. Through the doorway he could see a soldier's bayonet ripping through the buttercup curtains. A musket crashed through one of the front windows. The tinkling of breaking glass joined the sound of heavy boots tromping over wooden floorboards. In a moment the teapot smashed to the ground and broke into a hundred pieces. Jonathan watched as water pooled over the floor and seeped through the cracks in the boards. The soldier didn't even pause. In two strides he reached the paintings and lifted his bayonet.

"No!" Jonathan cried.

The blade fell, ripping the first painting from corner to corner. The soldier pawed through the frame. Then he tore through the remaining paintings. With each swipe of the bayonet, Jonathan felt the blade cutting across the memories of his heart. In the bedroom he could hear the other soldiers pulling clothes from the wardrobe. The sounds of rending fabric echoed out to the porch. The cradle tipped and fell, spilling its blankets into the hallway.

In minutes the cottage his mother had built as her refuge lay in ruins. Helplessness surged through Jonathan and left him shaking. One by one the soldiers left the cottage, marching past him without a glance.

Jonathan turned and stepped inside. Bits of buttercup cloth mixed with shards of glass and pieces of painted canvas on the floor. A breeze blew in from the broken window, rustling the shreds of curtains. Coals from the fire smoldered on the floor and caught a piece of canvas. A small flame flickered up. He walked over and extinguished it with his boot.

Outside, he heard the soldiers' feet thumping down the steps of the porch. "Nothing, warden," one them called.

A shout pierced the air. "Let go of me!" Kwelik yelled.

Jonathan raced out of the cottage.

Kwelik stood beside a soldier. His hand held her arm in a firm grip while her other arm held the baby.

"Found her running out the back with the babe in her cloak," the soldier reported.

Kwelik yanked her arm away from the soldier and stood tall, her chin raised. Her stance reminded him of the woman who long ago stood on a slave platform, unyielding and unafraid.

Jonathan hurried toward his wife and child. Anger obscured his vision. A soldier stepped in front of him, blocking his path. The butt of a musket jabbed into his ribs. His breath came out in a quick burst. He doubled over.

"Who would not run, sir," came Kwelik's voice, strong and confident, "with you great oafs stomping through our dwelling like bears gone mad?"

Brenna began to wail. Kwelik's jaw was set in firm lines, and her eyes seemed to burn like fire. She glared at the soldier beside her. "Now see what you've done."

To Jonathan's surprise, the soldier appeared embarrassed.

She stormed over to the warden. "Is this the practice of the English, sir, to raid the homes of honest, God-fearing mothers? To frighten babes in arms?" Her voice raised over the sound of Brenna's cries.

The warden sniffed, then pulled out a handkerchief and fluttered it in the air. His nose wrinkled. "Search her," he commanded.

"What?" The word sputtered from Jonathan's lips. He stepped forward. A second soldier grabbed his arm. He twisted but could not break free. The other soldier lowered his bayonet until it pointed at Jonathan's stomach.

Kwelik did not move. "You'll find nothing," she stated with a voice as steady as rain in a thunderstorm.

A soldier approached and lifted the baby carefully from her. He smiled down at the bundle in his arms and clucked his tongue. Brenna's cries ceased. As the man rocked her gently against his chest, Jonathan found his breath coming more evenly. Another soldier quickly searched Kwelik. His eyes remained half averted from his task.

Kwelik never looked away from the warden. "You should be ashamed," she told him.

The soldier finished his search and shook his head. The warden's face turned red. He threw his crop on the ground. "What have you done with it?" he screamed.

Jonathan glowered at him but didn't answer. Kwelik took the baby back from the soldier. She smiled. "Thank you," she said politely, as if he had taken the babe out of courtesy. Then she turned back to the warden. "If you have completed your search, sir, I would like to go back inside and see if your men," her voice hardened, "have at least left the child's cradle intact." She bowed slightly and then swept into the cottage like a queen entering her castle.

Jonathan's heart swelled with love. Nothing, not even this obese warden with his toy soldiers, could make him forget how God had honored him with her love. They could smash windows and tear through curtains, but they couldn't touch the bond between them.

"Until next time, Jonathan Grant." The warden's voice slid over him like mud from a bog. "Don't try to leave England." He hoisted himself back onto the pony and motioned for the soldiers to follow.

As they trotted away, Jonathan turned back to the wreckage of the once-cozy cottage. He walked inside. Kwelik stood by the fireplace with Brenna still tucked in her arms. Jonathan looked into the wide eyes of his daughter.

"Are they gone?" Kwelik asked.

Jonathan nodded.

"Well, that, at least, is a blessing." She sighed and looked around the room. She shook her head. "Did they have to break *everything?*"

Jonathan stepped over a broken vase. He leaned over and picked up the slashed painting of his mother. His eyes watered. He ran his finger over the painted brim of her hat and then tossed the ruined picture into the fire. Flames licked up the canvas. The paint peeled and turned black. Then the image was gone, devoured by the unmerciful heat, by a fire that didn't know the memories it swallowed.

"This is all Richard's fault," Jonathan muttered to no one. "He never should have sent her away." As he spoke, old bitterness became as vivid as the flames, devouring the bits of peace he had painted for himself over the past ten years.

Kwelik's voice shattered his thoughts. "Where's Justin?"

～

"They failed." Elizabeth crumpled up the message and threw it into the fire. "I couldn't have made it easier, and yet they failed."

"I don't want to hear your feeble excuses." A slender man in a snow-white wig and finely tailored coat walked in front of the fire.

Shadows played over his high cheekbones and Roman nose. Heavy draperies hung over the windows, blocking all but the light from the fire. "I never should have trusted a woman to do a man's job."

Elizabeth whirled toward him. Her dress caught on the mahogany desk behind her. She reached back and freed the material. "Don't bait me, Simon." The cloth wrinkled in her hand. She smoothed it along her hip and pursed her lips. "William will soon be the sole heir to the Grant lands. You simply need to be patient. "

"I've been patient enough. Richard has not been hanged, and now this brother has come back from the colonies to foil the plan."

A log fell in the fire, spewing sparks over the grate. Elizabeth dug her fingernails into the velvet at her waist. "They will both pay," she muttered, "and I will do all that I promised."

"But there's a son."

"Nothing will stand in our way. I swear it."

Simon pulled out his pocket watch, stared at it, then snapped it shut. "I must go. My wife grows restless. I fear she suspects."

Elizabeth frowned. "Eva is a fool. She knows nothing beyond the brewing of her ridiculous perfumes."

"Perfume-making busies her. But she has eyes, she has ears. If she knew that Richard is my half-brother—"

"No one knows that but you and I."

"And that's the way it must remain." Simon stared into the fire. "My father was a fool to love the woman Harlan Grant had chosen." He turned back to Elizabeth. "But no one suspected that Harlan didn't father her first child. Not until you discovered it."

"Mama?"

Elizabeth looked over her shoulder to see Katherine standing in the doorway. "What do you want?"

Katherine swayed back and forth as if afraid to enter the room. She glanced at the man by the fire and then back at her mother. "The baby is crying."

Elizabeth gasped. "What did you do to him?"

"Nothing, Mama. I promise." She backed up slowly until she was swallowed by the shadows. A moment later her footsteps raced down the hallway.

Elizabeth hurried toward the door. She glanced back. "We'll continue this conversation later, Simon. I trust you know the way out."

"And the way back in again," Simon smirked. "Remember that."

She hurried up the stairs, barely noticing the gleam of lamplight on the rich wooden banister or the faint smell of pipe smoke rising from the kitchen or the dark eyes of Frederick Grant staring down at her from the portrait on the wall. All that mattered was the baby, her baby, the son who would be heir to the Grant estate.

In the nursery she leaned over and picked up the child. His cherub face looked up at her with watery gray eyes. She clutched him to her chest. He sniffed and pulled at a strand of her hair.

"It's all right. Mama's here," she cooed.

The boy quieted.

"Look." She moved him onto her hip so that he could see around the room. Toys littered the corners while brightly colored pictures decorated the wall. A rocking chair sat on one side of the room. A blanket lay over the arm. Elizabeth walked over, plucked the blanket from its place, and carefully wrapped it around her son. "All this is yours," she muttered. She glided to the window and pulled back the drapes. "And soon everything you see will be yours as well. I promise it."

The baby gurgled in her ear.

Determination hardened within her. "I will not fail you," she whispered.

"Ma-ma-ma-ma," he babbled.

Elizabeth smiled as she lifted the boy over her head. "Mama loves you. Never forget that."

He giggled.

She turned and looked again out the window. Standing beside the trellis in the garden was a woman who looked up at her with eyes as cold as winter ice.

NINETEEN

~

Hatred, fierce and wild, boiled in Annie until she could feel nothing but the raw power of it. She lunged at Pontiac, her fingers like talons. She aimed for his face. But before she could reach her goal, White Wolf stepped between them. Her nails scraped his neck and chest. Four thin lines of blood oozed from the cuts. He caught her arm and pulled her close to him. The musky smell of sweat filled her senses.

"Not now!" he whispered harshly in English. "You'll get us killed."

She drew a sharp breath and pushed down her hate until it formed a hard lump in her stomach. She could feel it there, lodged like a heavy stone beneath her heart. White Wolf set her away from him. His eyebrows drew together in a dark frown.

Behind him Pontiac stood motionless. Firelight glinted off the hawk feathers tied in his hair. "She is still the fighter, I see." His voice held a hint of mockery.

White Wolf's hand tightened on her arm. "A worthy prize for a chief."

"Perhaps," Pontiac drawled.

The muscles tensed in Annie's neck.

White Wolf's eyes flashed to hers, then back to Pontiac. She read the warning in his gaze. "*Quiet*," it said. "*Wait*."

So she waited.

White Wolf and Pontiac gripped arms in greeting. They spoke a few words she couldn't hear. Then White Wolf nodded. Suspicion flamed through her. He was one of them. Could she trust him? She didn't know, but now she had no choice.

"Come, join us," said Pontiac. He motioned toward the fire. "And bring the woman."

As they entered the camp, the braves turned from the glow of flames. Shadows played over their faces, making them appear even more sinister. Annie purposely averted her gaze from the fire and looked at Sarah. For a moment Sarah lifted her face. Hope seemed to shine in her eyes. Then as she saw Pontiac and White Wolf, her head again fell. Strands of matted hair dropped across her eyes. She did not look up again.

"Our brother Waptumewi," Pontiac was saying to the others, "has come with a gift for the tribe." He strode over to her, grabbed her arm, and shoved her toward the braves.

She stumbled, then righted herself. The Indians stared at her without blinking. Then one of them hooted, a long, stuttering whoop that grew in intensity. The others joined in until the camp rang with the sound of their voices. Annie stiffened her body as if standing against a gale. The braves' cry stopped suddenly, leaving only the sound of the crackling fire.

White Wolf stepped beside her.

Annie glanced around the camp. Pontiac stood several feet away with his back to the fire. The braves still sat encircling the flames. Annie held her breath. The time for action had come. With a quick move she snatched the knife from her waistband and grabbed White Wolf around the neck. She pressed the blade into his throat. A startled gasp sprang from his lips.

"Don't move," she hissed. Then she spoke more loudly. "I'll kill him. No one come near us."

Pontiac lifted his spear. The braves leaped up, blocking her view of Tucker. Slowly they inched toward her. She stepped back, drawing White Wolf with her. "I expect to die here tonight," she said in the Algonquian tongue. "I will take him with me and as many of you as I can." She pressed the knife into White Wolf's skin, careful not to draw blood. She knew that he could easily break her grip, but he chose to stand still beneath the blade.

Pontiac held up his hand. The braves stopped their approach.

"No one else need die here tonight." White Wolf spoke from behind the knife.

"Let the woman and child go." Annie's voice carried over the camp.

Pontiac crossed his arms. "I must have a gift for Chief Tewea. I have promised him a woman."

"Let them go," Annie repeated.

"I will not go to Chief Tewea empty-handed." Pontiac remained calm.

He was baiting her. Annie's grip loosened on the knife. Frantically she tightened it.

"I do not think you will harm him," came Pontiac's voice, smooth and confident.

Annie felt her limbs start to shake.

"There is something that draws you two together. You will not kill him. It is in your eyes."

Annie squinted. A bead of sweat trickled down her temple.

Pontiac crossed his arms with the spear still in his hand. "Nevertheless, I will let the woman and child go."

"What?" The knife slipped lower on White Wolf's neck.

Pontiac uncrossed his arms and rubbed his hand up and down the shaft of his spear. He stabbed the weapon in her direction. "I will let them go if you will take their place."

Annie felt as if someone had punched her in the stomach. Frantically she fought for breath. Beside her White Wolf shifted from one foot to the other.

"I will." The words, spoken quickly, were like arrows in her heart.

Pontiac studied her for a moment. "You will come willingly?"

"Yes." She forced out the promise. As she did, she heard White Wolf's quick intake of breath.

"What're you doing?" he whispered from the side of his mouth.

"It's the only way," she whispered back.

Pontiac threw back his head and laughed. "Done!" he shouted. "It is a good trade." He turned toward his warriors. "Release the woman."

Two braves walked over, pulled out their knives, and severed Sarah's bonds. Sarah finally looked up. Bewilderment marked her features.

"Go, woman." Pontiac's voice boomed over the camp.

Annie nodded to Sarah. "Follow the river back to the settlement. Run."

Sarah wobbled to her feet with the babe still clutched to her chest. "But . . ."

Annie shook her head. "I'll be okay. Now go. Hurry."

Sarah gulped. Then she rushed off into the trees. Annie watched her go. When the sound of her footsteps faded, she released White Wolf.

His jaw was set in a firm line. "That was stupid." He bit out the accusation in a hushed undertone.

Annie's voice was equally quiet, equally fierce. "I freed her, didn't I? I did what we came to do."

"But at what cost?" His question cut through her like a blade. He turned away.

"Bind the woman," Pontiac called. He strode toward her, his hand extended.

Annie laid her knife in his palm. His fingers closed around it. Then it was done. She was his prisoner.

The two braves that had freed Sarah tied Annie's hands behind her. She felt the rope bite into her wrists. The magnitude of her choice swept over her. What had she done? Had Kwelik felt this way when she had been bound against her will? Kwelik had found peace by looking to God. Annie wondered where she would find her peace.

"We will head north tomorrow at dawn," she heard Pontiac say.

Beside him White Wolf stared at the body of Tucker, now black within the flames. White Wolf shivered.

"Does the sight trouble you, brother?" Pontiac asked.

White Wolf turned away as he answered. "It does. Is it not enough to simply kill him?"

Pontiac jabbed his spear into the ground. "This is necessary."

"Necessary? Are we then the savages they call us?"

"You're brutes. Devils. Worse than savages!" Annie shouted.

Pontiac ignored her. "This is war, Waptumewi. We do what we must."

White Wolf didn't respond.

Pontiac continued, "The English descend like a horde of grasshoppers. They push us back, devour our land."

White Wolf looked into Pontiac's face. "The war goes badly?"

Pontiac pulled his spear from the dirt and twirled it in his hand. "We are too few. We are not united. But by this we gain the strength of fear on our side." He pointed to Tucker. "The woman will go back and tell what she's seen. They will be afraid of us, and that fear may hold them back, at least for a time."

White Wolf nodded slowly. "Fear is a strong ally, but beware lest it turn and betray you."

"I will never be afraid of you!" Annie yelled. "Never!"

This time Pontiac glanced in her direction. "We shall see," he called. Then he motioned to the braves. "Take her to the fire."

Protest burst from her mouth. "No! You said . . ."

Pontiac didn't flinch. "Let us see if her heart is as strong as her words."

Two braves took her arms and hauled her toward the fire. Then they forced her to sit at its edge with the flames only an arm's length from her face. Heat seared her skin.

Annie turned her head and closed her eyes, anything to keep from seeing the remains of Tucker still burning in the fire. But she couldn't keep out the smell of burned flesh. It assaulted her, tore through her, until she gagged on it.

Suddenly she felt fingers tightly holding her chin. She opened her eyes to see Pontiac leaning over her. "Look and see, woman," he spat. He wrenched her face toward the flames.

The fire burned through the rope holding Tucker's hand. It fell to the embers beneath. The fire seemed to grow in intensity until it blocked out everything around her—the braves, the woods, the moon, Pontiac, White Wolf. All were gone. Only her hatred remained; only her fury burned hotter than the flames. *They will rue this night*, she told herself. *Here is where my revenge begins*.

The words rang in her soul. Suddenly she knew she had taken a step into darkness. She did not turn back.

～

Fear like Jonathan had never known pounded through him. *Justin!*

"He should have been back by now." Kwelik spoke quietly beside him. She walked over to the window. He could hear the concern in her voice. "You don't think the soldiers . . ."

"No!" Jonathan spoke more loudly than he intended, as if the volume of his denial would chase away his fear. *They wouldn't have; they couldn't have.*

Kwelik turned. Her bottom lip was held between her teeth.

"If he'd seen the soldiers, he would have come running. Where could he be?" Jonathan ran his hand through his hair.

"He said he was going down by the creek, but he might have gone to the pasture. I'll look there. You try the stream."

Jonathan nodded and hurried outside. "Justin, Justin!" he called at the top of his voice. He put his fingers to his lips and let out a long whistle. The sound echoed back to him, followed by silence. Only the cry of a crane in the distance answered him. He waited, listening, for a moment longer. Then he ran toward the creek. The wind blew in his face as fear made him run faster. "God, let me find him there. Let him be there by the creek. Let no harm come to him. Just let me find him, please. God, please help us, please . . ." Jonathan prayed rapidly in rhythm with his footsteps. He reached the creek, but Justin was not there. Again he called and whistled. Again nothing but the crane called back to him.

Cattails swayed at the edge of the water while small water bugs skimmed over the surface. Waves splashed over algae-covered rocks and swirled past a broken log that lay crosswise in the middle of the stream.

Jonathan squatted down to study the mud at the creek's edge. He searched for footprints, for indentations in the grass along the bank, for reeds broken by a small hand, but the terrain looked as if no one had come there in years.

A frog plopped in the water downstream and scrambled onto a green rock. It reminded Jonathan of the frog he'd seen at the prison. Ever since then everything had gone wrong. Was God punishing him for failing to help Richard? Would He take away his son just because of his refusal to forgive his brother? Was God like that?

Jonathan shivered, then stood. "Justin!" he shouted one more time, following with another long, shrill whistle. He waited. Silence. "Where are you?" he whispered. "God, help me find him, please."

Jonathan searched up and down the creek three more times and then headed back to the cottage. Kwelik was on the porch waiting for him. He noticed her shoulders droop when she saw that he was alone. Panic began to rise within him.

"He wasn't in the pasture either," she called. "I'm going to look up the road."

He nodded. "I'll try the gardens."

Calling for Justin, Jonathan rushed through the paths of lilacs and lilies, sprinted to the pond and around it, searched behind the wall of yews and inside the latticed gazebo. He hunted through the rose garden and in the stables, but still found nothing, not even a hint that Justin had come that way.

Despair and desperation bit at his heels as he returned to the flower garden. Vines of scented jasmine and bright yellow crocuses lined the path. Their beauty mocked his mood. Bees buzzed around his head, the sound of their flight like the hum of the panic within him. He sat on a stone bench near the pond and put his head in his hands. Around him he could hear the quiet lapping of water against stone and the whisper of leaves rustling in the wind. He strained his ears, strained every part of him, to hear the sound of his son's voice calling to him. But he heard nothing but the bees, nothing but the water, nothing but the wind in the trees. Then, like a sound from a dream, came the soft patter of feet down the path. His head flew up. "Justin?"

The form of an old woman met his gaze. Her head was covered with a gray cape that shaded her face and dropped over her shoulders. Black boots peeked from beneath a plain gray dress. No other adornment marked her garb except for a single silver cross that hung from a chain around her neck. Quietly she came and sat beside him.

"Why, sir, do you weep?" Her voice was soft, muted.

Jonathan attempted to catch a glimpse of her face beneath the folds of her cape, but she turned her head away from him. "I'm not weeping," he answered.

"Not on the outside."

The scent of lavender floated around him, reminding him of his childhood. He closed his eyes and breathed deeply of the fragrance, hoping it would calm him and help him to think more clearly. "My son is missing," he said. "He is six years old. Have you seen him?"

He thought he heard her gasp. "I have," she replied.

Jonathan felt a jolt of hope, but it died with her next statement: "But not today."

He dropped his head. His voice lowered. "I fear the soldiers took him."

Her head tilted toward her hands. "They did not."

"How do you know?"

Her answer came quickly. "I watched them. Justin was not with them."

Jonathan leaned forward. "You know him?"

Her hand rose to her necklace. She twisted the chain around her finger, then dropped it. "He comes here to the garden to visit me. We plant flowers together, and he tells me of his life on the frontier." She paused as if considering what to say next. "He's a good boy, filled with kindness and honor. You have done well, Jonathan Grant."

"How do you know me?"

"I have always known you."

"Are you a servant from my childhood?"

"You could say that, I suppose." From her tone he could tell she was smiling beneath the cape.

He did not smile in return. "I'm sorry I don't recognize you. Perhaps if I could see your face."

The woman pulled the hood tighter around her. "Not today," she murmured. "But tell me of your son. How long has he been gone?"

"Since this morning. I've searched everywhere."

She shook her head. The smell of lavender again wafted over him. "He has not come to me today though he promised he would. He told me he had found something, but he would not say what. Today he was to share his secret."

Jonathan stared at the gold-colored crocus at his feet. "What am I going to do?" He spoke more to himself than to the woman beside him.

Her hand reached out from beneath the folds of her cape to rest on his arm. He looked down. The hand was wrinkled and spotted with age, but not as much as he would have expected. She was not as old as he'd first thought. Her touch, warm and gentle, comforted him.

Then her voice washed over him. "You will pray and search and hold your wife in your arms while she weeps. You can do no more than that." She gave his arm a slight squeeze and then removed her hand.

Jonathan allowed his gaze to wander across the pond. When he looked back, the woman was gone.

∼

It was no use. No matter how hard Katherine tried, the tears still seeped from the corners of her eyes to make cold trails down her cheeks. Her eyelids were sore from rubbing, and her nose kept running. She clenched a small rag in her fist and wiped her upper lip for the hundredth time. "Mama doesn't hate me. She doesn't," she whispered to herself.

But she didn't believe it. She could stay here huddled in the corner of the kitchen all night, and Mama would never notice. The fire crackling so merrily in the open oven could go out, the dishes sitting on the shelves above her could fall and break, the stew bubbling over the flames could grow cold, and still no one would come in to see if she was okay. It hadn't always been that way, she remembered. Once Mama had cared, at least a little. But that was before.

Footsteps echoed down the hallway outside the kitchen. Katherine rose to her knees. "Mama?"

No one answered.

She crept to the doorway and peeked around the corner. Mr. Bains strode down the dark corridor. He slapped his hand along his breeches as he walked. Was it true that he was Papa's brother? That her Grandfather Harlan wasn't Papa's father at all? How could that be? Her eyebrows furrowed. Sometimes the grown-up world didn't make sense at all.

She watched Mr. Bains until he disappeared through another doorway.

"Mama's still upstairs," she told herself. "With the baby." She was always with the baby, cooing over him, talking to him, even singing to him, as if Katherine didn't exist at all.

She sniffed and wiped the dirty rag beneath her nose. She would have liked to hate the baby, but she couldn't. It wasn't his fault that Mama didn't love her anymore. He was just a little baby, and he *was* her brother. She didn't blame her mother for loving him, with his wide hazel eyes, just like Mama's, and his button nose and sweet smile. She loved him too. Sometimes she'd sneak into the nursery just to watch him sleeping. But she was always careful not to let Mama catch her.

Katherine scooted back to the corner and gazed out the window beside the outside door. Clouds drifted lazily across the gray sky. One cloud was shaped like the picture Justin had drawn of an Indian's tomahawk. She smiled slightly as she thought of her cousin. He, at least, cared about her. He was kind. He was her friend, him and the woman who stayed in the garden.

But where was Justin now? Had he too forgotten her? He'd promised to meet her here hours ago. Just that morning he'd made her swear to wait for him. "I've found something out, a secret, I think," he said. So she'd waited and waited, until the sun dipped behind the window ledge and cast long shadows over the tile floor. But no one had come.

"Katherine, dear, come here." She heard a voice from the outer doorway.

Katherine scrambled to her feet and hurried outside. There on the steps the woman from the garden stood. "Have you seen Justin?" Katherine asked.

The woman shook her head. "I've seen nothing today but a man consumed with fear and a woman eaten by hate. Justin is missing."

Katherine wrinkled her forehead. Her voice dropped to a whisper. "You don't think Mama . . ."

PART TWO

Darkness

~

TWENTY

~

Western Pennsylvania, August 1755

One step after the next, after the next. Heat and humidity pressed down on Annie's shoulders like heavy weights as she followed White Wolf along the twisting trail. Three other braves walked behind her while the rest drifted as silently as spirits through the trees ahead. She could scarcely see Pontiac, who led the group around rocks and underbrush without leaving a single mark to show that he had passed.

Somewhere to the west the Allegheny River rumbled southward to meet the mighty Ohio. Annie could hear its quiet roar although she could not see the water.

She lifted her hands, still bound at the wrists, and wiped away the moisture from her cheek. Her tongue licked over cracked lips and tasted the salt dried there. The bottom of her dress, wet from crossing a stream moments before, flapped around her ankles. Her stomach rumbled. The smell of raw bear meat floated over to her from the pack on White Wolf's back. Annie scowled. White Wolf had not said a word to her in the three days they had been traveling. She couldn't tell if he was angry with her or if he had decided she was no longer important now that he was back with his own people. Her eyes bored into the back of his head. *Turn around,* she willed him, *face me. Tell me the truth—did you plan all this? Did you know I would be captured?*

White Wolf did not turn. He simply continued walking, one step after another, until the rhythmic plodding made Annie feel as if she were going mad.

The jingle of a harness on the path ahead interrupted the monotony. She looked up. The braves stopped in their tracks, and some melted into the forest like a faint mist, ready to reappear if needed. Pontiac raised one hand. Silence descended over the war band. In a moment a horse emerged from the trees carrying a thin man in a tattered shirt and worn brown hat. "Greetings, Red Men," the man called. Annie could see a flash of yellow teeth behind a bushy black beard.

As the horse drew closer, a small cart became visible. It bumped along behind the beast and rattled over a branch in the path. The man pulled up in front of Pontiac. From this angle she could see that the cart was filled with pots, pans, furs, and lumpy bags full of who knew what. A leather-wrapped package was tied to the back end of the cart. More furs and shiny cookware hung from behind his saddle, and on top of that lay a single musket.

Annie quickened her pace. The braves did the same, until most of them stood behind Pontiac. The man glanced at her and then down at the bonds around her wrists before his gaze slid over the war band and back to Pontiac. He swept the hat from his head to reveal frizzled graying black hair around a bald center. He squinted at them. "Any of you speak English?"

No one answered.

"Eng-lish? Speak-a Eng-lish?" The words dragged from his lips in a voice that was suddenly too loud.

The Indians' hands darted toward their tomahawks. Pontiac's grip tightened on his spear.

White Wolf stepped forward. "I speak English. What do you want?"

The man dropped from his horse and grinned, showing two teeth missing in the front. "Want? I don't want nothin'," he drawled. His voice carried in the afternoon air. "But I gots plenty to offer." He swung his arm toward the cart. "Copper pots to cook yer deer meat, blankets fer the winter, muskets . . ." He never got any further than that.

An Indian on Annie's right chortled a sharp "Aa-iii-ee" and raced forward.

The man dropped the horse's reins and reached for his musket, but it was too late. The Indian leaped on him. The two fell to the ground. As they rolled, Annie could see the tomahawk protruding from the man's collarbone. A sickening squeal issued from his lips as a second brave fell on top of him. Blood gushed over his shoulder.

Annie felt bile rising in her throat. She longed to turn away but couldn't. Something in the man's desperate struggle called to her and forced her to her knees. Pontiac stepped beside her. His hand gripped her hair. Tears welled in her eyes.

The other braves swarmed toward the cart. They pulled open the packages, spilled the pots on the ground, and ripped through the furs. Then they turned to the horse. It whinnied and threw its head in the air. The whites of its eyes shone in the afternoon sun. A brave grabbed the reins and held it while the others pawed through the goods on its back. Only White Wolf held back, his eyes averted from the melee.

"Only two guns," reported one brave. "And a horn of powder."

Pontiac loosened his grip on Annie's hair and walked over to the cart. Only the package tied on the back remained untouched. He took a musket in his hand. "Take whatever you wish. Leave the rest."

On hands and knees Annie crawled over to the bleeding trader. His eyes rolled up to her. His mouth moved as if trying to form words, but no sound came. Blood trickled from the corner of his lips.

She wiped it away. "I'm sorry," she whispered.

He closed his eyes and then opened them again. "The blanket," he choked.

"What?" Annie leaned closer.

"In leather. Back. Cart."

Her gaze slid to the bundle tied to the cart. "I see it."

He looked at her with sudden intensity. One hand reached up to clutch her arm. "Smallpox." His head fell to the side. His eyes closed.

Smallpox. The mere mention of the word sent chills over Annie's skin. "What do you mean?" she whispered.

The man only groaned.

Before he could say more, an Indian grabbed her shoulder and pulled her away. In one swoop he ran his knife around the man's head and yanked off his scalp. In the moments that followed, whatever secrets he held died with him.

Annie rose to her feet and sidestepped to the cart. Quickly she loosened the package bound to the back railing. She glanced around. No one was watching her. She tucked the bundle under her dress. As she did, cold vengeance swept through her. The taste was as sweet as blood.

∼

Breath, low and uneven, woke Philippe from a dream of sunlight on the towers of Notre Dame. He looked up. Ashton stood above him, staring at him. Philippe studied the boy's dark skin, black hair, and eyes that burned like matchsticks. For a moment neither of them said a word.

Then Ashton broke the silence. "You're French," he blurted and jabbed his finger at Philippe's chest.

Philippe sat up and swung his legs to the side of the bed. "*Oui.* I am French."

The boy took a step backward. A scowl marred his features. "French are the enemy. I should shoot you." He lifted his chin.

Philippe reached for his jacket. "You do not have a gun."

Ashton's brow furrowed, making him look so much like White Wolf that Philippe nearly smiled. "Then I will scalp you," he stated. "I'm an Indian, you know."

Philippe pulled his jacket over his back, adjusted it, and reached down and drew his boots from beneath the bed. He slid his right foot into a boot and wiggled his toes. Finally he looked at Ashton. "Nor do you have a tomahawk." He put on the second boot.

From the corner of his eye, he could see the boy pulling back his shoulders until he stood stiff as a fencepost in the wind. "Then I will claw out your eyes with my bare hands," Ashton nearly shouted.

Philippe smiled. "Two hands you have, but I will not let you claw out my eyes."

Ashton's shoulders slumped. "You talk strange."

"So do you."

The boy crossed his arms. "I hate my father."

Philippe stood, walked over to the basin, and splashed water on his face. "You do not know your father." He grabbed a towel and dried his cheeks and chin.

"You're supposed to tell me that it's a sin to hate anyone," came Ashton's reply.

Philippe turned, the towel still in his hand. "If you believe it is a sin, why do you do it?"

Ashton flopped onto the bed. He did not answer the question. "They say you're my father's friend. Are you?"

Philippe hung the towel carefully on a hook and blinked away a droplet of water that clung to his lashes. "*Oui,* your father is my friend."

"He's a coward."

"Why do you say that?"

"He was scared when the Indians attacked. He didn't even fight."

Philippe adjusted his collar. "Foolish is the man who feels no fear in battle." He walked over and sat on the end of the bed. His voice lowered. "Your father is a man of valor. Do not mistake reluctance to take life for cowardice."

Ashton stuck out his lower lip and turned his head.

"Honor is not found in shooting the musket or wielding the bayonet." Philippe laid his hand gently on the boy's foot.

Ashton would not look at him. Instead, he stared at the wall and blinked rapidly. He sniffed. "Then where?"

Philippe tapped him on the knee. "Rise and help me straighten the bedclothes."

Ashton rolled from the bed and stood on the other side. Together they pulled up the blanket and smoothed it. When they finished, Philippe sat down and patted the spot next to him. Ashton sat beside him, his face pointed toward the floor.

"Honor is found in doing what is right, in loyalty, and in friendship."

The boy rubbed his hand under his nose and sniffed again. "He left me. He doesn't care about me at all."

"He had to help the woman and her baby."

Ashton's head shot up. His cheeks were damp. He glared at Philippe. "Tucker is an idiot. He deserves what he gets."

Philippe frowned. "You should not say such things"

"Why not? It's true."

"That may be, but still you should not say it." Philippe stood and walked toward the door.

The boy kicked his foot against the bedpost. "Miss Rosie says I should pray for them."

"And so you should."

"Why?"

Philippe stopped. "So God will have mercy."

Ashton raised his head and pinned Philippe with a look straight from heaven's gates. "What do you know about God?" he asked.

Philippe's mouth went dry. The question echoed through him. At that moment he knew it was time to head east to France. There, only there, would he find the answer to the questions that raked through his soul.

~

The carpet squished beneath Jonathan's feet as he paced back and forth in front of the bedroom window. A portrait of Frederick Grant glared at him from the wall beside the bed while a crystal chandelier, unlit, sparkled from the ceiling. The bed, draped in elegant silk, was turned down for the night. Jonathan averted his gaze from the sight. Tonight sleep eluded him. He felt as if it would always elude him as long as he didn't have his son.

He glanced at the expensive vase from India that sat atop a rich rosewood table imported from France. He ran his hand over the velvet upholstery of the chair near the window. His fist clenched. Everything here reminded him of the things he'd always hated about the Grant mansion—its opulence, its greed, its excess. But with the cottage in shambles, there was nowhere else to go.

In the cradle near the bed, baby Brenna slept soundly, her quiet breathing the only sound to accompany his footsteps. Jonathan strode silently to the cradle and peered over the side. One tiny hand lay on her cheek, her fingers splayed across her mouth and chin. He watched the gentle rise and fall of her chest and sighed. It seemed just yesterday that Justin was a baby, sleeping with one finger in his mouth, his eyelashes so black against his baby-fair skin. Longing pierced Jonathan's heart. He groaned. *Lord, my son . . .*

He reached down and brushed a finger lightly over Brenna's downy hair. Tears dampened his cheeks. He pulled away and returned to the window. Outside, stars winked through a mantle of clouds that drifted across the half moon. Jonathan gripped the sill and leaned forward. Quietness, like death, lay heavily over the night. He glanced down. *Justin, where are you?*

Shadows stretched over the gardens and darted behind trees like children playing hide-and-seek. Nothing but the darkness moved. All was still, silent, dark. And somewhere out there his son waited for his father to rescue him. At least Jonathan hoped that he still waited.

He again raised his eyes to the sky. "What have You done to me, God?"

Silence answered him.

"I came here because I thought it was what You wanted, and now I have lost my son." A pained groan tore from his lips. "How could You let this happen? Why did You?" He turned from the window and threw himself into the chair. He listened to the gentle whisper of the flame in the lamp by the bed. He listened for the voice of God, but he heard nothing but the fire.

Jonathan gripped his hands tightly in front of him and dropped his head. "I trusted You, God, but now . . . now I don't know anymore." He lifted his head toward the ceiling. "Where is my son? Why have You allowed him to be taken from me?"

Justin's shirt sticking out from the trunk on the floor caught Jonathan's attention. He reached over and pulled it toward him. Slowly he brought the cloth to his face and breathed deeply. "God," he choked, "I can't bear it." He stood up and again began to pace before the window.

The quiet whoosh of the door startled him. He looked up to see Kwelik, her hair bound in a towel, entering the room. Water dripped down her cheeks. Her eyes appeared red and puffy beneath the white cloth.

She came and stood beside him and reached out to take his hand in hers. Her other hand trailed over Justin's shirt. She leaned her head against his shoulder. "I miss him so much," she muttered.

"Maybe tomorrow . . ." Jonathan began, but could not finish the thought.

"It's been three days."

"I know. We'll find him; we have to."

Kwelik turned and walked over to the bed. She sat on the edge and began to dry her hair with the towel.

"Where is God now?" he asked her.

Her only answer was a soft sigh.

Jonathan ran his fingers through his hair and resumed walking back and forth. "I thought the safest place for us would be in the center of His will."

Kwelik smiled, a sad little smile that barely lifted the corners of her mouth. "God is rarely safe," she murmured.

He turned back to the window. *Of course she would say that*, he thought. *How can I speak of safety to the one who walked into the fire for Him?*

"There is a cost to following Christ," she continued. "There is always a cost."

"Yes," he answered, "but I never thought the price would be my son."

"Nor did I." Her voice was barely audible.

Jonathan walked over and put his hand on the Bible that lay on the table near him. Lamplight flickered over the page. His eyes fell to the story of Abraham and Isaac on Mount Moriah. He closed the book and rubbed his son's shirt between his fingers. "I don't have Abraham's faith," he stated. "I can't endure the thought of losing my son." His gaze rose to the moon. "How, Lord, did You ever give up Yours?"

Downstairs someone screamed.

TWENTY-ONE

~

Katherine didn't mean to scream. She'd tiptoed downstairs to the kitchen ever so quietly, opened the cupboard without even a whisper, taken out a piece of bread, buttered it, and ate it as silently as moth's wings on glass. And that's when the big brown spider plopped down on her arm. She'd always hated spiders, so she couldn't stop the scream. And now she was in for it. If William woke up . . .

The thought had barely formed in her mind when she heard it—the high-pitched wail of a baby. Katherine cringed. Mama would never understand about the spider. Mama never understood about anything.

A door slammed somewhere above her, followed by footsteps heavy on the stairs. The baby continued to cry.

"Oh, William, stop," she whispered. "Go back to sleep." But the babe's cry only intensified until it became a furious shriek.

Voices echoed from upstairs. "Who was it?" "I don't know." "Katherine Elizabeth!"

Katherine didn't wait to hear more. Instead, she turned and fled out the kitchen door. It swung shut behind her. Her feet flew down the path, barely touching the cool earth beneath them. Long, dark shadows swooped over the lawn and across the path. At the far end of the pasture crickets chirped a melancholy tune. Katherine headed toward the sound. Dew dampened the bottom of her nightgown as she cut across the lawn. Still she didn't stop. She ran past the morning glories hiding their faces from the moon, past the quiet rose garden, past the black-green pond, past the tall yew trees to the very edge of the manicured lawn. Only then did she glance back.

Flickering lights shone from the nursery window. If she held her breath and listened very carefully, she was sure she could still hear the wail of a baby. She let out her breath and glanced down the hill into a dark grove of trees below. She knew where she needed to go, where no one would ever think to look, where she would be safe until Mama's anger receded. Out there her old hiding place, the abandoned well building, waited for her.

Katherine started down the hill at a jog. When she reached the bottom, she turned right and snaked through the trees like a wraith in the night. Finally she reached the small shack half hidden behind a huge oak. Once the building had been painted dark green. But now the paint was long worn away, the roof was partly caved in, and the single window held only a few shards of broken glass. Still the sight of it was comforting. She hadn't been here since the soldiers came for Papa. Yet everything looked the same. Everything always looked the same, as if time had visited in some earlier century and then forgotten to return.

Katherine hurried to the door and pulled it open. One hinge, nearly rusted through, squeaked loudly. Darkness met her gaze. She wished she had thought to bring a lantern. But at least in the darkness she wouldn't be able to see any spiders that might scuttle past. She blinked twice and waited for her eyes to adjust. Slowly the stone circle that was the well became visible in the moonlight. Katherine hurried to the short stone wall and huddled beside it. She wrapped her arms around her knees and pulled them toward her. The well was only fifteen feet deep and still had a little water on the bottom. She'd looked down there a hundred times and had never seen anything but an old bucket and some pebbles that she'd thrown down years ago. But now it seemed creepy to have a wide, dark hole behind her.

She drew her legs closer to her chest. It felt cold in here, colder than she'd ever remembered it. She shivered and rubbed her wrist over her eyes. She felt the moisture there. *Mama hates it when I cry,* she reminded herself. But Mama wasn't here. Her lower lip trembled. She sniffed and felt a tear trickle down her cheek. It wouldn't be so bad if Papa were home. But he was gone, probably forever. She would do anything to get him back. Anything. But it was no use. The letters she sent were never answered. The questions she asked were never noticed. The prayers she prayed seemed to bounce off the ceiling and crash back on her, unheard. No one cared. Not Mama, not William, not even God. She sniffed louder.

And then she heard the voice—cold, echoing, damp. "Is someone there?"

Katherine leaped to her feet. She turned toward the well. "Who's there?" Her voice trembled.

"Hello? Hello? Kat? Is that you?"

She leaned over and peered into the well's blackness. "Justin?" His name jangled hollowly down the well. Her heart beat faster.

"I'm down here!" he shouted.

Katherine felt like jumping up and down with joy, but instead she leaned farther over the edge, careful not to lose her balance. "Are you hurt?" she asked.

"Naw, just cold and sore," came his shaky answer. "Get me out of here!"

Katherine pulled back and glanced around the shack. Nothing but an old rake met her gaze. She leaned back over the hole. "How?"

"Isn't there a rope or something?" Justin called.

"Only in the garden shed."

"Go get it. Hurry back."

"Will you be okay?"

"Sure. As long as you get me outta here."

"I will," Katherine vowed. She hurried out of the shack. Excitement surged through her as she ran through the trees and back up the hill. *I found him, I found him*, she whispered to herself. *They'll all be so happy*. Maybe now someone would pay attention to her, care about her. She raced to the shed, pulled the rope from the hook, and ran back to the old well building.

"I got it," she yelled as she burst through the door.

"Tie it real good on something," Justin called.

Katherine hunted for something solid. Finally she found a metal crossbeam hidden under an old piece of wood on the far side of the well. With fumbling fingers, she tied the rope to the metal and laid it across the well's opening. Then she threw the end of the rope down into the darkness. "Pull on it real hard, Justin," she called. "Make sure it'll hold." She saw the rope go taut as Justin yanked on the other end.

"I'm comin' up."

"You sure you can do it?"

A grunt answered her, followed by heavy breathing, scraping, and thumping. Then, after what seemed like an eternity, Justin's head appeared at the top of the well. He was panting heavily, and his face appeared ghostly white in the moonlight.

Katherine reached down with both hands and hauled him over the edge. He collapsed beside her. She threw her arms around him and hugged tight. "I thought you were dead," she mumbled.

He hung onto her for a moment and then pulled back. "Don't crush me. I'm all right." He sniffled and wiped his hand across his nose.

Katherine noticed smudges, dark against his pale face. "Everyone's been so worried," she said.

"Not everyone," he muttered.

She frowned. "What do you mean?"

"Do you want to know how I got down there?" He pointed to the well.

"You fell, didn't you?"

He crossed his arms. "I was pushed."

Katherine caught her breath. "Really? Who did it?"

Justin shrugged his shoulders. "I dunno. I didn't see him." He fell silent.

She waited.

Finally he continued. "Someone in a big black cape started chasing me. I remembered you telling me about this place, so I ran here. But he must have seen me. I hid in here for a while. Then when I got up to go, someone rushed at me and pushed me right into the well."

"You don't look so bad for being in a well for three days," Katherine commented.

"I had sandwiches for you, me, and the garden lady in my pocket, and there's a little water down there."

"Still . . ."

"The frontier makes folks tough, you know."

"I suppose." She paused. "I wonder who did it. Could it have been—"

Justin interrupted her. "Look here," he said and pulled out a paper from inside his shirt. "I think he was after this." He smoothed it.

Moonlight glinted off the paper and illuminated the writing. Katherine squinted her eyes and leaned forward. It was too dark to read, but she could tell that the writing was her father's. "What does it say?"

Justin quoted from memory: "'Inspector Higgins,' it starts. He sounds important. 'I write to correct a griev-gri-greev . . .' I didn't know the next word."

"It's probably grievous," Katherine said.

"Grievous," Justin repeated. "'Grievous error. I pray thee. . .'" He paused. "I don't remember what comes after that. But at the bottom it says, 'My father was not Harlan Grant.' That's our grandpa's name," he added.

"So it's true," she muttered.

"What's true?"

"That Mr. Bains is Papa's half-brother." She leaned closer to Justin. "What else does it say?"

Justin continued. "'I have put myself forth as Lord Grant for lo these past fifteen years, but the lie presses down on me as heavily as the full weight of the heavens.' Here's the good part. 'What shall I do? Tell the truth at last? That my younger brother Jonathan is the true and rightful heir . . .' That's all it says. It was never finished." He folded the paper and put it back in his shirt. "Do you know what it means?" he asked.

Katherine didn't answer for a long time. Finally she spoke. "It means the estate really belongs to your papa. My papa stole it from him."

"Oh," Justin breathed. "All this is really ours?" His eyebrows bunched together. "That means it'll be mine someday."

She could tell that Justin was expecting her to deny it, but she was no longer thinking about the estate. Something of much greater importance occupied her thoughts. Slowly she turned toward him. "You know what this really means?" she said.

"What?"

"It means I'm not a Grant," she stated. Then she looked up. Her eyes caught his in the moonlight. "And neither is William." Her voice dropped to a whisper. "This changes everything."

~

It was almost like coming home. Wigwams sprawled in a loose circle. Deer hides dried between trees. Thin lines of smoke trailed from the tops of each home like wisps of memory drawing him back into simpler days. White Wolf closed his eyes and listened to the sounds—women grinding corn, children laughing, a dog gnawing a bone. It was so much like home and yet nothing like it. He couldn't hear Papa humming a hymn as he helped Black Hawk construct a hut. He couldn't hear Mama reading from the Bible with a group of children at her feet. He couldn't hear Kwelik giggling at him as she made the sounds of the cougar and bear. He opened his eyes. He should have known he'd never belong.

In front of him Pontiac strode through the middle of the village. Women stopped their grinding and stared. Children paused in their play. Even the dog stopped its chewing and lifted its head to watch them with suspicious eyes.

White Wolf and the rest of the war band followed Pontiac. One brave held the rope tied around Annie's wrists. He yanked her forward. She did not resist. White Wolf frowned. He'd noticed that she'd been acting strangely since the encounter with the peddler. She had not even tried to escape. Instead, she seemed subdued, quiet, like the eerie silence just before a storm.

"Ho, Chief Tewea." Pontiac's voice boomed across the village. "We have come with gifts!"

A short brave ducked through the opening of a wigwam on their left. A single eagle feather hung from his braided hair. White Wolf could see that he was missing one eye.

The chief raised a hand in greeting. "Chief Pontiac, you are welcome, with or without gifts."

Pontiac stepped forward and gripped the arm of the other man. "How goes the war, brother?"

"Look around you." Tewea motioned toward the huts on his left and right. "You can see the scalps are many."

White Wolf's eyes followed his gesture. Scalps hung from lodge poles all around the village. One held the long auburn hair of a woman. Another had the short brown hair of a man, while others were from the heads of children. The scalps swirled before White Wolf's vision—brown hair, black hair, blond, and gray. So, so many reminders of the tomahawk's deadly bite. He felt his own tomahawk hanging at his waist. It had been a long time since its blade had touched a human head. Had it been too long? Or not long enough? He inched forward until he was standing just behind Pontiac.

The other villagers shuffled closer.

White Wolf glanced at dark eyes filled with curious wonder, dark brows drawn together in doubt, dark braids spilling over bare shoulders. He stepped back. A woman edged forward. A small girl peeked around her skirt. Slowly the child moved to the front. A bunch of wildflowers were clutched in her fist. The girl looked up at Annie. She took one tentative step forward and raised the flowers.

For a long moment Annie stared blankly at the child. Then her hand extended to take the offering. A tiny smile brushed her lips. "Thank you," she murmured. White Wolf saw delight shine in the girl's eyes. She smiled shyly in return and then again ducked behind her mother. He turned his attention back to the chiefs.

"Copper pots and some blankets for the winter," Pontiac was saying.

The braves brought the gifts forward. Tewea looked them over. He motioned toward his wigwam. "Come, woman," he shouted.

A woman with streaks of gray through her hair, her belly round with child, waddled from the hut. She grabbed the pots and blankets from the arms of the braves, nodded once at Tewea, and scurried back inside the wigwam.

Tewea glanced at Annie. "The woman?" he asked.

"As I promised you," Pontiac answered.

Tewea stepped forward and examined Annie with his single eye. His gaze traveled from her head, to her chest and hips, all the way down to her feet. Then he walked behind her and repeated the scrutiny. Twice more he circled her, unblinking. Suddenly he grabbed her chin and forced her mouth open.

To White Wolf's surprise, Annie did not bite him. She didn't even try. Instead, she stood perfectly still beneath his grasp, though he could see the hatred burning in her eyes.

"Good teeth," Tewea said. "She will do."

Pontiac nodded. "A good wife."

"Wife?" The word slipped unbidden from White Wolf's lips. He clamped his mouth shut.

Pontiac turned slowly. His gaze pierced White Wolf's. "Do you object, brother?"

In the silence that followed Annie spoke. "I will not marry that old goat. I will slit his throat before I spend a night in his bed." She said the words as calmly as a recitation of ingredients for deer stew.

"Silence, Fire Tongue!" Pontiac roared.

Annie's gaze slid over Pontiac as if he were naught but a beetle in her path. "My name is Annie."

Pontiac's face hardened. "You are what I call you." He turned toward White Wolf. "Waptumewi? What say you?"

White Wolf attempted to sort the jumble of thoughts in his mind. *I should have suspected this. I assumed she'd just be part of the tribe again. What am I going to do? Should I do anything? What if I don't? But marriage? To the chief?* He shook his head. It was unthinkable. But why did he care? She was not his responsibility anymore. Yet he did care. Somehow he couldn't help but care. Despite his confusion, one thing he knew—Annie should not marry the chief. "She will make a poor wife," he finally answered.

Pontiac lifted an eyebrow. "She is strong, healthy."

Tewea waved his hand in the air. "No, no. I will not marry her."

White Wolf felt the knot begin to dissolve in his stomach.

"She is for my son."

The knot returned.

Tewea glared at Pontiac. "Why do you care what this brave thinks?"

"It is he who captured her."

Tewea came forward until he stood just inches from White Wolf's nose. The chief stared up at him. White Wolf smelled breath stale from brandy. "You say this woman, this Fire Tongue, is not fit for my son?"

White Wolf turned his head from the stench. "She is not."

Tewea lifted his hand and snorted. "It is of no matter. We have no others old enough since Moon Dance died of the strange fever last winter. This one," he jabbed his finger at Annie, "will have to do."

White Wolf knew he should back down. After all, what was Annie to him but a nuisance? And yet if she married the chief's son, he was sure the man would be dead by morning. Somehow Annie would manage it. And if she killed the chief's son, she would die. And so would he for bringing her. "No." He spoke the denial through clenched teeth.

For three breaths he and Tewea glared at one another. Then Pontiac stepped between them. He pinned White Wolf with a gaze like flint.

Tewea started to speak, but Pontiac stopped him with a quick flick of his wrist. Tewea fell silent. The entire village fell silent, until all White Wolf could hear was his own breath in his ears.

Then Pontiac spoke. "It is time for the truth, Waptumewi. Why should Fire Tongue not marry Tewea's son?"

White Wolf could feel the eyes of the villagers boring holes in his skin. He took two quick breaths. He couldn't think. He had to say something. He had to stop this. *Oh, God . . .* "She's promised to me." The words were out before he could halt them. "Since we were children," he finished lamely.

For what seemed like a lifetime, Pontiac said nothing. Then he leaned close to White Wolf. "The lie does not suit you, brother," he said in an undertone. "But I shall make it truth." He turned back to Tewea. "I will find you another woman. I will send ten women from my own village to replace this one promised to Waptumewi. And tonight we will celebrate together."

"Celebrate what?" Tewea asked.

Pontiac stared straight at White Wolf. "We celebrate the union of Waptumewi and Fire Tongue. Tonight the promise will be ful-filled!"

White Wolf felt his breath leave him in a rush. What had he done?

TWENTY-TWO

~

Women swarmed around Annie like a flurry of curious bees. She tried to pull away from them, but the rope around her wrists stopped her. Suddenly she felt ten years old again—captured, helpless, with a hundred villagers poking her, prodding her, staring with wide black eyes.

"Stop!" she screamed. "Get away from me!" No one seemed to hear. Annie pulled at the rope again. It didn't loosen. She twisted and turned. Hands grabbed at her arms. Voices, like the babbling of a dozen mockingbirds, filled her ears. A wave of panic rose within her. Just as she thought she would drown beneath it, she heard a woman's voice, clear and commanding, over the uproar.

"Shoo, shoo," the woman called in Algonquin. "Go back to your homes. Go."

The crowd melted away until Annie could see the woman standing before her. Wide-set eyes over a nose a little too large looked back at her. Long black braids decorated with bright beads fell over the woman's shoulders. The little girl who had given her the flowers peered around her skirt.

The woman smiled at Annie and then looked up at the brave holding her rope. Slowly she raised one hand. The brave gave her the end of the rope and stepped back.

"I am called Dawn Light," she said in rough English. "I will help you. You speak our tongue?"

Annie nodded.

"Come, we have much to do." She reverted to Algonquin. "I will not harm you." She held the rope lightly in one hand and placed the other gently on Annie's forearm. "You will come with me?"

Annie looked into brown eyes that crinkled slightly in the corners. "I will."

Dawn Light smiled again, and this time Annie noticed how the gesture transformed her face and made it beautiful. She started toward a wigwam at the far end of the village.

Annie followed. She tried to catch White Wolf's eye, but he avoided her gaze. She turned away. What was he thinking? Why did he again step between her and fate? His desperation to save her, his willingness to accept her, caught her by surprise. But that didn't mean she wanted to be his wife. Wife, indeed! She scorned the thought. She would go through with the ceremony tonight, but she'd never be his wife. She felt a tug on her dress and looked down to see the girl who had given her the flowers.

The child gazed up at her. "Are you going to stay with us?" she asked.

Strange warmth flowed through Annie's chest. She pushed the feeling aside. *I mustn't allow myself to find friends here. I can't let myself care.* She shook her head. "No, I'm not."

The child's face fell.

Dawn Light ducked through the flap of the wigwam and held it back for Annie to enter. She stepped through and immediately noticed the ears of corn hanging from the ceiling. A small fire burned in the center of the room. Clay pots with pointed bottoms were propped in the rocks around the fire. One side of the hut was dominated by a sleeping platform covered with a large deer hide. A single pair of moccasins peeked from beneath. Baskets and a couple of small copper pots hung from hooks on the walls, and beside them a flat bone knife lay on top of two sticks. Annie inched toward the knife.

"Sit." Dawn Light's voice, though gentle, still carried the element of command.

Annie sat on the narrow bed and placed the flowers beside her.

Dawn Light took the knife from the wall and approached.

Annie caught her breath. She could see the white serrated edge of the weapon coming closer and closer.

"I will not harm you." The words seemed meaningless.

Annie turned her head. Then she felt her arms lift. She turned back.

Dawn Light held the rope in one hand and the knife in the other. Her gaze held Annie's. "I will cut the rope off. You will not run away."

"I will not run away," Annie repeated.

Dawn Light sawed at the ropes until they fell away and landed with a thump on the floor. Then she straightened. "You will feel better now. It is not good to be bound like an enemy."

But I am an enemy. She didn't say the words aloud.

"You are Annie?"

"I am Fire Tongue." Bitterness laced her tone. She rubbed her wrists with her hands.

A soft chuckle danced from Dawn Light's lips. "I suspect it is an appropriate name, but it is not what you wish to be called."

Annie felt herself blush. "No."

Dawn Light sat on the bed beside her and motioned toward the girl. "This is my daughter White Flower. She has seven summers. I have no other children."

White Flower nodded shyly at Annie and then sat cross-legged at her feet.

"Someday she will grow up and marry a warrior. You must show her that it is not such a bad thing to marry a man."

"I don't think I can do that," Annie muttered.

Dawn Light studied her for a long moment. "He is wrong about you," she finally said.

"What do you mean?"

"You will make a fine warrior's wife."

Annie made a sound low in her throat.

Dawn Light only laughed. Then she stood and walked over to one of the baskets on the wall. She rummaged through it with one hand and pulled out a dress the color of buttercups bleached in the sun. "I think this will fit you." She returned and held up the garment beneath Annie's chin. Her lips twisted to one side. "No, it is not right." She shook her head. "The color is wrong. Green, I think, to bring out your eyes." She returned to the basket and pulled out a buckskin dress dyed the color of lichens. She again held it up to Annie. "Perfect. You would like to try it on?"

Annie frowned. "No. I would not."

Dawn Light returned the frown but only for a moment. Then her features softened. "It is hard to be here for you. I see it in your eyes. They say much, your eyes."

"What do they say?"

"They say you are unsure of who you are. You are angry and sad, lonely, and yet afraid to let anyone near. Am I right?" She paused, then looked away. "I am sorry; I have said too much." Her gaze dropped. "White Flower, bring me the headband in that basket." She pointed beneath the bed.

White Flower scampered to her feet. When she returned, she held a headband of green and blue beads woven onto a strip of leather and interlaced with purple wampum shells.

Dawn Light took the band from her hands. "I wore this on my wedding day," she said. "Now you shall wear it too. Come, let me put it on you."

Annie felt her resistance seep away like water from a cracked cauldron. She lowered her head and allowed Dawn Light to tie the band around her forehead.

Dawn Light adjusted it and pulled back to get a better view. "It suits you well."

"I don't want to look like an Indian."

"You look like yourself. Now would you like to put on the dress? Yours is torn."

Annie looked down at her tattered skirt. "I don't want to look like an Indian," she repeated.

Dawn Light put her hand on Annie's arm. "Nothing could make you look like an Indian. Look at us." She swept her hand between Annie and herself. "We are as different as . . . as . . ." Her gaze fell to the wildflowers on the bed. "As a daisy and a wild rose."

"Which am I?"

Dawn Light grinned. "You are the rose, of course. Beautiful, but beware of thorns."

Annie couldn't help but smile. "I will put on your dress." She stood and turned her back to Dawn Light. Quickly she pulled the leather-wrapped bundle from beneath her skirt and shoved it under the bed. There would be time to think about the peddler's blanket later, she told herself.

When Annie turned around, Dawn Light was watching her. She didn't say a word. Instead, she smoothed the green dress over the bed and flicked a bit of lint from its sleeve.

Annie slipped off her dress and put on the new one. It felt soft against her skin and reminded her of the days before Kwelik had married Jonathan. Those had been hard times, painful times, but Kwelik had been there to help. And now this woman was here too. What made her so kind to a stranger?

"Can you keep a secret?" Dawn Light's voice lowered to a whisper.

Annie leaned toward her. "I can." Her heart beat faster.

"You mustn't let anyone else see." She put her hand in the folds of her dress and pulled out a thin silver chain. She held it up so that Annie could see the cross that hung from the center. "You may wear this," she said, "to remind you of home."

The words pierced Annie's defenses. Suddenly she felt not comforted but afraid, afraid that God was indeed looking down on her and did not like what He saw. She averted her eyes as Dawn Light put the chain around her neck and tucked it beneath her collar.

"Good," she said. "Only we three will know it is there."

"You are a Christian?" The question seemed to stick behind Annie's tongue.

"Yes!" Dawn Light's face blossomed in a huge smile.

The knowledge weighed on Annie like an ill-fitting yoke. She had intended to hate everyone in this village, but now . . .

"I will see you later," Dawn Light said. "Rest. Tonight will come soon enough."

Too soon, Annie thought as Dawn Light slipped from the tent.

White Flower remained behind. She looked up at Annie. "I am glad you have come to us." She turned toward the door and then paused and looked over her shoulder.

"Was there something you wanted?" Annie asked.

The girl caught her lower lip between her teeth. After a few moments she spoke all in a rush. "May I touch your hair, please?"

Annie pulled a handful over her shoulder and glanced at her copper-brown curls. "You may."

White Flower walked over, tentatively reached out her hand, and brushed her fingers over Annie's hair. "It's so soft," she breathed. "I thought it was made of metal like the pots our braves brought home from war."

Annie tossed the strands back over her shoulder. "No, it is just hair."

Brown eyes stared into hers. "It is beautiful."

Dawn Light stuck her head back through the flap over the door. "White Flower, come! Annie must rest." She looked at Annie. "Call me if you need anything. I will be close." Then she was gone and the girl with her.

Slowly and yet too quickly the shadows that crept beneath the door grew longer and longer and were finally swallowed by the first moments of evening. The deep, resonant beat of a water drum thrummed through the air. Boom. Boom-boom. Boom. The sound made Annie shiver.

White Flower peeked in the door. "It is time." Then she disappeared.

Annie squared her shoulders and left the wigwam. Outside, a huge bonfire flickered in the descending night. Sparks spat upward and shimmered for a moment before dying in midair. Behind them the drummer sat on a log and beat a steady rhythm. He started to sing a low, solemn tune to call the women from their wigwams. Beside him half a dozen other men shook rattles made of gourds and turtle shells. They too joined their voices in song. Slowly the women gathered in small groups around the fire. Above them a few stars twinkled against the darkening sky. And behind, the drummer continued his steady thumping.

Pontiac and White Wolf, their heads bent together in deep discussion, stood between her and the singers. Tewea sat across from them, his one eye glaring at the twisting flames.

Dawn Light came out of a wigwam and approached her. "You look beautiful," she murmured. "Come. They await you." She led Annie toward White Wolf.

He turned and looked at her with dark eyes. Then he reached out his hand.

Annie hesitated.

White Wolf frowned. "Take it," he hissed under his breath.

Annie stepped closer and placed her hand in his. His skin felt warm and damp against hers. Her gaze dropped, and she noticed that his tomahawk was missing. She looked further and saw that it hung at Pontiac's waist.

"It's the bride price," White Wolf whispered in answer to her unspoken question.

A *single tomahawk*. The thought goaded her. *And not a particularly good one*. Was that all she was worth? Not that she cared, but had there ever been a bride sold so cheaply?

"It's all I had," White Wolf muttered.

Pontiac cleared his throat. The drum fell silent. The singers stopped their song. Annie could feel the eyes of the villagers on her. Pontiac turned to White Wolf. "You will have this woman for your wife?"

"I will," answered White Wolf.

"It is done," said Pontiac. Then he turned away.

"Is that it?" The question tumbled from Annie's lips.

"That is it. We are married," said White Wolf in a voice that contained no pleasure.

Pontiac clapped his hands and whooped. The others added their voices until the sky seemed to echo with the sound. Then the cry ended as quickly as it had begun. The drummer began a new beat and started to chant. The men with the rattles joined in. As they did, the village erupted with sound—women giggling, men talking, children scampering around the fire and squealing with delight.

Tewea stood and extended his hand toward his wife. She linked her arm with his. As if that were a signal, the others also joined arms and began to dance counterclockwise around the fire.

"Come." White Wolf's voice sounded in her ear. "We must dance."

Annie crossed her arms. "I will not dance with you. I'm not your wife."

"What is done is done," came his reply.

"Not if I can help it!" She turned and stormed toward the wigwam.

White Wolf caught up with her halfway. He grabbed her arm and turned her toward him. She lifted her chin in defiance. He took it between his thumb and forefinger, forcing her to look at him. Their eyes met, and she found herself pulled into the dark depths of his pain, his guilt. And there she saw her own reflection.

Slowly he loosened his grip. His eyes searched hers. "I know that you hate me," he said, "but we are in this together now. Don't make it more difficult than it already is." He dropped her arm.

For a moment they stood there, neither speaking. She wanted to tell him that she didn't hate him, that she understood. But she could not force the words from her lips. He dropped his gaze and turned back to the fire. His shoulders slumped as he walked toward the flames.

"Wait," she whispered. But the words fell and were lost. She turned back to the wigwam and rushed inside.

There White Flower was spreading out a blanket on the bed. An empty leather covering lay on the floor beside her. It took only a moment for Annie to realize what had happened. "No, get away from that!" she yelled. But somehow she knew it was too late. The devil had come to call.

TWENTY-THREE

~

"Papa, Mama, I'm back!"

Jonathan leaped from the chair by the window. Could it be? Kwelik jumped from the bed. Together they raced to the door. Jonathan flung it open to find his son standing before him. He scooped him up in his arms and held him close to his chest. "Thank God," he muttered and breathed deeply, smelling the musty odor of Justin's hair and the dampness that clung to his clothes. This was real. It wasn't just a dream. Emotion swelled within him. He looked up. Kwelik stood beside him, her arms around the both of them. Tears shone in her eyes.

Words failed Jonathan. He held his son for a few moments longer and then set him down and knelt before him. "Where were you? Where have you been?" He placed his hands on Justin's shoulders, almost afraid to let go lest the boy disappear again.

"He was down in the old well," Katherine answered.

Only then did Jonathan notice the girl standing near him. She stepped closer. "Someone pushed him in, Uncle Jonathan."

Rage surged through him. "Who would do such a thing?" He looked into his son's smudged face.

"I dunno, Papa. I didn't get a good look at him."

"The important thing is that you're back," Kwelik interjected. She hugged him again. "A warm bath, some hot soup, and to bed, and you'll be all right again." She brushed her fingers over his hair.

Justin snuggled into Kwelik's neck. His arms wrapped around her. He sniffled, and Jonathan saw a tear drip down the boy's face.

"What's the matter, Justin?" Katherine asked.

"Nuthin'," Justin mumbled.

As he spoke, Elizabeth came out of the nursery. "What's going on here?" she asked. "Katherine?" Her voice was sharp.

"Justin's back, Elizabeth," Jonathan said.

Her mouth rounded, and she sucked in her breath. "Oh, that's—that's wonderful." She came toward them, her eyes flickering from Justin to Jonathan. "Welcome back, Justin," she murmured. "You certainly gave your parents a fright."

"Someone pushed him into the old well." Jonathan's voice was hard.

Elizabeth raised her eyebrows. "Oh, come now. Are you sure he didn't just fall in? He shouldn't be playing down there."

Jonathan bristled. "If he says he was pushed, he was pushed."

"I *was* pushed, Papa, by someone in a black cape," Justin piped up.

Jonathan glared at Elizabeth. "Do you own a black cape?"

Elizabeth straightened her shoulders. "Are you accusing me?"

Kwelik stepped forward. "Of course not. We're all just a little overwrought right now."

For a moment Jonathan thought he saw guilt in Elizabeth's eyes, but now he couldn't be sure. One thing he knew—someone had tried to hurt his son. Someone had done the unthinkable. And if it was the last thing he did, Jonathan swore he would find out who.

"Take Justin into our room. I'll go draw the bath." Kwelik's voice reached out to him.

He took Justin and went back into his room. Katherine followed. The three of them sat on the bed. Jonathan looked at Katherine.

Justin followed his gaze. "She found me, Papa. I woulda died down there if she hadn't."

Jonathan put his hand on Justin's knee. "Don't talk about such things."

Justin's eyes grew wider. "I would have though. But I prayed real hard just like Mama always says. I prayed and prayed and prayed. I didn't think God heard me, but He must have because Katherine came."

"It was all the spider's doing," Katherine muttered.

"What?" Justin and Jonathan said together.

Katherine's face reddened. "The spider—it fell on me and made me scream. Then when the baby woke up, I ran away to hide." She took a breath. "Do you think God sent the spider?"

God answering prayer with a spider. The ridiculous practicality of it made Jonathan chuckle. "It would be just like Him, wouldn't it?"

Katherine and Justin grinned.

"And look at this, Papa." Justin pulled a piece of paper from his shirt and handed it to his father.

Jonathan read it silently, then folded it, and put it in his pocket. *So he was going to tell the truth at last,* he thought. *I wonder why.* He glanced at Katherine and then at Justin. "Thank you, son. I'll take this now."

"Okay, Papa."

A soft whimper rose from the cradle. Jonathan reached over and lifted Brenna from the blankets.

Justin put out his arms. "Can I hold her, Papa? Please?"

Jonathan looked at his son's dirty shirt, mussed hair, and dirt-smeared arms. Then he smiled. "Here you go." He handed him the baby and watched as Justin took her gently in his arms.

"Hello, baby Brenna. I missed you," he whispered.

The baby cooed. Then she swung her arm up and grabbed his nose.

Justin giggled and kissed her on the cheek.

The sight warmed Jonathan's heart. From the side of his vision, he saw Katherine edge toward the door. He turned. "Good night, Katherine, and thank you."

She blushed. "Good night, Uncle Jonathan."

He looked at the child who had brought him back his son, looked at her wispy golden hair, her round pink cheeks, her innocent eyes—like those of a young angel. "You have given us a great gift, Katherine," he said. "Is there anything I can do for you?"

She paused, then looked him straight in the eye. "You can get my papa out of prison."

Her request echoed in his mind, asked in a voice so guileless that he could hear in it the still, small whisper of God.

"I will," he answered. As soon as he said it, the promise became a shackle around his heart.

～

Elizabeth kneaded her fingers over her forehead and paced in front of the parlor's fireplace. The sounds of conversation rumbled from the room above. She could almost make out Jonathan's voice and the higher one of his son. She stopped and tapped her fingers on the mantel.

The voices stopped. Somewhere above, a door slammed shut. She listened as quiet footsteps pattered down the stairs and out the front door. Katherine! Why did that child have to interfere? Everything was going as planned. Justin had mysteriously disappeared, and Jonathan had gone nearly mad with worry. But all that had changed because of Katherine. *Curse the child!* Elizabeth pounded her fist once against the mantel and then spun away from the fire.

An eerie feeling of being watched crept over her. She shuddered and turned toward the window. Outside, a light glimmered from the gardens. She peered into the darkness. Yes, there was definitely a light. What was Katherine up to now?

Elizabeth strode from the parlor, flung open the front door, and hurried toward the garden. A slice of moonlight illuminated her path. In the dim light she thought she could see two shadowy figures side by side on the garden bench. She rushed toward them, but when she got there, Katherine was alone, with a single candle flickering beside her.

"Who was that with you?" Elizabeth demanded.

Katherine raised frightened eyes. "N-no one," she stuttered.

Elizabeth leaned over and gripped Katherine's arm tightly in her hand. She gave her a quick shake. "Don't lie to me. I saw someone with you."

Katherine looked away. "It was only the lady of the gardens."

"Does she have a name?"

"No."

Elizabeth squeezed Katherine's arm until the flesh turned white around her fingers.

"I don't know her name," Katherine squealed.

Elizabeth loosened her grip. "What does she want with you? Why is she here?"

Katherine's brows furrowed. "She's here to help us. I think she's an angel."

Elizabeth growled low in her throat. She thrust Katherine's arm away from her and placed her hands on both hips. "She is a beggar and probably a thief. I never want to see you talking with her again."

Katherine lowered her head. "But she just wants us to be happy."

"Happy?" Elizabeth choked on the word. She would never be happy until the estate was William's, until Jonathan groveled at her feet, until his horrible savage wife was shamed before them all. And she didn't need some strange woman to help her accomplish that. All she needed was to bide her time. Opportunity would come soon enough.

Elizabeth glanced down at her daughter and noticed how her hair shimmered in the moonlight. The sight of it softened her. "I only want what's best for us," she murmured. She reached out and laid her fingers gently on Katherine's head. As she did, something stirred in her, a small remnant of the child she used to be. *Let go*, it called in her mind. *Let go of the past.* She pulled back her hand. "It's too late," she whispered. "I will not turn back."

"It's too late," Katherine repeated.

And Elizabeth knew it was true.

~

For two long weeks Philippe fumbled around the forest, trying to find his way to the coast. "Follow the river," Tom had said. It sounded simple, but after just two days he'd lost the path. It would have been easier if he hadn't spotted a marauding group of Indians and fled into the forest. After that he couldn't find his way back to the water. The only thing he knew was that he was heading east. The sun, at least, told him that.

But now even the thought that he was a little closer to France didn't comfort him. His feet hurt, his back ached, and the supplies that Rosie had given him were running out. He shifted the sack across his shoulder and stopped. With one hand he shaded his eyes and looked up at the sun. It was almost noon, time to find some water, eat a few bites, and rest.

It took Philippe another hour to find water. When he did, he knelt beside the stream and splashed handfuls over his face. Droplets dribbled down his chin as he scooped water to his mouth. Then he settled by the creek and pulled out a slab of dried rabbit. He chewed slowly in an attempt to make it last. Too soon the meat was gone. He leaned back against a tree trunk and sighed. Green moss grew like a blanket over the stones in the stream. The color reminded him of Annie's eyes. He wondered how she and White Wolf were managing. Had they rescued Sarah from the Indians? Had they finally put aside their anger and become friends? Or were they still bickering over nothing?

Philippe stretched his legs. He missed White Wolf and Annie. He even missed Tom and Rosie. The thought of Rosie brought back her last words to him. "God's grace to you, laddie," she had said. "But, mark me words, if ye can't find God here, you won't find him in France either." He'd brushed aside her advice then, but now he wondered. Could God be found in the wilds of the New World? Could he ever find peace outside of France?

He closed his eyes and enjoyed the warmth of the sun on his face. He listened to the rumble of water over rocks and the call of a bird in the distance. Tranquility settled around him until he felt that maybe, just maybe, God could be here too. "Lord," he muttered, "I don't profess to know You or even what You expect of me, but I need help now. I don't know where I am. I don't know where I'm going. Help me to find my way home."

Philippe opened his eyes and stood.

Nothing happened. He repeated the prayer.

No divine revelation popped into his mind. No heavenly arrow pointed toward France. No sign appeared to guide his way. He threw the sack over his shoulder and started walking in the direction he assumed was east.

Just as the sun tipped halfway past its zenith, he heard voices and the stomping of booted feet through the underbrush. Red coats appeared in the leaves. "There, up ahead," he heard one of the men call.

Philippe gripped his sack tighter and ran.

"Halt!" the man shouted.

He stopped mid-stride.

"Turn slowly, or we will shoot."

He dropped the bag and turned. Six men, all dressed in British uniforms and carrying muskets, stood thirty feet behind him.

"Who are you?" the man who must have been the captain demanded. "What're you doing here?"

Philippe stuttered an answer. "I—I am going home."

"French!" the captain snarled. "Search him."

Two soldiers rushed toward him. The others also closed the distance between them. Then one man grabbed his arms while another searched through the bag at his feet.

"Look at this!" The second man pulled out the jacket of Philippe's French uniform.

"As I suspected," the captain grunted. "A spy."

"*Non!*" Philippe spoke his denial in French.

The captain's eyes narrowed. "I recognize you." He stepped closer. "You were at the battle at Fort Duquesne. You might even be the very one who shot General Braddock."

"No, I did not fight."

"Liar!" The captain's hand flew at Philippe and hit him in the jaw.

Philippe's head jarred. For a moment his vision dimmed.

"We'll take him for questioning," he heard the captain say.

The soldiers tied his hands behind his back and pushed him forward. "Washington will be interested in what this one has to say," one of the men muttered.

Philippe stumbled as he walked between the soldiers. His eyes glanced at his sack, now slung over the back of one of the men. He remembered Rosie. He remembered his prayer.

Was this God's answer to his cry?

TWENTY-FOUR

~

It took two weeks for the first small red spots to appear. For thirteen days Annie lived with a dread like she'd never known. For twelve days she walked from wigwam to wigwam with her breath half-held, afraid to look too closely, afraid to hope or even pray.

Then came White Flower's fever. It devoured her strength, withered her joy, until she lay in bed like a limp weed scorched by the sun. Next the spots appeared as a spattering over her face and grew until they covered her chest and arms.

Now four days later Annie knelt beside White Flower's bed. The odor of vomit and sickness permeated the air. She tried not to see how the spots were turning to angry pustules, how sweat beaded on the girl's forehead, or how her hair clung to her face in damp clumps. Annie cleared her throat. "Here," she murmured. "I brought you some tea. It will help settle your stomach." She lifted the cup.

White Flower reached out and took it. She brought the cup to her lips and struggled to take a single sip. Her hand shook and a splash of liquid spilled over her speckled skin. Her head fell back to the bed. "I'm sorry," she whispered.

"No, don't be sorry." Annie laid her hand on White Flower's arm. It felt as hot as a black stone at midday. Guilt squeezed her heart. "Oh, White Flower," she murmured. She leaned over until her forehead rested on the girl's arm. She wanted to cry, she needed to cry, yet the tears refused to come. She raised her head.

The girl attempted to smile, but the gesture faded halfway. "I missed our berry picking this week. I know I promised . . ."

"Shhh, it's okay. We'll go some other day." The lie slipped uneasily from Annie's lips. She knew there wouldn't be another day. She had seen this before, the slow burning fever, the rash, the sickness that ravaged the body like a hungry cougar, and the death that followed. But this time it was her fault. This time she was the death-bearer. The knowledge tore through her gut.

"Can you get me my doll?" White Flower's voice came weakly from the bed. She pointed to a carved wooden toy on the ground beside her.

Annie retrieved it and laid it next to her.

White Flower tucked the doll close to her and shivered. "I'm so cold," she muttered. "And my head hurts like a dozen horses are galloping through it."

Annie pulled up the blanket beneath White Flower's chin. "Close your eyes. Rest. It will be better if you sleep."

White Flower's head flopped to one side. She coughed. "I hope you don't get sick too."

Annie looked away. "Don't worry about that." She remembered six years ago when she had gotten smallpox. Snowbird and so many others had died from it, but Annie had pulled through. Some said you couldn't get it twice. She didn't know if that was true. But one thing she did know—those were terrible times. Why hadn't she remembered the horror of it? How could she have thought to bring this misery on anyone, even on an enemy? She hid her face from White Flower's view. One tear escaped and slipped down her cheek.

"I'm hot," White Flower moaned.

Annie dried her face and pulled a cloth from her pocket. She dipped it into a pot of water near White Flower's bed and smoothed it across the child's forehead.

"Will you pray for me, Annie?"

She looked into eyes blurred with pain, wide with silent fear. "I—I can't," she muttered. The realization hurt worse than a musket shot through her heart. What would White Flower say if she knew the truth? Would she look up with eyes of condemnation and hate? Would she pray for vengeance against the one who harmed her? Annie rubbed her damp palms over her thighs and dropped her gaze to the floor. *Oh, God, what have I done?*

White Flower turned her head and closed her eyes.

Then Annie heard the sound she had been dreading for days—

someone else vomiting outside the wigwam. *So it begins*, she thought. *How will I ever atone for this sin?*

"Mama?"

White Flower's call sent a chill of fear through Annie. *No, not Dawn Light too. Please, God, not her. Anyone but her.*

Yet Dawn Light was the one who stumbled into the wigwam. She wiped her mouth on a rag held between her fingers. Sweat trickled down her temple. She sat on the edge of the sleeping platform and rubbed her hand over the back of her neck. A damp strand of hair dropped over her eyes. She glanced at Annie. "How is she?"

Annie shook her head. Her throat closed. Finally she managed to squeeze one word from her dried lips. "Weak."

Dawn Light dropped to her knees beside White Flower.

"Everything aches, Mama," the girl muttered.

She dropped a kiss onto her daughter's forehead. "I know, love," she whispered. "I hurt too."

Annie put her hand on Dawn Light's shoulder. She sniffed. "It's the sickness. Lie down and rest."

Dawn Light shook her head. "No, I have much work to do. I must prepare soup for White Flower and wash her clothes and . . ."

Annie cut her off. "I will do all that. You must lie down." Panic rose like a tide in her heart. *If Dawn Light dies, if White Flower dies* . . . She didn't want to think of the consequences. Quickly she helped Dawn Light to the second sleeping platform and covered her with a blanket. She tried to be so gentle, as if her actions could somehow begin to make up for her mistakes. But how could anything make up for what she had done? "Don't worry about a thing," she choked. "I will do whatever needs to be done."

Dawn Light sighed and leaned her head back against the rushes. "Thank you, my friend."

I am no friend. The realization stabbed through her until she didn't think she could endure it. Quietly she slipped from the wigwam. A sob gathered in her throat.

She ran toward the creek and threw herself beside the water. A breeze rippled its surface and pulled a strand of hair across her face. Her fists pounded into the dark mud. "God, God, I didn't mean it. Oh,

God, what am I going to do?" She drew a shuddering breath between sobs. Her head lashed back and forth until the bulrushes beside the creek became no more than a blur of green. "I did this. It was me. And now nothing can make it right." She remembered her former fury, her need for revenge. She remembered the day she had tucked the leather-covered blanket under her skirt. The memory sickened her. She had had a choice then. For that moment she'd stood on the edge of hell and looked into its fiery jaws. Why, why had she chosen the evil over the good? Why didn't she recognize the high price of hate?

Damp earth oozed through her fingers. She lifted her hands and rubbed them on her skirt. Dark splotches spread over her thighs. She poked at the dirt. "I will never be clean again," she whispered. "This deed will always cling to me. How can God even look at me now? I have become worse than those I hated. A murderer of innocent women and children." Washington had been right. The sword of revenge had pierced her heart. And now it was too late to pull it free. She stood up and glanced toward the sky. An eagle passed in front of the sun and cast a shadow over the land.

Slowly Annie rose and wandered back toward the village. Her feet dragged along the path. Beside it a single daisy swayed in the breeze. She stopped and studied the flower. Once Dawn Light had likened herself to the daisy, with its clean white petals and bright friendly face. But now everything had changed.

She knelt down and took the flower between her thumb and forefinger. "Somehow I will make up for my sin," she whispered to the golden face. "I will find a way to atone for the evil." In the distance a coyote barked. To Annie it sounded like the devil's laughter.

∾

This time there were no frogs, only a low hanging mist that burned off at midday and left the air heavy with humidity. Jonathan pulled at his collar and peeked between the tall rushes alongside the road. Before him the prison rose cold and forbidding. In front of it a carriage waited with a sway-backed roan that snorted and stamped its hooves against the ground.

A fly buzzed around Jonathan's head and landed on his cheek.

Silently he brushed it away. It made one lazy circle around him before flying off toward the horse and carriage.

Jonathan focused on the prison's front gate. Ten more minutes crept by. Finally the gate swung open, and the warden appeared. He waddled toward the carriage. Jonathan could almost see the ground buckle beneath him. Eventually he reached the carriage and heaved himself inside. The driver flicked the reins over the horse's back. The carriage groaned as the animal took a step forward. The roan shook its head and stopped. The driver cracked the whip over its back until the animal lunged forward. Its harness jingled in the afternoon air. Slowly the horse and carriage rumbled by Jonathan and down the long road.

Jonathan watched it dip down a knoll and out of sight. Then he rose, smoothed his hand over the bottom of his shirt, and hurried toward the prison. Now only Tibbs and a few guards stood between him and his goal, and they wouldn't dare to arrest him without the warden's command.

In a few moments Jonathan slipped through the gated entrance, across the short walkway, and up to the front door. There he paused, drew a deep breath, then pulled it open. He stepped through. The same guards stood on either side of the doorway. The same blank gray walls rose on all sides around him.

Tibbs rustled in the shadows of the darkened hallway and hobbled toward him. "Jonathan Grant," he muttered.

Jonathan nodded. "Tibbs."

The man grinned. "You be a more daring man than I thought."

Jonathan lifted his eyebrows. "Or more foolish."

"Mebbe."

Jonathan crossed his arms. "You know why I've come."

"Aye, I'll take you to 'im." He rattled the keys at his belt, turned, and headed down the passageway.

Jonathan followed down the long winding staircase to the dungeon door. The moans and shrieks that echoed from behind it seemed more muted this time. The door swung open under Tibbs's hand. Jonathan walked through. Again the chill and the stench enveloped him like a fist. Tibbs scurried past and unlocked Richard's cell door.

Then, just as he had done before, Tibbs hung the lantern on the overhead hook and turned toward Jonathan. "Call when yer ready to go."

Jonathan nodded and stepped into the cell. Light flashed over the figure huddled in the corner. "Richard?"

The man raised his head. "Jonathan?" His voice was hollow. "Is that you?" A hand, gaunt and pale, lifted to brush back a mat of dirty hair.

Jonathan caught his breath. He hadn't expected his brother to look as if he belonged more to the netherworld than to this one.

"You came back." Richard ended the statement with a wracking cough.

Jonathan gathered his wits. *He tried to kill me*, he reminded himself. *He deserves this.* "I had no choice."

Richard's head bobbed back and forth. "Yes, yes. I know. God has drawn you here." His speech quickened. "Pulled you out of the mist and made you real." His eyes, wide and unblinking, seemed to be staring right through Jonathan to the wall beyond.

Jonathan took a step backward, away from the wraith that was supposed to be his brother. "I made a promise to your daughter," he answered. *A month ago.* It had taken him that long to follow through, that long to allow Justin out of his sight.

Richard spoke again. "My daughter. Yes, I had a daughter once." His voice dropped. "Her name—what was it?" He muttered something under his breath. "Ah, yes, Katherine, my darling Katherine. How is she?"

"She does as well as can be expected with her father in prison."

For a moment Richard focused. "And the babe? I had a son. I remember him. He cried when they laid him in my arms."

Jonathan felt pity rise within him. "He grows healthy and strong." He squatted down so that he was at eye level with Richard. "But I did not come to speak of them. I need to ask you some questions."

"Questions? Why?"

"To get you out of here if I can."

A strange smile tipped the corners of Richard's mouth. "Does this mean all is forgiven?"

Something hardened in Jonathan's heart. "No." He stood.

Richard stuck out his lower lip. His eyes again glazed over. "No forgiveness for Richard, no forgiveness for Richard," he chanted in a sing-song voice. "Richard has been bad. Richard is sorry. But Jonathan won't forgive him."

"I can't."

"Jonathan is not really angry with Richard."

"Stop talking like that!" Jonathan's voice turned fierce. "Stand up. Speak to me like a man."

Richard rose slowly to his feet. He swayed back and forth, then rested one shoulder unsteadily on the wall. He rubbed his hands over his eyes and looked at Jonathan.

"That's better." Jonathan crossed his arms in front of him. He opened his mouth to speak, but Richard's words came first, soft but clear: "It's not me you're angry with."

Jonathan stared at him. "Okay, then who?"

"Isn't it obvious?"

"No."

"Father."

The single word was like a punch to his gut. "He's dead."

"Hmmm, yes," Richard muttered. "But not, perhaps, in your heart." He frowned. "Or in mine either." He paused. "What's that bulge in your pocket, brother?"

Jonathan reached in his pocket and withdrew the tin soldier. "Only this."

"Father gave that to you when you were ten."

"And took it from me a week later."

"Why do you carry it?"

Jonathan frowned. "To remind myself of everything he did to us."

Richard swayed back and forth. "Why remember?"

"So I will never be like him."

Richard smiled. "A tin soldier can't do that for you, Johnny. Only God can do that."

A long silence dropped between them. Jonathan didn't know what to say, how to respond to this man who spoke one moment as a sane man and the next as if devils danced through his mind.

Richard broke the quietness. "I dream about him sometimes." He stared up at the corner of the cell.

"Who?"

"Father." His voice was ethereal. "He's coming at me with the riding crop they found. Do you ever dream of him, Johnny?"

"No," Jonathan said flatly.

"I think about him as I'm sitting here in the darkness and the spiders are spinning their webs. I wonder, why did he do the things he did? Why couldn't he care for us? Why did he hurt Mother?"

"I don't know. I don't care anymore."

"Don't you?" Richard coughed again.

Jonathan began to pace along the side of the cell. "Why think of him? It doesn't matter now."

Richard scratched his head. "It does matter. It always has."

Jonathan turned away. "Father was a devil."

"No, he was only a man," came the soft reply. Then Richard sighed. "Let us not argue, Jonathan. I'm too tired."

Jonathan turned back around. "I found your letter." He pulled it from his pocket and handed it to Richard.

Richard took it and studied it for a moment. "I never had a chance to finish it."

"Why did you even start?"

"To make things right."

"It's not like you."

"No, it's not." He sighed again. "Go home, Jonathan. It's too late for me. You can't save a dead man."

"You're not dead yet."

Richard attempted to laugh and failed. "Look at me."

Jonathan's gaze raked his brother's frame. Richard seemed so pale that Jonathan almost had a sense that if the light were right, he could see right through him. "I'll keep my promise to Katherine."

"Ah, always so noble." Richard paused. "Always the fool." Sad eyes turned on Jonathan. "Somebody did this to me, brother. Don't let them destroy you too."

His warning was like the whisper of temptation. Or was it reason? "Enough, Richard. I said I would help, and I will. So tell me, what enemies do you have?"

Richard picked at a piece of straw sticking from a tear in his shirt. "Besides you, you mean?"

Jonathan scowled. "I didn't put you here."

"No. I don't know who did that."

"Could it have been Elizabeth?"

"It could have. She's hated me ever since I brought her back from the colonies. For a time she tried to hide it. But I could see the truth. I could always see it." He twisted the strand of straw in his fingers. "But she was with me that night."

Jonathan grunted in frustration. "Then who?"

"I don't know."

Jonathan threw his hands in the air. "You've got to think, man!"

Richard remained calm, quiet. "What do you suppose I've been doing all these many months? I've thought until my head pounds and my stomach heaves. Yet I'm no closer to knowing the face of my enemy."

Jonathan sat on the moldy mattress. He drummed his fingers on his knee. "That's what I always hated about England. The enemy does not wear war paint and brandish a tomahawk. This is a vile place." He was not speaking of the prison.

"Vileness is not in a place but in the hearts of men." It was the sanest thing Richard had said yet.

Jonathan looked at him closely and saw that the madness had receded. "So what am I to do?"

"See Inspector Higgins."

"Who's he?"

"The one who sent me here. Only he knows the truth." Richard sounded sure, but Jonathan wondered.

"For Katherine I will. But know that I do not do this for you." He turned and strode from the cell.

Richard called out from behind him. "Watch your back, Johnny. I see Father standing there."

Jonathan whirled around. But there was nothing behind him but a spider spinning a web in the darkness and Richard cackling madly beside it.

TWENTY-FIVE

~

Each day more villagers fell sick. White Flower weakened, and Dawn Light rose less and less from her bed. Quietness hung over the village like a death shroud. No children played by the creek. No laughter broke the silence. Even the dog seemed to know that death would soon encamp among them. It slunk around the village with its tail between its legs, a quiet whine issuing from its throat.

Annie spent her days boiling water, serving stew, and trying to forget what she had done. But she couldn't. She would never forget.

White Wolf rarely spoke to her. The war party had left the village two weeks ago, but White Wolf had not joined them. Now he hunted during the day and skinned his kill in the evenings. At night they lay down on separate mats and went to sleep without speaking. Annie had considered trying to escape. There was no one left to stop her, but guilt held her to the village more strongly than a dozen warriors with tomahawks raised.

Eight days after Dawn Light first became sick, Annie entered the wigwam for the fourth time that day. Stale, hot air assaulted her senses. The smell of sickness enveloped her. She stumbled to Dawn Light's bed and leaned over her. White Flower lay asleep on the other side of the wigwam. The spots on Dawn Light's scalp had scabbed over, making it look like a dozen birds had pecked her while she slept.

Annie put her hand on Dawn Light's forehead. It burned like a stick in the fire. She wiped her hair back from her face and dabbed away the sweat with a clean rag.

Dawn Light groaned and turned toward her. She focused with effort. "Thank you," she whispered, then managed a slight smile. "You have been so kind to us. Like an angel sent from God."

The words were like a twist of a knife in a wound. With them guilt and shame burst over Annie so strongly that she could no longer deny them. She knelt beside Dawn Light and took the woman's hand in her own. It was time to tell the truth, time to face the hate. "There is something I must tell you. This is all my fault."

Dawn Light closed her eyes. "You are not to blame."

Annie sucked in a quick breath and tightened her grip on Dawn Light's hand. "No, you don't understand. I brought the sickness in the blanket wrapped with leather."

Behind her the flap that covered the wigwam door rustled. Annie turned. Was someone listening? Or was it just the breeze? She studied the covered opening for a moment and then returned her gaze to Dawn Light's pallid face.

Dawn Light's eyes fluttered open. "How can a blanket carry disease?" Her voice was weak.

"I don't know," Annie answered. "The peddler said it did." *Did he know then what I would do with the knowledge? Did he see it in my eyes?*

Dawn Light nodded slowly. Her gaze traveled to the wigwam's ceiling. "Why did you do it?"

Words stuck in Annie's throat. A thousand answers flew through her mind, but none seemed right. Why, why? The question struck at her like hawk's claws, leaving her scratched and bleeding. Dawn Light turned her head and pulled her hand from Annie's.

Annie gripped the blanket in her fist. "What can I do?"

"Nothing. It is too late."

Yes, too late. Too late to hope, too late to believe. I've gone beyond the hand of God. Too late.

Dawn Light's head lolled to one side. Her hand slipped off her chest.

Annie leaped to her feet. She grabbed Dawn Light by the shoulders. "No, don't give up. Fight. Live!"

For one moment Dawn Light looked up at her. "I forgive you," she whispered. Then she was gone.

Annie fell across her weeping. "No! God, no! I'm so sorry. Oh, God. Oh, God." She cried until her throat was raw, and her breath came in rattling gasps. But nothing helped.

Dawn Light was dead.

That night White Flower followed her mother to heaven. Seven others died the following week. Annie felt as if she had died too, died with those she once called the enemy. But now she had no enemy but the truth, no adversary but the raging guilt that threatened to consume her.

How would she ever learn to live with this pain?

～

It seemed too cold for autumn. Outside the window the leaves were just beginning to turn golden, but inside the room Philippe felt a definite chill. He stiffened his back and glanced at the man sitting behind the desk in front of him. The man was dressed in a blue coat with a shirt as white as the sun on snow. He wore no wig but had his brown hair pulled back with a tie. He tapped the papers on his desk and looked at the men standing on either side of Philippe. "Found him east of the Susquehanna, you say?" His voice surprised Philippe. For someone who looked in his early twenties, his tone carried the authority of a much older man.

"Caught him runnin', sir," replied one of the men.

Philippe frowned.

"Thank you, men. You may leave him to me."

"Aye, Colonel." The men stepped back but did not leave the room.

The English commander leaned back in his chair and folded his fingers. "I am Colonel Washington. Who are you?"

The name meant nothing to Philippe. He lifted his chin. "I am Philippe Reveau. I will tell you nothing." He rubbed his hands over the place on his wrists where the rope had chafed his skin.

Washington smiled. "Well, Philippe Reveau, you have already told me two things—you speak English, and you do not like to be bound."

Philippe glowered at the man and then clamped his lips shut and looked around the room. No pictures hung from the walls; no rugs softened the floor; nothing broke the stark appearance of a space recently converted for the purposes of war. Only a cold stone fireplace in one corner and the heavy pine desk before him broke the monotony. Was this the workroom of a powerful man? It didn't seem so. Even on the frontier French men of power had accommodations that reflected their status. None of the commanders he knew would ever settle for such a plain chamber.

Philippe's gaze fell to the single oil lamp on the desk. Next to it lay an inkwell and a stack of curled papers. Did those pages hold secrets precious to the English? Did they tell of battle plans and strategies?

Washington rose from his high-backed chair and quietly turned over the top sheet of paper so that it lay facedown.

Philippe averted his eyes. Light shone in from two bare windows on either side of the desk. Outside, he could see a horse cavorting in the fields with a dog chasing after it.

Slowly Washington stepped around the desk and approached him.

"He was at the battle at Fort Duquesne," one of the men murmured from behind Philippe.

Washington nodded. "So you saw Braddock fall?"

"I am a French soldier. I—I demand to be sent back to France," Philippe blurted.

Washington chuckled. "You're not in the position to demand anything. You're not with the army. You were not captured in battle. So you're either a spy or a deserter."

Philippe turned away.

"Ah, it is as I suspected." Washington rubbed his hand over his chin. "But you were at the battle they are calling Braddock's Defeat?"

Philippe did not respond.

Washington sighed. "That loss should never have happened. So many died and are still dying."

"But you survived." Philippe's eyes narrowed.

"Yes, with four bullet holes through my coat and two horses shot from under me."

"*Mon Dieu*," Philippe breathed. "Is it true?"

Washington nodded. "Yes."

"Who are you then that the very hand of God would protect you from the enemies' shots?"

"Just a man and a soldier."

"More than that, I think."

Washington shrugged off Philippe's words. "And so you realize why I'm interested in what happened in that battle. I wish to know how your commander surmised our coming. How did your troops know to ambush us?"

Philippe straightened his shoulders. "The French are clever in battle. We and the Indians fought bravely that day. The English scattered like frightened sheep."

Washington scowled. "That may be, but it does not explain your victory." He stepped closer to Philippe. His voice dropped. "Do you have any idea what that loss has done on the frontier? Innocents, women and children, slaughtered by Indians like animals. And not just the English."

"How is this my fault or the fault of the French?"

Washington slammed his hand on the desk in a sudden flare of temper. "You're as savage as the Indians! This is Montcalm's doing and Dumas's. They gloat over our losses as I ride hither and yon," he waved his hand in the air, "in the attempt to protect 700 miles of wilderness with only a few hundred irregulars." He shook his head. "So few, so very few, against countless swarming hordes of savages. It is deviltry, I tell you—madness." He crossed his arms.

Philippe raised his eyebrows.

Washington stepped closer. His eyes were like steel. "You can't imagine the horrors I've seen." He turned away. "The supplicating tears of the women and the moving petitions of the men melt me into such deadly sorrow that I would offer myself a willing sacrifice to the butchering enemy." He sighed. "If only it would save the people." He seemed now to be talking more to himself than to Philippe.

"I am sorry."

Washington picked up a handful of papers from his desk. "Are you? Then you're alone among your brothers. Here, I will tell you what your Montcalm has unleashed." He ruffled the sheets. "Twenty dead and eleven carried off to almost certain death on the east bank of the Susquehanna. Forty dead and nine carried off from Paxton. Fourteen dead, five missing near Reading. One hundred dead, thirty-four captured west of the Susquehanna. And the list goes on." He threw the papers back on his desk. "This is what you set loose at your Fort Duquesne. Does this news please you, Frenchman?"

Philippe looked away. His thoughts flew to the settlers he had helped to defend—Rosie with her kind, knowing smile. Tom with his hearty handshake and warm eyes, and Ashton, the son of the only real friend he'd ever had. Were they among those reported dead and captured? The possibility made Philippe's stomach roil. What would this Washington say if he knew that Philippe had fought alongside the English? What would he say if Philippe told him he had English friends?

"So you have no answer," Washington said.

Philippe rubbed his finger under his nose. "What is there to say? I have nothing to offer you for their relief."

"Would you, if you could?"

The question drove through Philippe like a spear thrown from above. He took a deep breath. "I would."

Washington rustled through the papers on his desk and pulled two from the pile. "I will let you see these. Then you tell me if they do not stir your memory of the days before the battle at Duquesne."

Philippe took the pages from his hand and looked at them.

> Sir, in the name of God, help us! We are in a dreadful situation. The Indians are cutting us off every day. At least 1,500 Indians, besides French, are on their march against us and Virginia, and now close on our borders their scouts are scalping our families on our frontiers daily.
> John Harris

The second letter was from Adam Hoops in Lancaster. He wrote in a bold, slanting script.

> We are in as bad circumstances as any poor Christians were ever in; for the cries of widowers, widows, fatherless and motherless children, are enough to pierce the hardest of heart. Likewise, it's a very sorrowful spectacle to see those that escaped with their lives, with not a mouthful to eat, or bed to lie on, or clothes to cover their nakedness, or

keep them warm, but all they had consumed into ashes. It is really very shocking for the husband to see the wife of his bosom with her head cut off and the children's blood drunk like water by these bloody and cruel savages. . . .

Philippe shivered and handed the letters back to Washington. "I am sorry. I did not realize."

Washington studied Philippe for a long moment. Then he spoke. "I was wrong about you. You are not the coward I first thought."

Philippe felt his face grow warm.

"Washington sighed. "But if you can't help us, then what shall I do with you? Send you back to your countrymen?"

Philippe ground his heel into the floor. "No, do not send me back." One thing he knew, he could not go back. He would be hanged or shot or worse.

"Take 'im out back and shoot 'im," muttered one of the men behind him. "Filthy Frenchie."

"Slimy traitor," mumbled the other.

Washington scowled. "Silence. We do not murder prisoners in cold blood. He may help us yet." He walked around the desk, sat, and again leaned back in the chair. "We believe there was treachery involved in the battle at Fort Duquesne. There is, we think, a traitor among us."

"No, not here."

Washington sat upright. "You do know something then."

Philippe let his gaze wander out the window. The horse was now grazing on the far side of the pasture. The dog was nowhere to be seen. "I can tell you only that the treachery comes not from the frontier but from England itself."

Washington nodded his head. "As I suspected," he whispered. "Enemies in England." He cleared his throat. "Then that is where I shall send you."

"What?"

"You'll go to England. There will be a trial. You will testify. Tell them whatever you will, as long as it's the truth."

"No. Do not send me to England."

"You said you wished to go to France. I can't send you there, but I can get you across the ocean."

Philippe groaned. England—the very heart of enemy territory. How would he ever get to France now? Nothing, it seemed, had gone right ever since he'd prayed.

Washington picked up a quill, dipped it in the inkwell, and wrote a quick note. He folded it and handed it to one of the men. "Take him to Captain Bradley. He should leave on the next ship." He turned back to Philippe. "Now you also are in the hands of God." He clapped Philippe on the shoulder. "Remember, He is our only sure trust." A small smile quirked his lips. "At least that's what my mother always said."

Trust God. The very thought made Philippe shudder. How could he trust a God who had led him directly into the hands of the enemy? How could he trust anyone who denied him the only thing he ever really wanted? "I just want to go home," he muttered. "Is that too much to ask?"

I will be your home. The words whispered through Philippe's mind and were gone.

～

Annie stumbled from her wigwam and headed down the worn path toward the creek. An empty bucket lay sideways on the grass. She stopped to right it. Three blackberries rolled in the bottom. Her hands shook. *White Flower.* There would be no more berry picking, no more wild flowers. Annie wrapped her arms around herself and squeezed. *Breathe. Don't think. You'll survive this.* The words spoke in her mind, but she didn't believe them.

She continued to the stream. There White Wolf squatted beside the water and scooped handfuls up to his mouth.

She stopped next to him. "Grey Owl died this morning."

"I know."

"He was blind at the end."

"Yes."

"I think Night Wind will live."

"Hmm."

Silence drifted between them. White Wolf brought another handful of water to his lips. Annie could feel her heart thudding in her chest. Quietly she waited. Finally he flicked the remnants of water from his hands and stared out over the stream's bank. "Is it true?" he asked.

She took a step backward. "What?"

"That you did this? Night Wind heard you say that you did." He spoke without turning.

Guilt flamed through her. Someone *had* been listening at the wigwam door. She dropped her gaze. "I didn't know—I thought . . ."

"So it is true." The disdain in his voice felt like a shard of glass in her heart. "You've taken your revenge at last." White Wolf stood and turned toward her.

Red spots covered his face.

TWENTY-SIX

~

Suffocating darkness swirled across White Wolf's vision and threatened to suck the breath from his lungs. He tried to shout, but only a groan issued from his throat. Desperately he clawed at the blanket covering him. It was hot, burning. Black flames like serpent's tongues licked over his flesh. He thrashed his head against the bedding and fought to focus on the dried corn that hung above him. For a moment he saw it clearly. Then the darkness came again, heavy and impenetrable. He felt himself falling deeper into the whirling night. Then he could no longer sense the bed beneath him, the blanket covering his chest, or the damp cloth over his forehead. He moaned and let himself slip further into delirium.

Disjointed images flashed across his mind. He saw his father opening a big black book and pointing to the page. Then his mother laughed and swung him up over her head. Kwelik joined them, with a ring of dandelions around her head. Behind him a dog barked. Suddenly the images faded into a cloud of grayness. Out of the cloud a man walked silently. In his hand burned a fire of bright blue.

White Wolf shrank back. Still the man came closer, until White Wolf found himself staring into dark, fathomless eyes that saw straight through him. Fear like he had never known gripped White Wolf. He tried to run, but his feet were rooted to the ground. The man stretched out his hand. The blue fire flared up, then dissolved into nothingness. Where it had burned, a scar marked the man's hand as if something had once punctured his flesh. Black eyes pierced White Wolf. He fell to his knees. Everything in him told him to look away, but he could not. The man stood over him. A voice like rumbling thunder rolled over him. "Come, follow Me."

White Wolf tore his gaze away. Then he could again see his family looking at him from out of the cloud. As he watched, his mother crumbled, his father fell with an arrow sticking from his chest, and flames licked up to devour Kwelik. "Save them! Do something!" he shrieked at the man.

"I have," the man replied. He turned over both palms. Twin scars throbbed deep red.

"It's not enough," White Wolf choked.

"Let go."

White Wolf looked down at his own hands and saw a writhing snake clenched in his fists. He tried to open his hands. He tried to drop it, but the snake's body wrapped around his wrists like iron shackles.

"Let go."

The snake twisted its head and bit White Wolf's arm. Fire shot through his veins.

"Trust Me. Let go."

"No!" White Wolf shouted. He could see the man's hands in front of him reaching for the snake. White Wolf pulled back. "Get away from me." He looked down. The snake glared up at him. He glared back into glittering eyes that changed before his vision, becoming darker, wider, until he was staring at a reflection of himself. White Wolf screamed. Someone was shaking him. A voice penetrated the darkness.

"Waptumewi, Waptumewi! Wake up! Come back!"

The vision faded. White Wolf opened his eyes to see Annie standing above him. He blinked and found himself trembling. He looked down at his wrists. Only red-speckled skin met his gaze. The snake was gone. Or was it? If he closed his eyes, he could still feel it there, cold and slippery, its grip growing ever tighter. Where was the man with the blue fire? Was he still watching him? White Wolf moaned.

Annie sat on the bed beside him. Quietly she removed the cloth from his forehead and replaced it with a cool one.

"Can you see him?" he murmured. "Is he still here?"

"Shhh."

White Wolf frowned. His head pounded, and the room spun

around him. A bead of sweat trickled into his eye. Annie's face swam before his vision. He tried to lift his hand to his cheek, but it continued to lie listlessly at his side. There was no man, he told himself. No man and no snake.

Annie brushed her fingers over his forehead. He attempted to focus on her eyes. The color of moss green danced before him. It occurred to him that there was a reason he should be angry with her, but he couldn't quite remember what it was.

She stood up and walked to the other side of the wigwam. He could hear her rustling around in the basket underneath her bed. Then he remembered. She had brought the sickness. The memory came back to him with a sense of bitter irony. So she would kill him after all, and the snake would devour him.

He supposed he deserved it, though the other villagers didn't. It was his fault too that they died. He had made Annie who she was. He should never have followed Taquachi. He should never have done so many things. But this was war, and she was the enemy.

And he remembered something else. She was also his wife. She, a white woman, his sworn adversary. The thought would make him laugh if he didn't feel so awful. Had so much changed since he had pledged vengeance against the white man? In all those years only he had paid the price for his hate—he and the woman he now called his wife. Of course, she refused to acknowledge the union. Yet they were married all the same. He should have detested the thought. But somehow he didn't. Somehow it seemed right.

Annie again leaned over him. Her face seemed pale. She pulled back the blanket and gently bathed his neck and chest with cool water. Her kindness troubled him. He missed her fiery spirit, the heated exchanges, the spark that never let him get away with deception. Was it only her guilt that had changed her? Or was it something more? If he were getting well, would she be so quiet, so gentle? Was he then on the brink of death? Was that the poison he felt coursing through his body? The thought made his breath come in short gasps.

"You're going to be all right," she murmured, her voice hushed as if he had already dipped partway to the spirit world. "You will get well, Waptumewi. You have to."

Yes, he had to. He had to fight the snake and the man who wanted to take it from him. Somehow he had to fight them all. He looked up at Annie with her copper-brown hair like a halo around her face, her cheeks flushed with concern. Did she know how beautiful she was? Did she know he would fight for her too?

Her face blurred before him, and he felt the darkness rush in on him again. This could be the last time he ever saw her.

"I—I . . ." The words died unspoken, and White Wolf slipped into the darkness.

∼

Jonathan tapped his foot briskly on the wooden floor. He drummed his fingers across his knee and shifted in his chair. The back rungs squeaked loudly. He stood and walked over to the open window.

One story below him a horse and carriage rumbled past. Jonathan watched as the driver rose from his seat and shouted at a dog that ran across his path. Jonathan sneezed. The noise of the city assaulted him like the steady buzz of a thousand bees ready to sting. The rattle of harnesses, the rat-tat-tat of trotting hooves over cobblestone, and the occasional bark of a mutt all combined to grind along his nerves and make him long for home. He yearned to hear the chirp of a bird, the quiet whisper of water over stone, or the sound of a soft breeze rustling through the leaves of an ash tree.

Jonathan sighed. In the distance he could just make out the waters of the Thames. A barge lumbered down its center. He watched it for a moment and then returned his gaze to the street beneath him. A man wearing a black coat turned the corner and strode down the sidewalk. Three women in brightly colored dresses burst from the milliner's shop down the way. Their voices, high and unintelligible, drifted up to him. Across the road the sound of a hammer banging against metal emanated from a shoemaker's shop. Jonathan glanced at the display of impractical pigskin slippers in the window and snorted. He took a deep breath and smelled the warm aroma of bread baking. A cat stalked from the door of the bakery and hissed at the women as they passed. He felt like hissing too, but instead he leaned against the window frame, closed his eyes, and tried to conjure a vision of the frontier.

Before he could do so, someone coughed behind him. He turned to see a thin man with glasses that sat precariously on his long nose. "The inspector general will see you now," the man squeaked. He stepped back from the door and motioned for Jonathan to enter.

Jonathan straightened his shirt and hurried through the door. Inside, the air was murky with pipe smoke. He rubbed his eyes and glanced at the man sitting behind an old desk, the man who had arrested his brother. Narrow-set eyes that seemed to miss nothing surveyed him. Slowly the man raised long fingers to remove the pipe from his lips. He twisted his mustache between his thumb and index finger as his gaze traveled up and down Jonathan's frame.

Jonathan looked around. Tattered books lined the walls, and crumpled papers littered the floor. Curtains, torn and ragged on the bottom, covered a small window to his right. The rug was worn, and the single chair had one arm missing. Only the carving of a galloping horse, beautifully wrought and perfectly polished, gave evidence to finer things. He strode closer until he stood directly in front of the desk. The horse sat inches from his hand. He flicked his fingers toward it. "That's a beautiful carving."

Inspector Higgins rose from his chair. "You're taller than I expected. Three-quarters of an inch taller, to be exact. As for the statue, I was a horse-lover as a child." He placed his pipe carefully in its holder and brushed a few stray ashes from his coat. "I can tell a gentleman's stallion from a dray at a mile away just from the sound of its hooves."

Jonathan placed his palms on the desk. The wood felt warm. "And are you as good at discerning the type of rider?"

"I am." The inspector stated the fact without a hint of boasting.

Jonathan leaned forward. "Like my brother?"

Higgins shrugged. "The crop gave him away." He tucked a stray strand of black hair beneath his wig. "Would you like to sit?" He motioned toward the stuffed chair in front of the desk.

"No. Thank you."

"I see you are not one for formalities." His deep brown eyes bored into Jonathan's. "Or pleasantries for that matter."

Jonathan inclined his head.

"Does the frontier cause this effect in all men?"

"In most."

Higgins turned his head and looked out the small window. "Ah, I should like to see the wilds of the New World someday. It must be a wonder to behold." He turned back and smiled so pleasantly that Jonathan felt himself relax. Slowly he lowered himself into the chair.

The inspector's smile broadened. "Would you care for a drink?" He picked up a decanter.

"No. I prefer my wits clear."

"As do I." He put the bottle away. "Now, about your brother."

"His case has not gone to trial."

"Not yet. But it will do so in precisely eighty-seven days."

"Three months. Why the delay?"

Higgins tugged at his mustache. "There is no delay. Sentencing will occur as scheduled."

Jonathan squared his shoulders. "He may not have committed this crime."

The inspector squinted. "As his brother, I would assume you would find him innocent, and yet you have hated Lord Grant for many years. He betrayed you and sent your mother back to Ireland. You escaped to the colonies to be rid of him." He tugged even harder at the hair on his upper lip. "So why now this change? Curious. Very curious."

Jonathan squirmed in his chair. "You know much about me."

"It's my job to know about everyone."

Jonathan grunted.

"Tell me, why do you think your brother is innocent?"

"I don't know that he is, but when I saw him, he spoke of treachery."

Higgins nodded. "And treachery is something your family knows all too well."

Jonathan scowled. This man knew more than he should, more than anyone ought to know about a stranger. "You're correct again."

"Of course." The inspector dropped his grip on his mustache and instead rubbed his hand over his chin. His eyes never left Jonathan's. "Now I'll tell you something. I have had my doubts as well."

Jonathan's eyebrows lifted. "You have?"

Higgins sat back in his chair. "Sometimes I think I've missed something. I've gone over it again and again in my mind. But for the crop . . ."

"May I see it?"

The inspector pulled the crop from his upper desk drawer and handed it to him.

Jonathan looked at it closely, examining the fine leather binding and the fiery lion's head insignia.

"Is that not your brother's?"

Jonathan handed the crop back to the inspector. "It is, but anyone could have carried it."

Inspector Higgins shook his head. "Not anyone—only a nobleman with access to your brother's stables and his horses."

"Are you sure it wasn't a woman?"

The inspector tapped his fingers on his desk. He waited a full ten seconds before answering. When he finally did, his voice was quiet. "I had not thought so, but it could be. Yet the rider had power in his swing. It would have been a strong woman."

"Why do you say so?"

Higgins pulled back his wig to reveal a half-moon scar at his hairline. "He gave me this."

"So you want revenge?"

Higgins chuckled. "No. Revenge is for fools. I only want justice."

"As do I."

"Then we shall help one another."

"How?"

"By finding out who wants you dead."

"What?"

Higgins tapped his fingers on the desk. "Someone, sir, kidnapped your son. Yes, yes," he waved his hand at Jonathan, "I know all about that too. I also know that your son has been returned to you. Therefore, since the kidnapper's scheme has failed, it's only logical that he will come after you next."

"After me? Are you sure?"

"This is not, I suppose, the first time someone has sought your death?"

Jonathan drew in a quick breath. "No, but that time it was . . ."

"Richard. Precisely."

"It can't be happening again." His mind flew back to the confrontation on the ship to England. He had almost died then. Could someone have been planning to harm him ever since he left the colonies? It didn't seem possible, and yet . . .

"It can, and I suspect that it is." Higgins gave his mustache one firm tug. "Soon, I imagine, you will meet with an unfortunate accident."

Jonathan tightened his jaw. "Unless we act first."

"Indeed, we must act. But in due time. Nothing shall be gained through haste."

For one breath Jonathan paused. Then he nodded. "If there is someone who seeks my death, how shall we uncover him?"

"Or her." Higgins smiled. "I will surely need your help."

Jonathan crossed his arms. "What must I do?"

Inspector General Higgins folded his hands and leaned forward in his chair. His eyes glittered. "Methinks you will have to die."

Jonathan's blood ran cold.

TWENTY-SEVEN

~

For Annie time passed like a caterpillar creeping over a dry leaf—inch by inch, moment by moment, with death surrounding her on every side. For a while she thought White Wolf would die too. Yet despite his raging fever and the pus that oozed from his sores, each day he seemed to grow stronger. As he did, five more villagers died of the pox, two could no longer see, and a few still hung in the balance between this world and the next. Annie had all she could do to feed them, care for those who would let her near them, and burn the dead. Tewea and his war band had never returned. Nor would they, she assumed, if word of the sickness reached them.

Most days she spent in the wigwam caring for White Wolf or walking silently in the woods hunting for herbs and rabbits and praying for a forgiveness that she didn't think would ever come. Sometimes as the sunlight drizzled through red and orange leaves overhead, she felt God near her, as if He were walking there beside her. But then she would remember her sin and remind herself that she had forever closed the door on His love. She had thought revenge would make her free, but now she could feel the chains of guilt on her heart as heavily as if they were made of real iron. She knew that she had placed them there herself, locked them with her own hate, destroyed the key with her own refusal to forgive. There was nothing she could do but attempt to make up for her sin.

Now, two weeks after White Wolf first fell sick, she wondered if she'd ever get a chance to atone. Water from the creek sloshed out of the bucket in her hand and dropped onto her feet. She stepped into the wigwam and closed the flap behind her. Then she walked over and began to pour water into the basin by the bed, but something stopped her. Her gaze flew to the bed. White Wolf was not there. She gasped and straightened.

"Don't fear. I didn't vanish into the air," came a voice from behind her.

She turned. White Wolf stood there, wearing clean buckskin pants and moccasins. Three eagle feathers hung in his hair, and a tomahawk was tied at his waist. "What are you doing?" she sputtered.

He motioned toward a bearskin bag at his feet. "I'm preparing to fulfill my promise."

Annie lowered the bucket, not caring if the water spilled. "You're not planning on leaving, are you?"

He reached up, pulled two ears of dried corn from a hook on the ceiling, and placed them in the bag. "Yes. I'm going to the coast to find Philippe."

Her stomach dropped. "You're not well enough."

"I am." He placed a small yellow squash in the bag.

"What about the others?"

He continued to place items in the sack as he answered. "I've spoken with Little Turtle. They will stay until the sick ones have died or become strong again. Then they will travel west to join his sister's village on the other side of the great river. As for me, I plan to leave today as soon as I'm ready."

"Without me?" Her voice was scarcely above a whisper.

White Wolf stopped his packing. "You would go with me?" For a moment she thought she saw hope dash through his eyes. Then he looked back down at the bag. "You'll want to go back to the white man's settlement."

Annie lowered herself to the edge of the bed. "Don't you want to go back too?"

"Why should I?"

His eyes seemed to be studying her, probing her intentions. Did he think she was asking for her own sake? Was she? The thought scared her. She clenched her hands in her lap and looked away. "What about Tankawon, your son?"

Annie heard the rustle of corn husks as White Wolf shoved another item into his sack. "The boy does not need a father like me."

The tremor in his voice made Annie look up at him. When she did, she could have sworn she saw fear in his face. A grown man afraid of his own son, a boy less than ten summers old? It seemed impossible. Yet maybe it was not the child he feared, but the past that the boy represented. That she could understand all too well.

Before she could fully examine the thought, White Wolf sat on the bed beside her. His fingers toyed with a piece of fuzz on his pant leg. "I haven't done much right in my life," he admitted. "When decisions have come to me, I've chosen poorly. But this time I want to do what's right. I want to keep my word to a friend."

"He's probably gone by now. He could already be halfway to France."

"I hope he is, but I'll go anyway. I'll look for him in case he has lost his way."

Annie twisted her fingers together. "Why must you?"

"He's my friend."

She nodded. People like her and White Wolf didn't have many friends. But Philippe had been one to both of them. "How will we find him?"

"We?"

"We," she stated firmly.

"Are you certain?"

She crossed her arms. "I can't let you go tromping off to the coast half sick and hardly healed from the pox, can I?"

White Wolf rested his arm on one knee. "Ah, so you *are* afraid for me after all." His tone held gentle mockery. "And all this time I thought you wanted me dead."

His words pierced her. "Don't say that, Waptumewi. Don't ever say that. You know I . . . I . . ." She couldn't finish the sentence.

He leaned closer. "I know. I'm sorry. If not for your kind care, I wouldn't be sitting here."

"It's my fault you were sick in the first place." Bitterness laced her voice.

"Yes. But I'm well now."

He shifted, and his arm brushed her shoulder. She smelled the scent of new leather and felt his breath on her cheek. His nearness made her heart beat faster. For weeks she had slept in the same wig-wam with him, fed him his meals, bathed him with cool rags. But this was different. He was no longer helpless, no longer weak. She cleared her throat and moved back. "How will we travel? It will take a month to get to the coast on foot."

"I have two horses."

"Two?" She raised an eyebrow.

White Wolf smiled. "Little Turtle agreed to give me the second one if I promised to take you away."

She snorted. "After I made his rabbit stew just the way he likes it too!"

"I don't think it was the stew he was complaining about."

She sighed. "I know. I don't blame them for wishing me gone."

White Wolf put his hand gently on her arm. His touch felt warm and comforting. "My father always said that hate is the heaviest bur-den we will ever carry." He shook his head. "But I've found regret to be even heavier." He removed his hand and stood. Then he folded a blanket and bent over to put it in the bag.

Annie lifted her hand toward him. "No, don't take that."

He paused. "What? Why?"

Her voice shook. "No blankets, please. I can't bear it."

Slowly he nodded. "So that is how the sickness came to us. I had wondered."

She lowered her head until she was looking at the ground.

Then she felt his fingers beneath her chin. He lifted her face toward him. "Let us no longer dwell on what has gone on before. We can't change the past. Come, let us find Philippe and help him go home to France." He looked down at her for a moment. Then he dropped his hand.

She sniffed and wiped her fingers over her cheek. Then she rose, turned, and picked up a small copper pot from beneath the bed. "Okay, let's do it. Together." She glanced over her shoulder at White Wolf behind her. A wisp of her old stubbornness stiffened her spine. "But this doesn't mean I'm your wife, Waptumewi. Don't forget that."

White Wolf grinned. "Of course not."

Annie smiled and shoved the pot into the bag.

～

It was time. Moonlight shimmered through the bedroom window and cast shadows over the wall. Jonathan pulled back the blanket and sat up in bed. Kwelik lay beside him, her lashes dark against her cheeks. He smiled and touched his fingers to her hair. It felt silky beneath his touch. She sighed and snuggled closer.

Jonathan stretched his arms over his head and rose. Silently he slipped into his shirt and breeches and pulled on his boots. Then he leaned over Kwelik and kissed her gently on the forehead. Her eyes fluttered open. "Get ready," he whispered.

"We're going now?" Her voice was as quiet as a butterfly's flight. She pushed herself up and swung her legs over the side of the bed. Then she dressed as quickly as he had. "I can't say that I'll miss this place," she whispered.

He smiled at her. "I should have done this sooner. We shouldn't have stayed even a day in this wretched mansion, especially after what happened to Justin."

"We'll be safe now with the inspector."

He hoped so. He wished he could be sure. Tonight's escape was only phase one of Inspector Higgins's questionable plan. This was the easy part, hiding his family away from those who might harm them. Being separated from them would be difficult. Even now he wished he were taking them back home to the frontier instead of sending them into hiding.

Jonathan walked to the adjoining door and quietly pulled it open. He stepped inside the small room where Justin slept and leaned over the bed. "Son, wake up. It's time to go."

Justin woke with a wide yawn. He threw off his blankets, and Jonathan saw that he was already fully clothed. Justin stood up and rubbed his eyes. Then he grinned and pointed at the shoes on his feet. "See, Papa, I'm all ready."

Jonathan ruffled his hair and smiled down at him. "Come. Quietly now. We mustn't make a sound."

"This is a real adventure, isn't it?" Justin whispered loudly.

"Shhh. Yes, son." Jonathan rested his hand on the boy's shoulder and directed him back into the main bedroom.

"Why can't Kat come too?" he asked.

Jonathan frowned. "I've told you. No one must know. No one."

"Kat won't tell."

"No one. Not even Katherine."

Justin sighed.

Kwelik turned toward them as they entered the room. She had a bag over one shoulder, and Brenna was still asleep in her arms. "We're ready," she whispered.

Jonathan nodded. "Come, let's pray. Then we'll go."

They knelt together in a circle and held hands, with Justin's left fingers just touching his sister's foot. Jonathan closed his eyes and began, "Father, we thank Thee for guiding our path, and we pray Thee to go with us tonight. Protect us, O Lord, and help us. Save us from our enemies." The prayer came easily to his lips, and yet his heart felt heavy, and God seemed distant. *First be reconciled to thy brother . . .* The words echoed in his mind. He mumbled a quick "amen." He was doing what was right. So why did it matter if he still harbored anger in his heart?

It matters, came the silent answer.

Jonathan dropped Kwelik's hand and stood. What more could he do? He'd come to England, stayed in this place he hated, spoken to his brother not once but twice, and almost lost his son. Now he had to hide his family. And for what? To help Richard because God wanted him to. Did he really have to forgive him too? Did he really have to forget everything that had gone on before?

He threw a satchel over his shoulder and eased Brenna from Kwelik's arms. The baby cooed and nuzzled into his chest. He motioned toward Kwelik. She nodded and slipped out the door with Justin just behind her. Jonathan followed. Quietly they tiptoed down the stairs. At the bottom a floorboard creaked beneath Justin's foot. Jonathan paused. Had anyone heard them?

Silence met his waiting ears. He let out his breath and hurried toward the front door. Outside, gravel crunched under their feet as they rushed down the path toward the waiting carriage. A driver in a dark coat sat atop the seat. In a moment they would be safe. Just a few more steps. Jonathan quickened his pace.

Before they could reach the carriage, a light glimmered from the garden gazebo. Jonathan stopped. There in the enclosure a woman's face was illuminated by a soft ring of candlelight. Jonathan could not make out her features, but he could tell she was watching them. He drew Brenna closer to his chest. For one breath he thought he saw the woman raise her hand toward him. Then the candle flickered out, and she was lost to his sight.

In moments they reached the carriage, climbed in, and closed the door. Jonathan heard the quiet slap of the reins, and the horse pulled away. He looked out the window, watching as the moon-bathed mansion shrank before his view. Just as it disappeared from sight, a cloud passed over the moon. Darkness fell over the landscape like a shroud. For that brief instant Jonathan felt safe at last.

∼

Katherine couldn't sleep. Something was wrong. She could feel it in the air. She held her breath and listened. Was that the creak of a floorboard downstairs? Was that the quiet whoosh of the front door opening? She shivered and hid her head beneath the covers. She counted to ten twice.

No other sound met her ears. She peeked from beneath the blankets. This was no time to be afraid, she told herself. She had to be brave. With one hand she pulled back the covers. Then she slipped from the bed and crept toward the window. Outside, she could see the shadows of three people rushing down the path.

She placed her hand on the windowpane. "Good-bye," she mouthed and leaned her forehead against the glass. She would miss Justin, Uncle Jonathan, Aunt Kwelik, and the baby. They had been kind to her. But she understood why they had to go. Things weren't right anymore—not with that awful man coming late at night and Mama paying him all that money. Not with Mama jumping at every stray noise. And not with that funny man sneaking around, pulling at his mustache all the time. Something was going on, something bad. If only she could find out what, maybe Uncle Jonathan and his family could come back again.

But one thing she was sure of: Justin wasn't lying about someone chasing him to the well. Yesterday she'd found proof—a black cape hidden beneath the floorboards in the stable, a cape that smelled like lavender perfume.

PART THREE

Behold, the Light

~

TWENTY-EIGHT

~

Eastern seacoast, Hampton, Virginia, October 1755

He hadn't thought it would be so vast. Azure waves, tipped with white, stretched to the end of world and disappeared into the bright horizon. Only a few tall-masted ships, dark against the sunrise, dotted the expanse. A breeze blew in from the ocean and ruffled the feathers in White Wolf's hair. He lifted his head and took a deep breath. The scent of salt water mixed with rotting fish nearly made him gag.

"It looks like it goes on forever." Annie echoed his thoughts.

He glanced at her standing there beside him with the wind tossing her curls across her face and the new day's sun making her skin appear golden.

"I suppose I thought we could look across and see France for ourselves."

"Kwelik's over there somewhere." His gaze returned to the water.

"I miss her too." Annie's voice was quiet.

Above, a seagull swooped across the sky and squawked petulantly to the waves. White Wolf sighed. "Sometimes I think if I could just see her again, everything would be okay. Somehow I would find my way back to how things used to be before . . . before . . ."

"Before we lost our way."

"Before I tasted evil." As he said it, he saw Annie tremble. How different she seemed lately, as if she carried a weight too heavy to bear. Still, sometimes he saw the spark that made her unique. But now there was a quietness too, a pain that went even deeper than loss. And because of it, he found that he understood her. Somewhere in the darkness of pain and guilt she had dropped the anger that had protected her for so long. And now they walked in the shadows together, each searching for the light, each knowing that freedom would only come with a miracle. He touched her arm and motioned down the hill. "Come, let's go down to the docks."

Together they walked down the long street, through the alleys, between old, ramshackle buildings, and out to a skinny pier that stretched over the water. There White Wolf paused and leaned against a wooden pillar. Beneath his feet the planks creaked and groaned.

"There's another ship carrying Frenchmen from Acadia." Annie pointed to a dilapidated vessel just turning into the harbor. "Some say they've already deported thousands."

"Thirty ships so far, I heard. We'll never find Philippe with all these French-speaking Acadians around."

"He's gone already. He has to be."

White Wolf crossed his arms over his chest. "But how can we know for sure?"

"I bet Captain Bradley's ship sailed weeks ago."

"How do we even know that Philippe was on that ship?"

From the corner of his vision, he could see Annie's brows draw together in a familiar frown. "Chadwell heard it from Colonel Washington himself."

White Wolf grunted. "Still, I wish we could be certain."

From behind them the clang of a bucket interrupted their conversation. White Wolf turned.

An old sailor hobbled up the pier toward them. His feet were bare, and his shirt was so worn that it looked more like a fish net than a man's garb. He began to whistle a jaunty tune that matched the cadence of his steps. He swung the bucket in time with the song. When he was ten feet from them, he looked up. His gaze fell on White Wolf. He stopped short. His lips froze in mid-whistle. "Yeee-iiii, it be a heathen savage from the wilds." He dropped the bucket.

Annie stepped in front of White Wolf. "It's okay, good sir." She raised her voice over the sailor's continued cries. "He's a civilized savage." She glanced back and whispered a low "sorry" under her breath.

The sailor shifted his corncob pipe to the other side of his mouth without using his hands. "Civilized, ye say?" He squinted at White Wolf with one eye.

Annie stepped back beside White Wolf and jabbed him in the ribs with her elbow. "Say something in English," she hissed.

White Wolf stuck out his hand in the gesture he knew was the white man's greeting. "Pleased to make your acquaintance, sir."

The man stared at White Wolf's hand, then edged forward, and tentatively stretched out his own. White Wolf had barely taken it when the man snatched it back. "Shakin' hands with a savage. What's become o' me?" His shoulders shook with disdain.

White Wolf bristled and stepped forward. His fists clenched. Before he could continue, Annie trod on his foot. "Don't," she muttered behind a smile too sweet to be real.

White Wolf stopped. Annie again moved in front of him, and from the tone of her voice, he could tell she was still wearing a false smile. "Pardon us, kind sir. This is our first visit to Hampton, and we were wondering if you might have news of a friend of ours."

No! White Wolf gritted his teeth and glared at the back of Annie's head. *Don't tell him we're friends with a Frenchman.*

"What friend?" The old sailor cocked his head to one side and removed the pipe from his lips.

White Wolf held his breath.

"Captain Bradley," Annie answered.

White Wolf released his breath in a quiet whoosh.

The sailor reached over and picked up his bucket. "Bradley's ship left near a month ago."

"Oh, thank you." Annie touched her fingers to her hair and started to turn back to White Wolf. As soon as her face was hidden from the sailor's view, she winked. White Wolf felt his muscles relax.

Annie looked over her shoulder. "By the way, I don't suppose you know if the captain carried a Frenchman on board? Rumor has it that he did."

The sailor scratched his head with one hand. "Aye, I believe so. Takin' him over for some big trial in England, I heard."

England? The word sent a chill of foreboding over White Wolf's skin.

"Oooh, that sounds very exciting. I'm sure the captain will tell us all about it when he returns," Annie giggled. She put her hand on White Wolf's forearm and began to lead him down the pier. "Thank you, Mr. Sailor," she called as they hurried past him.

A lilting whistle floated back to them as they stepped off the pier and turned a corner. Immediately Annie dropped her grip on his arm. "Whew, that was close," she muttered.

White Wolf frowned. "What were you doing back there?"

"Keeping us out of trouble and getting a little information."

"I could have protected us from one old man," he growled. "There was no need to be afraid of him."

"Not him but the others that might have come running if he'd put up a shout. The sailors around here don't have a reputation for kindness. It's best if we stay out of their way." She slapped her hands together and motioned away from the docks. "Come on, let's go back to the inn." She started in that direction.

White Wolf didn't move. "I'm a warrior, remember?"

Annie turned back and put her hands on her hips. "A barely-recovered-from-the-pox warrior, you mean. You aren't as strong yet as you were before." She wagged a finger at him. "Don't forget that."

"I'm not a sick old man halfway to the grave," he mumbled.

She looked at him for a long moment. "No, you're not."

Something about the way she said it made him stop his arguing. He looked back at her. "What do we do now?" He meant so much by the question. Now that Philippe was gone, would they too go their separate ways? Would she return to the settlement and he to wandering the wilds? Would they say their good-byes and go back to their own worlds? Would he try to stop her if she did?

"We should have breakfast, I think," came her reply. "I saw a market a couple streets down from here."

White Wolf nodded. Had she chosen to ignore the deeper meaning of his question? Was she reluctant to face it too?

"I'll go get us something. You head back to the inn. I'll meet you there in a few minutes."

"You'll be okay alone?"

"I think I'll have better luck alone than with a 'heathen savage' in tow." She smiled.

White Wolf rolled his eyes. "Go, woman. And quickly."

Still smiling, she turned and disappeared between buildings.

White Wolf headed away from the docks and toward the main street. Two tall wooden buildings rose on either side of the alleyway. A few wooden crates lined the outer walls. A cat slunk across his path, pausing only briefly to stare at him before it scooted behind a stack of broken boxes. A cold breeze swirled through the alley and caused a chill to race across his skin. He rubbed his hands over his arms and shivered. Behind him he heard a crate crash to the ground. He turned.

Four men stepped into the alley. Two were large and burly. Another sported a black eye patch, while the fourth held a short wooden plank in his right hand. Behind them the old sailor peeked around the corner. "That's him," he called and then ducked out of sight.

White Wolf crept backward. The men advanced.

"Well, well, what 'ave we here, men?" crowed the man with the eye patch.

"Methinks it's a poor savage who's lost his way, Patch," replied one of the big men.

"Yer a mighty long way from home, savage," piped up the man with the plank. He slapped it twice in his opposite palm and grinned.

White Wolf's hand traveled toward his tomahawk.

"Careful there, Injun," muttered Patch. He pulled a long knife from his waistband and twirled it in his hand. Then he moved closer. "What do ya think, boys—is fortune smilin' on us today?"

"Cap'n will pay us extra for this one."

White Wolf pulled the tomahawk from its holder and brandished it before them.

Patch shook his head. "I dunno. He looks kinda weak. Don't know if he'd even make the journey."

"Aw, wouldn't that be a shame," cooed the man with the plank. "One less devil with a tomahawk. Let's get him, boys."

White Wolf crouched down in a fighting position

Patch threw back his head. "Ha, ha," he roared. "The savage thinks he can take on all of us."

"Watch out. Them savages are crafty beasts. The last one nearly bit Brodie's finger clean through."

The plank thumped twice on the dirt, and the man smirked as White Wolf jumped. "We ain't got nuthin' to worry about, boys. He'll come along nice and quiet. Just needs a little convincin', that's all." He banged the plank again.

White Wolf's palms grew sweaty. His heart beat faster. There were too many for him. He glanced around. Nothing but crates and solid walls met his gaze. He whirled and tried to sprint toward the main street. Before he took three steps, they were upon him. A hand shoved into his back. He fell to the ground. Quickly he regained his feet.

Now the men encircled him. Eyes black as soot stared at him. One man grinned. A glint of gold shone from his mouth. "Come quiet, and we won't have to 'urt ya," he warned. The circle grew tighter.

White Wolf leaped at Patch. A hand, hot and hard, clamped onto his arm. Foul breath blew across his cheek. Steel flashed in the morning sun. He flailed with his tomahawk. It glanced off the man's shoulder. A streak of red splattered across his arm. Someone hooted.

Patch stumbled backward.

White Wolf tried to twist and escape, but in his weakness the maneuver failed. Annie had been right. He was not strong enough. He gripped the tomahawk tighter.

Patch advanced again. "Come on, savage," he muttered. "Show us what you've got."

White Wolf crouched lower. Patch flipped his knife from one hand to the other. Before White Wolf could move, something crashed down on the back of his head. *The plank,* he thought as he fell to the ground. His vision blurred. Nausea turned his stomach. He struggled to rise but could not. Somewhere, as if from across the sea, he heard a man laugh.

Hands gripped him beneath his arms and pulled him to his feet. "This'll make four savages," one of the men called. "Fetch a mighty good price back home. Lord Trembley paid a 'undred pounds for the last ones."

White Wolf's arms were wrenched behind him. The ground seemed to sway under his feet.

"Don't know what he wants 'em for," came another voice that White Wolf recognized as the man who had wielded the plank.

"Servants."

Patch hooted. "To show off, more likely. Mighty braggart is that Trembley. Tellin' the wimmin that he's tamed them hisself. Big fool. One of these days a savage will slit 'is throat."

"Might be this one. Never know," a big man muttered.

"Naw. He ain't got it in 'im. English fog'll finish 'im if the sharks don't get 'im first." Patch spat on White Wolf's foot. The men laughed.

Understanding penetrated White Wolf's haze. *England.* He was going to England. Horror swelled within him—and then was lost in a wave of darkness that swallowed even his fear.

TWENTY-NINE

~

Annie turned the corner just as White Wolf hit the ground. She looked at the four men surrounding him and slipped back out of sight. She couldn't confront them alone, but she could listen and figure out a way to get White Wolf out of their grip.

Voices drifted over her—talk of a Lord Trembley, payment, and English fog. She shuddered at their plan. Sneaking Indians to England? Savage servants? She had never heard of such a thing. She peeked around the corner to see White Wolf being dragged toward the docks. His head lolled to one side, and a small trickle of blood stained his temple. Quietly she followed them, being sure to remain out of sight.

The men dumped White Wolf into a small rowboat, climbed in after him, and began to row toward a masted ship anchored halfway out in the harbor. She watched until the men reached the ship and hauled White Wolf aboard. Then all of them disappeared from view.

Over the next few hours Annie sat on a crate and formulated a plan. Finally two sailors rumbled toward her. She jumped from the box and straightened her skirts. "Pardon me, kind sirs."

The sailors halted. One of them, with a red face and rotted buckteeth, leered at her. "I'll pardon ya all night, little missy."

The other sailor jostled him with his elbow. "Shut up, Brodie. That ain't no way to talk to a lady."

Brodie scratched his groin and spat. "She ain't no lady, Jiggs."

Annie reached for the knife hidden in her skirt. Her fingers closed around the bone handle.

The sailor called Jiggs scowled at his partner. "My mama taught me that all wimmin is ladies."

Brodie scoffed. "Your mama was a—"

Jiggs smashed him in the mouth with his fist. "Shut up, I told ya," he shouted.

Brodie stumbled backward, wiped his hand across his lips, and stared at the red streak across his knuckles. "Aw, now why did ya go and do that for, Jiggs?"

Annie loosened her grip on the knife.

Jiggs rolled up the sleeve on his left arm. "Don't you be talking about my mama," he warned, "or I'll do it again."

Brodie sniffed. "I didn't say nothin'." He turned away.

Jiggs looked at Annie and carefully removed his worn hat. "Sorry 'bout that, ma'am. Now what can we be doin' fer ya?"

Annie put on her most sophisticated smile and pointed toward the ship in the harbor. "I need to get over to that ship. Would you be traveling that way?"

Brodie guffawed and punched Jiggs lightly in the shoulder. "Told ya," he said. His breath smelled of liquor. "She's a . . ."

Jiggs clenched his fist and raised it. Brodie stepped back. While they stared at one another, Annie removed her knife. She rubbed her thumb over the handle. She glared at Brodie and slowly lifted the blade. His eyes widened as he saw it.

"You would be wise to hold your tongue," she warned, "lest you lose it altogether."

The Adam's apple in Brodie's neck bobbed. He didn't say another word.

Annie turned toward Jiggs. "Now, Mr. Jiggs, would you be headed toward that ship?"

Jiggs looked from her to the knife and back again. "Aye."

"Good. Would you be so kind as to take me with you? I have business with the captain."

He lifted his hands to his shoulders in a gesture of surrender. "I'll take ya anywhere ya wish, missy. Just put that knife away now like a good girl."

Annie flicked the tip toward Brodie. "Leave him here, and I'll be happy to."

Jiggs glanced at Brodie. "I'll come back and get ya," he muttered.

Then he swept his arm toward a boat tied to the pier. "After you, Milady."

Annie raised her chin and replaced the knife. Then she walked over and stepped into the boat. Jiggs followed. The boat tipped left and then right as he got in beside her. She shifted to maintain her balance. Then he untied the rope, threw it to the middle of the boat, and grabbed the oars. Annie listened to the thwack of wood against water as Jiggs settled into a rhythm. Within minutes they reached the ship.

Jiggs guided the boat to the side of the ship and grabbed a rope ladder that hung there. He handed the bottom rung to Annie. She took the wet, slimy thing in her hand and gave it a tug.

"Well, climb on up." He motioned toward the top of the ship.

She looked up. Three men peered over the edge at her. She frowned, gripped the rope, and put her foot on the bottom rung. Then she thought better of it. "You first." She handed the ladder to Jiggs.

He laughed. "Whatever you say, ma'am." He threw the boat's rope up to his mates, took the ladder from her, and climbed up nimbly.

It took her twice as long to reach the top. *Rope ladders*, she decided, *weren't made for climbing with skirts.* When she reached the ship's railing, arms reached down and hauled her over the edge. She landed in an unseemly heap at Jiggs's feet. Quickly she caught her breath and scrambled upright.

The sailors grinned at her.

She straightened her shoulders and smoothed her dress with one hand. "I wish to speak to your captain," she announced in a voice that she hoped was dignified.

A snicker sounded behind her. She spun around but could not tell which one of them had laughed.

A sailor with a patch over one eye stepped forward. "Sure thing, missy," he said. "I'll take ya to 'im. Jus' follow me."

"Thank you, sir," she said.

He led her below deck to the captain's cabin, a cramped little room with a cot on one side and a large desk in the center. Maps were tacked to the walls, and above them two lanterns sputtered and threw shadows over the figure standing behind the desk. The man was leaning over and studying what appeared to be a star chart. "But for an accurate timepiece," he muttered to himself.

The sailor cleared his throat.

The captain glanced up. His eyebrows raised as he noticed Annie. He straightened. "What's this, Patch?"

The sailor pushed Annie forward. "This woman says she's got business with ya, Cap'n."

The captain stepped around the desk. His eyes flicked up and down her frame, missing nothing. "Do I know you, miss?"

Annie felt herself swaying with the ship. She attempted to steady herself, but her legs felt like jelly beneath her. "Not yet, Captain," she answered. "My name is Annie Hill."

The captain bowed slightly. "Welcome, Miss Hill. I'd offer you a seat, but as you see, I don't have a spare one. So how can I be of service?"

Annie took a shaky step forward. "I understand that you have some Indians aboard."

"Ah, do you now?" He returned to his place behind the desk and tapped his fingers over the star chart. "And how is that any business of yours, may I ask?"

She took a long breath and tried to choose her words carefully. "It's not my business that concerns me, Captain, but yours, and how you may increase your profits."

The captain sat down, folded his hands under his chin, and placed his forefingers beneath his nose. "I'm listening."

"I've come to offer you my assistance." The ship pitched to the right, and Annie stumbled forward.

The captain chuckled. "And what assistance do you perceive that I need?"

She bent her knees slightly to help maintain her balance. "Your men say that these Indians are to be sold as servants."

"Perhaps." His eyes gave away nothing.

"A servant who speaks his master's language and is trained in the niceties of culture would be of much greater value, don't you think?"

He nodded.

Annie continued. "But you, as captain, don't have time to teach them such things. And your men . . ." Her gaze flickered over to Patch and back to the captain. "Need I say more?"

The captain smiled. "And so you propose?"

"I'll teach them and care for them as well. I'm fluent in the Algonquin tongue."

"How do I know you speak the truth?"

"*Wapanisham nillawi wemiwi olini.*"

"What did you say?"

"Leaving eastward, they crossed all together."

"Nicely said. What's your price?"

"Only the cost of my fare and food for the journey. I've always wanted to go to England."

The captain rolled up his star chart and placed it in a holder beside his desk. "I have no extra cabins."

"Surely there's room for a cot somewhere."

He shook his head. "Only down with the savages."

Annie nodded. "That will suffice."

"It's no place for a lady." A hint of mockery colored his tone.

"A lady makes sacrifices to obtain her goals," she retorted. "Now do we have an agreement?"

"Can you guarantee that they will be able to understand English by the time we arrive in Dover?"

"I can."

"Then it's done. I'll take you to England, and you'll teach and take care of the savages." He turned toward the sailor. "Patch, take her down to see her charges. Mayhaps after one look she'll change her mind."

"I will not, sir. I'm not afraid."

"Perhaps you should be."

Annie exited the cabin behind Patch. He stomped down a darkened corridor, opened a hatch, and pointed to a rickety ladder. "You go down there," he ordered.

"You first," she replied.

"I ain't got time to escort no fool wimmin who don't know how ta stay home and do what they're told. So go on now. When ya get to the bottom of the ladder, turn left, and you'll see another 'atch. Open it and go down. Keep goin' till ya can't go no further into the

ship's belly. Bones'll be there waitin' fer ya. He'll open the door and
let ya in."

Annie followed his directions, descending into the cold, damp
center of the ship, past barrels of foul-smelling water, past bales of
musty straw. Finally she could go no further, and there, as promised,
a skinny sailor sat on a barrel and whittled a stick with his knife.

Annie approached him. "Excuse me, sir. The captain sent me to
see the Indians."

He looked up. "Who be you? An angel sent to torture poor men's
souls?" His voice was high and squeaky.

"I'm Miss Hill. I'm here to see the Indians," she said in a louder
voice.

"The Injuns, you say?" He put a hand to one ear.

She leaned closer. "Patch said you'd open the door for me," she
nearly shouted.

"Patch sent ya? Why didn't ya say so?" He removed a set of keys
from his belt and flipped through them until he found the right one.
He slipped it in the door's lock, turned it, and pushed open the door.
"Here they are, missy. Though this ain't no sight fer a woman. Ya sure
ya want ta go in there now?"

"I'm sure," she hollered.

"Then come on." He pulled the door open wider and hobbled
down three short steps into the darkness. "Watch yer head now. Low
ceiling."

Annie ducked her head and followed after him. She heard a low
hissing sound. Then a flame sputtered to life. Bones lit a lantern, and
light flooded the tiny room. Along the walls four Indians sat with
chains around their wrists and ankles. Her eyes flew to White Wolf.
He looked up at her, and she could see a bruise discoloring his cheek.
Quickly she put her finger to her lips. Understanding flashed through
his eyes before he lowered his gaze to the floor.

Bones tottered over to an older Indian whose eyes were closed.
"Wake up, ya red devil," he shouted and kicked the man. "Got someone here to see ya." He turned toward the young boy shackled next
to him. "You behave, ya hear. Don't scare the pretty lady, or you'll
be sorry."

"*Nakowa*," hissed a middle-aged Indian woman from the other side of the room. Annie glanced at her. The woman's eyes narrowed. "*Makowini*." She spat on the floor.

Bones hurried toward her.

"No, stop," Annie sputtered, but Bones didn't hear.

He slapped the woman's face. The sound echoed in the small enclosure. The woman squealed.

Annie grabbed Bones's arm and forced him to look at her. From the corner of her eye, she saw White Wolf strain at his bonds. "I'm here to take care of them. Go on now, and leave them to me."

Bones wrenched his arm free of her grasp. "That's crazy talk."

"Captain's orders," she yelled.

Bones's eyebrows bunched in a look of confusion. Then he shrugged his shoulders. "Whatever ya say. Not like I envy ya the job." He headed toward the door. "I'm goin' 'bove deck. Come on up if ya need anything." He pulled the key from the ring and tossed it toward her.

She caught it in midair.

"Lock the door when yer done." He climbed the stairs and left the room.

Annie listened as his footsteps faded down the corridor. Then she hurried toward White Wolf and knelt beside him.

"You came," he whispered.

"I had to." She picked up his chain and studied the lock on it.

"It's too dangerous. You should not have risked it."

"You're welcome." She smiled up at him.

He made a sound low in his throat. "You did, at least, remember your knife?"

She pulled it from her dress. "Of course."

"Try it in the lock."

She placed the tip in the keyhole and wiggled it around. Nothing happened. She kept trying, but still the lock held firm. Finally she threw the knife on the floor and groaned. "It's no use. I need the key."

"It's kept in the captain's office," came a voice from behind her. She turned to see the old man looking at her through slitted eyes.

He did not move. He did not even blink.

"She will not help us. She is a white woman," hissed the woman from the corner.

"Silence!" White Wolf's voice was hard.

"I'll help you," Annie stated in Algonquin. "I'll get you out of here, all of you." Her gaze traveled from the old man with his eyes half-lidded, to the boy huddled beside him, to the woman staring at her with features as cold as stone. "Tonight I'll get the keys, free you, and we'll all swim to shore." She reached down, picked up her knife, and returned it to its hiding place.

"I—I don't know how to swim," the boy stuttered.

Annie scooted over to him and placed her hand on his hair. He regarded her with wide eyes. "We'll help you. Don't worry," she assured him. "Tonight you'll be free again."

"Then I can go home?"

His question was spoken so softly, so plaintively, that it shot to Annie's heart. "Yes," she answered. "We all can." She turned back to White Wolf. "Did they hurt you?"

"Yes. No. I'll survive. And I can swim."

She stood and walked over to him.

"I still say you should not have come," he muttered.

She again knelt beside him and touched her fingers to the bruise on his cheek. "We're in this together, remember?"

"Together," he repeated.

She brushed his hair back with her hand and saw that the bruise originated from the side of his head. "Does it hurt much?" she asked.

He lifted his hand and took her fingers in his own. "Look at me."

Her eyes traveled to his. They were smiling. She felt his breath on her skin, the warmth of him, close to her. His nearness made her tremble. But she did not pull back. "I can't believe I'm saving your skin again," she murmured. "But don't think . . ."

He put his finger over her mouth to stop her words. "I know," he whispered. "This doesn't mean you're my wife." His eyes captured hers in a moment of deep understanding. Then his hand slipped to the back of her neck. Slowly he drew her lips down to meet his.

THIRTY

~

For one brief moment Annie felt as if she had finally found home. Warmth spread through her and threatened to dissolve the tight knot of fear within her. Then she remembered—Dawn Light, White Flower, her parents dead beneath the savage tomahawk. Quickly she pulled away.

White Wolf's eyes, dark and stormy, pierced her defenses. Slowly he released her. The chains clanged at his wrists. He reached up one hand and touched her cheek with his fingers.

With everything in her, she wanted to melt into him and surrender, to allow herself to feel safe, comforted. But she knew she must not. They had too much standing between them. He was an Indian, and she was a killer. Her chest tightened. How could he forget that? How could he not hate her?

She opened her mouth to explain, but White Wolf stopped her. "Shhh," he whispered. "I know. Someday we'll both be free. Together."

Annie nodded and swallowed past the lump in her throat. "I— I'll go search for the key now," she choked. Yet she knew that release from physical chains was not the freedom he meant. Instead, he was again reading her soul and finding there chains heavier than the ones that bound his ankles and wrists. She dropped her gaze, knowing that she would not find the key to her bondage in the captain's cabin. She would only find it with God, but now she was too afraid to face Him.

The creak of the door startled her and brought her to her feet. She pressed her hand to her chest to steady her breathing.

Jiggs poked his head through the door's opening. "Got a cot here fer ya," he called.

Annie turned her back toward White Wolf. "Come, Jiggs. There's a spot here by the wall."

Jiggs grinned and shuffled into the room. He held a worn hammock in one fist and a hammer and nails in the other. "Won't take but a minute to put it up." He walked over to a pillar and rapped it with his knuckles. "Right here, don't you think?"

Annie nodded. "That will be fine."

Jiggs pounded a nail into the pillar and another into the wall behind it. Then he strung the hammock between them and gave it a firm tug. "That'll hold jus' fine. If you can stand sleepin' with them." He jerked his thumb toward White Wolf and the others.

"Thank you, Jiggs. I'm sure I'll sleep well."

Jiggs shook his head. "You got a lot of pluck, girl. Wouldn't catch me dead down here at night—not even if my own mama asked it of me. Ain't you scared they'll summon devils ta torture you in the dark?" He shuddered. "I heard tell they got the black arts. They just a-stare into the shadows, and out come the devils."

Annie touched her hand to the hammock's center. Then she gripped it and pulled. The rope stretched but held firm. She turned toward Jiggs. "I've learned, sir, that devils come not from the shadows without but from the darkness within. I fear these Indians less than I fear myself." She muttered the last words in a low voice. As she did, her eyes caught White Wolf's.

Jiggs cleared his throat. "Well, Cap'n says you can earn yer keep startin' now."

Annie put her hands on her hips. "If he thinks I'm going to—"

He cut her off with a snort. "Naw, it ain't that. He just wants ya to help Cook make supper tonight, that's all." He ran his hand over the back of his neck and his foot over the floorboard. "Guess you should know. Cap'n says yer here ta take care of these red devils, and we ain't ta touch ya."

Annie let out her breath. "Good."

Jiggs looked up. "But tonight he wants ya to help Cook all the same. Says the savages be fat enough for now. You don't need to feed 'em tonight." He stuck his finger up his right nostril and scratched. Then he removed his finger and wiped it on his pants. "Bit worried 'bout that last one though. Methinks he looks a mite pale." He waved his hand toward White Wolf. "Mouse hopes he'll survive the journey, or he won't be gettin' a cut of the profit like the cap'n promised for bringing 'im in."

"He'll make it. I'll promise you that."

"Mouse'll be glad ta hear it."

Annie clamped her teeth together and swallowed a scathing comment about Mouse.

Jiggs smiled at her, showing teeth rotted brown with two missing in the front. "Come on. Better hurry along now."

Annie glanced at White Wolf and followed Jiggs up to the ship's galley.

The next hours passed in a blur of vegetables, gruel, and ill-mannered sailors. Finally the work was done, and Annie stumbled above deck. The sky glowed like dying embers as the sun dropped into the watery horizon. She gasped and glanced left and right, in front of them and behind. But it didn't matter where she looked. Land was nowhere in sight.

~

Far in the distance the coastline dipped before Philippe's vision. For three long breaths, he watched it. Then it was concealed by the fog, as if some heavenly paintbrush had swept down to blot it from sight. So close and yet a world away. France—his dream, his hope. Gone.

The deck behind him creaked as someone approached.

"We'll be there by nightfall," said a low voice.

Philippe looked over his shoulder to see Captain Bradley. As always the man's uniform was perfect—his snowy white cravat, his polished gold buttons, his dark blue coat without a smudge or tear. Today his hair was pulled back with a matching blue tie. Not one strand was out of place. The captain stepped beside Philippe and put his hands on the railing. Philippe looked down at knuckles worn from weather and strong fingers stained with ink.

"I'm sorry we can't take you to France." The captain spoke without looking at him.

Philippe's gaze dropped to his own fingers, too pale against the railing's dark wood. "I am surprised to hear you, an English captain, say so."

Captain Bradley's eyes remained steady on the fog ahead. "I know what it means to yearn for home."

Home. Philippe sighed. "Perhaps after the trial . . ."

"Perhaps." The captain sounded doubtful.

"That Lord Grant will finally get what's comin' to 'im," someone muttered behind them.

Philippe turned to see a sailor coiling rope beneath the mast. "Lord Grant?"

The sailor paused and rubbed his nose. "Aye, 'tis his trial you'll be testifying at." He spat on the deck. "Bloody traitor."

Captain Bradley scowled. "You'll be cleaning that up, Charlie. You know the rules."

Charlie slumped his shoulders. "Aye, Cap'n." He trudged to the port side of the ship for a mop and bucket.

Philippe rubbed his hand over his chin. Grant. The name sounded familiar. Of course, it was a common name. He had probably heard it somewhere in his travels. Wait. His memory stirred. Wasn't White Wolf's sister married to a man named Grant, one with an aristocratic heritage? Weren't they in England now because someone was in trouble? Could it be? Philippe shook his head. The world was not as small as that. He turned toward the captain. "I wonder, does Lord Grant have a brother who lives in the colonies?"

Captain Bradley eyed him suspiciously. "He does. Do you know of him?"

"It couldn't be Jonathan." The name slipped from Philippe's tongue.

The captain's eyes narrowed. "You *do* know him."

"*Non,* no." Philippe realized his error too late.

"So the brother keeps company with the French. The court will be interested to hear your news, I'm sure." The captain tapped his fingers on the ship's railing. "Perhaps we have found the true traitor after all."

"No, I did not mean . . ."

Captain Bradley ignored Philippe's protest. "It's said that he's married to an Indian woman."

The sailor shoved the mop into a bucket of seawater and grunted. "And we all know the Injuns fight with the French."

Philippe looked away and listened to the sound of the mop sloshing across the wooden deck. He groaned. What had he done? Condemned an innocent man by his thoughtless words? What would White Wolf say if he knew?

"Ah, the net tightens," muttered the captain. He slapped Philippe on the shoulder. "Washington was right about you. I should not have doubted him."

Philippe turned from the railing and walked toward the ship's stern. He did not look back; he didn't dare. It was all he could do to endure the low chuckle of the sailor, the calm assurance of the captain, and the knowledge that he had in the space of a few moments betrayed a friend.

Perhaps, he thought, he did not deserve France after all.

~

So it had come to this at last. All the promises, all the denials, all the angry memories that had ever haunted him solidified in this one single moment. Jonathan had come to make peace with a dead man.

He placed his hand on the cemetery gate and pulled. The gate swung open with a low groan. A bit of rust came off in his hand and marked his skin like a shadow of blood shed in years past. He wiped the rust onto his pant leg and found that despite the coolness of the autumn morning, his palms were sweaty.

A low-lying mist floated over the ground and crept over the stone wall surrounding the graveyard. Wild rosebushes, their flowers long withered and gone, intertwined with the mist and cascaded over the wall. Jonathan stepped through the gate and closed it behind him. His gaze traveled to the tall poplar tree in the middle of the graveyard. Only a few dry leaves still clung to its branches, while the others covered the ground like an oriental carpet half-hidden by the mist. Headstones, gray against the morning light, rose out of the fog. All seemed quiet, eerie, and cold.

Jonathan brushed his toe over a weed in the path. In his youth the cemetery had been immaculate. But now with Richard in prison and so many servants gone, the grass had become overgrown. Weeds sprouted from cracks and peeked from behind headstones. The neglect troubled him.

He wandered through the graves, his gaze flickering from one name to the next. Frederick, Victoria, George, Evelyn, Harlan. He paused in front of the great stone angel that marked his father's tomb. One of the angel's hands pointed toward heaven. Dew marked her face like tears shed for the sins of the dead. Jonathan reached out a finger and wiped the wetness from her cheek. "Don't weep for him," he muttered.

He looked down at the small headstone over the grave next to his father's. It read simply "Brenna Grant," with no dates, no loving tributes, nothing but a small cross etched into the stone. Not even her body lay beneath it. Richard had never bothered to bring it back from Ireland.

A familiar thudding started in Jonathan's chest. His finger touched the cool stone and traced his mother's name. He remembered the last time he had come to this place just before he left England for the colonies. At that time he'd laid a single white rose on his mother's grave and had spat upon his father's headstone. He'd planned never to come back. But now as he stood here and saw his father's ornate tomb overshadowing his mother's small headstone, he realized that he had never left this place. Though he'd traveled across an ocean and carved out a life for himself on the wild frontier, the hatred for his father, the sorrow for his mother, had bound him to this site as surely as if he had made his home on this very ground.

Now, though, he had come to change all that. He had come to do the impossible. He reached into his pocket. His fingers brushed a piece of paper and the tin soldier beside it. He pulled out the paper and unfolded it.

Dearest Jonathan,

Tibbs has agreed to bring this to Inspector Higgins. I can only pray that it will find its way into your hands. There is something you must know. I am dying. Death visits me nightly. He looks out at me from eyes in the shadows, and I know he is coming for me soon. They say I have the scurvy. But it is more than that. It is the past that haunts me, mem-

ories that condemn me to die. I know that you will not mourn for me. Nor, I imagine, will anyone, except perhaps Katherine. I realize this is no more than I deserve, to spend my final hours in this place where the light never shines, and the air smells of my own urine and the droppings of vermin. I will die like the sinner that I am. I do not ask that you try to free me. It is too late for that. But, my dear brother, you must do this one thing for me. You must forgive me and forgive Father. Do not let him steal your life as he stole mine. Break free, Jonathan. Break the chains of our past and fly back to the colonies with your wife and children. Leave your anger, your hate, here. Be free, Jonathan. For me, for Mother, for our children who should never know the legacy of Harlan Grant.

Your humble servant,
Richard

Jonathan stood before the grave of the man he had hated for as long as he could remember. He clenched his fists and raised his chin. "I forgive you, Father," he said aloud. But the words bounced back to him, empty and meaningless. Despite his intentions, the old anger, the old hurt, still welled inside him.

Jonathan knelt in the damp grass and stared at Harlan's head-stone. Loathing for his father filled him until he nearly choked on the feeling. He dropped his head. "Oh, Lord," he muttered, "I thought I could just say the words, and it would be done. I thought I could simply forgive him through an act of my will." He put his face into his hands. "Yet here I am, helpless before the fury of a lifetime. Help me." He lifted his head.

A leaf fell from the tree overhead and drifted down onto Harlan's grave. Jonathan reached out and picked it up. He spun it between his thumb and forefinger and then crushed it in his fist. "We were like leaves in his hand. How often did he squeeze and we crumbled?" He raised his head further and stared at the angel above him. "I feel the bonds of unforgiveness, Lord, and I can't break free. How can I forgive a man who beat my mother, destroyed my brother, and filled my life with such anguish? How can I forgive him who was nothing but cold, heartless, and cruel?"

"He was not always like that." A voice, hushed and gentle, spoke behind him.

Jonathan turned to see a woman hidden within a gray cloak. For a moment he thought she was a part of the mist that had taken shape and formed from the desperation of his prayer. "You're the woman from the gardens?"

She nodded. "I am."

"How do you know what my father was like?"

She turned her face so that she was looking out over the hills. "I knew him when he was a young man, younger even than you are now. Back then he was kind, even tender at times. I think at the beginning he loved your mother very much."

"You were there? You knew them both?"

"Hmm," she sighed.

"You remind me of someone. Were you my old nursemaid?"

She turned toward him until he could just see her features dimly through the fog. She smiled at him. "I remember holding you to my breast as a baby and watching you take your first steps."

"I had almost forgotten you. Have you lived here all this time?"

"I left for a while, but now I have returned to help you do what God has brought you here to do."

He shook his head. "I tried. But . . ." He stared at the woman, wanting to see a glimpse of Harlan Grant as she had known him. "Tell me, why didn't you stop what he did to us? Why didn't anyone stop it?"

"I wasn't strong enough. I wasn't brave enough."

"I guess none of us were." The scent of lavender swirled around him and became like a balm to the ache within. The nursery, he remembered, had always smelled of lavender. "What happened to make my father the way he was?"

Her answer came as softly as a whisper spoken to the breeze. "Sin is like a disease, I think. It's passed from generation to generation. Harlan caught it from his father, but your mother hoped you would be spared. You were always so determined to do what was right."

"And now I find that I can't."

"Why?"

"There are too many questions. Too many memories."

She nodded. "Let me tell you what I remember best. I remember your mother's gelding Sir Charles. Your father loved that old horse. He would sneak out at night and talk to him in the stables. When Sir Charles nearly foundered, your father stayed with him all night until the horse pulled through. He never raised a hand to that horse in anger. Did you never notice how the saddle was always ready for you, that Sir Charles was always brushed and clean whenever you wished to ride him? Your father did that."

"So he loved a horse but not his own family."

"He loved you too, but he could not show it the way he could with Sir Charles."

"That's no excuse."

"No. But tell me, are you more angry with him or with your own helplessness to stop him?"

Jonathan scowled. "Both, neither. I don't know. But if you had seen all that I saw, you would hate him too."

"Would I?" Her shoulders rose and fell beneath the cloak. "Christ has seen it all, and yet He forgives; He loves. He has seen even into me and loves me still."

Jonathan brushed the fragments of leaves from his fingers. From somewhere deep within him bubbled questions he thought long suppressed, questions he had dared not ask until now. Even as he spoke them, his voice trembled. "If God cared for us, why didn't He change my father and make him kind? If God truly loved us, how could He sit by while a helpless woman was beaten, while a little boy was struck and made to watch his mother bleed?"

"I don't know. But one thing I do know: God longed to change Harlan's heart."

"Why didn't He?"

"Because your father refused to forgive."

"Forgive who?"

The woman plucked at a string in her cloak. For a moment Jonathan thought she would not answer. When she finally spoke, her voice was strained. "Your mother, I suppose, for loving another. Richard for being born. You for not making the pain go away. And . . . his own father for hurting him the way he hurt you."

Jonathan shuddered. Slowly he closed his eyes and found himself staring at the truth. The same unforgiveness that now lived in his heart had made his father into a cruel, heartless brute. Would it happen to him too if he failed to forgive? *God, help me. Forgive me. Save me from myself. I need You to set me free. I can't do it on my own.*

He glanced up at the woman. "I know who you are," he whispered.

Her shadowed face turned toward him.

"You're an angel sent from God."

She looked away. Her head tilted toward the sky. "Perhaps." With that she walked away.

Jonathan watched her go until her figure disappeared down a grassy knoll and out of sight. Then he turned back to his father's grave. He stood and reached into his pocket. Now it was time to do what he had come to do, not by his own strength, but by the One who had the power to set him free. "I leave you in God's hands, Father," he said aloud. "It's time to end the hate." He took the tin soldier from his pocket and placed it on the gravestone. "Good-bye, Father. Rest in peace."

Jonathan turned and walked toward the cemetery gate. He did not look back. As he reached for the gate's latch, he felt as if a great weight had slipped from his shoulders. He knew that God had done for him what he could not do for himself. Jonathan walked through the gate and shut it behind him. Outside, the woman sat on a boulder that had fallen from the wall.

"Thank you," he called to her.

She did not move. "Now you can do what God has asked of you."

Jonathan paused. Did she know? Did she guess the sacrifice that he must now make?

"Take care, Jonathan." Her voice drifted to him as if it came across a great expanse of time. "The most difficult test is yet to come."

Jonathan bowed his head and wondered if anything, even freedom, could prepare him for the days ahead.

THIRTY-ONE

~

Sometimes when the wind blew just right across the waves, the sails billowed overhead, and the clouds raced across the sky to darken the sun, White Wolf could almost remember what it felt like to be free. He could almost smell the scent of white pine dampened by rain and taste the deer meat hot from the fire. But then a sailor's shout would disrupt the dream, and he would feel again the weight of chains around his ankles and the sores where manacles had bitten into his wrists.

This day was no different. A breeze swept across the ocean's surface like a brush tipping the waves with white. Above, the mast creaked, and the sails blew out fat and full just as they had for most of the journey. For five weeks the ship had been driven by the wind across the endless expanse of water while he and the other prisoners were holed up in its belly like vermin. Every third day Annie was allowed to release them so they could clean the deck with seawater, empty and wash the sailors' chamber pots, and mend the ropes that had frayed.

White Wolf lowered a bucket over the side of the ship. The rope scraped against his skin as the bucket dipped into the water. He pulled it back up again, listening as it thumped against the hull. When it reached the top, he grabbed the handle and tossed the water over the deck. A few droplets splashed across the feet of a sailor who was coiling a rope near the mast.

"Watch it, savage," the sailor growled. He stood, and White Wolf recognized Patch.

His knuckles tightened on the bucket.

Patch glared at him. "You wanna start somethin', savage?"

White Wolf gritted his teeth and turned away. The chains rattled against the deck. The last thing he needed now was a fight. He lowered the bucket back over the side and tried to forget his anger. Atop the sterncastle Little Owl and Gray Hair worked side by side, scrubbing the deck on their hands and knees. Spitting Turtle mended ropes at the bow. White Wolf pulled up the bucket and glanced around. Patch was gone.

He set the bucket at his feet and stretched his back. He was getting used to the tip and sway of the ship beneath him, but he would never adjust to the cramped quarters, the chains around his ankles, and the stench of unwashed bodies all around him.

"Get back to work, lazy," a sailor shouted from the stern.

White Wolf glanced up to see Brodie staring down at him. He grabbed the mop and started moving water around the deck, all the while thinking about how much he hated that man's ratlike face, his buckteeth, his squeaky voice that barked out orders every time White Wolf paused.

From the corner of his eye White Wolf saw Annie exit the sterncastle. Sunlight glinted in her hair. She put her hand up to her eyes and looked across the water. White Wolf smiled as she stiffened her back as straight as an arrow fresh from the string.

After a moment she leaned over and spoke to Gray Hair. He nodded, set down his scrubbing brush, stood, and made his way into the sterncastle. The captain would be pleased, White Wolf assumed, at how much English the "savage" had learned.

Annie looked down at him and grinned. Then she walked toward the back of the ship. He continued to watch her as he pushed the mop over the deck. She alone had made this trip bearable. She cared for him, for all of them, with such kindness, such self-sacrifice that he barely recognized her as the same girl who had once stabbed him. Of course, she had always been kind when she chose to be. And ever since the pox, she wore a mantle of meekness that sometimes seemed to chafe. But she did not waver. Often she offered her own food so that the others would have enough. Last week she held Little Owl in her arms all night when he cried and wept for his mother. She bathed Gray Hair's ankles and feet where the shackles made blisters. She'd even brushed Spitting Turtle's hair and sang old Lenape songs when the woman had trouble sleeping. And when he was sick the first week, she cleaned up his mess without complaint. Now, though, he thought she seemed too pale, too thin. Guilt was a hard taskmaster. What she needed, what they both needed, was to find peace with the past. But how?

White Wolf looked at the clouds overhead. Was God really up there? Did He see? Did He care? *Is there hope for us, God? Can people like Annie and me ever find peace? Or is it already too late?* The mop swished across the wooden planks. He paused and listened to the sound of the wind in the sails.

"Come home," the breeze whispered. "Come back." *Home.* The word called to him, beckoned him, but it seemed all wrong. After all, he was not headed home but to England.

The sound of a hand slapping against flesh startled him. His gaze flew to the stern. There he saw Brodie's face, red with the impression of a handprint. Annie stood next to him, her cheeks alight with rage. Her hand raised again. "Do not touch me, sir," she warned.

Brodie rubbed his face and scowled. "I kin do what I want. You ain't strong enough ta stop me."

She lifted her chin in a familiar look of defiance. "The captain is. Remember his orders."

Brodie sneered. "Cap'n is below deck though, ain't he? Don't think there be anyone here ta protect ya."

"I can protect myself." She reached into the folds of her skirt and pulled out her knife.

Brodie laughed. "With that little thing? Yer gonna hafta get something bigger than that if you 'spect to scare ol' Brodie."

Anger boiled in White Wolf.

"Stay away from me, you—you—you filthy animal." She brandished the knife in front of her.

Brodie jumped toward her and knocked the knife from her hand.

The mop slipped from White Wolf's grip. He lunged toward them.

Brodie grabbed Annie's arm and pulled her against him. His head descended toward hers.

A sharp war cry erupted from White Wolf's lips. Fury clouded his vision. The distance closed between them as if the chains around his ankles were wings instead. He reached the top of the sterncastle and swung his fist at Brodie's jaw. Brodie howled in pain and released Annie. He stumbled backward.

White Wolf did not hesitate. He leaped on the sailor and pushed him down, using his enemy's body to break his own fall. Breath escaped Brodie's mouth in a rush. He twisted, and hands flailed at White Wolf's chest.

Anger, too long pent up, gave White Wolf strength. His fists pummeled the sailor's body again and again. "Do-not-touch-her." Each word was accompanied by a stinging blow. Blood spurted from the man's nose and stained White Wolf's chest. He pulled back and attempted to lock his legs around the sailor, to pin him to the deck, but the chains hampered his movements.

Brodie squirmed away. White Wolf reached out and grabbed the sailor by his shirt. He dragged him back to the deck beside him. Brodie squealed and tried to pull back.

White Wolf tightened his grip. Somewhere above them he was vaguely aware of Annie's voice calling his name. "No, Waptumewi. Stop. Stop." His grip loosened. Brodie broke free and scrambled to his feet. White Wolf dove toward him. He grabbed his foot with one hand and pulled.

Brodie fell to his knees, but as he did, his fingers closed around Annie's knife. The blade slashed toward White Wolf. The Indian heard a *whoosh* as it cut through the air. He released Brodie and rose to a crouch, his gaze never leaving the knife. From the side of his vision, he could see the other sailors beginning to gather around him. None of them intervened.

"Get 'im, Brodie," called a sea-roughened voice from behind him. On his left someone hooted.

White Wolf crouched lower and circled the enemy. Cold laughter drifted around him, spurring his anger. He lunged forward. His leg swung out and caught Brodie behind his knees. Brodie crashed to the deck with White Wolf on top of him. He wrenched the knife out of the sailor's hand.

"Look at that Injun fight. Didn't think he had it in him," cried someone who sounded like Patch.

He turned and saw a flash of Annie's face, pale against the blue sky. Then his hand gripped Brodie's hair. He yanked back until a throat, white and bare, filled his vision. He pressed the knife into soft flesh and reveled in the sight of terror in his enemy's eyes.

The sound of a cocking gun stopped the killing blow. White Wolf froze.

"Hold, Indian." The captain's strong voice silenced the others.

White Wolf looked up and found himself staring down the barrel of a pistol into hard blue eyes. For a moment he did not move. Then Annie stepped behind the captain. *Please*. She formed the word with her mouth.

Slowly he lowered the knife and rose to his feet. Brodie staggered up and stumbled toward his mates.

White Wolf stood before the captain. No inkling of remorse stirred in his heart, though he knew the punishment for his actions would be death. He was, after all, a warrior. He tilted his chin.

The captain raised the gun higher until it pointed directly at his chest. "You know the penalty, Indian," he murmured.

"Wait." Annie laid her hand on the captain's arm. "He was only protecting me."

The captain's voice did not soften. "He attacked one of my men."

"Only because your man attacked me first despite your orders. Any gentleman would have done the same."

The captain glanced sideways. "May I remind you, Miss Hill, this is no gentleman."

"He sure is some fighter though," mumbled Patch from the other side of the captain. "Sure hate to see all our profits get thrown to the sharks."

"Better fighter than any I seen in England, Cap'n," piped up Jiggs. "Bet he could whip even Fast Fists Rowley."

"Sure he could," said a sailor White Wolf didn't recognize.

The captain looked at Brodie's swollen face, already purpling beneath the eye. "He did this with his legs shackled?"

Jiggs nodded vigorously. "That's right, Cap'n. Like it was child's play, he did."

The captain rubbed his chin. His voice lowered. "You think he could beat Rowley, you say? That might be worth seeing." He gave a sharp nod of his head and holstered his gun. "Very well. Patch, you train him. Make sure he's ready to fight when we arrive in England."

Patch grinned. "I 'spect my cut ta double then, Cap'n."

"Done." He turned to Annie. "Miss Hill, you will continue with your duties. Double rations for this savage until we reach England. We will need to build his strength."

"Where will we get the extra food?" Brodie whined.

The captain smiled. "From your share, of course. A fitting punishment, methinks, for disobeying my orders." He snapped his fingers. "Patch, come with me. We will discuss the savage's training regime. The rest of you, back to your duties." He waved his hand in the air. Then he shook his head and muttered under his breath. "Beat that cockney Rowley—now there's something I'd pay to see."

A low laugh echoed back to White Wolf as the captain and Patch headed down the steps of the sterncastle. When they were gone, the other sailors dispersed, leaving him and Annie alone at the stern. Though he knew she was looking at him, he could not meet her gaze. He did not want to see the loathing in her eyes, for now it had started again—the fighting, the war, the rage. Only this time it was worse. This time he was to be a fighter for the white man's pleasure and profit. Perhaps it would have been better to die.

White Wolf glanced over the water and swore that it appeared like blood.

∽

The moon rose huge and luminous in the eastern sky. Jonathan watched its face for a moment and wondered if it was looking down at him and judging him a fool. For by any sane man's standards, what he was about to do was foolishness indeed. Yet it was not man's standards that concerned him now, but God's. He closed his eyes. *Help me, Lord, to be strong enough. Help me to stand firm, and if I must fall, to do so bravely.* He opened his eyes. Then he squared his shoulders, adjusted the collar of his overcoat, and walked out onto the bridge.

For once no fog obscured his vision. The sky above was clear, with only a few clouds illuminated by the moon. A cold wind whipped the tails of his coat and nipped at his face. Below, he could hear water tumbling beneath the stone arch. As he reached the top, he glanced over the side and watched a branch swirl in the black water. It spun left, then right, before tipping beneath the surface.

Jonathan shivered and glanced at the tall hedge on the far side of the bridge. Was Inspector Higgins hiding there even now? He hoped so, but there was no way to be sure. Three days ago he had sent a message to the mansion saying he could be contacted through the inspector. At the same time Higgins let it be known that Jonathan would soon be the rightful Lord Grant. "This will bring him to us," the inspector promised. And sure enough, two days later an unsigned note arrived by special carrier. "Meet me at Downey's Bridge at moonrise. I have news to help your brother," it said.

Inspector Higgins had pulled at his moustache especially hard as he read it. "I knew it," he'd said. "Whoever it is wants you Grants out of the way. First Richard, then Justin, and now the traitor will try for you." He gave his moustache a final pull.

And so Jonathan had agreed to tonight's encounter, knowing that the next hour would determine Richard's fate. If all went as planned, Richard could be free by nightfall. "For you, brother," Jonathan whispered. Then he pulled his coat tighter and waited.

Soon the steady clop-clop of hooves echoed through the night. A horse and rider appeared out of the darkness. The rider wore a cloak with a hood that covered his features. Jonathan straightened his shoulders. The rider dismounted with the ease of a man practiced in the fine arts of a gentleman. A glint of silver shone at his waist. Jonathan looked closer and saw that it was a pistol.

"Hello, Jonathan." A deep masculine voice spoke from the folds of the hood. "I didn't think you would come."

Jonathan's breath came more quickly. "You said you had information about Richard."

The man nodded. "Yes. He will hang at the gallows, and the Grant estate will be mine, or more technically, my son's."

"Your son's?"

The man chuckled. "Such a healthy babe. He will never know, of course. 'Tis a pity."

Jonathan stepped back until he felt the side of the bridge behind him. "Know what?"

"That his father is not that treasonous fool, Richard."

"William." Jonathan breathed the name.

"Of course."

Jonathan rested his hand on the cold stone of the bridge. So much made sense now—Elizabeth's coyness, Richard's reticence, Katherine's childlike sorrow. "So the child is to be Elizabeth's revenge on the Grants."

"Does it pain you to know that the estate will not pass to one of your blood, but of mine?"

"I don't care about the estate. I never have."

"More's the pity."

Jonathan pointed toward the man's hand. "You didn't bring your crop this time."

"This time I won't need it."

"Who are you?"

The man reached down and pulled his pistol from its holster. "Look and remember, Jonathan Grant." His voice turned as hard as the bridge's stones. "For mine is the last face you'll see."

Jonathan caught his breath. The moment of truth had come. Slowly the man reached up and lowered his hood. Jonathan gasped as moonlight illuminated the face before him. "Simon Bains!"

Simon raised his gun. "You should never have come back."

"Why are you doing this?"

The man smiled. "Don't take it personally, Jonathan. Really, this is all your father's fault. Don't blame me—blame Harlan." He pulled back on the trigger. A flash of fire spat from the end of the gun.

Jonathan felt the impact of the shot. Pain coursed through him. He heard himself scream. Then he was falling over the edge of the bridge. His body splashed into the water. Icy arms closed around him like the embrace of endless night. Then the darkness fell.

THIRTY-TWO

~

Inspector Higgins jumped as soon as the gun sounded. *No! It's too soon!* His hands shook as he reached for his pistol. He saw Jonathan tumble into the water. *No, stop!*

The caped figure leaned over the side of the bridge. "Good-bye, son of Harlan," he called.

Higgins leaped from the shadows. "Halt, in the name of the king!" The command echoed through the night air.

But the rider did not turn. Instead, he threw the hood back over his head, jumped on his horse, and spun into the darkness. It was just like before, but this time Higgins was ready. He steadied his gun and aimed at the traitor. He pulled back on the trigger. A puff of smoke rose from his pistol as the shot reverberated in his ears.

The rider swayed in his saddle. Higgins held his breath. The man righted himself and kicked his horse to a gallop. His cape billowed behind him, and the rattle of shod hooves over rocky earth filled the night.

Quickly Higgins holstered his gun, mounted his own steed, and pursued the retreating enemy. Trees overshadowed the path, casting a checkered pattern of moonlight over the back of the rider in front of him. He sat higher in his saddle, urging the horse faster and faster.

The rider was indeed a gentleman, Higgins decided, though not perhaps as finely bred as he'd originally thought. He rode as one well practiced and yet not natural to the saddle, as if he had first ridden as an adult and pursued the skill with vengeance. But one thing he could tell—the one he pursued was certainly a man. But which man? That is what he must discover.

The outskirts of London loomed ahead. He could just see tall buildings that rose with black alleys between. He needed to catch the traitor before he could hide in the shadows of the city. Higgins leaned forward until his chin brushed his horse's mane. The wind whistled in his ears. Closer, closer. He, the hunter, and his nemesis, the prey.

Dirt gave way to cobblestone as the road twisted toward London. Suddenly the right side dropped away toward the river, and on the left a tall wooden fence rose along the border of Lord Trembley's estate. Inspector Higgins squinted and urged his horse on. "I have you now," he muttered between clenched teeth. "There's nowhere to turn, nowhere to hide."

As if the rider could hear him, the horse ahead spurted forward, lengthening the distance between them. The road bent, and for a moment, they slipped from his sight.

Higgins rounded the corner just in time to see the horse and rider soar over the high fence. For one breath their outline shone dark against the sky. Then they landed on the other side as gracefully as a feather on the shore.

The inspector kicked his heels into his horse and pulled the reins left. The fence loomed closer. "Come on," he urged. The horse's muscles bunched beneath him. He leaned forward. *Now!*

The horse skidded to a halt, and Higgins found himself airborne, alone. His chin thudded into the soft dirt on the other side of the fence. Breath emptied from his lungs in a sudden spurt. His hat skittered off into the darkness.

Slowly he lifted his head. On a hill in the distance, he saw the horse and rider pause, their figures black against the moonrise. An eerie laugh drifted through the night. Then the rider turned and galloped into the trees.

Inspector Higgins picked up his hat and shook the dirt from the brim. Then he sat on the damp grass and put his head in his hands. The unthinkable had happened. Jonathan had been shot for nothing.

~

When White Wolf first set foot on the shores of England, he felt as if he had descended into the pit of Hades. Sailors jostled him on either side. Crates swung from ropes overhead. Men bustled beneath them. Shouts, harsh and indistinct, rang in his ears. The stink of horse dung and rotting fish assaulted his senses. Noise and chaos and stench and confusion. Not a flower, not a blade of grass, not a tree or a songbird anywhere within sight or earshot. Nothing could seem further from home.

Patch tugged on the rope that held White Wolf's wrists. "Come on, Injun." He yanked the rope again. White Wolf stumbled forward with Gray Hair, Little Owl, and Spitting Turtle tied behind him. The chains had been taken from their ankles and replaced with crude ropes, tied only long enough to allow them to hobble forward without falling.

"We ain't got all day," Patch sputtered. He shook his head. "Shoulda left ya in the hole till I sold the others. 'No time for that— take 'em all,' says Jiggs." He mimicked Jiggs's tone. "Shoulda known better than to listen to a fool."

White Wolf ignored Patch's ramblings and craned his head left and right. Where was Annie? He couldn't see her on deck nor on the docks around him. Surely she would join him soon. She couldn't just leave him, could she? *She doesn't care about you,* doubt whispered. *No one does. You're alone.* He shivered.

"I said, move it, savage," Patch hollered and pulled the rope so hard that White Wolf nearly lost his balance. He hurried forward. The others stumbled behind him.

"Where are we going, sir?" called Gray Hair.

Patch rubbed his finger on the side of his nose and growled, "Ain't none of yer bizness, savage. But since ya asked, yer gonna 'ave a new master now."

No one dared say more.

Patch headed toward a black carriage waiting by the docks. A fine line of gold tooling shone around the edge of the covered carriage, and two fat, sleek horses sported harnesses that had been polished to a brilliant shine.

As they drew closer, a man stepped from the carriage. He wore a perfectly tailored coat, breeches, and a white-powdered wig.

"These are the servants for my master?" the man sniffed.

Patch smiled. "Hullo, Jeffers. I see you 'aven't changed a bit."

"That is Mr. Jeffers to you, sir," he said in a voice that made White Wolf think of a coyote with its foot caught in a trap.

"Whatever ya say, Jeffers," Patch smirked. "Yep, these be the servants."

Jeffers looked them up and down with squinted eyes. "A rather mangy lot, aren't they?"

White Wolf glared at the man and was suddenly reminded of all the things he hated about the white man.

He saw Patch's hand tighten on the rope. "They be good and 'ealthy just like yer master ordered. A woman for the mistress, a boy to shine his shoes, and a man for work around the estate. And they speak English, too." He pointed to Spitting Turtle, Little Owl, and Gray Hair by turn.

"English, you say?" Jeffers's eyebrows raised. "And that one?" He flicked his fingers at White Wolf.

"He ain't fer sale."

"Why, he's the best of the bunch. How much will you take for him?"

White Wolf's pulse quickened. He clenched his fists and longed to wipe the smirk from Jeffers's face.

"Not fer sale, I said. He's goin' to the fights. We're gonna pit 'im against Rowley."

"I heard that Mr. Rowley had retired," responded Jeffers in the most arrogant voice White Wolf had ever heard.

Patch laughed. "He'll be comin' outta retirement for this one. I kin guarantee it."

Jeffers sighed. "Very well then. How much do you want for these others?"

"It'll be 200 each for the two adults and 150 fer the kid."

Jeffers managed an affected chuckle. "Oh, really, sir, surely you jest. They aren't worth more than 200 for the lot of them."

Patch stood taller. "Got a 'undred apiece fer the last ones, and we brought them over in the summer. Gotta charge more fer winter travel."

"It is hardly winter, sir."

"Almost December, it is."

Jeffers sighed again, louder this time. "Very well, 300 for all of them."

"These ones be trained—450."

"I'll give you 400, or you can take them back where you found them."

"Well, all right, it's a deal," Patch grumbled. He lowered his head and shook it, but White Wolf could see that he hid a smile.

Jeffers pulled a pouch from the carriage, counted out the silver pieces, and handed them to Patch. Patch pocketed the money and untied the other three. "Nice doin' bizness with ya," he muttered. He tugged on the rope to lead White Wolf back to the dock.

Briefly White Wolf's eyes met Gray Hair's. "Good-bye," he whispered.

"Be strong," Gray Hair called back.

White Wolf turned away. Sorrow and anger chased through him until he could no longer tell them apart. This was the white man's world, he reminded himself. The white men were devils indeed.

Behind him he heard the carriage creak and the jingle of harnesses as the horses pulled away. Slowly he followed Patch back to the ship. The captain stood on the dock near it. Again White Wolf's eyes searched for Annie. Again he didn't find her.

Patch approached the captain. "Got 300 just like before," he said and handed him the money.

The captain weighed it in his hand and nodded. "I trust the remaining money in your pocket will be enough to get you and the Indian to London, as well as cover your share."

Patch twisted the rope in his hand. "What other money, Cap'n?"

The captain's eyes narrowed. "I'm not a fool, Patch. I can see the bulge of it from here. Now do as I say, and take the Indian to London. I'll follow later."

Patch backed away. "Yes, sir. Right away, sir." He half bowed, then turned toward the line of carriages on the far side of the dock. "Hurry up, Indian," he growled, pulling on the rope. "We gotta bit of travelin' ahead of us."

White Wolf walked as slowly as he could. His gaze darted around the dock area. In a moment he would be gone, and it would be too late. Where was she?

Patch chose the last carriage and heaved himself inside. "Get in, savage," he yelled. "You got rocks in yer pants er somethin'?"

White Wolf swallowed hard and stepped up into the carriage. The walls seemed to close around him as he settled into the worn seat.

"London, west side," Patch called to the driver. Then they were off. The carriage jiggled back and forth as the horse started down the road. White Wolf gripped the seat until his knuckles turned white. So this was what it felt like to travel as a white man. He hated it, rumbling like a corpse in a white man's coffin.

Patch sat back and put his hands behind his head. "Yer gonna make me a lotta money, Injun. Jus' you remember that," he muttered and closed his eyes.

White Wolf sat forward and looked out the window. Slowly the docks fell away from his sight. As they did, his anger receded, leaving despair in its wake. Now there was no one left who knew him, no one who cared. Loneliness settled over him, so heavy that he could scarcely breathe beneath it. Moisture blurred his vision.

He lowered his head. *Bring her back to me, God,* he prayed. *Don't leave me alone in this hell.*

～

Jonathan was dead. The realization lodged in Elizabeth's heart like a barbed thorn. After all he had done to her, she should have been glad, but she wasn't. She'd wanted her revenge but not this. Never this. She pushed back and forth in the rocking chair and listened to the creak of the runners against wood. Soft light from a single candle draped over the nursery walls and chased shadows around the floor. William sat quietly near her feet and played with a stuffed rabbit. Elizabeth smiled down at him as he pulled at the creature's fluffy ears and turned it on its head.

"Bun-nee. Bang. Bang," he said, then laughed.

She reached down and brushed his feathery hair with her fingers.

"This is all for you, William. Never forget that," she whispered. "Everything I've done has been for you." She rocked faster.

The door swung silently open. A white cap over fuzzy yellow hair poked through the opening.

Elizabeth frowned. "Betsy?"

The maid scuttled into the room and curtsied. She twisted a strand of loose hair nervously around her forefinger. "Sorry to bother you, Milady."

Elizabeth stopped rocking. "I told you, never come in here."

"I'm sorry, Milady. It's just that I thought tonight . . ."

"What about tonight?"

Betsy released her hair and instead fidgeted with the lace at her collar. "Well, with the recent sorrow, ma'am. I was so sorry to hear it. Such a nice man. 'Tis a mighty shame." She rubbed her finger beneath her nose and sniffed. "Would you like a spot of tea perhaps? Shall I iron your black dress for you?"

Elizabeth's voice turned harsh. "Whatever for?"

Betsy's brow furrowed briefly. "For mourning, ma'am."

Elizabeth crossed her arms and looked away. "Why should I mourn for a man who was foolish enough to fall into a river?"

"They say he was shot, Milady."

"I don't believe it." Elizabeth spoke the lie quickly, as if by doing so she could convince herself that it was true. But she knew the truth. Jonathan had been killed to protect a secret and to pay for sins that were not all his own.

Elizabeth glanced back to see Betsy's eyes widen into round orbs. "Even so, Milady, you must mourn. Your own husband's brother, you know."

She waved her hand at the woman. "Enough. Get the tea if you must, but leave me alone."

Betsy stepped backward and again began to twirl her hair between her fingers. "Yes, Milady. Of course, Milady. It's just . . ."

"What?"

She spoke the next words in a rush. "I think Miss Katherine needs you, ma'am. She's a-weeping in her room something awful. Perhaps if you just saw her for a bit . . ."

Elizabeth rose from the chair. "Katherine?" Concern brushed over her and then was gone. After all, Katherine was the only one Richard truly loved, and Richard deserved nothing but contempt. "She's a child. A few tears won't hurt her." She threw her hands in the air. "Can't you see that I'm too distraught to be troubled with that girl's fits of temper?"

Betsy bowed her head. "Yes, Milady. I see, Milady. Sorry I mentioned it."

"Get out!"

Betsy curtsied again and hurried away. The door swung shut behind her.

Elizabeth lowered herself back into the chair. Guilt padded through her. "Katherine suspects the truth," it whispered. "You can't hide forever. Jonathan's killer should not walk free." She rubbed her hands over her arms. Suddenly the nursery seemed too cold. She rested her head on the back of the rocking chair and closed her eyes. Perhaps it was time to put old hurts aside and do what was right. Do it for Jonathan, for all of them. And yet . . . She glanced down at William with his wispy blond hair and rose-pink cheeks.

He looked up at her and grinned. "Ma-ma, Bun-nee." He pounded his fist on the rabbit's head.

Elizabeth reached down and scooped him up in her lap. "Mama loves you," she whispered. "She won't let anything hurt you." And the truth, she knew, would hurt if anyone found it out. If they knew what she had done, William would be labeled for life, despised and cast out from high society. And she would be shunned and called a loose woman or worse. She couldn't bear that.

She lowered her head and smelled the sweet fragrance of little William's hair. "I won't risk your future for anyone," she murmured, "especially for a dead man." Her lips brushed his temple. "No," she promised him, "I will play this nightmare out to the end and forget that I ever loved Jonathan Grant."

THIRTY-THREE

~

It wasn't supposed to be like this, this utter aloneness, this ever-growing fear, this wandering the English countryside searching for what could not be found—days of looking for White Wolf, nights of longing for peace—and finding neither. Caring for the Indians was supposed to change all that; it was supposed to atone for her sin. And for a time her guilt receded behind the mantle of service. But all her work, all her sacrifice, still could not lift the darkness from her soul. And now she was alone.

Annie leaned over and picked up a small stone from the path. She clenched it in her fist and focused on the cool smoothness. *Don't panic*, she told herself. *You'll find him soon. It can't go on like this forever*. She dropped the rock. *I can't go on like this*.

Before her the road wound along the banks of a small stream. Water bugs skimmed the stream's surface and darted between leaves fallen from the trees overhead. Reflections of bare branches, like wide cracks against the soot-gray sky, danced across the water. Before her an old wooden bridge arched across the creek, and beyond it she could see a few scattered cottages and a long fence that disappeared over a hill. In the distance she could make out the outline of a church steeple. She glanced up at the sky. Darkness would be coming soon. Perhaps she could stay in the church tonight. If she hurried, she could just make it.

For weeks she had been traveling toward London, searching for White Wolf. She'd slept in barns and beneath bridges and lived off the kindness of strangers—an odd job here, a meal given there. But no one could tell her what she wanted to know. Where was White Wolf?

She'd walked out from the ship to find him gone, and not one sailor seemed to know where Patch had taken him. "Goin' to the fights," was all they would say. And so she had begun this search, not knowing what else to do, unable to admit that he had taken her heart with him.

A drizzle of rain spattered on her cheek. She didn't bother to wipe it away. In this country dampness seemed a part of life, making the air smell like a blanket left too long in the weather. Above her a crow swept past and cawed twice before settling onto a branch on the far side of the bridge. She quickened her pace.

Soon she had crossed the bridge and climbed the hill beyond it. The church came into view just as the sky began to turn the color of mouse fur in the rain. A flicker of candlelight gleamed from the church window. Annie stumbled down the rock-strewn path toward it.

The light beckoned her until she stood at the church's door. She smoothed her hair with one hand and straightened her skirt. She pulled open the door. The warm glow embraced her. Then the sounds of an organ, sweet and clear, enveloped her and drew her inside. She took a deep breath and smelled the musty scent of old wood mixed with burning tallow. Before her rows of long benches led to the front of the sanctuary where a book lay open on the altar.

She stepped forward, her gaze drawn to the single stained-glass window above. The streetlight shone through the glass to illuminate the figure of Christ, his blood-stained hands reached out toward her. His feet and side were marked with the same bright red glass that shone from his palms. His eyes were open, and they looked at her with such pain, such longing, that she almost thought the image was real. Did He know what she had done? Did He accuse her even now? She dropped her gaze to the ribbons of multicolored light that spattered across the altar.

A man played a small pipe organ on the side of the sanctuary. Annie could just see his profile, his long, straight nose, his hair pulled back neatly at the nape of his neck, though half of him was hidden behind a tall pillar.

She sat on the last bench, pulled her knees up to her chest, and rested her head against the wall. Again her gaze was drawn to the image of Jesus. What would He say to her if He could? Would He condemn her? Would He scorn her for her sin and for the hate that had led her to it?

She closed her eyes. If only she could forget. If only she could be free. Then she could look upon the Christ-figure without feeling ashamed. But even good deeds had not washed the blood from her hands. She'd worked and worked and yet found herself not cleansed, but alone and afraid.

The organ's song grew louder until it swelled around her like the roar of ocean waves. A voice, strong and deep, rose over the music. "Arise, my soul, arise," he sang. "Shake off thy guilty fears. The bleeding Sacrifice in my behalf appears."

Annie opened her eyes and looked at the man. His focus was fully on the keys before him. He did not look up or, indeed, even seem to know she was there. Yet as the rich music enveloped her again, it was as if he were playing for her alone.

"Shake off thy guilty fears," the man repeated in his clear baritone. *Guilty fears.* The words condemned her. She shuddered. Was God speaking to her? The music pulsed through her so strongly that she began to tremble. God could not care about her, she reminded herself. He didn't even know her name.

"Before the throne my Surety stands," the man's voice boomed. "My name is written on His hands."

She looked up at the window. Christ's palms, blood-red, seemed to throb before her vision. Her breath came faster. Her name written there in blood? Could it be true? Did God know her? Did He see? If He did, He would know what she had done, and He would hate her as surely as she had hated the Indians.

Suddenly the man stopped, shook his head, and pushed down a single key. Then he picked up a quill and jotted something down on a piece of paper next to him on the bench.

Annie clutched her knees tight to her chest and rocked back and forth on the wooden pew. She'd been angry for so long—angry and afraid. The thought whispered through her—afraid that someone might discover the truth.

The man began again in a different key. "He ever lives above for me to intercede, His all-redeeming love, His precious blood to plead.

His blood atoned for all our race, His blood atoned for all our race and sprinkles now the throne of grace."

Not for me, Lord, surely not for me. The world seemed to fade away until there was only herself, the music, and the nail-scarred hands outstretched above her.

Again the song rose. "Five bleeding wounds He bears, received on Calvary. They pour effectual prayers; They strongly plead for me. 'Forgive him, O forgive,' they cry. 'Forgive him, O forgive,' they cry, 'nor let that ransomed sinner die.'"

Forgive . . . Her hands clenched into fists in front of her. *Let go, let go,* the words whispered through her soul. Yet she could not obey them. So much held her back. Pictures of her family flashed through her mind, followed by the image of White Flower, pale on the bier.

"'Forgive him, O forgive,'" came the song again.

Could she let go? Could she face the past and then release it forever?

The verse changed. "His blood atoned for all our race, His blood atoned for all our race."

For me too? Could it be? But I have blood on my hands.

"And sprinkles now the throne of grace."

But . . . . The memory spilled over, dark and painful, her secret hidden for so long. *It was my fault. I saw the Indians coming. I was angry with Papa. So I stayed silent. I could have done something. It's my fault they died. My anger condemned them . . .*

"Five bleeding wounds he bears . . ."

She looked up at the hands marked with blood. Understanding dawned through her. "He has taken my guilt," she whispered. "Taken it as His own." The blood on her hands had become the blood on His. Slowly she opened her fists. Her head bowed. "Forgive me, Lord. Forgive me for what I did not do for my family and for what I did do to the Indians. Make my hands clean."

The music softened and swirled around her like a breeze. For a moment, for an eternity, she was swept into the music, and it seemed that God stood before her with eyes not accusing but kind. She lifted her hands. *Take the anger that has been my life. Take the pain.*

Then the man began to sing again, his words like a balm on a wound long infested. "My God is reconciled; His pard'ning voice I hear. He owns me for His child; I can no longer fear. With confidence I now draw nigh and, 'Father, Abba, Father,' cry."

Tears streamed down Annie's cheeks. "'Father, Abba, Father,'" she repeated. She felt the burden of a lifetime slip away with the tears that cleaned her face. Love like she had never known filled her heart. *I don't deserve . . .* she began.

I love you anyway, came the silent answer.

You died to set me free. She wrapped her arms around herself and squeezed. *I never knew. I never understood before. I never dreamed . . .*

Yet something deep inside still weighed on her heart.

Minutes passed, and she realized that the room was silent. She looked up. The man stood beside her. His eyes crinkled into a warm smile. "Hello, friend. I didn't see you come in."

Annie blushed. "I'm sorry. I didn't mean to intrude."

"No intrusion." He sat on the bench in front of her. "Did you like the hymn?"

She straightened her legs and leaned forward. "It set me free."

His smile broadened. "Ah, so you know the call of our Lord." He folded his fingers and placed his hands in his lap. "It's a wondrous thing to be forgiven."

"Is it really like the song says?"

"Indeed, it is. 'In God we put our trust: If we our sins confess, faithful He is, and just, from all unrighteousness to cleanse us all, both you and me. We shall from all our sins be free.'"

"'From all our sins be free,'" she murmured. "Is that another hymn?"

"Alas, you have found me out." He smiled. "To me everything is a song."

"I never knew I could be free. Not after what I've done."

"'His presence makes me free indeed.'"

"Don't tell me . . ."

"That hymn's called 'I Know My Redeemer Lives.' It and the others were written by my friend Charles Wesley." He scratched his chin. "Though I think he got the key wrong on the first one."

Her eyes widened. "My friends Rosie and Tom sing hymns all the time by someone named Wesley. You know him?"

He bowed his head. "Indeed, I do. My name's Wakefield. John Wakefield. I don't suppose you've heard of me?" His lips twitched into a grin.

"No, I'm sorry."

"Don't worry, miss. I didn't expect you to."

She laughed. "My name is Annie, Annie Hill."

"Well, Miss Annie Hill, how can I help you tonight?"

"Tell me more about the freedom God gives."

"Perhaps this hymn says it better." He cleared his throat and began to sing. "He breaks the pow'r of cancelled sin; He sets the pris'ner free. His blood can make the foulest clean; His blood availed for me."

"Yes, that's it exactly. I've lived my whole life as a prisoner."

"Are you free now, Miss Hill? Truly, fully free?"

The question caught Annie off guard. She wanted to answer yes, but somehow she knew something was missing still. She had a feeling that something was left undone, like when she went to the stream to wash clothes and forgot to take the stew off the fire. Her voice lowered. "What more do I need to do?"

"What is it that keeps you from Him? What still holds you back?"

He said it, and she knew. The anger, the hate. But after what they'd done to her, to her family, how could she forget? Taquachi's face, dark with war paint, appeared before her mind's eye. He was a devil. Surely God wouldn't . . .

"Ah, I can see from your face that you've hit upon the answer."

"He asks too much."

"What does He ask?"

"That I forgive." Yet how could she forgive Taquachi, or even White Wolf?

He nodded. "Yes, it goes hand in hand. He forgives us, and we must forgive others."

Her shoulders slumped. "But I can't."

"Can't or won't?"

Her thoughts flew to Taquachi, to the day he had dragged her from her home and tried to make her into an Indian. She remembered the cold, black eyes, the glint of the tomahawk, her mother's scalp hanging from his belt. "Both."

Wakefield sighed. "You must choose. He will help you if you ask."

Annie lowered her head and remembered all the injustice she'd ever suffered, all the pain she'd endured, all the cruelty she'd seen. And yet it paled before what she herself had done, what God had forgiven her of. Again she clenched her hands tight and then released them. As she did, the hatred began to drift away, and the scenes of horror became less vivid in her mind. "Good-bye, Taquachi," she whispered. "I choose to forgive you. With God's help I will no longer carry you in my soul." His image slipped away like sand dribbling through her fingers.

She expected elation, joy, exuberance, but instead she felt none of those things. For the first time came a peace deep within her, a quietness, a rest that she had never known before.

Wakefield smiled. "'The bliss of those that fully dwell, fully in Thee believe, 'Tis more than angel tongues can tell or angel minds conceive.' Go, friend, God is with you."

His words made her remember why she had come. "I don't have anywhere to go."

His brows furrowed. "You have no place to stay?"

"I—I . . ." She paused, then spoke in a hurry. "I need to find where a man called Rowley fights."

Wakefield shook his head. "I know little of fighting. Why must you find this place?"

"I'm looking for my . . . husband." She barely breathed the word.

"I see." He nodded. "I'll take you to Mistress Brown's. You can stay there tonight. And in the meantime, I'll do what I can to find these fights you speak of."

"Thank you," she whispered. "Thank you for everything."

"Come." He motioned for her to precede him out the door.

Annie stepped into the cold night and found herself warmer than she'd ever been. For the first time in her life, she knew that God would help her to do what was right. She would find White Wolf and tell him the truth. She would be his wife if he would have her.

The only problem was, White Wolf would never understand what had happened this night. If only he too could be free.

THIRTY-FOUR

~

Pipe smoke hung in the air like a winter blanket, dimming the light of the oil lamp on Higgins's desk. He pushed back his chair, crumpled the paper he'd been writing on, and threw it on the floor. He pulled a fresh sheet from the top drawer of his desk, dipped his quill, and started again.

> *Sir Magistrate,*
> *I humbly request you to order the release of one Richard Grant, imprisoned for treason, as I now believe him to be innocent of the crime. I have discovered . . .*

No, it was still wrong. He dropped the quill back into the inkwell and shoved the paper away from him. "I have discovered nothing, absolutely nothing that can be proven," he groaned. And the trial was today. Soon it would be too late to free Richard.

He crinkled the paper and tossed it next to the other one. What he needed was proof, not suspicions. He needed hard evidence to implicate the true traitor. If Richard was to escape the hangman's gallows, someone would have to take his place. Tonight.

Higgins stood up and walked over to the window. He pulled at his moustache. Outside, the day was dreary, with no rain, no sun, nothing but a hazy grayness that obscured the sky as surely as shadows and darkness had obscured his investigation. He sighed and turned away from the glass. One thing was clear, however. The traitor was after the Grant heirs. First Richard, then Justin, and lastly Jonathan. He ran his hand absently along the smooth finish of the carved horse on his desk. Jonathan . . . It should have been so easy; he should have had the perpetrator that night. But everything had gone wrong. He shook his head. He didn't want to think about that now. Some mistakes could not be undone.

His thoughts returned to the facts. All the Grant men had been attacked—all but baby William, the easiest target of all. He twisted his moustache around one knuckle. It seemed then that the path was being cleared for William. But why? The most obvious answer was Elizabeth's desire for revenge. But somehow that didn't seem right. She was not the black rider, nor did she have the mental ability to carry out this scheme. No, the traitor wanted more than to avenge Elizabeth. He wanted to destroy the Grants.

Higgins rubbed the scar on his forehead. If only he had caught the rider at the first or had captured Rowley and made him testify against the traitor. But the rider had raced away, and Rowley disappeared into the darkness of the tavern. Higgins shook his head again. He should have been stronger, smarter, quicker that night last November. Then an innocent man would not be headed for the noose. But sometimes justice was a feather on the wind, blown just beyond his grasp. And this was one of those times.

"Begging your pardon, sir," came a voice from behind him.

He turned. "Ah, Bidwell. What have you found out for me today?"

The man pushed the glasses up on his nose and cleared his throat. "Good news, Inspector. Very fortunate. You'll be pleased, I'm sure."

"Speak quickly, Bidwell. What news?"

"Rowley's coming out of retirement, sir. Set to fight today at high noon at the old Darton warehouse."

Higgins caught his breath. "Rowley? Are you sure?"

Bidwell nodded. "'Fast Fists Rowley brought out of hiding by the fighter they're calling the New World Wonder, the Fighting Savage'—that's the news all over town."

Higgins smiled. Just the break he needed. Months of searching had come up with nothing, and now on the eve of disaster the man surfaced. If he hurried, if Rowley knew what Higgins hoped he knew, and if the winds of fate blew just right, then Richard had a chance at freedom. He grabbed his pistol and tucked it into his waistband. "You're a good man, Bidwell. Remind me to increase your pay."

Bidwell grinned. "You always say that, Inspector."

Higgins patted him on the back. "But you haven't seen even an extra farthing."

"No, sir."

"Well, maybe this time will be different." He donned his coat and buttoned it up to his neck. "Lock up when you leave, and don't tell anyone where I've gone."

"Yes, sir. As you wish, sir."

Higgins glanced around the room one last time. His gaze fell to the balls of paper on the floor. Perhaps, he thought, he would not need the letter after all. "Thank God for the Fighting Savage," he whispered. Then he remembered the fate of Rowley's last opponents. He shuddered. Even a bloody savage deserved a better end than that.

~

"Wake up, savage."

White Wolf felt a boot dig into his ribs. He opened his eyes to see Patch standing above him. The straw crackled beneath him as he pushed himself to a sitting position.

The tiny back room of the warehouse seemed even smaller and stuffier than it had at dawn. Now the late morning sun peered through the cracks in the walls to illuminate dust in the air. White Wolf groaned. "Go away. Leave me alone."

"Big fight's in less than an hour." Patch shoved a bowl of lumpy gray mush in front of him. "Gotta keep up yer strength." He grinned. "Yer making me a rich man today."

Not again. God help me, I can't fight again. He rubbed his hands over his eyes. For the last two weeks all he had done was fight. Three, sometimes four times a day, until his life had become a blur of fists and blood splattered against pale skin. Short men, fat men, men as big as mountains with missing teeth and black eyes . . . white men.

This is what I wanted, isn't it? The accusation rose in his mind. *To fight the white man?* A bitter scowl twisted his brows. *But not like this.* He stared up at Patch. "I'm not going to fight."

Patch laughed. "Scared of old Fast Fists Rowley?" His voice dropped. "You should be scared. You know what 'appened to the last two guys that fought 'im, don't ya?" He pushed the bowl of gruel into White Wolf's hands.

White Wolf's gaze lowered to the floor. He twirled the spoon in the bowl and lifted it to his mouth. "No, and I don't care."

"Ya should care. They both ended up dead."

White Wolf choked. Gruel sprayed over his feet. "Dead?"

Patch's grin broadened. "Knocked 'em out cold, he did, and they never woke up again." He thrust his fist against White Wolf's shoulder. "That could be you today, so eat up. We gotta get ya ready."

"I'm not going to fight, I said."

"Oh, yer gonna fight all right. We got ways of making ya, remember."

White Wolf did remember, and his stomach churned. Slowly he drew his legs together and set the bowl on his lap.

"I see yer comin' around. This is gonna be one whopper of a fight." Patch chuckled.

White Wolf took another bite of mush. A fight to the death. It seemed appropriate somehow. Kill or be killed was all his life had been since that day long ago when his village was attacked. It seemed as if it had happened a lifetime ago to another boy in another place at another time. But it was the decisions he had made that day that had brought him here, that changed him into a man who could only fight and fight, could win and yet never be victorious. The nightmare always continued. Was God mocking him or calling out to him? Was there a God at all?

Patch kicked him again. "Eat."

He shoveled in another mouthful. A rumble of sound came from outside the door.

"Ah, they're comin' already," Patch muttered.

Then White Wolf recognized the sound as boots on the wooden floor and the reverberation of rough voices against the walls.

Patch rubbed his hands together. "'urry up."

White Wolf sighed and finished his gruel.

Patch took the bowl and tossed it onto the floor. Then he

grabbed White Wolf's collar and pulled him to his feet. "Time to get ya ready, savage."

White Wolf shrugged off Patch's grip. "Get on with it." He removed his shirt.

Patch slapped his hands together and reached into his pocket. He pulled out a bottle of oil and dumped some onto his palm. Then he began to rub the oil onto White Wolf's back and chest. "This'll make the punches roll right off ya," he said. He hit White Wolf twice on the shoulder blades and grimaced. "You make sure ya beat 'im, savage. I got a whole pouch bet on this one." He snapped his fingers.

In the main warehouse the shouts of the crowd grew louder.

Patch recapped the oil bottle. "Rowley must have got 'ere. Guess it's time." He motioned toward the door. "Go on. Time ta fight."

White Wolf glowered at him, then opened the door, walked down a short hall, and entered the largest room of the warehouse. As soon as he stepped through the last door, a sense of chaos swept over him. A horde of raucous men littered the room. Tankards of ale swung from their hands and up to their lips. Laughter and chatter and the clanking of glass swirled together in a cacophony of sound.

"Takin' bets 'ere," shouted a man in a fur cap.

"Ten pounds on Fast Fists," came a reply.

"Five on the Injun."

"Fifteen that Rowley'll finish him off before Biddle drains his first mug o' ale."

White Wolf glanced from man to man—the white faces, the flushed cheeks, a thousand eyes, mean and squinty.

Then he saw his opponent. The crowd parted and formed a circle. A man as big as a bear walked through like a king before his subjects. His shoulders were cloaked in a shiny red material, and on his feet were boots the size of moose skulls. He reached the middle of the circle of men and lifted his arms. The cloak fell to the ground to show his bare chest and a long red sash around his waist.

White Wolf swallowed. Patch shoved him forward. "Remember what I told ya," he hissed. "Hit 'im low; hit 'im 'ard. Don't turn yer back to 'im."

A bell sounded. For one brief moment the room quieted.

"It's time." Patch's voice rumbled behind him like water over stones. Rough hands pushed him forward. The circle tightened and became a blur of bodies around him and his opponent.

"You know the rules," a man in a tall hat yelled over the noise of the crowd.

"There ain't none," someone called back.

"That's right," the first man barked. "The last man standing is the winner." He clapped his hands twice, and the fight began.

Rowley put up his fists. White Wolf circled cautiously. He felt naked without his tomahawk at his side. He had never fought a man so large or who came at him with such cold confidence.

Rowley smiled. "Come on, Injun. Don't be scared. I won't hurt ya but a little."

The crowd roared with laughter.

White Wolf lunged. A fist impacted his shoulder. He spun and stumbled back. The man was faster than he'd expected. He regained his balance and tensed the muscles in his back.

"I got more where that came from, Injun," Rowley taunted and clenched his fists tighter.

White Wolf crouched lower.

"Stand up like a man, savage. Or are ya jus' a dog after all. Come on, doggie. I got a bone fer ya."

White Wolf reached inside himself for the anger, the hate, that had sustained him in the past. He searched for the red-hot fury but found only weariness, only pain. So tonight he would die. But not yet. He circled the man one more time.

Rowley followed his movement. White Wolf darted closer and swung his fist into Rowley's side. The man grunted. White Wolf pulled back but not quickly enough. Rowley's arm caught him on the shoulder and spun him sideways.

"Don't turn yer back!" he heard Patch scream over the crowd.

Too late! A fist like a cannonball hit him just above his waist. His breath left him. Another punch and another. He strained for air. Pain shot through him. Rowley's arm twisted around his. Heat like a knife stabbed into his ribs. He couldn't breathe. He couldn't move. He couldn't even cry out.

Rowley loosened his grip. White Wolf staggered forward and turned. Rowley's body, huge and monstrous, leaned over him.

"What's the matter with you? Fight!" Patch bellowed.

White Wolf dodged under Rowley's next swing and followed with a hard jab to the ribs. *I chose this life*, he told himself. *Chose it with the blood of the wolf, the blood from Taquachi's cup, the blood of the first white man I ever killed. I built this prison myself.*

Rowley retreated. White Wolf pressed forward. Rowley swung again. White Wolf's head jarred to the left. Fire blazed through his jaw. He tasted blood and felt the hot trickle down his chin.

Blood. Always the blood.

"He's got 'im now!" someone shouted over the calls of the crowd.

The smell of sweat and blood flooded his senses. He saw a blur of flesh, and then knuckles crashed into his eye. His vision dimmed, then sharpened. His head throbbed. A hand grabbed his arm and twisted. He gasped at the pain. A vision of Rowley loomed above him. White Wolf ducked and felt the breeze as Rowley's arm passed over him.

"Fight like a man," came a voice from the crowd. "Look at 'im cowerin' like a girl."

White Wolf tried to stand straighter but failed. His body listed to the left. One arm hung limply at his side. He was sick, sick of the fight, sick of this life of war, hate, and yes, blood. But he could not escape it. He could not escape his sin. *His blood sets us free*, his father's voice whispered through him. *"Redemption through His blood, the forgiveness of sins."*

"But not for me," he muttered. "It's too late for that." It would soon be over. Soon the final blow would come, and the darkness would wash over him forever.

A shout rose from the crowd. "Get 'im, Rowley!"

"Stop this!" another man called.

White Wolf glanced up to see a man peering between two others. The man pulled at his moustache and struggled to push through the throng. Those in front of him elbowed him back, and his face was lost to view.

"Get back in there and *fight!*" yelled Patch's voice in his ear. Hands again pushed him mercilessly forward.

He swung at Rowley and missed. *I can't do this anymore. I'm tired of fighting the white man. . . .* "Seek the Lord, and his strength: seek his face evermore," came his father's voice again.

He bent low and rammed his body into Rowley's midsection. He had rejected God, he reminded himself. He'd turned his back and vowed never to return. And yet . . . what if it wasn't too late?

For one breath White Wolf pulled back from the fight. *God, show me Yourself! Let me see You,* came a cry from the depths of his soul. *Only You can set me free.*

At that moment Rowley's fist connected with his jaw. He crashed to the floor. A foot slammed into his gut. Blackness swirled across his vision and engulfed him. His head snapped left and right as Rowley hit him again and again and again. Pain exploded within him. He opened his mouth to scream. No sound came. The voices grew dim. And suddenly he couldn't feel the punches anymore. He couldn't feel anything. Only the darkness. Only the silence. Only a stillness as heavy as death.

Then the light came again—faint at first and growing brighter.

The voices sharpened. "He's out." "No, he's comin' to." "Get up, savage! Get up!" That one was Patch's. "White Wolf! Waptumewi, wake up." The last voice, gentler than Patch's, penetrated his haze. Someone was calling his name. Could it be?

He blinked and saw a figure leaning over him. A vision swam before him—moss-green eyes looking down at him with tender care. He lifted his hand to touch soft red-brown hair. *Annie?* Did he speak her name aloud?

"It's me." He could barely hear her over the shouts of the crowd.

"You're real. You found me."

Her fingers touched his cheek. "I love you." Her lips formed the words, though her voice was lost in the din around them.

Slowly her features came into focus, and in them White Wolf saw the face of God.

THIRTY-FIVE

~

Strength surged through White Wolf's frame. God had answered his prayer. Despite everything he'd done and everything he'd been, God had not forsaken him. He lifted his head and saw the path to freedom, and over it lay the shadow of a cross.

A tremor raced through his frame. It was time to come home. It was time to let go of the hate that had bound him for so long. But how? He rose from the floor and faced his opponent. One thing he knew. He must not die now, not here on the very threshold of freedom, not until he knew for sure if forgiveness could really be his.

He saw in his mind again the image of the cross. "Save me, Lord," he whispered. "Give me the strength to do what I must." His vision focused on the two men who held Rowley by the arms. When they saw White Wolf stand, they released their grip.

Rowley stepped toward him. "To the death, Injun," he muttered.

"Waptumewi?" Annie's voice sounded strained.

He glanced at her. "I must finish it."

She nodded.

He turned to Rowley. "To the death."

A shout rose from the crowd. "Finish 'im off."

"No!"

"Get back!"

"Get 'im!"

Rowley lumbered forward, fists flying. White Wolf countered with a punch of his own deep into Rowley's ribs. The crowd roared. White Wolf drew a quick breath. Jab, retreat, swing, duck. Dart left, then right. Hit low. Hit hard. Press forward, circle. Advance, fall back. Seconds dragged into long minutes as White Wolf returned blow for blow, not knowing what else to do, knowing only that he must live at least long enough to step into the shadow of the cross. Sweat beaded on his forehead. Again he swung and this time connected with Rowley's temple.

Rowley stumbled backward. A line of blood appeared from his ear. He spat and lurched forward. White Wolf stepped left. He swung again and missed.

Rowley coughed. "You can't win this, Injun. May as well give it up. Everyone 'ere knows it's just a matter o' time." His gaze shot over the crowd. His eyes rounded. He straightened. "Inspector?"

White Wolf leaped forward. His body crashed into Rowley's massive bulk. His fist jammed into the man's jaw. Blood spewed across the floor. Like a tree felled by an axe, Rowley thudded to the floor. His eyes glazed.

White Wolf smelled victory. He cocked his fist and leaned over Rowley's frame. Visions of every injustice he'd ever endured at the hand of the white man spun through his mind. The Adam's apple bobbed in Rowley's neck. One punch. Just one more hit right at that spot, and he would crush Rowley's windpipe.

To the death, the words whispered through his mind. His gaze met Rowley's.

Terror flamed in Rowley's eyes. He tried to rise and failed.

Sudden silence blanketed the room. Only breathing, harsh and hard, echoed in the quietness.

White Wolf looked down at his clenched fist. For a moment he thought he saw there the shadow of a snake. "No," he whispered. "Not again. I forgive them. I forgive them all." He opened his hand and lowered his arm.

Rowley choked, "What are you waiting for?"

Slowly White Wolf stood upright. He stared down into Rowley's face, into the face of a white man, and knew that at that moment God had performed a miracle. The hate was gone. The snake had vanished beneath the shadow of the cross. "In the name of Jesus Christ, I spare your life as He spared mine." He stepped back and looked into the eyes of the men around him. His gaze rested on Patch. "I will fight no more. God has given me my freedom."

Patch did not say a word.

White Wolf turned to Annie. He stretched his arm toward her.

Tears glistened in her eyes as she placed her hand in his. He drew her to his side. The crowd parted before them.

"*Our* freedom," she murmured.

"Together?"

"Always . . . husband."

He squeezed her fingers and smiled. Papa had been right after all.

～

The air shimmered with dread and expectation. Breath, visible in the coldness of the courtroom, hung like a dim fog over the faces of the watchers. Philippe's own breath, heavy and rapid, rose in white puffs before his eyes, obscuring his vision. He shifted in his chair and glared at the man in front of him. "I do not know, I tell you."

The man toyed with his watch fob and paced back and forth between the judge and Philippe. He adjusted his spectacles and touched one finger to his wig. Silver buttons glittered from his coat as the man again turned to face him. "We don't believe you. You admitted that you knew one Jonathan Grant, that you received secrets from his brother, Lord Richard Grant."

"*Non!* I mean, no. *Mon Dieu,* how many times must I say it?" He threw his hands in the air. "I do not know Jonathan Grant. I have never met the man. And I do not know his brother either." He crossed his arms and looked out over the courtroom. There hundreds of eyes stared back at him. Men in wigs, women in tall hats—a blur of faces crammed together to fill every corner of the courthouse.

Philippe blinked and focused on the first few rows. In front sat a woman with features as cold as ice, and next to her was a young girl whose cheeks were damp with tears. For a moment Philippe felt a desire to reach out and wipe away the moisture. She rubbed the back of her hand over her nose and looked away. Behind them a black-haired Indian woman studied him with puzzled eyes—eyes the color of the summer sky.

Philippe leaned forward. It couldn't be. And yet . . . yet he would know that face anywhere, even a dozen years after he had seen it last. How many Indian women were there with eyes like blue topaz? Only one. But how could she be here now? Perhaps she was not. Perhaps she was only a figment in his memory, sent now as a vision to remind him of the man he'd once hoped to be—a good man, honest and upright. He would be that man now. He would not be afraid.

"Pay attention, sir!"

The voice penetrated his thoughts. He returned his gaze to the man before him.

"Now." The prosecutor shook his forefinger in the air. "How did your captain receive the information from Lord Grant?" His finger jabbed at a huddled figure on the side of the courtroom.

Philippe glanced at the scarecrow of a man with his untidy hair and haunted, hollow eyes. Once a proud English aristocrat, now he was no more than a shadow. Prison had not been kind, and this trial, it seemed, would be no kinder. "I do not know what you speak of."

Murmuring rose from the courtroom. The judge tapped his knuckles on the wooden bench in front of him. The room quieted.

The prosecutor's voice broke the silence. "Your captain received information, did he not?"

Philippe sighed. It seemed as if he'd been sitting in this hard chair forever, though it had probably been less than two hours. Other witnesses had gone before him, but none of them had received the scrutiny reserved for the "enemy spy." He rubbed his hand over the back of his neck. "So I was told." His memory flitted back to that night so many months ago when he had sat by the fire with Jean-Pierre. He'd been focused on getting salve for White Wolf's wound, but the old healer had wanted to talk. Hadn't he said something about an English aristocrat? About information given for no more than a promise and a pittance? Could Richard Grant be that informant? Philippe didn't know, and he didn't care.

"And were you also told the identity of the traitor?"

"No. I told you. I do not know."

"Do not know or will not say? We can, you know, have you shot as a spy."

Philippe's eyes narrowed. "Yes, I know."

Before the prosecutor could answer, a flurry of wind and snow swirled through the door as it pushed open. A thin man in glasses slid through the opening. He stomped the snow off his boots and brushed his hands over the shoulders of his coat. Everyone in the courtroom turned. The man removed his hat and approached the bench.

The judge raised his eyebrows. "Well? What say you, Mr. Bidwell?"

Bidwell shook his head. "I couldn't find him, sir. He's disappeared."

"Are we then to resolve this man's guilt without the inspector general? His testimony is crucial."

Bidwell bobbed his head up and down. "Yes, Your Honor. I know, Your Honor. But I did bring this." He pulled what appeared to be a riding crop from his coat.

The judge smiled. "Ah, the famous crop. Very well. Bring it to me."

Boot heels clicked against the floor as Bidwell approached the bench and handed the crop to the judge. The courtroom was quiet as the judge examined the leather instrument beneath the light of an oil lamp. Someone scuffled his feet over the wooden floor. Another coughed and sniffed. A chair squeaked. Finally the judge lifted his gaze. "Yes, I see the insignia. Quite clear, it is. Thank you, Bidwell. You may find a seat."

Bidwell bowed his head and retreated to the far side of the room.

"May I continue the questioning now, Your Honor?"

The judge turned to the prosecutor. "If you must, Sir Riley, but make haste, if you will."

Riley turned back to Philippe. His features hardened. "Tell us, how did Lord Grant transfer his information to your captain?"

Philippe scowled. "I tell you again, I do not have the information you require. I do not know if that man," he waved his hand toward Richard, "is guilty or not." He tipped forward. "I am, sir, just a simple Frenchman who wants to go home."

"A Frenchman, yes." Riley slurred the word. "We are at war with the French, and yet you expect us to believe you?"

"I have no reason to lie."

"But you will not tell us how you know this man or his brother?"

"I do not know them!" Philippe's voice raised to a shout.

"Silence!" The judge slammed his hand into the bench. His face reddened. "Silence, I say. This is getting us nowhere."

"But, judge—"

"I've heard enough! We have the crop, and we have the miserable defeat of Braddock's troops in the wilderness. The crop alone is enough to testify against this man."

A sob issued from the crowd. Philippe looked up to see the young girl bury her face in her hands. The woman next to her shifted in her chair. Hate glinted from her eyes. Behind them a man stared at the prisoner. A small smile twisted his lips. *The English are a strange breed*, Philippe thought, *to rejoice in the pain of others*.

The judge continued, "I declare Lord Grant guilty of treason against England and against the king, and I sentence him to—"

"Wait!" A man in the middle of the crowd stood. A hat shadowed his face. Every head pivoted toward him. He strode forward. When he reached the front of the courtroom, he stopped. His voice rang through the room. "Lord Grant is innocent of the crime. I have proof."

Someone gasped. Whispered questions sprang from every corner. "Who's that?" "Did you see him come in?" "Lord Grant is innocent?" "No, he's guilty. He must hang!" This last from the man with the smirk.

The judge again pounded his fist on the bench. The questions ceased. Slowly the judge stood. "Who are you?"

The man's shoulders straightened. "Let Lord Grant go. I will take his place."

"You are guilty of the crime?"

"I will bear the guilt." The man's voice did not waver.

The judge leaned forward. "Show us your proof."

"Here." He stepped up to the bench and took a paper from the folds of his overcoat.

The judge took the paper and read it aloud:

"Bonjour, mon ami.
    "We received your information. Braddock will find a surprise waiting when he gets to Fort Duquesne. . ."

"No, it can't be," someone hissed.

Philippe looked over the faces in the courtroom. One had turned pale. The woman with hate in her eyes now looked afraid. Her lips trembled. Tears glistened, bright and full, from the eyes of the Indian woman. Philippe looked back at the bench. The judge's gaze rested on the face beneath the hat. "The seal is authentic. Where did you get this?"

"Does it matter? I take responsibility."

The judge's voice lowered. "You know what this means?"

The man's head lifted. "I know."

The judge frowned. "Approach the bench, sir."

The man came closer until only he and Philippe could hear the judge's next words. "Surely you have seen the gallows outside?"

"I have." The man's voice did not waver.

"And the mob as well?"

"Yes."

"Then you know that someone must hang today, or the people may riot. This," he tapped on the parchment before him, "is not enough to convict you."

"It's enough."

For a long moment, the judge stared into the eyes of the man in front of him. Finally he nodded. "As you wish." The words dropped like the sound of a mallet on a coffin lid. He turned. "Release Lord Grant," he boomed.

Guards hurried to comply.

The judge stood and pointed at the man before him. "You, sir, are guilty of the crime of treason. You shall be hanged by the neck at sundown. Take him away."

The guards stepped forward. The man turned. As he did, he removed his hat, and Philippe saw a flash of amber eyes set in a face as strong as steel. Whispers skittered through the courtroom, punctuated by a child's voice, clear above the rumblings: "Uncle Jonathan?"

THIRTY-SIX

~

Higgins held his breath as the Indian leaned over Rowley's still body. He saw the savage cock his fist. A shout rose in his throat, but an invisible hand smothered it and kept him silent. He pressed forward. *No, God, stop him! Don't let Rowley die!*

Suddenly the Indian straightened. "In the name of Jesus Christ, I spare your life."

The men standing near Higgins gasped. "He ain't gonna do it," someone whispered.

"He's a bloody Christian," another muttered.

Without a word the Indian extended his hand toward a woman in the crowd. She took it, and for a moment the two looked at each other as if the room had melted away, and no one else existed in the world. Then the men around him pushed back, and the two passed untouched through the crowd.

"We'll find Jonathan and Kwelik," the woman was saying. "Then we can go home."

The words penetrated Higgins's mind. Jonathan? Kwelik? "Wait, stop!" He reached his hand between the men in front of him and touched the woman's shoulder. She turned.

"I can help you."

"Look at that Rowley, skulking off like a dog with its tail 'tween its legs," called the man in front of him.

Higgins caught his breath. His eyes sped to Rowley. There halfway across the warehouse, the man slithered toward the back door.

"Stop him!" Higgins shouted. "Halt, in the name of King George!"

No one listened, least of all Rowley. Higgins shoved aside the men in front of him. This time, he vowed, his prey would not escape. He grabbed the pistol from his belt and shot toward the ceiling. "Stop, I say."

Silence dropped over the crowd like water from a bucket. All eyes locked on Higgins. Rowley froze. Slowly he turned back. "Inspector General Higgins," he called.

The room again erupted in sound, dozens of voices jabbering like a flock of mockingbirds. "It's the inspector." "Inspector who?" "What's he doin' here?" "He ain't gonna catch me." "Let's get outta 'ere."

Men fled toward the doors in a flurry of coats and the jostle of elbows. Higgins stood stunned as men vanished like cockroaches before the light. For a brief instant, Rowley looked back at him and grinned. He touched his finger to his brow in a mocking salute and then joined the throng headed for the back door.

"Oh, no you don't," Higgins whispered. "Not again." He sprinted toward Rowley.

Men skittered out of his way as he closed the distance between them. Rowley glanced over his shoulder. His eyes widened. "Get outta the way," he shrieked. But the mass of bodies in front of him stayed solid.

Higgins threw himself at Rowley's back. The man tumbled to the floor. Higgins jammed his knee into Rowley's spine and wrenched his arm behind him.

Rowley squirmed beneath his grip. "Don't move," he yelled, "or I'll break your arm."

Weakened from the fight, Rowley became still. "Leave me alone," he grunted. "I ain't done nuthin' wrong."

Higgins noticed the sudden quietness in the room. He glanced up. The warehouse was empty except for the Indian and the woman coming toward him. Dust scuttled across the floor where men's boots had so recently passed. He returned his gaze to Rowley. A splash of light dripped in from a window overhead and drizzled across Rowley's face. A trickle of blood still stained his cheek.

Higgins pressed his knee deeper into Rowley's back and quickly reloaded his pistol. Then he pointed it at the man's shoulders and stood. "Get up, and don't try to run."

Rowley clambered to his feet and glared at him. "I ain't tellin' you a bloody thing. You ain't got nuthin' on me."

Higgins scowled. "I've got my two eyes that say you're a traitor, and my two ears that tell me you've sold secrets to the French. I was there, Rowley. I saw it all."

Rowley turned paler yet. "It weren't me, I tell ya."

"Admit it."

"I don't know what yer talkin' about."

"You'd better remember quick, or you'll find yourself wearing a rope around your neck."

Rowley hung his head. "Yer gonna string me up anyway. It don't matter what I say."

A hand brushed Higgins's shoulder. He turned to see the Indian standing behind him. "I'll help," he said. "What do you need from him, and why do you need it?"

Higgins paused. Could he trust this man? "Why do you offer?"

"Because you said you would help us. You're the first man in England to do so."

Higgins looked deeply into the brown eyes before him. Slowly he nodded. "Today an innocent man will hang from the gallows unless Rowley here will identify the true traitor." He waved his pistol at Rowley's chest.

The Indian turned toward the man who'd been his opponent. "I spared your life, white man. Now do what's right."

Rowley sniffed and took one step backward. "I don't know who it was. I never seen him before."

Higgins jabbed his forefinger toward Rowley. "But you saw him that night."

Rowley didn't answer. The Indian moved closer. Tension coursed through Higgins. His hand tightened on the pistol. The boom of a bullet split the air as the gun accidentally fired. The shot sped over Rowley's shoulder. Everyone jumped.

Rowley's eyes grew round. "All right, all right," he sputtered. "I saw 'im. Little guy, big nose."

Higgins rubbed his hand over his upper lip. He turned toward Rowley. "Could you identify him if you saw him again."

Rowley shrugged. "I s'pose so. For a pardon, mayhaps I could."

"Testify against the informer, and I will see that you walk free."

Rowley's eyes slipped from Higgins to the Indian and then back again. "I'll do it for the pardon and fer the Injun here who spared me."

Higgins nodded and tucked the pistol back in its holster. "Then come. We must hurry." A vision of the hangman's noose darted through his mind. Were they already too late?

～

Fear, like a wave of darkness, spilled over Jonathan and left him shaking. Slowly he removed his hat and fought against the panic within him. The time of decision had passed. God had called, and he had answered. And in doing so, the final fetters of unforgiveness broke in his heart. He knew he was free at last. Love, and sacrifice, had conquered the hate for good. But at what cost?

He turned toward the courtroom. The buzz of whispered questions darted around him. His gaze locked with Elizabeth's. *Speak now. Tell the truth,* he willed her. For a moment he thought she would.

Her mouth opened. Shock registered on her features. Then she averted her eyes, and Jonathan knew that the moment was gone. The gallows awaited him.

Beside her Katherine gasped. "Uncle Jonathan?" Her words seemed to echo in the sudden quietness of the crowded courtroom. Then the room again erupted with sound.

Jonathan lifted his chin. Guards rushed toward him. He felt their hands on his arms, their breath on the back of his neck. His arm twisted behind him. Manacles, thick and cold, were clamped around his wrists. He closed his eyes. Now it would come. The dichotomy of freedom—his soul set free, his body bound.

Yet he had done what God asked of him. He had done it though he had not planned to when he'd arrived at the courtroom that morning. Weeks ago Higgins had pulled him, bruised and freezing, from the river's belly. The metal plate over his chest had done its work. As the days sped by, they had sought proof to free his brother and found nothing. He'd come today to face his failure. Instead, he would face his death.

The moment the judge pronounced his brother's guilt, everything had changed. Suddenly he knew what God demanded, knew it as surely as if a voice had spoken in his ear. *Greater love hath no man than this, that a man lay down his life for his friends . . . for his brother.* And so it came, the test of his faith, the test of what God had done within him that day in the graveyard. And he knew he must not fail lest his soul be captured once more. Then as if to confirm it, he'd reached into his pocket and found there the letter. For all this time he'd kept it, not knowing that God would use it to set Richard free and send him to the gallows.

"Move on, Grant," muttered a guard behind him.

Jonathan opened his eyes and shuffled forward. He knew Kwelik was out there somewhere. He could feel her gaze on him, questioning, searching. Would she understand what he had done even if he could explain it? Would she know why he had to do this thing that seemed like madness?

Just that morning he'd watched them build the gallows. Muscular men wielded hammers and carried thick planks of wood. A thin man had brought a new rope, tied it, and tested its strength. He never dreamed they were building it for him, but God knew. For now, forever, that would have to be enough.

A guard shoved him in the back. He stumbled, righted himself, and turned. There on the side of the courtroom Katherine ran into the arms of her father. Even from across the room, he could hear her sobs. Richard glanced up, and their eyes met. Confusion and bewilderment shone in Richard's gaze. Then he dropped his head and buried his face in his daughter's hair.

Peace swelled in Jonathan. He had done what was right. He had kept his promise to Katherine and to her father. He had chosen God's will above his own. And now he knew that God had completed the work in his heart.

He turned back toward the door and found himself staring into a face he had seen before—the face of the traitor himself. "Simon," he whispered.

Simon's eyes narrowed. "You fool," he hissed.

Jonathan did not respond. Today victory wore the mask of defeat, and gain donned the mantle of loss.

Simon leaned closer. "This time there will be no escape . . . Lord Grant."

Lord Grant. So he knew that Richard was not a Grant at all. What else did this traitor know about his family?

"This time you really die."

Jonathan looked into Simon's eyes and knew he spoke the truth. No metal plate over his chest would save him this time. Now death was real. And yet he did not regret his action.

Lord Grant. The words echoed in his mind. He'd spent his whole life running from that title, but now at his death he would accept it. He would wear it like the noose around his neck. Today Lord Grant would die. Perhaps it was right that it was so. A guard grabbed his arm and shoved him toward the door. Simon's face fell from sight. A dozen more steps, and the door swung open before him.

Outside, people jammed the courtyard and poured from the building behind him. Urchins dressed in gray rags, women in old shawls, ladies in embroidered dresses, men with glittering watch fobs, others with rotting teeth and shabby clothes—all glared and jeered and called out foul names until the air trembled in the melee.

"Out of the way!" a guard shouted.

The people pushed back until a path formed to the gallows. Jonathan looked up at the hangman's noose silhouetted against the setting sun. Slowly he marched through the crowd, their faces a blur of anger and hate.

"Death to the traitor!" someone called.

"The devil's got ya now, French lackey," screamed another.

"Take that, ya bloody turncoat!" A woman spat in his face. The spittle dribbled down his chin to his neck. He could not wipe it away.

Then in his mind, he pictured Jesus walking beside him, walking toward the cross on Golgotha. And he remembered that freedom was won through obedience, through surrender . . . even unto death. They could steal his life, but they could not take his soul. He would die a free man.

A rock struck him in the cheek. He felt a trickle of blood on his skin. "That's fer General Braddock," someone shrieked. "The devil take ya, traitor!"

Jonathan lifted his head. They could not touch him now. He was in God's hands—God's alone. The stairs loomed in front of him. One step forward, two. A tomato splattered against his chest. Three. Four. Something hit the back of his head. He raised his foot and placed it on the first step. Richard was free—he mustn't forget that. Above, the noose swung back and forth in the breeze. A hand touched the back of his arm. He turned. Kwelik.

The pain in her eyes brought tears to his. He fought them back. For this one moment he wanted to see her clearly. He wanted to fix her features in his mind for all eternity.

I love you. Her lips formed the words.

And he knew she understood. His gaze traced the scar on her cheek where the flames of her own freedom had left their mark. If anyone knew the price of freedom, it was her, his beloved bride, who had walked into the flames for Christ, just as he walked to the gallows now.

Her gaze caught his in a moment so deep that words vanished. He tried to speak but could not. And yet he knew that she could read his love, could see it like a brand across his face.

Fingers dug into his flesh and compelled him forward. Up another step, and another, and another, until he stood atop the platform. He turned back to the crowd. The guards gripped his arms and positioned him beneath the noose. His gaze again fell on Kwelik, and he drew from her strength. He was glad she had not brought the children. He couldn't have borne it if they had been here too. To see her was enough to remind him of all he was about to lose and all that he hoped to gain.

Behind her Richard's gaunt face looked up at him with eyes still marked with wonder. As Jonathan watched, the hardness melted away, and Richard was again the young boy he'd once known, the brother he'd once loved. Jonathan saw a lifetime of hurt and hate built by their father's cruelty crumble and knew that Richard too had finally been set free.

Harlan Grant was dead at last.

Jonathan's gaze flickered over Katherine, Elizabeth, and a woman who seemed hauntingly familiar. Was she the one from the graveyard, from the gardens of the Grant estate? For one breath his eyes lingered on the stranger. Then they passed to the man standing beyond her. The traitor, like the devil himself, watched and waited for the moment of his revenge.

A man stepped in front of Jonathan, blocking his view. He unrolled a short piece of parchment. The crowd hushed. "For betraying the king and his loyal subjects." The man's voice rang over the gathering. "For selling secrets to our enemies. For the vile act of treason against your own countrymen, you are forthwith sentenced to death by hanging." He placed the rope around Jonathan's neck. "Have you any last words?"

Mercy, God. Save me. The plea rose in his heart. He tipped his head back and listened with his soul. But the heavens were silent. A minute passed, then two. The sun slipped lower. A sea gull dipped into view. Jonathan watched its flight—free, unfettered, at peace with the wind and sky. He closed his eyes and willed himself to soar too, to fly to heaven, higher, higher, until he felt himself caught up in the perfect peace of God. "Unto God alone do I commit my spirit," he cried. "He alone sets me free."

The rope tightened.

THIRTY-SEVEN

~

Higgins knew he was too late the minute he saw the crowd. Anticipation hung around them like a dark mist. To his right a baby cried. A dog barked. People leaned forward and craned their necks for a better view. Voices, like the rumbling of stones down a mountain, filled the air and became indistinguishable. In the distance, black against the sky, he could see the gallows and a man beneath them. He pushed closer to the backs of the watchers.

"Let me through." His shout bounced off the bodies in front of him and died unheard.

No one moved. A woman with a goat in her arms glanced over her shoulder. "Stop yer pushin'," she called. The goat bleated.

Higgins grabbed a man by the shirt and yanked him out of the way.

"Who do ya think ya are?" the man sputtered.

Higgins raised his voice. "I am Inspector General Higgins. I must get through."

The man squinted. "Sure ya are, and I'm the king's mother." He shrugged out of Higgins's grip and wiggled back into place.

"It's no use," muttered Annie from beside him. "They've already got the noose around his neck."

Rowley tapped him on the arm and motioned toward the gallows. "That ain't 'im, Inspector. He ain't skinny enough."

Higgins took a closer look. His breath stopped halfway. It wasn't Richard.

Annie stood on her tiptoes. She gasped. "It's Jonathan!"

Higgins groaned as he too recognized Jonathan's silhouette.

White Wolf leaned over and spoke in his ear. "You must shoot your gun again as you did at the fights. There may still be time. Quickly."

Higgins nodded and pulled the pistol from his belt. He aimed at the sky, closed his eyes, and squeezed the trigger. Nothing.

"What happened?"

He stared at the silent barrel. "Empty. It's empty. I never reloaded."

Annie stared at him. "Well, do it! Hurry. They're reading the death sentence now."

Higgins's fingers trembled as he pulled the powder horn from his pocket. Tiny pebbles scattered over his hand and wrist as the powder spilled into the gun. He shoved in the wad and packed it down. Annie dug into his pocket and grabbed a lead ball. "Here." She pushed it into his hand.

It slipped from his fingers and rattled onto the ground in front of him. He grabbed another bullet from his pocket. Quickly he dropped it into the gun's barrel, raised the pistol, and shot into the sky. The sound ricocheted off the buildings around him.

A few people turned. No one else even moved.

"It isn't enough!" he shouted. He shook his head. Pistol shots were all too common in this part of the city, as common, it seemed, as the bark of a dog.

"What're we going to do?" Annie moaned.

Higgins looked up to see a man tighten the rope around Jonathan's neck. The man's hand moved toward the lever that would collapse the planks beneath Jonathan's feet. "It's too late."

Suddenly a sound unlike anything Higgins had ever heard rose from beside him. Piercing, bloodcurdling, like the howl of a demon set loose from the pit. The hair on Higgins's arms stood on end. He pressed his hands to his ears.

The crowd fell silent. Every eye turned toward them. Higgins lowered his arms and stared at the Indian beside him.

White Wolf put his hands on his hips and looked toward the gallows. "How many times must I save that man?" he muttered.

～

Jonathan heard the cry—savage, guttural—a sound that could only have come from the throat of a Lenape warrior. It seemed to echo from the frontier of the New World, across the ocean, to the shores of England, like a call from the past. A shiver prickled his skin.

The crowd froze in place. Jonathan looked over their heads to see the proud face of an Indian brave, his chin lifted toward the sun. And beside him stood Inspector Higgins. Jonathan felt the muscles in his back relax.

Higgins raised his arm. "Stop! Stop the hanging! Let us through!"

The crowd pushed back to form a path between Higgins and the gallows. Jonathan watched as the inspector strode toward him, followed by the Indian, a man as tall as a tower, and a woman who reminded him of Annie. Closer they came, until he could see the firm set of the inspector's jaw.

"Let that man go," Higgins ordered. "He's innocent, I tell you."

The man who had read the sentence stepped to the front of the platform. "Sorry, Inspector," he called. "Orders is orders. This man's gotta hang."

Jonathan's breath came more quickly.

The man returned to the side of the gallows. From the corner of his eye, Jonathan could see a hand reaching toward the lever.

Higgins pointed his finger directly at the man. "Pull that lever, Wallace, and I'll see that you're the next to hang."

The man raised his hands and moved back. Higgins took the stairs two at a time until he reached the top. "You." He pointed to a guard. "Get the judge. Tell him the case is reopened, and we need his presence posthaste."

The guard nodded and hurried toward the courtroom.

"He's a bloody traitor," yelled a voice from the crowd. "He's gotta hang."

"Hang the traitor! Hang the traitor!" Several took up the chant.

Higgins turned and pulled the rope from Jonathan's neck. "What did you do?" he muttered.

Jonathan stepped back away from the noose. "I confessed."

"What?"

"It was the only way."

"Hang him! Hang him!" The cry grew louder.

Higgins turned to the second guard. "You there—do you have a knife?"

"Aye, sir." The guard drew a blade from his pocket and handed it to Higgins.

He took it and cut the bonds around Jonathan's wrists. Jonathan rubbed his chafed skin and leaned closer to Higgins. "Do you have the proof we need?"

Higgins smiled. "Better. I've got Rowley."

Hope surged through Jonathan.

"Is Bains here?"

"Behind Elizabeth."

Higgins touched his moustache. "As I suspected." He turned toward the crowd. "Silence! Silence, I say."

The crowd quieted.

"The traitor must pay for what he's done," a man called.

Higgins nodded. "Justice will prevail, good sir. The traitor will hang."

A cheer rose from the crowd.

Higgins again lifted his arms. "But this is not the traitor."

"He confessed." "Heard it myself." "Bloody turncoat," came the cries from the crowd.

"Patience, friends."

Jonathan's gaze dropped to Kwelik, but she was not looking at him. Instead, she was embracing the Indian. Then she opened her arms to the woman who looked like Annie. Somehow her actions comforted him, told him that everything was all right, and God was with them. He looked past her to see the tall man moving through the crowd. Rowley. He held his breath as Rowley drew closer and closer to Simon. *Don't move*, he willed. In a moment all would be right again. Just a few more steps, and Rowley would see the traitor.

Higgins moved back and placed his hand on Jonathan's arm. "I suggest you stay up here." He spoke from the side of his mouth and kept his eyes on the crowd. "I may have stayed your execution, but I can't control the mob."

"Got 'im, Inspector!" Rowley's shout echoed over the calls of the crowd. "This be the guy who gave me the secrets."

Jonathan's gaze shot to his enemy's face. Horror flashed through Simon's eyes as Rowley lifted him by his collar. Higgins crossed his arms and moved to the front of the platform. He looked down at the traitor. The murmurings of the crowd ceased, as if all held their breath for the inspector to pronounce his judgment. Even the animals were silent.

Higgins's voice boomed through the air. "Simon Bains, you are under arrest for the crime of treason."

Simon twisted in Rowley's grip. "I don't know what this man is speaking of," he whined.

"He's speaking of your guilt, sir." Higgins leaped from the platform and strode toward Simon. "You've eluded me twice, but this time justice demands her due."

Jonathan could see Simon tremble. "You'll take the word of this idiot over a respected nobleman?" His voice cracked.

Higgins did not hesitate. "You're no nobleman, Simon Bains. Nor was your father."

Simon's face turned red. "My father was a good man! He was a saint until *his* father destroyed him." He threw his arm toward Jonathan. "I will have justice, justice for that devil's sin!" He wrenched his shoulders out of his coat and twisted out of Rowley's grip.

Rowley dropped the empty coat and lunged toward him. Simon reached behind his back. A pistol appeared in his hand. He pointed it at Rowley's chest. "Stay away!" he screamed.

Rowley stumbled backward. His gaze darted to Higgins. "I told ya I'd help ya, but I ain't going up against no madman."

Behind him Katherine bent down and picked up Simon's coat.

Simon spun toward Higgins. He jabbed his gun at the inspector and then pointed it wildly around the crowd until his aim finally rested on Elizabeth. "You," he cried. "You did this. You'll pay for betraying me."

Elizabeth's face turned white. "No," she breathed. "I didn't say a word."

Simon sneered. "Liar! You, with your lily-white hands and your perfectly coifed hair. You play the fine gentlewoman, but I know what you really are."

Elizabeth's voice turned to a whimper. "No, Simon. Don't . . ."

"You were not a gentlewoman in my bed, you . . . whore!"

"No," she shrieked. The feathers on her hat swayed.

Simon's voice raised to a strident shout. "Tell them, tell them what you've done. Tell what your precious little William really is."

Elizabeth's head thrashed back and forth. "No," she moaned. "Simon, please . . ."

He turned to the crowd. "William. William Grant is a bast . . ."

Elizabeth's scream covered the word. She backed away. Her gaze flashed left and right to the faces around her.

The muttering of the crowd grew to a muted roar. Fingers pointed in her direction. Finely dressed men shook their heads, and elegant women whispered behind gloved hands.

Elizabeth fell to her knees. Her head dropped into her hands. Even from the platform, Jonathan could hear her wracking sobs.

"That's enough, Bains." Higgins's command cut through Elizabeth's wailing.

Simon threw back his head and laughed. "You can't win. I've already beat you all." His pistol swung from Elizabeth back to Higgins.

Higgins did not even flinch. "Put that down, Bains," he ordered. "Don't make this worse for yourself."

"Lavender!" Katherine's shout carried above the voices of the crowd.

Jonathan looked down and saw her waving Simon's coat in the air. "It smells like lavender," she repeated. "It is him!" She pointed at Simon.

Jonathan saw Higgins's brows draw together in a frown. "What are you talking about, Katherine?"

Katherine turned toward him. "The cape beneath the floorboards in the stable. It smells like lavender." The words tumbled from her lips in a rush. "I thought it was the nice lady, but his coat smells that way too." She shook the garment. "He's the one who pushed Justin down the well. I know he is."

Now Higgins's eyebrows lifted toward his hairline. His hand raised toward his upper lip. He turned to Simon. "Your wife makes perfume, does she not?"

A bead of sweat appeared on Simon's forehead. "What difference does it make?"

Higgins stepped closer. "Now there are two who testify against you."

"An idiot and a child. It proves nothing."

Jonathan cleared his throat. "And an English Lord."

"Give up, Bains."

Simon spun toward Jonathan. "No! I won't let you win. Harlan must pay for his crime!"

Jonathan's voice softened. "Harlan is dead."

"No, not till you pay. Not till you all pay."

Higgins raised his voice. "Is that what all this is about? How Harlan hurt your father?"

Simon's eyes narrowed. "What do you know about my father?"

"I know that he loved Brenna Grant. I know that he fathered a child by her, and I know that child was Richard Grant."

Surprised whispers fluttered through the crowd. Simon's hand trembled.

Higgins continued, "I also know that your father killed himself."

"He went mad after Harlan married her. That thief robbed my father of everything he ever cared for. He destroyed my father. I'll never forgive him for that. I'll never forget."

"Your father made his own choices, Bains."

"Do you know what it did to him to watch his lover abused and know he could do nothing?" The gun shook as he spoke. "He wasted away right there before my eyes, as if I did not matter at all. Only his precious Brenna mattered, only the son that could never know he was not a Grant." His voice became shrill. "What about me, I ask? They took him from me. Now they will pay. Revenge is mine!"

"You only have one bullet." Higgins spoke as calmly as if he were commenting on the weather. "You can't shoot us all."

"Then I choose him." He jabbed the gun toward Jonathan. "Harlan's only son."

Jonathan looked down the barrel of Simon's pistol into the eyes of a man consumed by pain, and in that moment he understood the enemy. Hate and anger had chewed away at his mind until nothing was left but the need for revenge. *That could have been me,* he thought. *But for God's grace and mercy, I could be the one standing behind the gun, about to shoot an innocent man.* A chill raced through him. Of all the things God had done for him, saving him from becoming like Simon was perhaps the greatest. Near, so near, had he come to losing his soul.

The woman from the gardens stepped in front of the pistol, positioning herself between Simon and Jonathan. "That's enough, Simon," she said.

"It is I that you want, Simon." Richard's voice rose from the crowd. He stepped from behind Rowley. "Am I not the one who betrayed you . . . brother?"

Simon's face flushed. "Yes. You knew the truth, and yet you did nothing. You kept the name of Papa's killer and wore it proudly. You should have honored our father, been proud of *his* name. But instead you despised him."

"I didn't know."

"Didn't know? Or didn't care?"

Richard's chin lowered. "Both, I'm afraid."

Simon nodded. "You're not worthy to be his son."

A shot exploded from the pistol. Smoke filled the air. Richard spun and fell to the ground.

"No!" The shout tore from Jonathan's throat. He jumped from the platform.

Rowley and Higgins leaped on Simon and wrestled him to the ground.

The woman from the gardens reached Richard first. She bent over him and gathered him in her arms. Jonathan knelt behind her. Richard's breath came in ragged gasps. His hand pressed over the wound in his stomach.

"Shhh," the woman whispered. "I'm here. Everything will be all right."

Blood gurgled from Richard's lips and spilled over his chin. His mouth struggled to form words but failed. He coughed and lifted a shaking hand toward the woman's face. "How?" he murmured.

"It doesn't matter now."

His head tipped from side to side, but his eyes remained steady on the woman's face. "I'm so sorry."

"Shhh," she repeated and placed her fingers over his lips. "I love you. I always have."

Richard closed his eyes, and for a moment Jonathan thought he was gone. But then his eyes again fluttered open and this time fixed on Jonathan. "Thank you, brother."

Tears dropped down Jonathan's cheeks. "I'm sorry I couldn't save you."

Richard smiled. "You did save me, Johnny. You saved me twice."

"It wasn't enough."

For three long, labored breaths, Richard couldn't speak. When he finally did, his voice was only a whisper. "I die a free man. It *is* enough." His head lolled to one side, and his eyes glazed.

"No!" Jonathan lifted Richard's body from the woman's grip and rocked him back and forth in his arms. He felt a hand on his shoulder and Kwelik's voice, soft and comforting, somewhere above him.

Then the voice of the woman replaced Kwelik's. Arms encircled him. "Shhh, shhh, son," someone whispered in his ear.

Jonathan pulled back. He looked up into the woman's face, fully lit for the first time. "Who are you?" he breathed.

Her features softened, and her eyes glistened with tears. "Still you don't recognize me? Oh, Jonathan." Her voice quivered. "The missing queen has come home."

His mind flashed to the yew chess figures leading to the cottage. The truth washed over him, sweet and unbelievable. "It can't be!"

She touched his face. "It is."

"Mama?" Her hair, graying now, her eyes, wide and soft, her mouth, curved in a gentle smile. How had he not recognized her? And yet there was something different about her too, something new in the way she held her head, the set of her jaw, the confidence that surrounded her. The years had made her into a different woman.

"But the letter—it said you were dead."

"I was very ill, but God granted me life."

"Why didn't you tell us?"

"Oh, Jonathan." Her fingers brushed his cheek. "Don't you see?

I couldn't have you coming after me. And when I returned here, I couldn't tell you the truth. Not until the traitor was caught."

Jonathan knelt there with a mix of sorrow and wonder rushing through him, his mother's arms around him. The mother he'd thought dead, the reason he'd hated his brother so fiercely, the pain he'd carried with him for so long—she was here. She was alive! Today was truly a day of miracles.

Where hate had once filled him, forgiveness had come to reign. Where anger had lived, mercy now flourished. Somehow God had taken his pain and made something beautiful.

In that moment as Jonathan breathed in the lavender scent of love, the final shadows lifted, and he was filled with light.

Epilogue

Lockwood, England, April 1756

The roses were in bloom again. Pink, white, and yellow—their fragrant faces testified to the end of winter. Philippe rested his hand against the window. Outside, a blackbird hopped across the lush lawn of the Grant estate and then spread its wings and flew out of sight. He sighed. A misty circle appeared on the pane. He pressed his forefinger into the center and wiped away the moisture.

A shriek tore through the rafters above him. Philippe shivered. *Elizabeth*. After all these months, he should have become accustomed to the screams, but each time, though it happened a dozen times a day, the sound of her madness still chilled him.

"The carriage is here."

Philippe dropped the curtain and turned from the window. White Wolf stood behind him. "It's time."

Philippe looked into the face of his friend as if to imprint it on his memory. "Yes, I know."

White Wolf stepped toward him and placed a hand on his shoulder. "This war will be over soon. Then the magistrate will let you return home."

"I hope so," Philippe muttered. "But in the meantime, I'll do my best to take care of the children and the estate. At least until Tobias returns and can hire help. Then . . ."

White Wolf sighed. "It's so much to ask. Jonathan and Kwelik . . ."

Philippe smiled. "Never have I seen a man so yearn for the frontier. It will kill him to stay here any longer. We have discussed this before."

White Wolf glanced away. "I know, but I promised to help you get to France, and now . . ."

Philippe patted him on the arm. "It's okay, my friend. Go home. Do what God has asked of you."

"Yes." White Wolf's eyes became unfocused. Philippe knew his friend was seeing his dream, a dream of going back to his people and telling them about God, just as his father had done before him—and a dream of being a real father to Ashton, his son.

"You know this is the only way."

White Wolf nodded. "But what about you?"

"It is enough for me to see how God has changed you."

White Wolf grinned. "And gave me a new hope to replace my old anger."

"Come on." Philippe motioned toward the door. "It's time for you to go."

Minutes later they joined the others in front of the Grant mansion. The carriage door stood open before them like a portal to the future. The scent of rose blossoms filled the air. The horse snorted and shook its mane.

White Wolf glanced at Jonathan. "We're ready."

Jonathan nodded and extended his arm toward Philippe. Solemnly Philippe took Jonathan's hand in his own and squeezed.

Jonathan's gaze pierced his and then swept up the wall of the mansion. "I never thought I'd regret leaving this place, but a part of me will mourn it." His grip relaxed, and he smiled. "But I'm pleased to be leaving it in such honest hands. You're a good friend, Philippe Reveau. I'll never say a bad word about the French again."

Philippe grinned. Jonathan dropped his hand and walked to the carriage door.

Jonathan's mother approached. "Thank you, Mr. Reveau. Because of you, I will finally see the land my son loves so much." She took his face between her hands and kissed him on both cheeks. When she pulled away, her eyes were moist.

Kwelik took her place. Tears rolled down her face. "My friend," she murmured, and could say no more. Her fingers brushed his cheek. "May God give you your heart's desire and withhold none of His love." She sniffed. "It seems I'm always leaving you behind."

She stepped back, and Annie threw her arms around him and hugged him fiercely. "You'll get to France yet," she said in his ear. "I know you will." Her arms dropped from around him, and she hurried into the carriage.

Then there was no one left but himself and White Wolf.

"If you ever need me," White Wolf began.

Before he could finish, Philippe grabbed him and pulled him to his chest. He thumped him on the back. "You take care of that wife of yours and say hello to Ashton for me."

"I will," White Wolf promised. Then he stepped away, climbed into the carriage, and shut the door behind him.

The driver flicked the reins, and the carriage pulled away from the mansion. Just as it passed the rosebushes, a small hand slipped into Philippe's. He glanced down to see Katherine standing beside him.

"I'm going to miss them," she whispered.

"So will I."

"I'm glad you stayed."

Philippe's gaze traced the gentle curve of her cheek, her eyes damp with tears, her chin lifted bravely. His heart swelled. "As am I." His eyes raised to rest on the far horizon.

Somewhere out there France still waited.

About the Author

Besides being a freelance writer, Marlo Schalesky (B.S., Chemistry, Stanford University) is a partner in a mechanical engineering firm in California. She has published more than four hundred articles in prominent Christian magazines and is working toward a Master's of Divinity at Fuller Theological Seminary. Marlo enjoys many outdoor activities such as hiking and horseback riding. She and her husband, Bryan, have been married for twelve years and have a daughter named Bethany Ann.